Home Matters

Home Matters:
Longing and Belonging, Nostalgia and Mourning in Women's Fiction

Roberta Rubenstein

palgrave

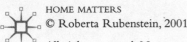

HOME MATTERS
© Roberta Rubenstein, 2001

First published 2001 by
PALGRAVE
175 Fifth Avenue, New York, N.Y. 10010 and
Houndmills, Basingstoke, Hampshire RG21 6XS.
Companies and representatives throughout the world

PALGRAVE is the new global publishing imprint of St. Martin's Press LLC Scholarly and Reference Division and Palgrave Publishers Ltd (formerly Macmillan Press Ltd).

ISBN 0-312-23875-4

Library of Congress Cataloging-in-Publication Data

Rubenstein, Roberta, 1944-
    Home matters : longing and belonging, nostalgia and mourning in women's fiction / Roberta Rubenstein.
       p. cm.
    Includes bibliographical references (p.) and index.
    ISBN 0-312-23875-4
    1. American fiction—Women authors—History and criticism.
2. Domestic fiction, American—History and criticism.   3. Women and literature—United States—History—20th century.   4. Women and literature—Great Britain—History—20th century.   5. American fiction—20th century—History and criticism.   6. English fiction—Women authors—History and criticism.   7. English fiction—20th century—History and criticism.   8. Domestic fiction, English—History and criticism.   9. Nostalgia in literature.   10. Desire in literature.   11. Grief in literature.   12. Home in literature.   I. Title.

PS374.D57 H66 2001
813'.509355—dc21   00-051487

A catalogue record for this book is available from the British Library.

Design by Westchester Book Composition, Danbury, CT USA.

First edition: February 2001
10 9 8 7 6 5 4 3 2 1

Printed in the United States of America.

For Chuck, especially,

and for Vanessa and Joshua

and my mother, Sarah

Contents

Part IV: Nostalgia for Paradise

Acknowledgments

I am especially grateful for the helpful suggestions and supportive encouragement of friends and colleagues who read earlier versions of this project and whose comments helped me find my way to the final shape of my thinking. I thank Ruth Saxton and Ellen Cronan Rose, whose valuable suggestions on earlier drafts of the manuscript challenged me to sharpen my thinking. I also appreciate the astute readings of individual chapters by Jean Wyatt and Marianne Noble. Thanks especially to my husband, Charles R. Larson, for being—as always—my most supportive reader and my keenest critic.

This book grew from ideas first expressed in print in several articles. I gratefully acknowledge the following publication permissions for earlier versions of the following chapters: the chapter on Virginia Woolf and Doris Lessing originally appeared in *Woolf and Lessing: Breaking the Mold*, copyright © 1994 by Ruth Saxton and Jean Tobin, editors. Reprinted with permission of St. Martin's Press, LLC; the chapter on Barbara Kingsolver's *Animal Dreams* originally appeared in *Home-making: The Politics and Poetics of Home*, copyright © 1996 by Catherine Wiley and Fiona R. Barnes, editors. Reprinted by permission of Taylor & Francis, Inc./Routledge, Inc., http://www.routledge-ny.com; a version of the chapter on Toni Morrison's *Jazz* originally appeared as an essay with a different focus in *Mosaic*, Vol. 31, no. 2. This was a special issue titled: Part 2, "The Interarts Project: Cultural Agendas" (June 1998).

◇ ◇

Home Matters:
Longing and Belonging

Home is where one starts from. As we grow older
The world becomes stranger, the pattern more complicated
Of dead and living.

—T. S. Eliot, "East Coker," *Four Quartets*

◇

you have been miles
away, after all,
while I have been
making myself at home.

—Martha Collins, *"Homecoming"*

◇

Get to a good place, turn around three times in the grass,
and you're home. Once you know how, you can always
do that, no matter what.

—Loyd Peregrina in *Animal Dreams,* Barbara Kingsolver

Not merely a physical structure or a geographical location but
always an emotional space, *home* is among the most emotionally
complex and resonant concepts in our psychic vocabularies,
given its associations with the most influential, and often most ambivalent,
elements of our earliest physical environment and psychological experi-

ences as well as their ripple effect throughout our lives. More than two mil-
lennia ago, Homer tapped this motif on an epic scale: Odysseus's encounters with monsters, temptations, and challenges prepare him for his ultimate
return to the point of his original departure where, to invoke a passage
from Eliot's *Four Quartets,* he knows the place for the first time. Twenty
years after his departure from Ithaka, both Odysseus and home have been
transformed.

Countless writers have followed Homer's lead, with resolutions to the
archetypal theme of homecoming ranging from Thomas Wolfe's conclusion that "you can't go home again" to Dorothy's realization when she
returns from her sojourn in Oz that "there's no place like home." However,
in most of the centuries since Homer sang the details of Odysseus's adven-
tures and his triumphant return to Ithaka, women—even if not, like Penelope, directly affected by her spouse's extended absence at war and
adventure—have more typically associated home with a different set of
meanings shaped by the reality of domestic obligations and confinement.
Indeed, it is precisely the construction of home as an oppressive rather than
a nostalgic space that underlies the modern feminist movement. Influenced
by Simone de Beauvoir's exploration of the "second sex" and Betty Friedan's
articulation of the "feminine mystique" during the 1950s and 1960s,[1]
many women came to regard home as a restrictive, confining space. Chal-
lenging deeply-imbedded cultural scripts that defined women in terms of
familial and domestic roles, they viewed home not as a sanctuary but as a
prison, a site from which escape was the essential prerequisite for self-
discovery and independence.[2] "Homesickness," stripped of its nostalgic
associations, became synonymous with "sick of home."

Given the heterogeneous nature of the feminist discourse that has
evolved since the second wave of the women's movement, scholars and
critics are much more aware of the impossibility—and the fallacy—of pre-
suming to speak for all women or of assuming that any critical or theoretical position is inclusive. In a fragmented postmodern world in which exile
and migration are increasingly common and as entire populations are displaced by ethnic wars, genocide, famine, and other destructive forces both
human and natural, the definition of home—and the meaning of homesickness—may depend on where one stands not only psychologically and
ideologically but geopolitically.[3] In the new millennium, one may hope for
a cultural pluralism that acknowledges the multiple consequences and
meanings of exile and displacement from home.[4]

In undertaking the current study, I acknowledge my debt to the influential paths charted by feminist scholars before me, who inspired my inter-

est in mapping intersections of gender and space, along with psychological and cultural differences.[5] Although the notion of home appears in the more recent of my two previous studies of contemporary women writers, in that book my principal focus was the correspondences between material and psychological or cultural boundaries in narrative representations of female selfhood by authors of different ethnicities.[6] Questions of space, place, and race have continued to interest me as I have discovered other dimensions of the emotionally resonant topos of home in women's writing.

In pursuing the current project, I have tried to answer a series of questions for myself. Given the advances in women's opportunities and feminist consciousness that began during the 1970s (or, to qualify the statement, the advances that became disproportionately possible for white, Western, middle-class, heterosexual, and younger women, as against women who did not belong to those categories), how do narratives by contemporary women writers reflect such social changes? Have fictional female characters succeeded in jettisoning at least some of the negative baggage associated with home in its incarnation as confining domestic space? Why, despite cultural and ethnic differences, despite different stages in the life course of the authors themselves as well as the characters they create, do notions of longing and belonging retain such significance within female experience?

There are both cultural and psychological sources for these preoccupations. The American experience in particular has been distinguished from its beginnings by the centrality of immigration and assimilation and the related experiences of exile, cultural dislocation, and the inevitability of homesickness. Typically, the desire to recover/return home is regarded as the expression of a regressive wish to retreat to a less complicated moment in history or personal experience. However, within recent fiction by women, that longing may be understood as a culturally mediated response to significant changes in female experience in particular as a result of the social transformations generated by feminism during the 1970s and '80s. Many women, both academic feminists and writers, who have shaped and have been shaped by the second wave of feminism, have experienced conflict between being daughters and mothers and lovers—whether heterosexual or lesbian—on the one hand and successful professionals on the other. That is, during the last third of the twentieth century and into the current century, women have felt the tension between private and public identities—between securing a professional life and honoring a private life that embraces elements of what is traditionally called "home-making." Once domesticity became aligned with confinement and oppression, and once *home* became associated with a politically reactionary backlash against feminism, homesickness went underground, as it were. In this sense, longing for home may be understood as a yearning for recovery or return to the idea of a nurturing, unconditionally accepting place/space that has been repressed in contemporary feminism. Narratives that excavate and recover the positive meanings of home and nostalgia in effect represent "the return of the repressed" in that they foreground, confront, and attempt to resolve that subversive longing.

This tension at the heart of feminist consciousness appears at the psychological level as, on the one hand, the impulse toward autonomy and self-realization and, on the other, the pull of interdependence, if not dependence. Belonging is a relational, reciprocal condition that encompasses connection and community: not only being taken care of but taking care. Paradigm-shifting feminist revisions in theories of female psychological development altered the way many women understood their own experiences in emotionally significant relationships: as daughters, lovers, and mothers. Accounting for gender differences in the understanding of the developmental dynamic of union and disengagement between mother and child, these feminist revisions of psychoanalytic theory prompted a major shift in focus.[7] One effect of that shift was an unconscious *idealization* of the maternal as understood from the (nostalgic) daughter's perspective.[8]

As I considered narratives in which female characters long for or ponder their emotional distance from home, I realized that nostalgia encompasses something more than a yearning for literal places or actual individuals. While homesickness refers to a spatial/geographical separation, nostalgia more accurately refers to a temporal one. Even if one is able to return to the literal edifice where s/he grew up, one can never truly return to original home of childhood, since it exists mostly as a place in the imagination.[9] Although the meaning of nostalgia itself has changed over time, essentially it has come to signify not simply the loss of one's childhood home but the loss of childhood itself.[10] As the intellectual historian Jean Starobinski traces the shifting meaning of the idea of nostalgia from its original meaning as an organic disease to its current meaning as a form of emotional disease, he notes that "what a person wishes to recover is not so much the actual *place* where he passed his childhood but his youth itself. He is not straining towards something which he can repossess, but toward an age which is forever beyond his reach."[11] In a sense, then, nostalgia, or homesickness, whose meaning remains so closely allied with it, is the existential condition of adulthood. While "exile" is a freighted term within the context of postcolonial awareness, we are all—regardless of gender, homeland, or place of origin—exiles from childhood.

Although both homesickness and nostalgia may be responses to the universal inevitability of separation and loss—the unavoidable human journey from rapture to rupture—I propose that the dis-ease "manifests" itself in different degrees of intensity and yearning, depending on whether or not the experience is associated with psychic pain. In the deeper register, nostalgia is painful awareness, the expression of grief for something lost, the absence of which continues to produce significant emotional distress. Most individuals experience such loss not merely as separation from someone or something but as an absence that continues to occupy a palpable emotional space—what I term the *presence of absence*. The felt absence of a person or place assumes form and occupies imaginative space as a presence that may come to possess an individual. Nostalgia in this sense is a kind of haunted longing: figures of earlier relationships and the places with which they are associated, both remembered and imagined, impinge on a person's emotional life, affecting her or his behavior toward current experiences and attachments. Implicit in the deeper register of nostalgia is the element of grief for something of profound value that seems irrevocably lost—even if it never actually existed, *or never could have existed,* in the form in which it is "remembered."

The yearning of painful nostalgia is thus closely related to—indeed, a form of—mourning, the process whereby an individual gradually works through the intense grief experienced when a loved one dies.[12] Moreover, other kinds of profound losses, including displacement from an emotionally vital domicile or cultural community, may catalyze grief and mourning.[13] I use the phrase *cultural mourning* to signify an individual's response to the loss of something with collective or communal associations: a way of life, a cultural homeland, a place or geographical location with significance for a larger cultural group, or the related history of an entire ethnic or cultural group from which she or he feels severed or exiled, whether voluntarily or involuntarily. In literary representations of cultural mourning, the figure who expresses that sense of collective loss may be either a character or, implicitly—through the narrative's framing of that loss—the author herself.

Thus, I argue that the authors considered in the following pages employ nostalgia and the tropes of *home* and *homesickness* to represent certain relationships between psychological and cultural experience, including displacement and the potentiality for imaginative repair. The idea of reparation presupposes damage or injury. Within the argument of this study, that damage may be understood as emotional/psychological—the narcissistic "injury" of separation that inevitably occurs during infancy and childhood, and from which most of us endeavor to recover. Later, as women age, they may experience another kind of psychological displacement, expressed in the need to reassess past experiences and to reconcile the loss of youth with forward progress in life. In another context, culturally displaced or exiled people may mourn their separation from home/land, community, language, and/or cultural practices that contribute to identity.

In the chapters that follow I argue that, in contrast to the conventional view of homesickness and nostalgia as sentimental if not also psychologically regressive modes of feeling,[14] both may have compensatory and even liberating dimensions within the frame of narrative. Several writers evoke nostalgia or the longing for home to enable their characters (and, imaginatively, their readers) to confront, mourn, and figuratively revise their relation to something that has been lost, whether in the world or in themselves. Through it, they may move beyond nostalgia's initially regressive pull to override, neutralize, or transmute loss and achieve a new level of awareness. Narratives that engage notions of home, loss, and/or nostalgia confront the past in order to "fix" it, a process that may be understood in two complementary figurative senses. To "fix" something is to *secure* it more firmly in the imagination and also to *correct*—as in *revise* or *repair*—it. Even though one cannot literally go home again (at least, not to the home of childhood that has been embellished over time by imagination), it may be recoverable in narrative terms. Through their characters, authors may (figuratively) reconstruct and thus restore or repair the emotional architecture of that multivalent space. Excavating the meaning of the yearning for re/union that overlays the reality of loss and the related process of mourning, they may mediate—and traverse—the gap between longing and belonging.

A few words are in order here regarding the principle of inclusion for what may seem an eclectic group of writers and texts. All but two of the writers are American; all but one are contemporary writers, although of several different generations. Because of the thematic organization of this study, several authors—Virginia Woolf, Doris Lessing, Barbara Kingsolver, and Toni Morrison—are represented by more than one text; Morrison appears in more than one section. The opening chapter on Woolf and Lessing, the only British writers included in this study, establishes a framework for the discussion that follows. In my view, there are no twentieth-century American literary foremothers who have had an influence comparable to that of Woolf and Lessing. Woolf, writing several decades before de Beauvoir interrogated the notion of the "second sex," and Lessing, who began to write in the midcentury period during which the second wave reached its crest, have both had an indelible and enduring influence on the consciousnesses of a large population of female readers—and writers—over succeeding decades and generations. Their fiction broke new ground not only formally but substantively: both writers insisted that women's inner lives and consciousnesses—in addition to their social experiences—were the *central subject.* In the fiction and autobiographical writings of Woolf and Lessing, I identify the tensions that frame this study: complementary constructions of longing or nostalgia. I juxtapose Woolf's longing for the idealized lost mother of her childhood and the lost landscape of home with Lessing's construction of a compensatory idealized mother quite distinct from her actual mother and a home/land distanced not only (like Woolf's) by time and memory but by geography. Woolf's and Lessing's writings reflect the tension between self-realization and the contrary pull of longing for mother and home; between nostalgia as a comforting recollection and nostalgia as a deception of memory; between profound emotional loss and imaginative reparation and healing.

The two authors represent complementary positions in another sense. Woolf, the daughter of a prominent Victorian critic and herself a major figure in the evolution of modernism, occupies the position of a cultural "insider." Lessing, a generation younger and a British "colonial," occupies the position of the exile, the "outsider" for whom home, both geographically/politically and psychologically, is a conflicted site. Raised in southern Africa, where she lived until the age of 30, Lessing emigrated to England and subsequently was named a "proscribed citizen," barred from returning to her homeland for nearly three decades.

The six American writers of later generations considered in the chapters that follow elaborate in diverse ways these oppositions between home and exile, insider and outsider, longing and belonging. Illuminating the dialectic between loss and reparation, each writer takes up and complicates one or the other (or both) positions expressed in the fiction and autobiographical writings of Woolf and Lessing regarding the lost landscape of home and its imaginative recovery in fiction. Thus, subsequent sections of this study focus on psychological and/or cultural displacement as they shape notions of home and loss and embody diverse representations of individual and/or cultural mourning. In *Animal Dreams*, Barbara Kingsolver extends the notion of home to the idea of homeland, with the emphasis on the land itself. Working through mourning for her lost mother and her own lost motherhood, the emotionally displaced Codi Noline ultimately discovers a deeper knowledge of her true place. In linked novels about Taylor Greer and her adopted Cherokee daughter, Turtle, Kingsolver redefines the terrain of home and of the mother-daughter relationship as a cross-cultural one with political as well as psychological ramifications. Imagining unorthodox constructions of family and belonging, she addresses several dimensions of cultural dislocation and exile within a multicultural America. Taking up another strand of the multicultural construction of American experience, Julia Alvarez focuses explicitly on geopolitical exile, including the accommodations and losses that derive from the additional effects of linguistic dislocation.

As women age, the nature of their emotional and imaginative distance from home—their longings and losses—evolves as well. Homesickness and nostalgia function as tropes for a different kind of yearning, embodied in the recognition of lost youth and of versions/visions of the self that have been outgrown. Again, both Woolf and Lessing anticipated the preoccupation with "coming of age," not in the traditional sense used to describe novels of initiation into adulthood, but in the sense Simone de Beauvoir gave the phrase: the coming of *age*. The narratives I consider here by Anne Tyler, Paule Marshall, and Toni Morrison focus on characters who negotiate the limits and possibilities of midlife and beyond, accomplishing a passage through nostalgic mourning for lost dimensions of self as well as (in the latter two authors) cultural mourning for lost communities and histories. In Marshall's *Praisesong for the Widow* and Morrison's *Jazz,* characters work through previously unresolved grief as, through them, the authors themselves mourn the loss of historical homelands, communities, and cultural traditions.

The final section of this study, focusing on Gloria Naylor's *Mama Day* and Toni Morrison's *Paradise,* follows the tropes of home and homesickness, and the links between home and mother, into a metaphysical geography. Both narratives reflect a division between matriarchal and patriarchal conceptions of the world that extends to the conception of Paradise itself; both emphasize maternal figures with special powers who facilitate (or, at least, attempt to) spiritual homecoming for their symbolic daughters. Both narratives explore the nostalgia for Paradise, understood as a spiritual home with strong maternal associations, located in a liminal space where past and future converge.

I make no claim for the representative nature of the group of writers considered here. Others, including women of other ethnicities and nationalities, might well have been included, since the longing for belonging and notions of home, nostalgia, and mourning are obviously not exclusive to this small sample of texts. I write about these authors and texts because they represent so clearly a locus of concern to women in particular, beginning with the resonances of home and relationship but extending to matters of cultural dislocation, ethnicity, language, moral responsibility, aging, and spiritual longing. In a number of the narratives, the (usually female) central character finds herself at a significant crossroad between home and a problematic "elsewhere," a place/space that is figuratively located at the intersection of different geographies, cultures, languages, life stages, or spiritual conditions. At the imaginary intersection of time and place, the characters discover—as their authors narratively render—the multiple ways in which home matters.

Part I

Is Mother Home?

◇

◈ 1 ◈

Yearning and Nostalgia:
Fiction and Autobiographical Writings
of Virginia Woolf and Doris Lessing

[W]e are sealed vessels afloat on what it is convenient to call
reality; and at some moments, the sealing matter cracks; in
floods reality; that is, these scenes—for why do they survive
undamaged year after year unless they are made of something comparatively permanent?

—Virginia Woolf, "A Sketch of the Past"

Every writer has a myth-country. This does not have to be
childhood. . . . Myth does not mean something untrue, but
a concentration of truth.

—Doris Lessing, *African Laughter*

A central impulse in the work of a number of the writers considered
in this study is nostalgia—the expression of yearning for an earlier
time or place or a significant person in one's past history, the memory and significance of which or whom contributes to the sense of the self
in the present moment. That impulse is especially noteworthy in the fiction
and autobiographical writings of two influential figures in the tradition of
fiction by women in the twentieth and early twenty-first centuries, Virginia Woolf and Doris Lessing. More than simply expressing a preoccupation with the past, both writers recurrently explore the emotionally

saturated meanings of two categories of memories in particular: of place (*home*) and of person (*mother*). These memories are filtered through and inevitably revised by particular consciousnesses, including those not only of fictionalized characters but of the authors themselves as they reflect on places and people significant during earlier phases of their lives. Thus, while a number of Woolf's and Lessing's characters embody the authors' respective representations of nostalgia, each author has also written autobiographical accounts describing important figures, places, and experiences in her life that corroborate and underlie her fictional renderings of homesickness.

More than Woolf, Lessing consciously acknowledges that memory itself is an elusive, fluid, and often unreliable component of consciousness, whose manifestations depend on the shifting relationship between any present moment and an always-receding past. Anna Wulf of *The Golden Notebook* (1962) observes with exasperation that trying to remember her experiences during her formative years in southern Africa is "like wrestling with an obstinate other-self who insists on its own kind of privacy. Yet it's all there in my brain if only I could get at it. . . . How do I know that what I 'remember' was what was important? What I remember was chosen by Anna, of twenty years ago. I don't know what this Anna of now would choose."[1] More recently, Lessing has remarked, "you see your life differently at different stages, like climbing a mountain while the landscape changes with every turn in the path. . . . I try to see my past selves as someone else might, and then put myself back inside one of them, and am at once submerged in a hot struggle of emotion, justified by thoughts and ideas I now judge wrong. . . . *How do you know that what you remember is more important than what you don't?*"[2]

Similarly, as Woolf phrases it in her autobiographical essay, "A Sketch of the Past," "It would be interesting to make the two people, I now, I then, come out in contrast. And further, this past is much affected by the present moment. What I write today I should not write in a year's time."[3] Yet elsewhere Woolf affirms a view of recollection that runs counter to this observation. She describes as one source of her fiction-making impulse a number of vivid memories that are preserved as "scenes," apparently unaltered by her evolving relation to them over time: "I find that scene making is my natural way of marking the past. Always a scene has arranged itself: representative; enduring . . . for why do [these scenes] survive undamaged year after year unless they are made of something comparatively permanent?" ("Sketch" 122)[4]

If, as Woolf so memorably declares in *A Room of One's Own,* "we think back through our mothers if we are women,"[5] it is also instructive to approach her writing from the other direction: to think back through one of her "daughters," as it were. The presence of nostalgia in Doris Lessing's writing—not only as emphatically resisted by (the suggestively surnamed) Anna Wulf but elsewhere and more ambivalently as both the domain of unreliable memories and a harmonious unitary world—ultimately casts a critical light on the ways in which nostalgia functions in Woolf's fiction and autobiography: if not as a "lie," at least as a scrim that revises and softens the sharp edges of haunting memories.

Lessing, born of English parents in Persia (now Iran), was reared in Southern Rhodesia (now Zimbabwe) and emigrated to England (still England) when she was thirty. As a result of her leftist political activities, she was listed as a "Prohibited Immigrant"[6] and proscribed from re-entering her African homeland for more than twenty-five years. Both of her autobiographical narratives, the significantly titled *Going Home* (1957) and *African Laughter* (1992), record her successive returns "home" to Zimbabwe, providing unique intertexts for the expressions of nostalgia that occur throughout her fiction as well.

Lessing's first experience of literal homesickness, if not the nostalgia that colors adult recollections, occurred when she was still a child, living away from home in a convent boarding school in Salisbury; while there, she was "always ill at school and not only with homesickness."[7] Recapturing that experience through her fictional persona, Martha Quest, Lessing highlights the uneasy quality of nostalgia as sixteen-year-old Martha, isolated in a darkened room because of infectious pinkeye, awaits her matriculation exam. The narrator describes an October day, bright with light and pungent with the scent of flowers, as Martha feels "the waves of heat and perfume break across her in shock after shock of shuddering nostalgia. But nostalgia for what?"[8] Although offered as Martha's experience, the passage transparently expresses Lessing's own yearning for features associated with the site of her emotionally complicated childhood; Martha, not yet having left home (or Africa) as Lessing had done by the time she wrote the first novel of *Children of Violence,* could not have known such "shuddering nostalgia." Later, when Martha does leave home to take a secretarial job in Salisbury, Southern Rhodesia, she falls ill with a "dubious" illness and sardonically resists acknowledging a likely source of her malaise: "One might imagine I was homesick!" (*Martha Quest* 209).

When Martha drives across the open veld with Douglas Knowell (the man she soon marries), her voice again disappears into that of the narrator's in her celebration of the "naked embrace of earth and sky. . . . [T]his frank embrace between the lifting breast of the land and the deep blue warmth of the sky *is what exiles from Africa dream of; it is what they sicken for, no matter how hard they try to shut their minds against the memory of it*" (*Martha Quest* 240, my emphasis). Again, it is not Martha Quest but Lessing, the exile from Africa, who associates the land with an idealized, embracing mother and whose voice we hear in that expression of longing.[9] Martha's earlier query, "nostalgia for what?", is ostensibly answered in *A Proper Marriage* (1952) when, newly pregnant, she fatalistically attributes her odd confusion of anxiety and excitement to "nostalgia for something doomed."[10] The paradoxical expression of retrospective foreknowledge is, once again, more revealing of the exiled Lessing's knowledge of loss than of the still-adolescent Martha's.

The yearning for a place—and for a past—that is simultaneously real, ideal, and true is rendered in considerably more complex terms in Lessing's subsequent fiction, particularly for Anna Wulf of *The Golden Notebook,* for whom such nostalgic proclivities are especially problematic. As Anna considers the experiences of her formative years in Southern Rhodesia—from a greater distance in both time and space than does the young Martha Quest—she struggles to find a "true" perspective within her romanticized memories; she determines that nostalgia must be resisted, for it distorts and falsifies memory. Early in the Black Notebook, Anna confesses her feeling that her first and only novel, *Frontiers of War,* utterly falsified rather than rendering honestly her deepest emotional experiences. She virtually repudiates it as an "immoral novel" because "that terrible lying nostalgia lights every sentence" (*Notebook* 63), capturing not the authentic version of events at Mashopi but "something frightening, the unhealthy, feverish illicit excitement of wartime, a lying nostalgia, a longing for license, for freedom, for the jungle, for formlessness" (*Notebook* 63).[11] At her most cynical, she even characterizes this complex of self-deceiving feelings as a "nostalgia for death" (*Notebook* 287).

One challenge a reader faces in attempting to understand the meaning of what Anna Wulf terms "lying nostalgia" is the impossibility of comprehending such observations independently of the Anna who records them. In the multiple notebooks and time frames of Lessing's narrative—encompassing Anna's memories from the 1940s, when she lived in Zambesia (Southern Rhodesia), to her experiences in London during the 1950s, when she tries to record more recent and current events in her life—she attempts to capture both the "raw" experiences and their myriad transmutations, only some of which she acknowledges as fictions. All of her memories are observed through a fractured lens whose distortions are produced not only by the passage of time but by the difficulty of finding the "correct" emotional distance from them. "Lying nostalgia" becomes a judgment about the difficulty—in fact, the impossibility—of recovering, through either memory or fiction, the "authentic" version of past experiences. Among the many strands that draw the multilayered narrative of *The Golden Notebook* into a kind of coherence, the unstable relations between past and present, between experience and language, between fact and fiction, and between subjectivity and authenticity pervade Anna's struggle with her various "selves" and thus occupy a significant place in the novel's multiple meanings.[12]

It is revealing to juxtapose Anna Wulf's struggle with "lying nostalgia" in her accounts of her experiences at Mashopi with Lessing's later actual visits to the land of her formative years. In 1982, her first visit "home" since 1956, she returned to several emotionally significant places of her young adulthood, hoping to "sort out memory from what [she] had made of it" (*Laughter* 66). When she actually encountered specific places, she found that she could not disentangle her memories from her fictionalizations of them. Visiting the Macheke Hotel, fictionalized in *The Golden Notebook* as the Mashopi Hotel, Lessing discovered that her fictitious version of it was so deeply installed in her memory that she could not even recall the proprietor's true name (*Laughter* 76).

> What happened in Macheke I described, changed for literary reasons, in *The Golden Notebook*. But how much changed? All writers know the state of trying to remember what actually happened, rather than what was invented, or half invented, a meld of truth and fiction. It is possible to remember, but only by sitting quietly, for hours or sometimes for days, and dragging facts out of one's memory. . . .
> Mashopi was painted over with glamour, as I complained in *The Golden Notebook*. (*Laughter* 72)

Interestingly, the "I" who thus complained was Anna Wulf. Here, Lessing acknowledges the objection to "lying nostalgia" as her own, further demonstrating the effect of time's passage on the already-blurred boundaries between fictionalized and autobiographical versions of her experience.[13]

In each of her autobiographical accounts of her visits to her original homeland, Lessing struggles over whether to return to emotionally significant places that have shaped her imaginative vision of herself and her past. Seven years after her emigration to England, during her first return home in 1956 (and the last before she was prohibited from re-entering Southern Rhodesia for more than two decades), she visited towns and areas that were important to her during her childhood and youth.[14] However, she could not bring herself to return to the location of her childhood home in the bush. The house itself, constructed of mud, cow dung, and trees, was no longer there, having been destroyed by fire some years before. Knowing that fact, Lessing determined that she could only preserve her inner imaginative record of home if she did not have to confront the visual proof of its absence. At the same time, she wishfully fantasizes that she might make her way back to that site and find it "still there after all."[15] The language conveys a site preserved not in space but in time, through memory and imagination.

Indeed, rather than returning to the actual location of that now-vanished childhood home, Lessing recovers it imaginatively, rescuing it from erasure through an interior salvaging operation:

> For a long time I used to dream of the collapse and decay of that house, and of the fire sweeping over it; and then I set myself to dream the other way. It was urgently necessary to recover every detail of that house. . . . I had to remember everything, every strand of thatch and curve of wall or heave in the floor, and every tree and bush and patch of grass around it, and how the fields and slopes of the country looked at different times of the day, in different strengths and tones of light . . . . Over months, I recovered the memory of it all. And so what was lost and buried in my mind, I recovered from my mind; so I suppose there is no need to go back and see what exists clearly, in every detail, for so long as I live. (*Going Home* 55–6)

Nonetheless, the nostalgic vision of home—and of "going home"—persisted. When Lessing returned to southern Africa in 1982 after a twenty-five-year absence, she once again attempted to locate the Southern Rhodesia of her childhood. In *African Laughter,* as in *Going Home,* she simultaneously measured the progress of the contemporary Zimbabwe that has replaced it. During her reunion with her younger brother, Harry, who had remained in Zimbabwe, she was astonished that her sibling had no memory of experiences, still extraordinarily vivid to her, that they had shared during childhood. Harry's mention of their childhood home precipitated her deepest nostalgia for a place that no longer existed. Nonetheless, she resisted returning to the most emotionally powerful site of her past:

In 1956, I could have gone to see the farm, the place where our house had been on the hill, but I was driving the car and could not force myself to turn the wheel off the main road north, on to the track that leads to the farm. Every writer has a myth country. This does not have to be childhood. I attributed the ukase, the silent *No,* to a fear of tampering with my myth, the bush I was brought up in, the old house built of earth and grass, the lands around the hill, the animals, the birds. Myth does not mean something untrue, but a concentration of truth. (*Laughter* 35)

During her six weeks in Zimbabwe in 1982, Lessing once again avoided visiting the site of her childhood home. Finally, on her return in 1988, she resolved to override her longstanding resistance and her brother's caution that going there would "break [her] heart" (*Laughter* 314). Unaware of her enduring struggle with her feelings about their family home in the bush, his remark refers more literally to the disappearance from the bush of entire groups of wild animals, casualties of the transition to more commercially viable farmland.[16] Nonetheless, Lessing finally determined that she "had to go back to the old farm" (*Laughter* 301), in order to confront her own "myth-country":

This business of writers' myth-countries is far from simple. I know writers who very early build tall fences around theirs and afterwards make sure they never go near them. And not only writers: all the people I know from former dominions, colonies, or any part of the earth they grew up on before making that essential flight in and away from the periphery to the centre: when the time comes for them to make the first trip home it means stripping off new skin and offering exposed and smarting flesh to—the past. For that matter every child who has left home to become an adult knows the diminishing of the first trip home. (*Laughter* 301)

One of Lessing's unanticipated discoveries was that the material improvements that had occurred in Zimbabwe since her departure in 1950 ironically deprived her of the full impact of her return to the veld. Paved roads accelerated her approach to a landscape she had hoped to re-enter as slowly as the original rutted dirt lanes of her childhood had required. From the nearby town to the location of the old family house in the bush—the place that would "[confirm] so many dreams and nightmares" (*Laughter* 312)—the journey has shrunk from an hour (or two, by foot) to a few minutes.

Approaching with trepidation that emotionally saturated place where yearning and resistance had long mingled, she mused, "Suppose one was able to keep in one's mind those childhood miseries, the homesickness like a bruise on one's heart, the betrayals—if they were allowed [to] lie in the mind always exposed, a cursed country one has climbed out of and left behind for ever, but visible, not hidden . . . would then that landscape of pain have less power than I am sure it has?" (*Laughter* 305, Lessing's ellipsis). However, finally encountering with relief the actual place, "one not imagined or invented" (313), Lessing confronted her deepest nostalgia for the physical landscape of her childhood. "I stood there, needless to say limp with threatening tears, unable to believe in all that magnificence, the space, the marvel of it. . . . I lived here from the age of five until I left it forever thirteen years later. I lived *here*. No wonder this myth country tugged and pulled . . . what a privilege, what a blessing" (314–15, Lessing's final ellipsis and emphasis).

What distinguishes this more recent autobiographical statement of Lessing's return to the landscape of her youth from the tormented struggles of her fictionalized persona, Anna Wulf, is the softening of the idea of nostalgia as a "lie." There is less sense of loss than of recovery, even of wonderment, and acceptance of both what has been forgotten and what has been remembered, albeit inevitably colored by complex emotional shadings. Although Lessing sensed the strong presence of her parents' "ghosts" (*Laughter* 317) at the site of the family farm, she recognized that her sense of loss was not only personal but general; "every day there are more people everywhere in the world in mourning for trees, forest, bush, rivers, animals, lost landscapes . . . you could say this is an established part of the human mind, a layer of grief always deepening and darkening" (*Laughter* 318, Lessing's ellipsis).

The impulse to return to, reconstruct, or recover such lost landscapes of the past in some sort of "pure" form uncontaminated by the alterations of time or later experience and understanding is a central preoccupation expressed elsewhere in Lessing's oeuvre. In *Briefing for a Descent into Hell* (1971), the locations that Charles Watkins, a professor of classics, visits during several hallucinatory journeys also suggest the ambivalent grip of nostalgia. His inner journeys are juxtaposed with the medical establishment's efforts to penetrate his amnesiac condition. In fact, amnesia functions in the novel as the antithesis of nostalgia. If nostalgia is the yearning to recover the self one knew in earlier, happier circumstances, amnesia is its involuntary erasure; the complementary conditions might be described as memory of loss and loss of memory. Thus, at various moments, Watkins struggles to *remember* something vitally important—who he "is" and what his "mission" is—but the details continually elude him.

A central aspect of nostalgia—and a central point of connection between Lessing and Woolf—is a longing for such an ideal, harmonious world that is preserved through emotionally saturated memories of the past. If, as the Jungian analyst Mario Jacoby has phrased it, "to 'know' what Paradise means presupposes knowledge of its opposite, of the burdens and sufferings of earthly existence" and if "the very idea of Paradise contains simultaneous grief over its loss,"[17] then Lessing's *Briefing for a Descent into Hell* expresses not only personal yearning for significant lost places or persons but also a kind of collective human yearning for Paradise and the lost innocence of a prelapsarian world. Several of the locations in Charles Watkins's interior travelogues suggest this compensatory, lost/desired Edenic place, "a country where hostility or dislike had not yet been born."[18] Its contours and characteristics invoke the "myth-country" of Lessing's nostalgically recalled African childhood. In the first representation of this "lost landscape," golden leopardlike beasts become Watkins's companions in an idyllic terrain of lush forests, rivers, and savannas, recalling Lessing's nostalgic memories of childhood in the African bush, teeming with wildlife ("Impertinent Daughters" 65). Eventually, after Watkins explores his domain and discovers the outlines of a vanished city,[19] he realizes that evil has somehow entered the idyllic place and understands his archetypal fall from innocence into the knowledge of good and evil: "I had arrived purged and salt-scoured and guiltless, but . . . between then and now I had drawn evil into my surroundings, into me . . ." (*Briefing* 60).

The pattern of descent or entry into an idyllic location that is ultimately poisoned by human aggression or evil is repeated several times during the narrative, concluding with Watkins's lyrical "recollection" of an interlude with Partisan soldiers in Yugoslavia during the Second World War. He describes an Edenic world of "vast mountains, in which we moved like the first people on earth, discovering riches at every opening of the forest, flowers, fruit, flocks of pigeons, deer, streams of running splashing water full of fish . . ." (*Briefing* 233). A close friend asserts that Watkins in fact never served in Yugoslavia. In effect, Watkins "recovers" a nostalgic memory of an experience that he never actually had—one that reflects Lessing's own memory of abundance in her childhood landscape.

Through the absolute discrepancies between who Watkins "is" to his relatives and friends and to himself—in his lyrical unconscious voyages and in his prosaic recovered identity (the latter restored through medical intervention)—Lessing explores, among other issues, nostalgic memories that are congruent with the fantasy of a collective Edenic past. Moreover, it is the shifting and selective nature of memory itself that is explored in the narrative through representations of complementary, if not contradictory, dimensions of Watkins's reality. Inevitably, by the time the professor of classics is "restored" to his pre-amnesiac self, he has "lost" virtually all memory of his experiences in the interior realm, suggesting that each domain somehow cancels out the other. As he ruefully acknowledges to another psychiatric patient, "They say I lost my memory because I feel guilty. . . . I think I feel guilty because I lost my memory" (*Briefing* 259).

The yearning to return to an idyllic place in the past persists on an intergalactic scale as Lessing turns from "inner space" to "outer space" fiction. In *Shikasta* (1979), for example, the Canopean emissary Johor returns after a long absence to the colonized planet Shikasta—a place he recalls as the paradisal Rohanda. His pre-journey briefing includes a strong warning about the hazards of the now-degraded planet's innermost zone, Zone Six: its most characteristic feature is "a strong emotion—'nostalgia' is their word for it—which means a longing for what has never been or at least not in the form and shape imagined."[20] Johor knows that Zone Six is "a place that weakens, undermines, fills one's mind with dreams, softness, hungers that one had hoped . . . had been left behind forever" (*Shikasta* 7). Nonetheless, he and several other emissaries from Canopus submit themselves to the negative aura of Zone Six in order to influence selected inhabitants; their mission is to avert even further degeneration on the planet. Through documentary records of the emissaries' sojourns on Shikasta, the reader encounters Lessing's paean to a paradisal past along with her thinly disguised critical history of our own "Century of Destruction." Thus, Anna Wulf's—and even Johor's—critical judgment notwithstanding, *Shikasta* encompasses Lessing's ambivalent attitude toward nostalgia as both the domain of debilitating, falsifying memories and the inextinguishable yearning for a harmonious prelapsarian world.

A "myth country" located in the past—and in the imagination—also figures centrally in both Virginia Woolf's autobiographical writings and her fiction. The epiphanic "moments of being" that invigorate her fictional characters often originate in a yearning to return to or recover an idyllic scene or site. For the fictional Clarissa Dalloway, one such defining place is Bourton, where she spent the summer when she was eighteen. Recalling her passionate attachment to Sally Seton during that summer, she can still invoke the precise qualities of her feelings, preserved as if without alteration or distortion. "The strange thing, on looking back, was the purity, the integrity, of her feeling for Sally. It was not like one's feeling for a man. It was completely disinterested, and besides, it had a quality which could only exist between women, between women just grown up."[21]

The central encounter in the narrative between Clarissa and Peter Walsh, with the ensuing ripples of recollection that it releases for both of them, pivots on nostalgia: their overlapping but differently tinted memories and yearnings for the emotional intimacy and intoxication of their youthful romance at Bourton. "Do you remember the lake? [Clarissa] said, in an abrupt voice, under the pressure of an emotion which caught her heart, made the muscles of her throat stiff, and contracted her lips in a spasm as she said 'lake'" (*Mrs. Dalloway* 43). For Peter the image brings an inner wince of pain as well, as he is forced not only to confront his loss of Clarissa to Richard Dalloway all those years ago but to acknowledge that he still loves her. In late middle age, both Clarissa and Peter look nostalgically to the past, regretting the erosion of the freshness, the intensity, of their youthful passions. Still, Woolf, who believed that certain vivid memories retained their exact impressions intact in the mind, unmodified by the passage of time—"these scenes—for why do they survive undamaged year after year unless they are made of something comparatively permanent?" ("Sketch," *Moments* 122)—permits Clarissa to preserve some of that vital fire of emotional truth into her adult life. The exhilaration she had experienced with Sally at Bourton survives in memory as the "radiance . . . the revelation, the religious feeling" (35–6) of their youthful encounter, a "moment of being" that she savors several times during the single day that forms the novel's present time.[22]

The most emotionally saturated "myth country" in Woolf's writing is not Clarissa Dalloway's Bourton, however, but the environs of St. Ives, Cornwall, where Virginia herself vacationed with her family during summers of her early childhood. Not only her first but, in her own estimation, her most central memory is associated with that landscape:

> If life has a base that it stands upon, if it is a bowl that one fills and fills and fills—then my bowl without a doubt stands upon this memory. It is of lying half asleep, half awake, in bed in the nursery at St Ives. It is of hearing the waves breaking, one, two, one, two, and sending a splash of water over the beach . . . of lying and hearing this splash and . . . feeling . . . the purest ecstasy I can conceive. ("Sketch," *Moments* 64–5)

Later she emphasizes her feeling that nothing else in her early childhood was as valuable as the gift her parents gave her of those summer holidays in

Cornwall—"the best beginning to a life conceivable" ("Sketch" 110). The account of St. Ives continues for several pages as Woolf describes in meticulous detail Talland House, its luxuriant gardens, and its "perfect view—right across the Bay to Godrevy Lighthouse" ("Sketch" 111). Eventually, she succeeded in recapturing and immortalizing that view and experience in *To the Lighthouse* (1927), achieving one of the sublime literary expressions of nostalgia.

Woolf digresses briefly to examine the memory-making process itself, as she mulls over "how many other than human forces affect us" ("Sketch" 114). She considers whether memory is an accurate record or "whether I am telling the truth when I see myself perpetually taking the breath of these voices in my sails, and tacking this way and that, in daily life as I yield to them . . ." ("Sketch" 115). Although she suspects this train of reflection "to be of great importance," Woolf puts it aside as "a vein to work out later" ("Sketch" 115) and returns to her imaginative reconstruction of St. Ives. Thus, she does not pursue the discrepancies between "truth" and recollection, as Lessing's Anna Wulf does so insistently. Woolf's idyllic memories of St. Ives are more significant when viewed against her decidedly unnostalgic and unidealized descriptions of her childhood home at 22 Hyde Park Gate, London. Memories of that environment are not softened by the scrim of nostalgia, for it was there that Woolf suffered not only the deaths of several members of her immediate family—her mother, stepsister, younger brother, and father all died within an eleven-year period beginning when she was thirteen—but also the sexual advances of her two half-brothers.[23] Through memory and imagination she preserved the image of her mother in particular, as well as other vanished members of her family, as shields against a site so "tangled and matted with emotion" that she felt "suffocated by the recollection."[24]

To the extent that nostalgia may signify not only homesickness or the yearning for an emotionally significant place but also the longing for an absent, emotionally important figure who is strongly associated with it, memory traces of *home* are inevitably linked with those of *mother*.[25] Both Virginia Woolf's and Doris Lessing's fiction and autobiographical writings demonstrate this central emotional connection. Undoubtedly the fullest expression of nostalgia in Woolf's writing occurs in passages, both autobiographical and fictional, in which she attempts to recover memories of her mother, Julia Stephen, who died when Virginia was thirteen. In "A Sketch of the Past," written when she was in her late fifties, Woolf admits that she remained haunted by the image of her mother until she was in her forties—until, in fact, she wrote *To the Lighthouse*. Before that time, "the presence of my mother obsessed me. I could hear her voice, see her, imagine what she would do or say as I went about my day's doings. She was one of the invisible presences who after all play so important a part in every life" ("Sketch" 80). Later she adds, "of course she was central. I suspect the word 'central' gets closest to the general feeling I had of living so completely in her atmosphere that one never got far enough away from her to see her as a person" ("Sketch" 83).

Moreover, Woolf associated the death of her mother with the loss of the idyllic St. Ives. One summer, the Stephen family returned to Talland House to discover that the incomparable view of the lighthouse and bay had been spoiled by the construction of a hotel; soon, a realtor's sign appeared on their own lawn. "And then mother died. . . . Our lease was sold . . . and St Ives vanished forever" ("Sketch" 117). In *To the Lighthouse,* Woolf imaginatively transforms homesickness by rendering into a consummate work of fiction her experience of the loss of the idyllic setting of childhood as well as the (idealized) mother with whom it was inextricably associated. Like her mother, Julia Stephen, Mrs. Ramsay is an emotionally commanding presence whose image remains equally indelible in her absence, years after her death is matter-of-factly announced in the novel's middle section. Moreover, through a fictionalized persona, the artist Lily Briscoe, Woolf explores the pain still associated with the loss of that idealized mother. In her autobiographical commentary, Woolf observes, "if one could give sense of my mother's personality one would have to be an artist" ("Sketch" 85). However, the motherless Lily of the first part of the novel worships Mrs. Ramsay in a manner that would characterize few actual mother-daughter relationships; idealizing the older woman, she literally desires to merge with her.[26] "What device [was there] for becoming, like waters poured into one jar, inextricably the same, one with the object one adored? . . . Could loving, as people called it, make her and Mrs. Ramsay one? for it was not knowledge but unity that she desired . . . intimacy itself, which is knowledge. . . ."[27]

In the novel's middle section, the bracketed, understated announcement of Mrs. Ramsay's sudden death clearly mirrors Julia Stephen's unexpected death in 1895 at the age of forty-nine. Other bracketed statements of the deaths of Prue and Andrew Ramsay echo the loss of Virginia Woolf's half-sister Stella and her brother Thoby to arbitrary, premature deaths. While "Time Passes," the Ramsay house in the Hebrides—modeled after Woolf's mythologized St. Ives—remains empty and dark. The sense of literal and emotional absence represented through descriptions of the deteriorating, unoccupied house lyrically revises Woolf's less poeticized view of the years immediately following Julia Stephen's death: "With mother's death the merry, various family life which she had held in being shut for ever. In its place a dark cloud settled over us; we seemed to sit all together cooped up, sad, solemn, unreal, under a haze of heavy emotion" ("Sketch" 93).[28]

In the novel's final section, Lily returns ten years later with the remaining Ramsays to the house in the Hebrides and confronts the presence of absence: the undiminished power of Mrs. Ramsay's personality remains despite her death. Lily's yearning is embedded in the effort of completing a (new) painting that, rather than capturing a realistic representation of Mrs. Ramsay, abstractly crystallizes her own feelings of attachment, longing, and loss. If nostalgia may be distinguished from simple memory by the presence of painful longing that betrays uncompleted mourning and by a desire for the (impossible) restoration or recovery of that which has been lost, Lily experiences those feelings as she grieves for Mrs. Ramsay and longs to recover her presence. Ultimately, in the novel's concluding passage, Lily experiences a cathartic, healing moment as she moves from expressions of anger and longing to the transmutation of loss through creative expression. Adding the final line that resolves the emotional dilemma pursued through her grieving, and its aesthetic equivalent pursued through her painting, she achieves the moment of release: "I have had my vision" (*Lighthouse* 209).

Thus, in the first part of *To the Lighthouse* Woolf creates a multifaceted but nonetheless idealized vision of her mother fabricated out of her own unrequited longing and loss, placing Lily to worship, childlike, at the maternal woman's knee—the way Woolf did (or imagined she did) as a child. In her autobiographical account, however, Woolf acknowledges more critically, "Can I remember ever being alone with her for more than a few minutes? Someone was always interrupting. When I think of her spontaneously she is always in a room full of people . . ." ("Sketch" 83). The novel's middle section, "Time Passes," lyrically equates *mother* and *home* as the death of Mrs. Ramsay reverberates through the destruction and collapse of the magical intimate space with which she is associated; in the novel's final section, the house (if not Mrs. Ramsay) is brought back to life again. In the last section, nostalgic yearnings are balanced with a critical perspective and a degree of anger toward her vanished mother that Woolf was incapable of acknowledging for nearly thirty years and that Lily Briscoe was incapable of acknowledging ten years earlier in the first section of the narrative. Lily, recalling what she regards as Mrs. Ramsay's excessive willingness to subordinate herself to the needs of her emotionally demanding husband, reflects, "Giving, giving, giving, she had died—and had left all this. Really, she was angry with Mrs. Ramsay" (*Lighthouse* 149).

The true source of Lily's anger is not Mrs. Ramsay's emotional "giving" to Mr. Ramsay but what any mourner feels toward the lost object of her or his attachment: anger toward the departed for the absolute and irrevocable fact of her death, which has severed the bereaved survivor from that vital object of affection. "Here was Lily, at forty-four, wasting her time, unable to do a thing, standing there, playing at painting, playing at the one thing one did not play at, and *it was all Mrs. Ramsay's fault.* She was dead. The step where she used to sit was empty. She was dead" (*Lighthouse* 149 50, my emphasis). The emphasized phrase and the repetition of the statement, "she was dead," bring to mind a child's diction, also captured in the indiscriminate angry complaint, "it's all your fault."

Phrased another way, the Mrs. Ramsay of the first part of the novel is an idealized figure rendered from Virginia Woolf's nostalgic memories and fantasies, preserved from childhood, of her mother's *presence.* For the Mrs. Ramsay of the final part of the novel, Lily is the vehicle for Woolf's more critical exploration of the reverberations of her mother's *absence:* the emotional traces of nostalgic mourning along with the belated expression of anger triggered by irrevocable loss.[29] Registering the cathartic effect of the process that she ultimately filtered through Lily Briscoe, Woolf analyzed the significance that writing about her mother (and father) in this novel had on her decades-long obsession:

> I suppose that I did for myself what psycho-analysts do for their patients. I expressed some very long felt and deeply felt emotion. And in expressing it I explained it and then laid it to rest. But what is the meaning of "explained" it? Why, because I described her and my feeling for her in that book, should my vision of her and my feeling for her become so much dimmer and weaker? ("Sketch" 81)

Although Woolf does not explicitly answer the questions she raises in this passage, it is obvious that *To the Lighthouse* is the answer. Her narrative achieves a double memorialization, through art, of the lost mother: the masterpiece of language rendered by Woolf that contains the more modest visual equivalent created by her fictional stand-in, Lily Briscoe.[30]

At the age of sixty-four, Doris Lessing—only a few years older than Woolf when she wrote the first of her autobiographical memoirs—also attempted a "sketch of the past," no doubt prompted by her return to southern Africa after an involuntary decades-long absence. In it, she acknowledges the difficulty of articulating her earliest, painful memories as she attempts to achieve a balanced recollection of her parents, particularly her mother. Interestingly, one striking image of her parents reads as if it could have come from Woolf's *To the Lighthouse,* when Mr. and Mrs. Ramsay confront their mutually exclusive perceptions of the journey to the lighthouse and of the world itself. As Lessing phrases it,

> I have an image of them, confronting Life in such different ways. He looks it straight in the face, with a dark, grim, ironical recognition. But she, always being disappointed in ways he could never be, has a defiant, angry little air: she has caught Life out in injustice *again.* "How can you!" she seems to be saying, exasperated, to Life. "It's not right to behave like that!" And she gives a brisk, brave little sniff. ("Impertinent Daughters" 57–8, Lessing's emphasis).

Ultimately, however, Lessing's unsentimental and unidealized recollection of her mother is antithetical to Woolf's: Emily Maude Tayler, far from being the self-sacrificing "angel of the house" embodied in Julia Stephen, is—from the daughter's perspective—the quintessential rejecting mother. Lessing's memories are tainted by a conviction from early in life that she was an unwanted child—that her mother, as she phrases it, "didn't like me" ("Impertinent Daughters" 61). Having wished for a first son, Maude Tayler made no secret of her disappointment with her daughter, for whom she had not even chosen a name at birth (the attending physician suggested "Doris") and for whom she had "no milk"—"I had to be bottle-fed from the start and I was half-starved for the first year and never stopped screaming . . ." ("Impertinent Daughters" 61). Lessing acknowledges that her memories of her mother are "all of antagonism, and fighting, and feeling shut out; of pain because the baby born two-and-a-half years after me was so much loved when I was not" ("Impertinent Daughters" 61). Not surprisingly, as she admits, "Writing about my mother is difficult. I keep coming up against barriers, and they are not much different now from what they were then. She paralysed me as a child by the anger and pity I felt. Now only pity is left, but it still makes it hard to write about her" ("Impertinent Daughters" 68).[31] In the more recently published first volume of her autobiography, *Under My Skin* (1994), Lessing provides a fuller overview of her parents' lives both before and after she was born. Once again, she emphasizes the rift between daughter and mother, claiming, "I was in nervous flight from [my mother] ever since I can remember anything, and from the age of fourteen I set myself obdurately against her in a kind of inner emigration from everything she represented" (*Under My Skin* 15).

Some years before Lessing published two essay-length autobiographical memoirs and two volumes (to date) of her biography, she attempted a symbolic one: when *The Memoirs of a Survivor* (1975) was published, she described it as her "attempt at autobiography."[32] Thus, her fictionalized representations of intergenerational female relationships deserve especially close scrutiny. In fact, in certain ways Doris Lessing's significantly titled *Memoirs of a Survivor* is for Lessing what *To the Lighthouse* is for Woolf: a memoir (or construction) of the "lost mother" of childhood who is associated with the image of an idyllic vanished landscape of paradise or wholeness. However, the "lost mother" of Lessing's fiction is based less on her actual negative, rejecting mother than on a compensatory fantasy: the perfect parent of the imagination who offers unconditional love and acceptance.

As the unnamed narrator of *Memoirs* tries to make sense of the collapsing social world outside her window, she another of Lessing's travelers in "inner space"—journeys symbolically through the wall of her flat to enter into another domain in space and time. Among other details that gain resonance in the context of Lessing's conviction that her mother had rejected her from birth, the unnamed narrator of *Memoirs* describes "the sobbing of a child, a child alone, disliked, repudiated; and at the same time, beside it, I could hear the complaint of the mother . . ." (*Memoirs* 148). As the inner world the narrator apprehends beyond her wall becomes her "real life" (*Memoirs* 18), the domain she visits "beyond the wall" ramifies into different layerings and emotional hues of experience and possibility. On the one hand it embodies the confining experiences of someone's actual past: variously, a girl Emily in different stages of emotional development as well as other females in the narrator's past, including her mother and her own earlier self at various stages of maturation. Significantly, both Lessing's mother and her maternal grandmother were named Emily.[33]

The location beyond the wall of the narrator's flat is understood as "a prison, where nothing could happen but what one saw happening . . . with no escape but the slow wearing away of one [minute] after another" (*Memoirs* 42). Certain rooms trigger a powerful "tug of nostalgia for . . . the life that had been lived there" (41). A claustrophobic "child-space" (43), although apparently comprising Emily's experiences, is a location "as close to me as my own memories" (47). The narrator yearns at times to escape permanently into the inner realm, "simply to walk through the wall and never come back. But this would be irresponsible . . ." (24). Instead, rather than dismissing nostalgic memories as distortions that lie (as did Anna Wulf) or giving in to their painful but sentimental appeal, she determines to explore them and thus neutralize their debilitating power.

Hence, the domain beyond the wall also offers sites of potentiality, alternatives to the suffocating past enshrined in memory. "The space and knowledge of the possibility of alternative action" (*Memoirs* 42) offers the narrator the prospect of "restoration": revisions of experiences and locations both recalled and forgotten. She accepts responsibility for Emily as if she were her own daughter. Her choice may be understood, in light of Lessing's autobiographical admissions, as her attempt to achieve emotional reconciliation with her mother—herself a "poor girl brought up without affection" ("Impertinent Daughters" 55)—by reversing the generational obligations of the filial relationship. In an ironic mirroring, Lessing's mother also experienced "homesickness"—but for her, "home" was the England she had left behind before Doris's birth. In *Memoirs,* Lessing conflates her mother's nostalgia with her own: one of the narrator's fantasies or "fables" is pictured as a farm in Wales, far away from the collapsing city, characterized by "love, kindness, the deep shelter of a family" (34).[34]

Late in *Memoirs,* the rooms beyond the wall that the narrator has helped to restore open out into terraces of Edenic gardens that contrast sharply with the deteriorating, contaminated world she observes outside her flat. Ultimately, all walls dissolve and the nostalgic locations transmogrify into a place she can enter in present time. With Emily and others of their group, she is led "out of this collapsed little world into another order of world altogether" (217). The paradisal world they enter represents the satisfaction of the desire to ameliorate homesickness, to return to the state of ultimate harmony first known in the infant's attachment to her (or his) mother.

The figure who leads the narrator and the others into the ineffable is described in lyrical language reminiscent of Virginia Woolf's idealized fantasy of the lost mother of childhood. (Probably coincidentally, the passage also contains an echo of the significant final phrase of *Mrs. Dalloway):* "the one person I had been looking for all this time was there: *there she was.* No, I am not able to say clearly what she was like. She was beautiful. . . . I only saw her for a moment, in a time like the fading of a spark on dark air— a glimpse: she turned her face just once to me, and all I can say is . . . nothing at all" (*Memoirs* 216, emphasis and ellipses, except for the final ellipsis, are mine). Suggesting an all-encompassing symbolic embrace that resolves the "longing for the mother as the 'containing world'," [35] "the world fold[s] itself up" (*Memoirs* 216) around the nameless female figure who leads the narrator and the others into the blissful state that is the imagination's antidote to homesickness. Thus do the nostalgic memories of *home* and *mother* become imaginatively figured as Paradise.

Nostalgic longing and mourning remain central matters two decades later in Lessing's most recent and less admittedly-autobiographical fiction, *Love, Again* (1995). Through the prism of aging, Lessing maps the territory of the affections from the vantage point (or *dis*advantage point, as it were) of post-middle-age. Matters of the heart—and a deeper scaffolding of unacknowledged longing—continue to challenge even an emotionally self-sufficient older woman as she finds herself struggling to reconcile claims of autonomy with the overpowering pull of emotional intimacy and sexual desire that unexpectedly enmesh her. While the reawakening of eros catalyzes the central character's reflection on her past and obliges her to consider the interconnections among aging, gender, desire, and loss, Lessing's narrative also reprises the complex nostalgia that marks her previous fiction.

Sarah Durham, an attractive widow in her mid-sixties, is a scriptwriter for a theatrical agency who, in the process of working on a romantic opera, finds herself infatuated with several men in the production, all young enough to be her sons. Eventually, as she struggles with her irrational feelings, she finds herself recalling events from much earlier in her life, even dating back to infancy. Grieving in response not only to the suicide of a friend with whom she has collaborated on the opera but to the painful reawakening of the whole gamut of primitive sensual and erotic feelings, she relives the experience of "Absolute loss. As if she had been dependent on some emotional food, like impalpable milk, and it had been withdrawn."[36]

Among other emotionally saturated moments in the history of Sarah's affections are several experiences that concern her younger brother, whom she recognizes was the true object of her mother's affections during their childhood. Late in the novel, Sarah observes a scene in a park that mirrors her own (and, presumably, Lessing's) experience of being catapulted out of her mother's emotional orbit by the birth of a much-wanted son. In the scene, a young child is cruelly excluded from her mother's totally-absorbed infatuation with her infant brother. In the vain hope of claiming her mother's attention, the child lavishes affection on the adored baby. Sarah, privately empathizing, even identifying, with the excluded child's desolation, acknowledges their mutual habitation of an "eternity of loneliness and grief" (346). Through her fictional protagonist's attempt to trace the vagaries of desire back to their source in the primary mother-child relationship, Lessing demonstrates the power of negative nostalgia as the unappeased phantoms of earliest experience converge with the not-entirely appeasable demons of advancing age.

Following her return to Macheke/Mashopi to determine whether she could know the place apart from her imaginative transformations of it in *The Golden Notebook,* Lessing wrote, "Memory in any case is a lying record: we choose to remember this and not that. . . . When we see remembered scenes from the outside, as an observer, a golden haze seduces us into sentimentality" (*Laughter* 72). As a description of the nostalgia-producing aspect of imagination, the language here is especially pertinent: the "lying record" of memory results from the inescapable filters of time and experience that separate the current self who recalls—"from the outside, as an observer"— from the younger self whose experiences are recalled. Lessing's conviction that memory inevitably "lies" sharply contrasts with that of Woolf, who validates the undistorted accuracy of certain scenes from her childhood. While Woolf considers but ultimately resists the likelihood that, over time, even indelible memories are transformed by the evolving perspective of the observer self, Lessing discounts the possibility of recovering a "pure" version of any scene or experience in one's past. Indeed, it is this difference in orientation, partly shaped by their different historical moments, that most distinguishes between the operations of nostalgia in Woolf's and Lessing's oeuvres. The modernist Woolf wrote during a time period in which collective loss—the devastations of one world war and a second one impending, the erosion of cultural stability, and the loss of the certitudes of traditional narrative form itself—corroborated the experiences of profound loss within her own personal history. In both her fiction and her autobiographical writing, she attempts to "fix" the past in both senses—to repair and to secure—at least in part by excavating and resolving nostalgic memories. By contrast, Lessing is an exile who, reflecting (and reflecting on) her own life, chronicles the dislocations of female experience as they overlap with contemporary experience—geographical as well as psychological and temporal. Thus, while the past may be unequivocal for Woolf, it is entirely equivocal for Lessing, who questions the very fixity of the past that Woolf attempts to fix. Yet despite the challenge to "lying nostalgia" that Lessing articulates so persuasively through Anna Wulf in *The Golden*

Notebook, a number of her other fictional and autobiographical writings betray the powerful grip of the lost landscape and the idealized lost mother of her own formative years.

For both Woolf and Lessing, nostalgia is the imagination's attempt to override, neutralize, or cancel loss. For both, that impulse fuels a desire not only to retrieve emotionally resonant memories but to "fix" them: to "make of the moment something permanent" (*Lighthouse* 161) and also to transmute the losses it represents into something more consoling. Thus, nostalgia is not simply, as Gayle Greene argues, "a forgetting, merely regressive, whereas memory may look back in order to move forward and transform disabling fictions to enabling fictions . . .".[37] Rather, the emotional reparations that both Woolf and Lessing achieve through their aesthetic representations demonstrate the transformative significance of their autobiographical and fictional explorations of longing and loss, whether focused on idealized persons or places, or both. Though shaped by radically different historical, geographical, and personal circumstances, both authors explore and illuminate the writer's "myth-country"—"not . . . something untrue, but a concentration of truth" (*Laughter* 35)—as they transform the lost landscape of home and the lost mother of childhood into art.

Part II

Displacements of/from Home

◇

◈ 2 ◈

Home is (Mother) Earth:
Animal Dreams, Barbara Kingsolver

You can't know somebody . . . till you've followed him home.

—Codi Noline, *Animal Dreams*

I f the fiction and autobiographical writings of Virginia Woolf and Doris Lessing reveal a nostalgic preoccupation with the idealized or fantasized lost mother and the lost landscape of home that is associated with her, a number of narratives by contemporary American women writers complicate those preoccupations in diverse ways. Nostalgia, whether "lying" (in Lessing's terms) or the trace of "enduring" memories (in Woolf's), represents a saturated emotional private history as it perpetuates and, over time, may eventually resolve the process of mourning. In its literary representations, nostalgia thus functions as a means of rendering and figuratively repairing the lost past by transmuting its pain. The narratives discussed in this section—Displacements of/from Home—were authored by writers a generation or two younger than Woolf or Lessing—their figurative daughters and even granddaughters. Each novel constructs the central character's longing for belonging in relation to particular places or figures in the past that continue to color her understanding of herself. In Barbara Kingsolver's *Animal Dreams* (1990), *The Bean Trees* (1988), and *Pigs in Heaven* (1993), and in Julia Alvarez's *How the García Girls Lost Their Accents* (1992), the female protagonists find themselves either far from what they regard as home or longing for a home/land or language from which they have been estranged. The expression of nostalgia suggests that the effort to "fix" the past continues to influence and shape women's recent fiction.

The process of mourning in response to loss may be elicited not only by nostalgia or homesickness for a particular place or person but also by an individual's severance—whether voluntary or involuntary—from a larger cultural community. Throughout this study I use the phrase *cultural mourning* to signify the literary representation of mourning that results from cultural dislocation and loss of ways of life from which an individual feels historically severed or exiled (such as the circumstance produced for African Americans by the profound dislocations of slavery, for Native Americans by displacement from their original lands to reservations, and for political exiles by voluntary or involuntary dislocation from their home/lands). The narratives discussed in this section elaborate on the central character's longing for belonging in two senses: not only for the idealized lost mother and her association with the lost home/land but for connection to a collective cultural history and home (and, for Alvarez, a language) that extends beyond the protagonist's individual experience.

In *Animal Dreams,* Barbara Kingsolver develops the theme of longing—for the absent mother and for home—with reference to other stories of quest and return, most prominently *The Odyssey.* The idea of home/land is complicated by allusive references to a more recent classical Western text, *The Waste Land,* as well as to Native American conceptions of home and cosmos. The figure of the father also functions importantly in the equation of loss. One of the suggestive resonances with home and homeland that structure *Animal Dreams* is the allusive presence of the father of narratives of homecoming, Homer. (For English speakers, the notion of home is embedded in the poet's very name). Indeed, the first point of view introduced in the novel is that of Doc Homer, father of the protagonist, Codi Noline. Through misguided pride rather than malice, Doc Homer has disguised and misrepresented the identity of home for his daughter since her earliest childhood. The voices of father and daughter alternate throughout the narrative, providing a double perspective for the several intertwined narrative motifs. Although the Spanish version of Homer's name, *Homero,* heads each of the narrative sections told from his perspective, the full meaning of that fact only becomes clear late in the narrative. Codi and her younger sister Hallie represent not only complementary embodiments of the quest but complementary dimensions of the Odyssean universe: readers learn that Cosima (Codi's full Spanish name) signifies "order in the cosmos" while Halimeda (Hallie's full name) translates as "thinking of the sea."[1]

Animal Dreams is structured through three overlapping narrative dimensions, each of which depends on the pattern of the quest and/or the return home. The most fundamental is the emotional and psychological cluster that concerns the attachments and losses in Codi's own family history and represents her belated but ultimate recovery of her own lost self in the aptly named town of Grace, Arizona. Codi's mother died when she was three years old and her sister Hallie was only an infant. Although Codi has vague memories of her mother as a "strong and ferociously loving" figure (*Animal Dreams* 49), she remains "an outsider to . . . nurturing" (46), not even certain whether she witnessed or only imagined the helicopter that conveyed her departing mother, who died even before the vehicle could "lift itself up out of the alfalfa" (49).

Since childhood, Codi's widowed father has been nearly as absent to her. The community's respected doctor, Homer Noline is, ironically, unable to heal his own family. Numbed by grief over the loss of his wife, he has remained in a state of perpetual mourning, raising his two daughters in a clinical, detached manner based more on the correct orthopedic shoes than on the expression of affection. His perception of his daughters as young children, expressed in the first section of the novel, underscores the way his own emotional losses have continued to delimit the world for Codi (though not for Hallie). Recalling the two girls sleeping like small animals huddling together for warmth, Homero conflates their past and future lives, reflecting "how close together these two are, and how much they have to lose. How much they've already lost in their lives to come" (4).

Thus emotionally unparented from an early age, as children Codi and her sister had played a game they called "orphans," in which they fantasized about who among an anonymous crowd of people might be "our true father or mother[.] Which is the one grownup here that loves us?" (72). Codi's sense of isolation continued into adolescence, when she grew to be nearly six feet tall; her acute self-consciousness about her height still makes her feel "out of place" (228). When she was fifteen, she became pregnant by her boyfriend—a Native American youth who never knew of her pregnancy—only to lose the child during the sixth month. Her father, aware of both her pregnancy and the stillbirth, had even witnessed Codi's burial of the fetus in a dry riverbed without ever revealing that fact or attempting to comfort her in her loss. Although at one point he recalls an imagined conversation with her—"Do you know what you have inside you?" (98)—he had voiced neither those words nor any other acknowledgement of her condition or its termination.

Shaped by these fundamental losses of mother and of child, Codi regards herself as "bracketed by death" (50). In fact, her surname, "no-line," signals her separation from generational continuity, compounded by her view of herself as an outsider. As a result of her father's misrepresentations, she believes her parents came from Illinois and therefore that Grace is not her true home. Although she does not name her condition—a prolonged depression precipitated by unresolved mourning—most of the early images of the narrative figure her emotional deadness: bones and skeletons, graves and graveyards. The actual skeleton that Codi finds in a storage room in the high school where she teaches biology signifies the emotional skeletons in the closet that she must discover as prelude to the reclamation of her past and her discovery of her way back home.

Less adventuresome and less optimistic than her politically idealistic sister, Codi suffers from a sense of estrangement when she first returns to Arizona. "I *was* a stranger to Grace. I'd stayed away fourteen years and in my gut I believe I was hoping that had changed: I would step off the bus and land smack in the middle of a sense of belonging . . . home at last" (12). Instead, she continues to feel "dislocated" (47); having "spent my whole childhood as an outsider . . . I'd sell my soul and all my traveling shoes to *belong* some place" (30, Kingsolver's emphasis). Poignantly and ironically, what has brought Codi back to the "memory minefield" (46) of her home-town is not her own memories but her father's accelerating memory loss. Each of the sections of the narrative told from Homer's perspective demonstrates the dissolution of a sense of time, so that events from the past become indistinguishable from current events. Because he holds many of the secrets to his family's history, his mental erosion and confusion make Codi's quest more urgent and difficult.

Like Codi's inner being, the land around Grace is at risk; a major stage in Codi's eventual discovery of her true place as an "insider" in Grace is her political awakening to that fact. The people in the community talk about "poison ground" and the "fruit drop" (63) that is killing the orchard trees; concurrently, Codi ponders the mystery of her own "family tree" (173). Through her temporary job as a high school biology teacher, she accidentally discovers that the river water and the land are literally "dead" as the result of unchecked chemical pollution from a nearby mining operation. Codi, galvanizing the women of Grace to rally against the mining company by opposing the dam that would divert their river and perpetuate the pollution of their land, also initiates her own inner reparations. One woman affirms the necessity of action, arguing that their menfolk won't see the struggle to reclaim their land in the same terms as the women do. "They think the trees can die and we can just go somewhere else, and as long as we fry up the bacon for them in the same old pan, they think it would be . . . *home*" (179, Kingsolver's emphasis). Through that comment, Kingsolver suggests that both men and women of the community around Grace regard home not simply as a particular place but as a symbolic space defined through women's traditional domestic tasks and emotional investments.

Yet, increasingly in the narrative, home is associated with the land, which carries its own emotional history and memory. As Codi pursues her personal history, attempting to tap her father's memories even as they recede from coherence, she explains to her biology students, "People can forget, and forget, and forget, but the land has a memory. The lakes and the rivers are still hanging on to the DDT and every other insult we ever gave them" (255). Codi's claim reflects both Kingsolver's training as a biologist and her appreciation for a Native American perspective in which the land is an organic entity that supports communal identity. As she has explained in an interview, "I think biology is my religion. Understanding the processes of the natural world and how all living things are related is the way that I answer those questions that are the basis of religion. . . . [T]he Christian creation myth, which says the world was put here as a little garden for us to use, goes a long way in explaining how we've really devastated that garden."[2]

In *Animal Dreams,* the intertwined explorations of individual and collective memory and the land's "memory," as each bears on the idea of home, provide the narrative's most mythically resonant dimension. The parallels between Doc Homer's and Codi's inner dis-ease and the disease of the land allusively suggest both T. S. Eliot's *The Waste Land* and its antecedent, the legend of the Fisher King whose sterility signifies the land's inability to flourish.[3] The cycle of death and fertility also figures prominently in a number of traditional and contemporary Native American narratives, most visibly in Leslie Marmon Silko's novel, *Ceremony* (1977), set in the Southwest.[4] Although in Kingsolver's contemporary rendering of the story Doc Homer is not literally a king, he functions symbolically in the narrative as the ailing Fisher King, incapacitated by old age and accelerating memory loss. A figure of authority in the town, Doc Homer presides over life and death as both doctor and coroner. As Codi characterizes her family's isolation from the community her father serves, "everyone in Grace was somehow related except us Nolines, the fish out of water" (71). Moreover, Homer Noline acknowledges his spiritual malaise. When, midway through the narrative, Codi confronts him with her discovery in the town graveyard—a gravestone that provides a central clue to her family's buried history—Doc Homer responds, "Perhaps I am dead" (169).

What gives Kingsolver's narrative of quest and return its originality is the interweaving of Western and Native American mythologies of the land, and her fresh embodiment of the wasteland legend of sterility and regeneration, through the creation of a female rather than a male quester who is heir to the "king's" malaise. Codi Noline mirrors her father's emotional sterility, a condition compounded by the traumatic events of her own childhood and adolescence as well as by her experience as an "outsider" painfully estranged from the community in which she grew up. Before she returns to Grace, "anesthetized" by pain (89), she has maintained a sterile relationship (in Crete, another allusion, perhaps, to Odysseus's travels) with an emergency room surgeon named Carlo—"a man who reattached severed parts for a living" (38)[5]—ostensibly seeking but actually fearing genuine emotional attachment. Her only true attachment is to her sister, whom she idolizes, comparing herself unfavorably to Hallie at every opportunity. As she phrases it in one of many efforts to articulate the differences between them, "It wasn't a matter of courage or dreams, but something a whole lot simpler. A pilot would call it ground orientation. I'd spent a long time circling above the clouds, looking for life, while Hallie was living it" (225). Codi's inner torpor is thus figured not only in the sterility of the land around Grace but in her sense of radical disconnection from it—her lack of "ground orientation."

In some versions of the wasteland legend, there is a third figure besides the injured king and the quester whose task is to aid in his recovery: a healer.[6] However, Codi is as much in need of healing as is her father. In Kingsolver's reworking of the legend under the influence of both classical Western and Native American mythologies, it is the quester herself, not the king, who is ultimately healed. Ironically, Codi, the daughter of a doctor, studied to enter the medical profession herself until, during her residency in obstetrics-gynecology, she suffered a failure of nerve during a complex delivery and withdrew from further training. Rather, the role of healer falls to Loyd Peregrina, the Native American man who unknowingly impregnated Codi years before.

Loyd is in many ways Codi's antithesis. Although he too has suffered emotional losses of those close to him—his twin brother died at about the same time that Codi lost her baby and, later, his marriage collapsed when his wife ran out on him—Loyd is sustained by his strong family attachments and his Native spiritual tradition. Deeply connected both to people and to the land, he has access to a deeper understanding of home—not so much a literal place as a spiritual location—and a vision of the cosmos that

Codi only slowly acquires through his nurturing affection for her. Loyd's role in the narrative as Codi's spiritual guide is signaled by his names. His surname, *peregrina,* is the Spanish word for "pilgrim"; his given name, Loyd, suggests his "alloyed" state. Like his endearing coyote-dog Jack, he is of mixed blood: Pueblo, Navajo, and Apache. The different tribal legacies embody complementary orientations in the world, roughly—as Loyd characterizes them—"homebodies" and "wanderers" (213). Despite his hybridity, Loyd identifies himself not as an Apache, or wanderer (as Codi had assumed during their brief adolescent relationship) but as a Pueblo, or homebody.

Codi, at this point still believing that her family originated far from Arizona, concludes that she is a member of the "Nothing Tribe" (213).[7] Elsewhere she is humorously characterized by her friend Emelina as the opposite of a homemaker, a "home ignorer" (77). Becoming more fully acquainted with Loyd only after she meets his extended family of nurturing female relatives in the Santa Rosalia Pueblo, Codi discovers that "You can't know somebody . . . till you've followed him home" (231)—indeed, until you know his community. According to Paula Gunn Allen (herself of mixed—Laguna Pueblo and white—blood), among the Keres (Laguna Pueblo) people in particular, the association between home and tribe constitutes a vital dimension of identity. The individual knows who he/she is within a communal context of connectedness to others and to tradition. Moreover, as Allen interprets the Pueblo belief system, the figure who embodies that connection is Mother: "Failure to know your mother, that is, your position and its attendant traditions, history, and place in the scheme of things, is failure to remember your significance, your reality, your right relationship to earth and society. It is the same as being lost—isolated, abandoned, self-estranged, and alienated from your own life."[8] Juxtaposing Loyd's spiritual "groundedness" with Codi's lack of "ground orientation," Kingsolver assimilates the Pueblo conception of home not as a regressive place but as a spiritual space within which one is vitally linked to a larger community. Against Codi's defensive ethic of personal loss shaped by a history of unresolved mourning—"Nothing you love will stay" (233)—Loyd Peregrina's healing teaching and profound concern for her enable Codi to discover her capacity for intimacy and a more encompassing meaning of home as a state of mind, where nothing is ever lost.

William Bevis observes that in a number of novels by Native American authors, "coming home, staying put, contracting, even what we call 'regressing' to a place, a past where one has been before, is not only the primary story, it is a primary mode of knowledge and a primary good."[9] Additionally, "'identity,' for a Native American, is not a matter of finding 'one's self,' but of finding a 'self' that is transpersonal and includes a society, a past, and a place. To be separated from that transpersonal time and space is to lose identity."[10] According to Bevis, that view of the individual as part of larger collective identity derives from three assumptions of tribalism that are common to diverse Native American tribes: "the individual is completed only in relation to others," "respect for the past," and "place."[11]

Versions of these communal/tribal values are assimilated in Kingsolver's narrative: the disaffected, alienated, "homeless" white female protagonist, under the spiritual guidance of her Native American lover, ultimately recovers the meaning of her past and discovers her place in the community. Repeatedly in *Animal Dreams,* affirmative Native American images and attitudes are placed in contrast with Codi's or her father's ambivalent or negative attitudes toward themselves and their community. These distinctions further illustrate Kingsolver's effective synthesis (and juxtaposition) of Western and Native American mythologies. For example, in Homer's *Odyssey,* Odysseus's wife Penelope embodies the virtues of loyalty and patience, one demonstration of which is her strategy of weaving by day and unweaving by night in an effort to stall her suitors. In traditional stories common to both Pueblo and Navajo traditions, Spider Woman, the weaver, is celebrated as the creative principle itself. By contrast, Doc Homer, in one of his disjointed reveries, views himself as enmeshed in a negative web: "His family is a web of women dead and alive, with himself at the center like a spider, driven by different instincts" (98).

As Codi's guide to the more positively interrelated web of the Pueblo universe, Loyd takes her to a secret location in the desert, Kinishba, where ruins of ancient pueblo dwellings visibly express the connection between physical and spiritual spaces. When Codi asks him, "Is there anything you know of that you'd die for?" Loyd responds, "The land" (122). According to Paula Gunn Allen, the bond with the land is "the fundamental idea that permeates American Indian life; the land (Mother) and the people (mothers) are the same. . . . The land is not really a place, separate from ourselves, where we act out the drama of our isolate destinies. . . . Rather, for American Indians . . . the earth *is* being, as all creatures are also being: aware, palpable, intelligent, alive."[12] In *Animal Dreams,* Codi and her sister Hallie find themselves engaged in parallel political endeavors on behalf of the land: helping to rescue it from chemical pollution and contamination. Codi rallies the women of Grace to oppose contamination of the nearby land from mining tailings. Hallie, grandly committed to changing the world, has gone to

Central America to work with Nicaraguans to defend their land against imported toxic agricultural chemicals. Although Hallie never appears directly in the narrative, her voice enters it through her idealistic letters to Codi from Nicaragua.

Not long after Codi and Loyd exchange their views about the meaning of the land, they move toward sexual intimacy. Codi acknowledges—in language that adumbrates the wasteland motif—"just being held felt unbelievably good, the long drink I'd been dying for" (130). Following love-making, Codi feels as if her body has been "renewed. I felt like a patch of dry ground that had been rained on" (130). Later, Loyd explains to her his conception of home as one's spiritual location of oneself in the cosmos. As he expresses it,

> "The greatest honor you can give a house is to let it fall back down into the ground. . . . That's where everything comes from in the first place."
> I looked at him, surprised. "But then you've lost your house."
> "Not if you know how to build another one. . . . The important thing isn't the house. It's the ability to make it. You carry that in your brain and in your hands, wherever you go." (235)

Loyd stresses that, in contrast with white people, who regard home as a material concept (and some of whom insist on hauling their mobile homes around with them), Native Americans travel light, like coyotes: "Get to a good place, turn around three times in the grass, and you're home. Once you know how, you can always do that, no matter what" (235). He adds, "It's one thing to carry your life wherever you go. Another thing to always go looking for it somewhere else" (236). His observations emphasize the Pueblo Indians' sense of home less as a literal place than as a spiritual space, an inner center of being. Codi, initially resisting Loyd's wisdom along with the vulnerability his affection for her exposes, admits to herself, "I wasn't keeping to any road, I was running, forgetting what lay behind and always looking ahead for the perfect home . . . where no one you loved ever died" (236). In Codi's view, home is the place associated with mother and safety, where no one—least of all the mother herself—ever dies. But because Codi has never fully mourned either the loss of her mother during her childhood or her stillborn child during adolescence, she carries within her the presence of absence: the condition of emotional emptiness and unsatisfied longing.

Other images in *Animal Dreams* extend the correspondences between the quest for home and the wasteland motif while bridging the several dimensions of the narrative I have suggested: psychological or emotional, political, and mythic dimensions. Of these, the most prominent is that of vision/blindness. Figurative eyes appear everywhere in *Animal Dreams*. According to local legend, the residents of Grace descended from the Gracelas, nine sisters who came from Spain to Arizona in the nineteenth century to marry miners. They brought with them a population of peacocks, the wild descendants of which roam freely in the orchards of Grace. Fittingly, in the collective effort to oppose the mining company dam that would divert the river away from their town, the female descendants of the Gracelas also are linked with the wild birds: they make and sell papier mâché peacock piñatas that incorporate the "eye" feathers from actual peacocks. Supporting the motif of spiritual quest that structures *Animal Dreams,* peacocks are symbolically associated with wholeness, immortality, and the soul.[13]

The narrative counterpoint to eyes and vision is blindness. Recalling the Teiresias figure of Greek mythology who also appears in Eliot's *The Waste Land*—and perhaps also the Cyclops whom Odysseus blinds in the *Odyssey*—Codi suffers, if not actual blindness, a deeply imbedded fear of it. Pertinently, she regards her sister Hallie, whose clear moral vision she envies, as "more precious than an eye" (46). Jesting to a colleague, she describes her teaching method as "the blind leading the blind . . ." (153). In a recurrent nightmare, she experiences "a paralyzing freeze frame: there's a shattering pop, like glass breaking, and then I am blind" (74). Later, she speculates that the dream is not simply about losing her vision but, even more terrifying, about losing herself, "whatever that was. What you lose in blindness is the space around you, the place where you are, and without that you might not exist. You could be nowhere at all" (204). Through this correspondence between loss of vision and loss of self and place, Kingsolver articulates a central connection between Codi's literal and spiritual placelessness. Without a home, understood as an emotional and spiritual center, she is "nowhere"; she can neither locate nor secure her place in the cosmos. Loyd, her guide toward integration, understands and attempts to ameliorate her condition of spiritual homelessness.

Only near the very end of the narrative, after Codi has progressed in her healing journey and has suffered still another devastating emotional loss—her sister, Hallie, dies in Nicaragua—does she identify in her father's deceptive revision of the family's history the source of her nightmare of blindness. Doc Homer's lifelong hobby of photography characterizes his objective approach to life as he endeavors to "photograph the past" (138). Like his own contrived self-image, his carefully constructed photographic images are composed to resemble something other than the actual objects being recorded on film. Years earlier, he had used his camera in a self-initiated research project in which he documented the local genetic pool. As a result of generations of inbreeding, virtually every child born in Grace comes into the world with eyes distinguished by "whitish, marblelike irises" that only later turn pale blue (42). The allusion to the "sea-change" of *The Waste Land*—in turn an echo of Ariel's song in Shakespeare's *The Tempest* ("Those are pearls that were his eyes"[14])—suggests the pattern of death, rebirth, and transformation that shapes Codi's journey and unifies Kingsolver's narrative.

To document his findings, Homer Noline photographed each newborn's eyes shortly after birth. Ultimately, Codi discovers her father's photographs of her sister and herself as newborn infants. Through this visual proof, she determines that, in contradiction to Doc Homer's falsified history of the family's Illinois roots, both of her parents were direct descendants of the Gracelas—in fact, second cousins who married each other, to both families' dismay. "I held the two photographs up to the light, mystified. The eyes were unearthly. We were two babies not of this world. Just like every other one in the stack of photos; two more babies of Grace. He was doing exactly the opposite of setting himself apart. He was proving we belonged here; we were as pure as anybody in Grace. Both sides" (284).

When Codi's longstanding conviction of being an "outsider" gives way to the certain knowledge that she indeed belongs "inside" the community from which she has felt herself estranged, the old nightmare recurs as an illumination that literally blinds her: she "heard the broken-glass pop of the flash and went blind" (284). Her temporary blindness figuratively suggests her shift in focus from "outside" to "inside": from external to inner vision. Shocked into awareness of the meaning for her own identity of her father's duplicity, Codi finally *sees* her place within the community of Grace and within the interconnected web of life and generativity inspired by Loyd's Native American spiritual principles.

Indeed, the cycle of renewal in both organic and spiritual senses that underlies the wasteland legend is reiterated in *Animal Dreams* through the frequent juxtaposition of organic icons of life and death. Images of blossoms and bones, orchards and skeletons, flowering fruit groves and graveyards, recur throughout the narrative, recalling that the original wasteland story has its source in fertility legends.[15] Moreover, numerous folklore beliefs specifically link death and burial rituals with fertility. According to Weston, "This view . . . [may be] at the root of the annual celebrations in

honour of the Departed, the 'Feast of Souls,' which characterized the com-
mencement of the winter season, and is retained in the Catholic conception of November as the month of the Dead" (Weston 85).

In *Animal Dreams,* specific references to or celebrations of the beginning
of the "month of the Dead"—the Day of All Souls—occur at the beginning, middle, and end of the narrative, marking successive stages in Codi
Noline's spiritual renewal and her journey home. The first appears as the
novel's opening sequence, "The Night of All Souls" (3–4), in which Doc
Homer's recollections of his young daughters are interwoven with multiple
images of graves, skeletons, corpses, and death. During the second Day of
All Souls, Codi accompanies several women of the community and their
families to the town cemetery. There, she remembers that, years before, her
father had prohibited her and her sister from participating in the annual
celebration, remarking, "Those great-grandmothers aren't any of your
business" (160). Of course, the exact opposite is true, as the identity of
Codi's relatives becomes her urgent business. When she stumbles on the
neglected gravestone of one Homero Nolina, Codi begins to suspect her
father's true connection to Grace. Her puzzlement about the "no-line" of
her family history—her sense of exclusion from the hereditary line con-
necting generations both before and after her—accentuates her acute longing for belonging. "More than anything else I wished I belonged to one of
these living, celebrated families, lush as plants, with bones in the ground for
roots. I wanted pollen on my cheeks and one of the calcium ancestors to
decorate as my own" (165). Through her discovery of her ancestors' Spanish surname, Codi ultimately recovers her connection to her legitimate
"family tree," as Kingsolver further conflates the narrative's imagery of fertility and vegetation. The *nolina* plant is a desert species related to the yucca
plant; producing a flower spike as large as a Christmas tree, it is capable—if
moisture is insufficient—of surviving for years between flowerings.[16] As
Codi slowly evolves from "*noline*" to "*nolina,*" Kingsolver fittingly signifies
her potentiality for blossoming after an extended period of dormancy.

One further important representation of the associations between burial, fertility, and renewal concerns the death and interment of Hallie. Earlier, Codi has characterized her sister as "the blossom of our family, like one
of those miraculous fruit trees that taps into an invisible vein of nurture
and bears radiant bushels of plums while the trees around it merely go on
living . . . the *semilla besada*—the seed that got kissed" (49). Inevitably, the
idealized Hallie dies during the narrative, a victim of kidnapping and ter-
rorism in Nicaragua. Profoundly grieved by Hallie's death, Codi regards
herself not only as "a skeleton with flesh and clothes and thoughts" (302)

but also as "a hard seed beyond germination" (307). Yet, symbolically, her sister's death allows Codi to assimilate the lost/denied dimensions of her better self—caring, passion, and vulnerability—that Hallie embodied. As she articulates that psychological truth at the ceremonial funeral for Hallie, "Everything we'd been I was now" (328).

However, between the news of her sister's death and her burial, Codi experiences a temporary failure of nerve stemming from fear of her growing attachment to Loyd. While airborne on her way to Denver in ambivalent escape, she discovers a decisive sign in the airplane's unscheduled landing for mechanical reasons. Her new perspective vividly corroborates the "sea change" as well as the evolution toward a Native American awareness that has occurred in her. From the air, Codi initially observes the "bone-dry" (320) paths that mark the empty creeks. Then, in an image that suggests a baptism in vitality, she observes the

> watercolor wash of summer light [that] lay on the Catalina Mountains. The end of a depression is that clear: it's as if you have been living underwater, but never realized it until you came up for air. I hadn't seen color since I lost Hallie.
>
> . . . .
>
> Just past the railyard was a school where a double row of corn-colored school buses were parked in a ring, exactly like one of those cheap Indian necklaces made for tourists. Bright backyard swimming pools gleamed like turquoise nuggets. The land stretched out under me the way a lover would, hiding nothing, offering up every endearing southwestern cliché, and I wanted to get down there and kiss the dirt.
>
> I made a bargain with my mother. If I got to the ground in one piece, I wasn't leaving it again. (320–21)

At last recognizing her true home in her deeper connection to the land and/as her mother, Codi returns to Loyd by train, a more "grounded" mode of travel. Suggestively, she feels as if she had "been on that train for the whole of [her] life" (322). Just before she reveals her presence to Loyd, she acknowledges her altered understanding of the relation between inside and outside and the implicit sense of arrival home: "I was on the outside, in a different dimension. I'd lived there always" (323). It is not Codi's destination but her vision of it that has changed. Having begun to accept that she cannot participate fully in life without accepting the reality of loss and death, she makes Hallie's memorial service in Grace an occasion for celebration of her life rather than a somber rite emphasizing its cessation. By Hallie's own prior request, the body remains behind in Nicaragua, underscoring the fertility motif that unifies the narrative: "She said Nicaragua could use the fertilizer" (303). The ceremony takes place in early summer, in an orchard where peacocks curiously eye the events and where "every tree in every orchard looked blessed" (324), signifying the restoration of fruitfulness as well as Codi's recovery of a legitimate location on her own Nolina family tree. Through her awakened capacity for love and her reunion with her community and its land, Codi herself becomes a *semilla besada.* Her sister's philosophy—"It's what you do that makes your soul, not the other way around" (334)—ultimately describes the moral understanding and spiritual growth that occur in Kingsolver's protagonist.

Prompted by the memorial ceremony for her sister, Codi endeavors to lay to rest—and to reconnect with—the spirits of others she has lost. The ritual reburial of her lost child is described both through Codi's intense emotion and Doc Homer's confused overlapping memories of past and present events. Moreover, the equation between buried corpses, fertility, and renewal suggests not only the wasteland motif but Eliot's poem in particular. The lines from *The Waste Land,* "That corpse you planted last year in your garden,/Has it begun to sprout? Will it bloom this year?"[17] reverberate in Codi's unknowing participation in precisely this cycle of death and renewal when, at fifteen, she had buried the corpse of her stillborn child in a dry riverbed. Retracing those steps nearly twenty years later, she achieves reunion with the land and with her own inner being—that prematurely buried part of herself that might be characterized psychologically as her lost inner child—and ultimately begins to blossom and mature.

A common motif in myths of quest and return (although one not explicitly present in the wasteland legend) is the quester's reconciliation with his or her parents, signifying the acceptance and assimilation of adult roles; *Animal Dreams* concludes with these culminating reconciliations. The final celebration of the Day of All Souls that concludes the novel extends these central correspondences between death and renewed life, quest and arrival home. Near the end of Eliot's *The Waste Land,* the Fisher King, with "the arid plain behind" him, wonders, "Shall I at least set my lands in order?"[18] Homer Noline, now deceased, has joined his Nolina ancestors in the cemetery where "the spirits of all those old bones [are] being tended by their children" (339). His daughter Codi rejoices that, on behalf of Homer Noline/Homero Nolina and in fulfillment of the auspicious name he gave her at birth, she'd "brought some order to his cosmos finally" (340).

More profoundly, affirming the meaning of her name, Cosima, she has brought order to her own cosmos. The sense of motherlessness, the presence of absence that has fueled Codi's protracted mourning and longing to belong, is ameliorated through her discovery of a true community, "fifty mothers who'd been standing at the edges of my childhood, ready to make whatever contribution was needed at the time" (328). Through the nurturing support of many women—including her friend Emelina, who, when Codi first returned to Grace, offered her a place to live and who provides a model of flourishing family life—Codi achieves the healing of loss, the resolution of mourning that enables her to accept that "all griefs are bearable" (327).

As in one sense of "fixing" the past that I have proposed in connection with the fiction and autobiographical writings of Virginia Woolf and Doris Lessing, the protagonist of Kingsolver's *Animal Dreams* mends her vision of her family history and remedies her longing for her lost mother by recovering and then repeating a part of her own history in a more affirmative form. As Codi repairs the threatened "no-line" of her family history, she relinquishes her fixation with loss and death, turning her attention from past generations to future generativity. At the age of thirty-three, she becomes pregnant again—this time willingly—through her reunion with the man who fathered the child she lost during adolescence. Symbolically regenerating that lost child, she is able, this time, to share the knowledge of her pregnancy with its father, Loyd.

On the final Day of All Souls that concludes the narrative, Codi visits the location from which her mother departed years before and concludes that she indeed had actually witnessed, rather than only imagining, the helicopter that carried her mother's body, "ris[ing] like a soul" (342). That discovery marks Codi's understanding that her mother's vanishing—into the air, as it were—is a true memory of a real event and not the product of her childish imagination. Surrendering her impacted grief at her mother's absence from her life, Codi thus relinquishes her view of herself as motherless child and childless mother. Knowing that she has found her place within the community—and also within the state—of Grace, she affirms her "ground orientation" (225) and embraces, at last, her true home.

◇ 3 ◇

Home/lands and Contested Motherhood: *The Bean Trees* and *Pigs in Heaven*, Barbara Kingsolver

I don't even know anymore which home I miss. Which level of home.

——Estevan in *The Bean Trees*, Barbara Kingsolver

The protagonist of Barbara Kingsolver's first novel, *The Bean Trees* (1988) (discussed here out of publication sequence as one of two narratives that focus on the same central characters; the dates of publication straddle that of *Animal Dreams*) is, like Codi Noline, a quester. Like her (traditionally male) predecessors in American fiction, she sets out from home, "going west" to see the world, where she ends up creating a new home for herself. Along the way she renames herself and passes from the state of young adulthood to motherhood. She leaves her original home—no father but a loving, supportive mother who accepts "whatever [she] came home with"[1]—because she wants to avoid the limiting and limited fate of her female peers: adolescent pregnancy and early marriage (typically in that order). Ironically, the most decisive and destiny-altering event in her life is her unconventional entry into motherhood.

Departing from rural Pittman County, Kentucky, "Missy" (Marietta) Greer throws her lot to destiny, determining that she will acquire a new name and a new place to live based on where her decrepit '55 Volkswagen

Bug stops running; "wherever it ran out, I'd look for a sign" (11). She narrowly avoids being named after Homer, Illinois (a name and a place that Kingsolver reserves for significant roles in the novel that she published three years later, *Animal Dreams*), making it as far as a place called Taylorville before she runs out of gas. Her next stop is considerably more fateful. On a Cherokee Indian reservation in Oklahoma—a place with significance for her since her great-grandfather was a full-blooded Cherokee—Taylor finds herself the custodian of a Native American child who is deposited in her car during the night. The woman who delivers the child in this unprecedented manner implores Taylor to "take this baby" (17), indicating that she is the child's aunt and that its mother is dead. As a result of this unorthodox "delivery," Taylor finds herself responsible for the welfare and well-being of a child somewhere in age between "a baby and a person" (17), much the way any new mother does, although in this instance without the customary contributions of either parturition or a father.

Through these events early in the narrative, Kingsolver establishes the tone and direction of her story. Initially, Taylor follows her arbitrary destiny, signified by the child's unorthodox arrival in her life, and only later recognizes the challenge to shape or "tailor" the child into a person. Her first significant choice is to accept the Indian child rather than to return her promptly to the reservation. As Taylor remarks of her initial encounter with the child left for her, "From the first moment I picked it up out of its nest of wet blanket, it attached itself to me by its little hands like roots sucking on dry dirt" (22). In fact, the child clings so tenaciously to Taylor that she names her Turtle, "on account of her grip" (36). From that literal attachment, the novel traces the growth of a true emotional bond as the relationship develops from Taylor's view of the child as "not really mine . . . just somebody I got stuck with" (52) to her affirmative decision to become the child's legal mother.

When Taylor arrives in Arizona, her unconventional family expands further to include the owner of the incongruously named business, Jesus is Lord Used Tires. Competently assisting Taylor in the repair of the two flat tires her car has developed during the long journey from Kentucky to Arizona, Mattie also serves (as her name hints) as a kind of surrogate *mater*, beginning with her first offer, "Just make yourself at home" (43). In sharp contrast to the austere Southwestern landscape Taylor first encounters in Arizona, Mattie's tire enterprise beckons as a startlingly flourishing environment, an incongruous but almost Edenic garden with global geographical references—"a bright, wild wonderland of flowers and vegetables and auto parts. Heads of cabbage and lettuce sprouted out of old tires" (45).

The purple bean vines in this garden-run-amok grew from seeds brought from China decades earlier by one of Mattie's neighbors. Seeking a place to live through the Want Ads, Taylor meets Lou Ann Ruiz, a young woman also transplanted from home; their "hometowns in Kentucky were separated by only two counties . . ." (72). Lou Ann affirms her instant kinship with Taylor, remarking, "You talk just like me" (76). In her struggles with the demands of new motherhood and single parenting following her husband's defection, Lou Ann functions as a kind of sister and double to Taylor; her exaggerated anxieties, guilt, and fear of life form a comic counterpart to Taylor's earnestness and plucky independence. Taylor, affectionately observing her new friend and companion attempting to shield her baby, Dwayne Ray, from all of life's hazards, concludes that, "For Lou Ann, life itself was a life-threatening enterprise. Nothing on earth was truly harmless" (84). Taylor recognizes that Lou Ann is actually less a phobic personality than the possessor of an overly vivid imagination. Her true fear is the "fear that the things you imagine will turn real" (102).

Taylor's new life expands to include a job at Mattie's, where she encounters two Guatemalan refugees who have fled their country because of political persecution and torture. Only later does she discover Estevan and Esperanza's connection to Mattie: Jesus is Lord Used Tires is also a safe house in an underground system of sanctuaries for Central American political refugees. Taylor, a foreigner in the Southwest—though not nearly as isolated by differences of language and culture as are the Guatemalan couple—strongly empathizes with their feelings of dislocation and "home sick[ness]" (103); ultimately, she learns the deeper sources of their misery. When they travel together from Arizona to Oklahoma to reach another safe house, Taylor asks Estevan, who was once an English teacher in Guatemala City, "Do you miss your home a lot?" Elaborating on his displacement from his geographical, ethnic, and linguistic origins, Estevan articulates the complex and overlapping meanings of home for the exile. He replies, "I don't even know anymore which home I miss. Which level of home" (193). Later he defines his sense of longing from the exile's position: "What I really hate is not belonging in any place. To be unwanted everywhere" (195).

The homeless exile Estevan is the moral center of *The Bean Trees*, introducing Taylor to both the reality of geopolitical displacement and the spiritual maturity of one who has been punished by an arbitrary destiny. At an early gathering of the friends who evolve into Taylor's extended family, Estevan offers a parable of nurturance, mutuality, and community. First, he describes a place called hell, where the occupants are starving. Although a pot of delicious stew is available, no one is able to eat. "They only have spoons with very long handles. . . . [T]he people can reach into the pot but they cannot put the food in their mouths" (108). In the other place, called heaven, although the circumstances are identical—a pot of stew and long-handled cutlery—the occupants are well-fed. Estevan dramatically demonstrates how that result is accomplished by "reach[ing] all the way across the table to offer [a chunk of pineapple] to Turtle" (108). Significantly, for this exile, heaven is associated with both nurturance and communal sharing.

The possibilities and limitations of nurturance—and their inevitable associations with both *mother* and *home*—constitute a central issue in *The Bean Trees*. When the child, Turtle, begins to speak in English, her first word is "bean," later expanded to "humbean" (human being)—uniquely suggesting the organic continuum of all living things. As Turtle's vocabulary expands, she names and focuses insistently on vegetables and vegetation; her favorite activity is to plant and "bury" seeds. Bean trees and their look-alikes appear several times in her experience, including once when Turtle identifies a seed-bearing wisteria vine as a bean tree. Taylor, marveling at the resemblance Turtle has perceived, regards it as a "miracle": "the flower trees were turning into bean trees" (144).

Although on the surface Turtle seems as "healthy as corn" (120), she is herself a kind of miracle. During a pediatric exam, Taylor learns that the child has been seriously abused, so damaged by fractured bones and prior injuries recorded in "secret scars" (127) that her physical growth has been seriously stunted. As the pediatrician explains, "sometimes in an environment of physical or emotional deprivation a child will simply stop growing, although certain internal maturation does continue. It's a condition we call failure to thrive" (123). Taylor, stunned by this revelation of an innocent child's suffering, directly glimpses a world in which evil and injustice exist. Yet, in the harsh desert environment of southern Arizona, a countervailing image offers itself. Taylor, averting her focus from the X-ray images of Turtle's damaged body that the doctor places against a window for illumination, "looked through the bones to the garden on the other side. There was a cactus with bushy arms and a coat of yellow spines as thick as fur. A bird had built her nest in it. In and out she flew among the horrible spiny branches, never once hesitating. You just couldn't imagine how she'd made a home in there" (124). Taylor later discovers other examples of tenacity, survival, and the maintenance of home even in the face of deprivation, learning from others and from her own observations that many species of desert plants and animals that appear to be in the condition of "failure to thrive" in fact have developed the capacity to remain dormant until the conditions for growth are more propitious. (The idea recurs in the image of the tenacious, drought-resistant *nolina* plant—and, by association, Codi Noline—of Kingsolver's *Animal Dreams*.)

Turtle's innocent suffering is linked to another strand of the narrative. In explanation of a suicide attempt by Esperanza (whose name ironically means both "to wait" and "to hope"), Estevan reveals to Taylor that the source of his wife's pain is the loss of their young daughter, who was forcibly taken from them in Guatemala. When Taylor realizes her own good fortune by comparison with Esperanza's, she feels guilty, as if her "whole life had been running along on dumb luck and [she] hadn't even noticed" (137). When Taylor touches Esperanza, the woman's skin feels "cold and emptied-out, like there was nobody home" (149). That experience parallels Taylor's own feeling of emptiness when she imagines the abuses in Turtle's early life.

The final third of *The Bean Trees* focuses on a cluster of ideas associated with attachment and loss as well as with home/land and mother. When a social worker advises Taylor that she has no legal claim to the child to whom she has become so attached, the threatening alternative to the unorthodox but "perfectly good home" (174) that Taylor and Lou Ann have created is an institutional "state home" (175) where Turtle would be sent as an orphan. Taylor finds herself in a position that resembles both her friend Lou Ann's chronic fear of danger and loss and Esperanza's actual loss of her child to forces beyond her control. Mattie advises her, "Nobody can protect a child from the world" (178). Taylor, believing that she may lose Turtle if she does not at least attempt to locate the child's relatives and gain their legal consent for her de facto motherhood, determines to return to the place where the child was left to her, at the same time conveying Estevan and Esperanza to a more secure safe house.

As the two pairs—Taylor and Turtle, Estevan and Esperanza—travel to Oklahoma as a "family" in Mattie's borrowed car, the lines of relationship are not always clear. In fact, Taylor agonizes about the growing affection between Turtle, who refers to Esperanza as "Ma," and Esperanza, who sees in the child her own lost daughter. The Guatemalan couple chooses to accompany the child further than is necessary because, as Taylor observes with mixed feelings, they are "getting attached" (203). En route, Taylor also discovers another crucial detail of Turtle's history. The Cherokee child's association of "Mama" with cemeteries explains the meaning of her peculiar habit of "planting"—now understood as burying—dolls and other objects as well as seeds: she had obviously witnessed the burial of her mother. The organic link between life and death, between human and vegetable "burial" and growth, is thus reinforced as Kingsolver insists on the larger cycle of life and death in which human beings figure as only one species among many.

When Taylor is unsuccessful in her attempt to locate Turtle's Cherokee relatives, she takes the next step toward claiming the child as her own. Estevan and Esperanza, whose dark skin and Mayan Indian features resemble Turtle's, pose before a notary with their names anglicized as Steve and Hope Two-two, the child's "parents" who willingly give her up for adoption. Taylor realizes both the risk and the gift of mutuality that the couple's generous act represents. "Of all the many times when it seemed to be so, that was the only moment in which I really came close to losing Turtle. I couldn't have taken her from Esperanza. If she had asked, I couldn't have said no" (215). Instead, however, the procedure that enables Taylor to claim Turtle, albeit illegitimately, also enables Esperanza to resolve her mourning for her own daughter. The staged procedure of giving Turtle up for adoption symbolically permits Esperanza to achieve "catharsis . . . as if she'd really found a safe place to leave Ismene behind" (220). As the emotional price for keeping Turtle, Taylor must give up someone she loves as well. Feeling a much deeper affection for Estevan than she can reveal, she acknowledges, "all four of us had buried someone we loved in Oklahoma" (220). Accepting the risks of love and loss—risks revealed to be even greater in the face of injustices and evils that she had never previously imagined—Taylor knows that she is, in her own way, as much a "survivor" (226) as are Estevan and Esperanza.

The organic world again offers a model for Taylor's moral growth, as Kingsolver reprises a central idea of her narrative: the "miracle" of mutuality and community that makes both home and attachment possible. The wisteria vine—which, confirming Turtle's earlier intuitive observation, is indeed a member of the bean family—is able to thrive in inhospitable soil because of a microscopic organism that aids the plant's growth by transforming nitrogen gas into fertilizer. Taylor regards the arrangement as a kind of "underground railroad" that mirrors, in natural form, the human one in which she has participated on behalf of Estevan and Esperanza, "a whole invisible system for helping out the plant that you'd never guess was there. . . . It's just the same as with people. . . . The wisteria vines on their own would barely get by . . . but put them together with rhizobia and they make miracles" (227–8). Some of what Taylor discovers about life and the significance of rhizobia is also absorbed by Lou Ann, who relinquishes enough of her fears to form a new attachment with a man, find a job, and claim, with newfound wisdom, "nothing on this earth's guaranteed . . . everything you ever get is really just on loan" (231).

As Taylor heads back to Arizona with Turtle, she explains the meaning of adoption and asserts that she is now the child's only mother. Significantly, Turtle's response is "home, home, home, home" (232). Taylor thinks she means "that house where we live with Lou Ann and Dwayne Ray" (232), the place they have created together out of love and trust. But for Turtle, home is not only a physical location but also an intangible safe space in which she knows she is loved: "she was happy where she was" (232). Taylor is gratified to realize that in Turtle's vegetable-soup song—which, over the course of the narrative, has been successively elaborated to include names of all of the people to whom the child feels attached—Taylor herself is "the main ingredient" (232).

Although *The Bean Trees* concludes with Taylor en route home to Tucson with Turtle, all of the certainty established by Taylor's contrived adoption of Turtle unravels in the sequel, set three years later. In *Pigs in Heaven* (1993), Kingsolver further explores the intersecting meanings of home/land, family, and community as these categories bridge two distinct cultures, Caucasian and Native American. Like *The Bean Trees,* this narrative focuses on the moral implications of attachment, both the one between mother and daughter—in this case, Taylor and not only her daughter but her mother—and across cultures. Both Taylor and Alice Greer (a minor character in the first novel who figures more prominently in the sequel) are single mothers who are deeply attached to their daughters. Both mothers participate in the narrative's central moral conflict: how does one act in a child's best interest when different cultures disagree fundamentally on where she belongs, on what is her true home?

Kingsolver has acknowledged that her decision to write a sequel to *The Bean Trees* was based on her realization that she needed to correct the moral myopia of the first novel. "I realized with embarrassment that I had completely neglected a whole moral area when I wrote about this Native American kid being swept off the reservation and raised by a very loving white mother. It was something I hadn't thought about, and I felt I needed to make that right in another book."[2] The sequel, *Pigs in Heaven,* expresses more explicitly Kingsolver's cultural mourning on behalf of displaced Native Americans. When a young Cherokee lawyer enters the lives of Tay-

lor and Turtle to reclaim the child for the tribe, the adoption itself is
declared invalid as matters of identity and ethnicity are raised anew.
Annawake Fourkiller, who was "schooled in injustices"[3] from an early age,
also regards herself as a rescuer of those who have been separated from
their tribal home/land for one reason or another. When her impoverished
family, including four brothers and Annawake, was broken up during her
childhood, she and her twin, Gabriel, were separated. Gabe was adopted by
a white family in Texas; eventually he determined that he belonged in neither white nor Native American cultures. His acute sense of displacement
led to a life of desperation and crime; Annawake knows where her twin is
only when he is in prison. As she phrases it with bitterness, Gabe was
"stolen from the family and can't find his way home" (60).

As a result of the traumatic breakup of her family, Annawake has
become committed to reclaiming Cherokee children whose displacement
from their culture of origin through adoption by white families represents
the continuation of a destructive process in Native American historical
experience. As she later explains to Alice Greer the sad history of the
Cherokee removal known as the Trail of Tears, which occurred in 1838,

> We were forced out of our homelands in the southern Appalachians. North
> Carolina, Tennessee, around there. All our stories are set in those mountains,
> because we'd lived there since the beginning, until European immigrants
> decided our prior claim to the land was interfering with their farming. So
> the army knocked on our doors one morning, stole the crockery and the
> food supplies and then burned down the houses and took everybody into
> detention camps. Families were split up, nobody knew what was going on.
> The idea was to march everybody west to a worthless piece of land nobody
> else would ever want. (281)

Kingsolver, herself of Cherokee blood through her great-grandmother,[4]
has acknowledged the legacy of the historic Cherokee displacement and
honored her cultural heritage in the short story, "Homeland." The story's
young narrator, Gloria, is fascinated by her Great-Mam (great-grandmother) Ruth, who tells her Cherokee stories and instructs her in her people's belief in the interrelatedness of all living things. Gloria's family take
the elderly Ruth (whose Native name is Green Leaf) back to Cherokee,
Tennessee, for a visit to her "homeland." There, she is repelled by the commercial exploitation of her culture, evidenced in the proliferation of cheap
souvenirs and a phony dancer who performs for tourists in ceremonial
dress and feather war bonnet. Rejecting the place as offering no semblance

of her cultural homeland, Great-Mam refuses even to leave the car, proclaiming, "I've never been here before."[5]

In *Pigs in Heaven*, Annawake Fourkiller's effort to reclaim Turtle for her tribe is based on her view that the threatened Cherokee culture must be defended from such exploitation by the surrounding white culture. Thus, in her view, tribal identity must take precedence over attachments across cultures. No matter how good and loving a mother Taylor is, no white mother can give the Cherokee child the intangible sense of "where she comes from, who she is" (77) within her cultural heritage, a concern that, Annawake argues, becomes increasingly important as a child matures. Taylor, resisting the implications of Annawake's beliefs concerning cultural identity and historical loss, defensively responds, "My home doesn't have anything to do with your tragedy" (75). However, as Taylor ultimately discovers, it does.

Along with details of Taylor's crisis of motherhood, Kingsolver interweaves the stories of Alice, Taylor's own mother, who has Cherokee blood on her mother's side, and the full-blooded Cash Stillwater, who (Taylor finally learns) is the widowed father of Turtle's mother, who died in an auto accident. Alice Greer returns to another site of the Cherokee homeland, traveling to (the perhaps-too-obviously named) Heaven, Oklahoma, to help her daughter Taylor defend her emotional claim to Turtle against Annawake Fourkiller's legal challenge. The emphasis on community that underscores *The Bean Trees* is extended in *Pigs in Heaven* as Kingsolver explores the implications of conflicting cultural attitudes toward family structure and communal responsibility. For Annawake, the most problematic dimension of Taylor's relationship with Turtle is the communal Cherokee family organization. As Annawake explains, because several related families share the responsibility for children and people sometimes "share the kids around" (223), "it's not a big deal who's the exact mother" (227).

A Cherokee cultural legend illustrates the matter of communal responsibility. The story of the "pigs in heaven"—the star constellation known in Western European cultures as the Seven Sisters or Pleiades—concerns six brothers who, according to Cherokee legend, neglect their tasks because they would rather play than work. As punishment, they are turned into pigs as they ascend into the heavens.[6] After hearing the story, Taylor's lover, Jax, concludes that the "moral" encoded in the legend is a guiding myth of communal responsibility for the Cherokee people: "Do right by your people or you'll be a pig in heaven" (88). In contrast, the message underlying the mainstream American myth of success is closer to "do right by yourself" (88).

Later in the narrative, the story of the pigs in heaven acquires still another interpretation. Annawake, speaking this time with Taylor's mother, Alice, suggests that the story's moral is "to remind parents always to love their kids no matter what . . . and cut them a little slack" (314). When Alice insists that she sees seven rather than six stars in the constellation, Annawake modifies her interpretation still further to include not only "The Six Pigs in Heaven" but "the one mother who wouldn't let go" (314). In fact, Annawake's evolving interpretation suggests her own changing attitude toward the legal proceedings she has initiated. Implicitly, she understands that Taylor is "the one mother who wouldn't let go"—a "turtle" (like her daughter), who clings so tenaciously to the child to whom she has become attached that she cannot willingly yield to the Cherokee tribal position.

Annawake, caught between the legal argument and her growing moral awareness of the damage that might accrue to the child if the legal proceeding is successful, secretly launches an alternative strategy: a "match" between the child's Cherokee grandfather, Cash Stillwater, and Taylor's mother, Alice. The tactic is ultimately (and comically) successful, as the legal issue is resolved through a decision to assign Turtle's custody jointly to people representing complementary aspects of her "best interests"—Taylor by history of their relationship and Cash Stillwater, Turtle's Cherokee grandfather by blood. As Annawake phrases the argument in court, the "outside press" will only be interested in one issue: "what is in the best interest of the child? But we're Cherokee and we look at things differently. We consider that the child is part of something larger, a tribe. Like a hand that belongs to the body. Before we cut it off, we have to ask how the body will take care of itself without that hand" (338).

Through this solution, all three generations of the Greer females come to accommodate themselves to a larger conception of home/land: a place defined not only by the nuclear family—even one as unorthodox as Taylor and Turtle's—but by a larger cultural community. In the narrative's resolution of these competing versions of family and home, Alice recovers her Native American roots along with an accommodating Cherokee husband. Through him, his granddaughter, Turtle, gains access to her tribal heritage and her Native community. However, Alice and Turtle have more to gain from this arrangement than Taylor. Inevitably, Taylor regrets the loss of her exclusive bond with the child she has loved and raised for three years. Nonetheless, in keeping with sharing as a moral principle as well as the principle that shapes the equilibrium of the natural world—sooner or later, life's gains are paid for by losses—she accepts the collective tribal wisdom that modifies her legal relationship with Turtle to accommodate a more culturally sensitive and communal vision of identity, family, and home. In a moment that exemplifies the narrative's focus on the value and necessity of communal connections, Taylor runs a red light in order to remain within the procession of cars leaving the courthouse, reflecting to herself that "if she gets separated from the others now, she'll never know how her life is going to come out" (342).

Both *The Bean Trees* and *Pigs in Heaven,* like *Animal Dreams,* explore the larger cultural forces and ethical beliefs that influence the meanings of mother and home/land, attachment and loss, longing and belonging. For Taylor Greer, motherhood, rather than occurring as an unproblematic biological event, must be fought for in moral as well as emotional terms, defended against competing claims of cultural identity and communal as well as personal responsibility. In both narratives, children are displaced from their home cultures and/or their biological parents, "given" to other couples through illegitimate adoptions. The symmetry between the circumstances of Esperanza's daughter, lost to probable adoption by "military or government couples who cannot have children" (*Bean Trees* 137), and Turtle, originally thrust into Taylor's care and ultimately adopted by her against Cherokee claims of compromised cultural identity, enables Kingsolver to express a complex dilemma in which children figure as innocent pawns in a larger struggle for ethnic survival and identity.

Additionally, both narratives explore the reverberations of homelessness and political displacement and exile for Native peoples. Estevan and Esperanza in *The Bean Trees* and Annawake Fourkiller in *Pigs in Heaven,* foils to Taylor's contested motherhood, are voices of cultural mourning, grieving for their personal losses within the context of their respective people's historical loss of homeland, family, and identity. Homeless people, Estevan and Esperanza are classified as illegal aliens in the United States where they have sought sanctuary from political persecution in Guatemala. Mayan Indians and Cherokee Native Americans are represented in Kingsolver's narratives as subject peoples who have suffered political oppression and social exploitation sanctioned by the power elites in their respective countries. The loss of home/land persists in the challenges to cultural continuity and community posed by exile, geographical displacement, and cross-cultural adoption.

The resolution of *Pigs in Heaven,* despite its somewhat contrived plotting, is Kingsolver's way of acknowledging the implications of such questions. Her two narratives imaginatively address an aspect of the issue of multiculturalism in the United States and its complications when a child is displaced, even for apparently benign reasons, from her ethnic and cultural community and home/land. Motherhood and home are understood as terms with not only private but cultural ramifications: one person's happiness may well be predicated on another person's (and another culture's) misery and loss. In *The Bean Trees,* when Estevan explains to Taylor that, despite his grief, he could not have sought his missing daughter in Guatemala without risking the lives of many other people he cared about, the shocked Taylor replies, "I can't even begin to think about a world where people have to make choices like that." Estevan responds, "You live in that world . . ." (137). Through her narratives, Kingsolver enables the reader to see that we all live in that world.

Inverted Narrative as the Path/Past Home:
How the García Girls Lost Their Accents,
Julia Alvarez

> They will be haunted by what they do and don't remember. . . . They will invent what they need to survive.
>
> —Chucha in *How the García Girls Lost Their Accents*

The condition of exile, as described from the exile's own perspective, introduces a different set of issues in relation to the notions of home and nostalgia. For the culturally displaced person, self-division is inevitable. Torn between preserving her language of origin and acquiring the language of her adopted culture to facilitate assimilation, the exile may harbor ambivalent feelings toward both her home of origin and her adopted domicile. The culturally displaced person constructs her identity in relation to two distinct, if not also antithetical, sites in time, space, and memory. As Amy Kaminsky phrases it, "Whether forced or voluntary, exile is primarily from, and not to, a place. It thus carries something of the place departed and of the historical circumstance of that place at the moment of departure, making the exiled person no longer present in the place departed, but not a part of the new place either. . . . Language tells us that exile is its own location: people living out of their homeland are '*in* exile.'" [1] Moreover, nostalgia for one's homeland is virtually inevitable, as the exile appraises present circumstances against a vanished past that encompasses conflicted meanings of place and, frequently, language. As Kaminsky adds, "Exile writing is a discourse of desire, a desire to recuperate, repair, and return" [2]

Barbara Kingsolver's *The Bean Trees* touches on several of these ideas through Taylor Greer's friends, the Guatemalan political exiles. Through their plight, Kingsolver highlights the problem of cultural displacement that Taylor only begins to grasp when she realizes the complexity of her relation to the Cherokee child she "adopts." However, while sympathetic to the emotional costs of exile and displacement, Barbara Kingsolver writes as an "insider," born and raised in America. By contrast, Julia Alvarez writes from the position of cultural and linguistic "outsider," as one whose family was compelled to leave their home/land, and language of origin for fear of political reprisals. As Alvarez describes the impact of her family's precipitous flight from their home in the Dominican Republic in 1960 in response to Trujillo's reign of terror, "Overnight, we lost everything: a homeland, an extended family, a culture, and . . . the language I felt at home in."[3] In *How the García Girls Lost Their Accents* (1991), the experience of exile is not secondary but primary. Moreover, the narrative is recuperative and retrospective in more than one sense: its trajectory of reparation and return is expressed not only narratively but structurally through the inversion of chronology. Beginning in 1989 and ending in 1956, the narrative formally reflects the pattern of nostalgia as well as the two senses I have suggested of attempting to "fix" (secure/repair) the past: the return home is accomplished through a reparative imaginative vision, not in the actual world.

The narrative's principal narrating eye/I is Yo—Yolanda García—whose nickname functions as a linguistic pun, since *yo* is the Spanish word for *I*. Of the fifteen stories, approximately half are told from the first-person perspective, of which Yo narrates four as either "I" or "we"; each of her three sisters narrates one or two stories. The remaining stories, with the exception of a brief portion of one told by a retainer of the García family in the Dominican Republic, are in the voice of a third-person narrator, implicitly Yo. Each of the three major sections of the narrative is comprised of five stories or vignettes. The first encompasses episodes in the lives of the four García sisters during young adulthood, narratively "followed" by the college years; the second focuses on the García family during their first decade in the United States "followed" by their early days as immigrants; the final section is set in the Dominican Republic during the early childhood of the four García sisters.

Alvarez literally places the end at the beginning, opening the narrative with Yolanda's conflicted return to her home/land as a young adult in 1989. That she is estranged not only from her country of origin but from herself is signaled by the third-person point of view: Yolanda is split between her roles as observing narrator and acting subject of the story—between the present and the past. Her homecoming after a five-year absence is weighted by the feeling that, despite her powerful yearnings to return to her country of origin, she does not feel "at home" in the Dominican Republic. Not only has she has literally lost her Spanish accent but, as she stumbles in her native language, she fears that she is losing her mother tongue altogether. The opening episode, "Antojos," turns on a Spanish word that Yo does not recognize. Various García relatives who still reside on the Island explain that *antojo* means *craving*, "like a craving for something you have to eat."[4] Additionally, *craving* connotes longing or yearning for something absent, an orientation that underscores Yolanda's nostalgic relation to a place and a relinquished past that she can never entirely either re-enter or recover.

One stimulus for Yolanda's visit is her secret longing to return permanently to her homeland. "Let this turn out to be my home" (11), she wishes. However, the rest of the narrative contests that possibility. In this first vignette, Alvarez juxtaposes details drawn from Yo's two domiciles, emphasizing the self-division that complicates the life of exiles. Yo's nostalgia for the home/land of childhood is repeatedly undercut by reminders of crucial differences between her past and present domiciles, including characteristics that she observes from the altered perspective of her years of living in America and becoming culturally assimilated. "This is not the States. . . . A woman just doesn't travel alone in this country" (90), others caution her. When she disregards that prohibition by traveling by herself into the foothills in search of her *antojo*, guava fruit, the bucolic scene initially prompts her nostalgic response: "This is what she has been missing all these years without really knowing that she has been missing it. Standing here in the quiet, she believes she has never felt at home in the States, never" (12). However, darker emotions surface when she fears that she is lost in the rural countryside. "The rustling leaves of the guava trees echo the warnings of her old aunts regarding the real dangers that await women foolish enough to travel alone: you will get lost, you will get kidnapped, you will get raped, you will get killed" (17).

When her car develops a flat tire out in the country, Yolanda feels further endangered, her anxiety heightened by the approach of two men carrying machetes. "She considers explaining that she is just out for a drive before dinner at the big house, so that these men will think someone knows where she is, someone will come looking for her if they try to carry her off. But her tongue feels as if it has been stuffed in her mouth like a rag to keep her quiet" (19–20). The image vividly signals the sense of peril, victimization, and female violation that characterized Trujillo's reign of terror. What "saves" Yolanda from giving in to her paralysis of fear is her pretense to the men that she is an "Americana"—that she knows no Spanish. "And as if after dragging up roots, she has finally managed to yank them free of the soil they have clung to, she finds she can move her own feet toward the car" (21).

Her response highlights a central preoccupation of Alvarez's narrative and of Yolanda's inner division in particular: the inseparability of identity and language and the consequences and implications of "losing one's accent" or losing one's "mother tongue" (13) as a result of separation from one's original homeland. In an autobiographical essay, Alvarez describes her confusion when she first came to the United States as a child and discovered that everyone, "maids, waiters, taxi drivers, doormen, bums on the street, all spoke this difficult language," English; when her mother explained that their fluency came with "mother's milk," Alvarez had naively thought that "a mother tongue was a mother tongue because you got it from your mother's breast, along with proteins and vitamins" (*Declare* 27). Since a new identity must be constructed in exile from—and frequently against—the language and traditions of one's origin, that new identity inevitably evolves in relation to deeply felt loss. The mother tongue represents both refuge and impasse. Elsewhere, Alvarez has revealed "the most frightening" aspect of her linguistic displacement in its early stages was the loss of her first language before she attained fluency in the second: "I was without a language."[5] In *García Girls,* Yolanda recalls a conversation with a Dominican poet who argued that "no matter how much of [one's language of origin] one lost, in the midst of some profound emotion, one would revert to one's mother tongue"; he poses the question to Yolanda, "What language . . . did she love in?" (13)

That unanswered question is partially answered in the narrative's subsequent episodes, as Alvarez explores and exposes the complicated intersections of language, identity, love, and loss. When Yo first becomes sexually intimate with the white American man whom she later marries, she is afraid to respond in kind to John's words, "I love you." "Once they got started on words, there was no telling what they could say" (70). A symptom of the related failures of language and communication between the lovers is the fact that, from the beginning, John mispronounces Yo's nickname, anglicizing it as "Joe." When Yo feels the rift widening between them, she runs "like the mad, into the safety of her first tongue, where the proudly monolingual John could not catch her, even if he tried" (72). Eventually, as the fissures in the relationship widen to a chasm, John hints that Yo is going crazy and Yo compliantly accepts his view that their estrangement is a result of her mental instability. Her breakdown is represented as inseparable from the breakdown of language itself. First, "she could not make out [John's] words. . . . He spoke kindly, but in a language she had never heard before" (77). As she separates from John, her own self-estrangement intensifies. When she determines to leave the marriage, she signs her parting message to John with "his name for her, *Joe,*" since "her real name no longer sounded like her own" (79). Her breakdown leads to an interlude in a psychiatric facility where she attempts to mend her painful inner division—exacerbated by her husband's tendency to separate and categorize his own ambivalent feelings toward her—and recover "one whole Yolanda" (80). When her parents query her about what happened to a marriage they had assumed was a happy one, Yo responds with a statement that, while a colloquial oversimplification, is nonetheless accurate: "We just didn't speak the same language" (81). But even after the marriage ends, the problem of language persists, with Yolanda developing a "random allergy to certain words. She does not know which ones, until they are on the tip of her tongue . . ." (82). The word "love" triggers an acute allergic reaction; emotional pain is expressed not only in the words themselves—in both English and Spanish—but in the body's own language.

Alvarez's reverse chronology inverts (and subverts) the idea of "development" in either the narrative sense—the traditional bildungsroman form—or the psychological sense—the development of identity. Effects precede causes. Indeed, because the narrative moves backward in time as the reader moves forward through it, the effect is an excavation of the layered strata of memory that exposes and retraces experiences and language to their earliest sources. The reversal of chronology makes each vignette a recuperative story of something originally lost. Thus, the failed relationship between Yolanda and John recounted in the vignette titled "Joe" is described from the perspective of its dissolution, but also from Yo's later insight into the sources of its failure. The chronological inversion also produces narrative irony, as in the episode in which Yo reveals that she has lost her identity as a writer. In the vignette that follows, she describes her appearance at a poetry reading as a practicing writer, reading bold love poems before an audience that includes both her lover and her bemused mother.

In the same vignette ("The Four Girls"), Yo recounts knitting a blanket for her sister Fifi's new baby as she articulates the metaphorical relationship between knitting and living. She admits that she is "addicted to love stories with happy endings, as if there were a stitch she missed, a mistake she made way back when she fell in love with her first man, and if only she could find it, maybe she could undo it, unravel John, Brad, Steven, Rudy, and start over" (63). Her observation serves as a vivid metaphor for the narrative as a whole as Alvarez, through Yolanda, moves backward to unravel—and to "fix" or reknit in a more deliberate and coherent design—the interrelated meanings of language, identity, and loss.

Accordingly, in "The Rudy Elmenhurst Story," Yolanda retraces her first love relationship, her involvement with a shallow and crude young man. Drawn to him in a college creative writing class in which they are assigned to write love poems, Yo is introduced to an entirely different vocabulary for love—or rather, for sex. Once again (from the reader's perspective, though for Yo it is the first time), she discovers that she and the young man to whom she is attracted don't speak the same language. While Yolanda, regretting the "immigrant origins" (94) that still color her behavior and speech despite her efforts to suppress her Latina identity, relishes the first blossoming of romance and sexual desire, Rudy Elmenhurst's far more prosaic goal is simply to get Yolanda into bed. The central differences between them are symbolized by their entirely different languages for "love": "His vocabulary turned me off even as I was beginning to acknowledge my body's pleasure. If Rudy had said, *Sweet lady, lay across my big, soft bed and let me touch your dear, exquisite body,* I might have felt up to being felt up. But I didn't want to just be in the sack, screwed, balled, laid, and fucked my first time around with a man" (96–7, Alvarez's emphasis).

The problem of terminology is compounded by Rudy's parents. Even before Yolanda meets them, she learns, through Rudy, that they patronizingly regard her as "a geography lesson for their son. But I didn't have the vocabulary back then to explain even to myself what annoyed me about their remark" (98). When she does meet them, they call attention to her foreignness by complimenting her on her "accentless" English (100). Soon afterwards, Rudy drops Yolanda, having realized the inaccuracy of his stereotypical view of hot-blooded Latina women whom he had assumed would be easy "lays." The reader, having already encountered Yo's "allergic reaction" to the vocabulary of love in her (earlier-described but later-occurring) relationship with John, now understands its deeper sources.

A central theme of the first section of *García Girls* is loss expressed in terms of the complex intersections of language(s) and eros; a central issue of the middle section is the interrelated meanings of home and homesickness, longing and displacement. Encompassing the García family's first ten years after their exile from the Dominican Republic, the vignettes focus on the shift between "waiting to go home" (107) and the realization that, for political reasons, they will never do so: "we were here to stay" (107). Initially, the four siblings "[whine] to go home" (107). Their standard of living as recent immigrants to the United States is markedly lower than the manner to which they were accustomed as the family of a prosperous doctor of the elite class in the Dominican Republic. In their life on the Island (as Mami reflects in a later episode), "there had always been a chauffeur opening a car door or a gardener tipping his hat and half dozen maids and nursemaids acting as if the health and well-being of the de la Torre-García children were of wide public concern" (174). New York, once regarded as the magical place from which the girls' father and grandfather had returned with magical toys and gifts, becomes a far less romantic location where they are able to afford "only second-hand stuff, rental houses in one redneck Catholic neighborhood after another, clothes at Round Robin, a black and white TV afflicted with wavy lines" (107). More disturbing, at school in Brooklyn, the girls are continually reminded of their otherness by racist epithets delivered by their white American peers.

However, when the García girls begin to attend boarding schools, they discover freedoms they had never imagined—"dance weekends and football weekends and snow sculpture weekends. . . . We began to develop a taste for the American teenage good life, and soon, Island was old hat, man. . . . By the end of a couple of years away from home, we had *more* than adjusted" (108–9, Alvarez's emphasis). Concurrently, the García parents fret that the girls are becoming too assimilated. To counter the ominous possibility that their daughters will eventually fall in love with and even marry American men, they advance their own "hidden agenda"— "marriage to homeland boys" (109)—by sending the girls back to the Island each summer to reimmerse them in the traditional culture and language.

The plan backfires when the youngest of the four sisters, the teenaged Fifi, indeed falls in love with an Island man, an illegitimate cousin who embodies all of the Island culture's deeply entrenched patriarchal and macho attitudes toward women. Carla, the oldest sister and a budding psychologist, labels Fifi's uncharacteristically submissive relationship with her boyfriend as "a borderline schizoid response to traumatic cultural displacement" (117). Although Alvarez uses the abstract clinical phrasing partly to satirize Carla's inflated academic pretensions, the underlying reality of the trauma of "cultural displacement" is entirely accurate. The three older García sisters, conspiring to spring their youngest sibling loose from her infatuation and the very real threat of her entrapment in an oppressive

relationship, expose her liaison with a man so steeped in antiquated patriarchal attitudes that he actually believes—or, at least, tries to persuade the
naive Fifi to believe—that "condoms cause impotence" (125).

In an autobiographical essay, Alvarez offers a complementary vignette,
describing one of her summer visits to the Island as a teenager as she
emphasizes even more clearly the connection between emotional and linguistic dislocation. When aunts and uncles on the Island beg the Alvarez
sisters to speak to them in Spanish, the girls find it increasingly difficult to
do so. "By now, we couldn't go back as easily as that. Our Spanish was full
of English. Countless times during a conversation, we were corrected, until
what we had to say was lost in our saying it wrong. More and more we
chose to answer in English even when the question was posed in Spanish.
It was a measure of the growing distance between ourselves and our native
culture—a distance we all felt we could easily retrace with just a little practice" (*Declare* 64).

However, as she continues, "it wasn't until I failed at first love, in Spanish, that I realized how unbridgeable that gap had become" (64). When a
young man who was more romantically interested in the teenaged Julia
than she was in him began to talk to her about their "future" together, she
realized that she, "not having a complicated vocabulary in Spanish . . .
didn't know the fancy, smooth-talking ways of delaying and deterring"
(70). As a result of that unhappy experience, she "never had a Spanish-only
boyfriend again. Maybe the opportunity never presented itself, or maybe it
was that as English became my dominant tongue, too many parts of me
were left out in Spanish for me to be able to be intimate with a potential
life partner in only that language" (*Declare* 70–1).

As imaginatively reconstructed in *García Girls,* the widening schism
between feeling and the language through which it is expressed is drama-
tized not through Yolanda but through her more naive and susceptible
younger sister, Fifi, who fails to see the danger of emotional surrender to
her macho Island boyfriend. Although the sisters' rescue of her is successful
and their mother determines never again to send the girls back to the
Island for the summer, their "revolution" (107) is achieved at a cost. As the
narrator concedes, speaking—in newly acquired colloquial English—for all
of the sisters, "We are free at last, but here, just at the moment the gate
swings open, and we can fly the coop, [their Island aunt] Tía Carmen's love
revives our old homesickness" (131).

The García family's ambivalent relation to home is signaled by this and
other references to homesickness, paired with the girls' efforts to assimilate
and to mask their differentness from their verbally abusive and often racist

American peers. In a sense, the narrative's inverted chronology heightens the sense of homesickness, since it increases as the reader moves forward through the narrative and the vignettes move backward in time. Yo's father's newly established medical clinic in Brooklyn is "thronged with the sick and the homesick yearning to go home again" (139). The daughters, questioning "why . . . they [had] come to this country in the first place" (138), simultaneously long for home and, to their parents' dismay, wish "to become Americans" (135). As Alvarez has elaborated in her autobiographical essay on the dilemma of assimilation for the exile/immigrant, "the problem was that American culture, as we had experienced it until then, had left us out, and so we felt we had to give up being Dominicans to be Americans" (*Declare* 167).

Narratively, the sense of loss "overtakes" the desire to assimilate as the fictional narrative moves still further back in time to describe the García family's celebration of their first year in America. When each family member is invited to make a wish over a candle anchored in a flan, Carla wonders to herself, "What do you wish for on the first celebration of the day you lost everything? . . . She should make an effort and not wish for what she always wished for in her homesickness. But just this last time, she would let herself. . . . 'Let us please go back home, please,' she half prayed and half wished" (150). Yolanda's particular strategy of survival (like that of Alvarez herself), "since the natives were unfriendly, and the country inhospitable," is to "[take] root in the language" (141). By this point in the narrative, the reader is well aware of the complications as well as the irony of such a strategy, for, as disclosed not only in the opening vignette but in succeeding ones, language functions ambiguously for Yo (as for the author): as both sanctuary and quandary.

The final section of *How the García Girls Lost Their Accents,* set in the Dominican Republic during the four years that precede the García family's flight to the United States as political exiles, is the culminating exploration of the tensions between nostalgia and loss, language and feeling, childish innocence and adult awareness. In this section, Alvarez discloses that "home" is already a compromised site. In a politically repressive state, unconditional safety and security are precisely what are at risk. As described in the ironically titled vignette, "The Blood of the Conquistadores," the Garcías' home in the Dominican Republic contains a secret compartment where Papi hastily retreats when the secret police, flaunting guns and wearing reflective mirror sunglasses that obscure their expressions, arrive on a surprise visit. Mami insincerely invites the *guardias* to "make yourselves at home, please" (203), all the while worrying that they will discover her husband's hiding place and that he will be hauled off to jail—or worse. Alvarez reminds us of "the national language of a police state: every word, every gesture, a possible mine field, watch what you say, look where you go" (211).

When Mami learns that the family's exit papers have been secured and that they will leave the island within forty-eight hours, "everything she sees sharpens as if through the lens of loss . . ." (212). The second daughter, Sandi, voices that sense of personal and cultural mourning on behalf of all of the sisters—indeed, on behalf of all exiles. When each girl is told that she may select only one special toy to accompany her on the one-way journey to the United States, Sandi feels that

> nothing quite filled the hole that was opening wide inside [her]. . . . Nothing would quite fill that need, even years after, not the pretty woman she would surprise herself by becoming, not the prizes for her school work and scholarships to study now this and now that . . . not the men that held her close and almost convinced her when their mouths came down hard on her lips that this, this was what Sandi had been missing. (215)

All of the Garcías except the youngest, Fifi, have disturbing memories of their "last day" (217) on the island; Fifi only remembers Chucha, the family's ancient Haitian servant. Chucha's odd practice of sleeping in a coffin—in rehearsal for her final slumber—represents the approaching death of the Garcías' old life. Significantly, Chucha is the one non-García character in the narrative whom Alvarez grants a first-person voice. In her monologue, she foresees the decay and destruction of the family home:

> Now I hear the voices telling me how the grass will grow tall on the unkempt lawns. . . . Chino and I will be left behind in these decaying houses until that day I can see now . . . that day the place will be overrun by *guardias,* smashing windows and carting off the silver and plates . . . . They will strip the girls' shelves of the toys their grandmother brought them back from that place they were always telling me about . . . a bewitched and unsafe place where they must now make their lives.
> . . . They will be haunted by what they do and don't remember. . . . They will invent what they need to survive. (222–3)

As if to actualize those events that haunt the childhood memories of the García sisters, the remaining stories in Alvarez's narrative are imaginative reconstructions of what the girls "do and don't remember" of childhood in their homeland, ranging from the simplicities of early experiences before threat and danger precipitated their cultural dislocation to somber discoveries regarding hypocrisy, class differences, the body, sexuality, and sexism. The final vignette of the narrative, "The Drum," is an especially haunting one. The narrator is "Yoyo," a nickname for the child Yolanda with a double meaning that encompasses her eventual predicament as an exile moving back and forth between two cultures. Yolanda reconstructs the story of her acquisition of a toy drum and her fascination with a litter of kittens. Too young to understand the import of her actions, she removes one of the newborn kittens from its litter in the coal shed and conveys it inside her drum as she beats incessantly on the membrane. Soon tiring of the captive kitten's pitiable wails, she removes it from the drum and tosses it out a window to its certain death.

If the end is in the beginning in *How the García Girls Lost Their Accents,* so also is the beginning in the end. The adult Yolanda, "collapsing all time" (289) at the end of the final story of the narrative, admits that her careless and destructive treatment of the kitten, although committed in childish ignorance, continues to haunt her dreams and invade her nightmares. That phantom figure and its accusatory wail have become the very source of her creative relation to language. Recalling the ghosts that shaped the consciousness of Maxine Hong Kingston (whose influence on *García Girls,* here and elsewhere, is visible[6]), Yo/Alvarez describes growing up as

> a curious woman, a woman of story ghosts and story devils, a woman prone to bad dreams and bad insomnia. There are still times I wake up at three o'clock in the morning and peer into the darkness. At that hour and in that loneliness, I hear her, a black furred thing lurking in the corners of my life, her magenta mouth opening, wailing over some violation that lies at the center of my art. (290)

The word *violation,* suggesting desecration, defilement, even rape, echoes the image of the narrative's opening vignette when Yolanda returns to the Island and, while alone in the countryside seeking her *antojo,* fears for her safety. The losses experienced by Yo and her sisters and recorded in Yo's narrative comprise both gender-specific dangers and more general cultural losses. *How the García Girls Lost their Accents* fuses homesickness with its antithesis: the recognition that, beneath the scrim of benign nostalgia lie guilt-inducing phantoms and disruptive memories. Alvarez' narrative is both a construction and an unraveling of the process of return. Revisiting the home/land in imaginative form both recuperates home and unmasks what homesickness may disguise. Each of the vignettes in the narrative's final section is an exposure of secrets and violation, whether of hidden compartments in the family home or violations of trust, succor, and sexual innocence. The narrative act of exposing such duplicities at the heart of innocence enables the narrator to relinquish nostalgia. "Fixing" the past enables her to move beyond it to authorize her life in the present as a writer by naming and accepting, in her acquired tongue, the phantoms that have shaped it.

The other secret that Alvarez' narrative exposes, the loss that it mourns equally, is the loss of innocence itself—that irrecoverable state that can only be recognized in the fact of its loss. In expressing the author's cultural mourning for a lost time, place, and culture, *How the García Girls Lost Their Accents* represents the form of nostalgia that Jean Starobinski associates with recognition of the universal exile from childhood.[7] Alvarez, looking back after several decades of assimilation into American life and the achievement of success as a writer, is still susceptible to the "old yearning" that remains in the heart of most exiles: "what would my life have been like if I had stayed in my native country?" (*Declare* 72)

However, having learned to honor the richness of her inescapably hybrid identity, Alvarez can also claim that her self-described label of "Dominican American writer" is

> not just a term. I'm mapping a country that's not on the map, and that's why I'm trying to put it down on paper. It's a world formed of contradictions, clashes, comminglings—the gringa and the Dominican[—]and it is precisely that tension and richness that interests me. Being in and out of both worlds, looking at one side from the other side . . . a duality that I hope in the writing transcends itself and becomes a new consciousness, a new place on the map, a synthesizing way of looking at the world. (*Declare* 173)

These words are part of an imaginary conversation with an older Dominican writer who once chastised Alvarez for writing in English rather than in her native tongue. In response, Alvarez defends her choice as the only honest one for her, articulating her own personal resolution of the dilemma of the exiled writer who must come to terms with linguistic and cultural displacement: "Doña Aída, you who carry our mixtures in the color of your skin, who also left the island as an exile many times and so understand what it is to be at home nowhere and everywhere, I know I don't really have to ask your pardon or permission. Beneath our individual circumstances and choices, we have fought many of the same struggles and have ended up in the same place, on paper" (*Declare* 175).

The four texts considered in this section represent different expressions of displacement from home/land and of cultural mourning. Both Barbara Kingsolver and Julia Alvarez, focusing on female protagonists in young adulthood, render the connections between home and loss, longing and belonging. For Kingsolver's Codi Noline, displacement from home is both geographical and emotional. Her journey home requires a revision of the false history of her origins given to her by her father and the acknowledgment of—and mourning for—of multiple emotional losses: the mother she lost during childhood, the unborn child she lost during adolescence, and the sister she loses during the narrative. Kingsolver's two narratives that focus on a cross-cultural mother-daughter relationship project the resolution of mourning into a larger cultural framework where "history" is not simply the story, whether true or false, of one family's history. As Taylor Greer discovers the high personal cost of displacement for both her Cherokee daughter and her Guatemalan friends, Kingsolver juxtaposes conflicting value systems across cultural and political differences and highlights the intersection of past histories and current practices. The paired novels articulate losses that both encompass and transcend the personal domain, expressing cultural mourning not only for family members but for lost home/lands and cultural autonomy. Julia Alvarez, writing in her second language, amplifies the notion of cultural mourning as she traces the forms of loss for the political and geographical exile who chooses assimilation into a new language and culture. Each of these narratives represents the author's attempt to repair or revise the past. Positioning her character in the liminal space between longing and belonging, each author employs nostalgia to achieve a new comprehension of the relationship between private history and cultural displacement.

Part III

Midlife Nostalgia and Cultural Mourning

◇

◇ 5 ◇

Home/sickness and the
Five Stages of Grief:
Ladder of Years, Anne Tyler

Grief is a circular staircase.

—Linda Pastan, *The Five Stages of Grief*

There are other kinds of displacements besides cultural ones, including those precipitated not by exile or geographical relocation but by phases of the life cycle itself. For some, advancing age catalyzes its own unique dislocations, whether literal—relocating from one's home to a retirement community, for example—or psychological—the discomforting necessity of acknowledging and letting go of earlier roles and previous phases of self-definition and identity. However, the biological process of aging, while inevitable, does not affect everyone in the same way, particularly since it is influenced by a multitude of factors ranging from economic circumstances and social/cultural cues to gender and personal emotional history. Anne Tyler's *Ladder of Years* (1995), Paule Marshall's *Praisesong for the Widow* (1983), and Toni Morrison's *Jazz* (1992) reflect different renderings of the dislocations of aging as they express the longing for belonging at different stages along the life cycle. Additionally, both Marshall's and Morrison's novels combine midlife nostalgia and "homesickness" with cultural mourning for a lost past that encompasses but also extends beyond personal history and memory.

Mourning in response to loss may be elicited not only by nostalgia or homesickness for a particular place associated with emotional succor and by grief for the loss of a particular person from whom an individual is severed by death but also by a person's separation—whether voluntary or involuntary—from a larger cultural community and history. As described in the preceding section, *cultural mourning* signifies the literary representation of grief that results from cultural dislocation and loss of ways of life from which an individual feels personally or—by association with a particular cultural group—historically severed. Through their exploration of nostalgia and the process of mourning as it intersects with the matter of aging, the three authors whose narratives are considered in this section imaginatively revise or "fix" the past, both by mending and by imaginatively securing it.

Initially, Anne Tyler's *Ladder of Years* may seem out of place in the context of other narratives considered in this study, not only because of its comic tone but because, while the others focus on female protagonists who long to return home and/or who suffer from homesickness, nostalgia, or cultural dislocation, Tyler's novel decisively inverts the pattern. Rather than nostalgically seeking to return, either literally or imaginatively, to a place associated with succor and wholeness, the forty-year-old protagonist of *Ladder of Years* suffers (initially) from never having left home. If Delia Grinstead can be said to be homesick, it is in the ironic sense of being *sick of home*.[1] She has "never lived anywhere else"[2] besides her house in a comfortable residential area of Baltimore. The youngest of three daughters of a successful family doctor who was widowed when she was four years old, Delia later became the wife of another doctor, who inherited her father's practice, and the mother of three children of her own, currently in various stages of adolescence. Remaining a homemaker and homebody, Delia has, uniquely, inhabited the same house/home for her entire life.

The event that propels her away from her stagnant life is her chance encounter in a grocery store with a young man whose wife has recently left him. The stranger, having spotted his former wife in a nearby aisle with her current partner, impulsively asks Delia to pretend she's with him to mislead his errant spouse. Indeed, the novel (like most of Tyler's novels) is full of such accidental moments, of women who have left their marriages and homes either literally or emotionally, of people pretending to be someone else. The young man in the grocery store makes Delia aware of herself for the first time "from outside, from a distance" (27).

Soon afterward, she finds herself wondering whether her husband Sam, whom she married when she was seventeen and he was thirty-two, married her primarily because it gave him an entrée into her father's established medical practice. Having worked for years as unpaid receptionist and secretary for her father and husband, Delia has come to feel invisible and unappreciated. Those feelings are exacerbated not only by the recent death of her father but by the drift of her three children from dependence on her into lives of their own. Their indifference makes her feel inconsequential, "like a tiny gnat, whirring around her family's edges . . ." (23). Later in the narrative, Delia ponders the accident of timing that dictates that "aged parents die exactly at the moment when other people (your husband, your adolescent children) have stopped being thrilled to see you coming" (129).

Although *Ladder of Years* is in many ways a comic novel with a somewhat improbable plot that concludes with reunion and even an impending marriage, its undertone is considerably more somber. As the narrative progresses, the reader comes to understand that Delia is in a state of denied bereavement, not only for her recently deceased father but for her self. Only when she actually leaves home and establishes herself in a new environment—ironically, one that comes to duplicate a number of features of the roles she initially sheds—does she properly acknowledge those losses, begin to recover a deeper knowledge of who she is, and become aware of the nature of the home/sickness that has forced her to revise her life.

Although her chance encounter with the young man in the grocery store offers the opportunity for a romantic liaison, Delia quickly pulls back from the possibility. Rather, Adrian, who edits a newsletter about time travel, becomes the catalyst for Delia's rather different mode of travel in both time and space. Some weeks after an innocent but potentially compromising encounter with Adrian, Delia finds herself, during a family vacation at the Delaware shore, reminiscing about the early years of her marriage and motherhood. She recalls the intensity of honeymoon passion (now lost) and the years when her children still believed that she was "so important in their lives" (72). In contrast to her nostalgic musings, a belittling comment from her husband compels Delia to see Sam's detachment and to regard their "entire marriage unroll[ing] itself before her: ancient hurts and humiliations and resentments, theoretically forgotten but just waiting to revive . . ." (74).

Impulsively, wearing only her swimsuit and her husband's robe, Delia walks away from her family on the beach and—becoming another of Tyler's "accidental tourists"—keeps traveling until she finds herself miles away, in a small town in Maryland. Actualizing the escapism offered by the formulaic romance fiction that she reads compulsively as a way to flee the "grinding gears of daily life" (29), Delia literally "runs away from home" (210) the way children occasionally—but mothers virtually never—do. What is most noteworthy about her "escape" is its capriciousness, its utter lack of premeditation. Although something within her clearly prompts her to keep going without turning back, she never fully examines her impulse for deserting her family with scarcely a backward glance or a pang of guilt. Once the new trajectory is set into motion, Delia, although driven more by chance than design, finds herself for the first time in her life making intentional choices about who she will be in her new circumstances as an independent woman. Much of the narrative traces her efforts to shed her former life and start over again at a new location not only on the map but within herself.

One aspect of Delia's travel away from her husband and family at the beach is a hitchhiked ride in a handyman's van that doubles as his home. Delia envies the "beautiful, completely stocked, entirely self-sufficient van that you could travel in forever, unentangled with anyone else. Oh, couldn't she offer to buy it?" (80) The van, besides offering an entirely different vision of home/self than the one in which Delia has become trapped, also suggests the underlying incentive for her journey: the necessity to achieve self-sufficiency and to disentangle herself from the stultifying embrace of home. Taking a boarding house room in the small town of Bay Borough and securing a position as secretary to a local attorney, Delia soon establishes new routines and savors the very spartan qualities of her new life as "Miss Grinstead": only two changes of clothes; a room so bare and bereft of personal possessions that she can look around with satisfaction and "detect not the slightest hint that anybody lived here" (97). Affirming her choices as part of the "impersonal new life she seemed to be manufacturing for herself" (96), Delia exults in her isolation, reflected back to her in the room's "starkness" (93). Her spare surroundings actualize the fantasy of a character in an earlier novel by Tyler, who ventures the opinion that "our whole society would be better off living in boarding houses. . . . Everyone should have his single room with a door that locks, and then a larger room downstairs where people can mingle or not as they please."[3]

Delia Grinstead's retreat to a bare room that signifies psychological as well as physical escape from the comforts of home allusively suggests Doris Lessing's story, "To Room Nineteen."[4] In that story, a dissatisfied woman also walks out on her husband and (younger) children, intermittently withdrawing to a stark, anonymous hotel room in order to disengage from her enmeshed life as wife and mother. However, tracing a much darker trajectory than does Tyler's narrative, Lessing's story leads not to the woman's psychological liberation and reunion with her family but to irreversible withdrawal and absolute spiritual despair that culminates in suicide. By contrast, Tyler's Delia climbs the stairs to her bare room in the boarding house, thinking, "*Here comes the executive secretary, returning from her lone meal to the solitude of her room.* It wasn't a complaint, though. It was a boast. An exultation" (96, Tyler's emphasis).

The professional persona that Delia projects in the first salaried position of her life is cool and efficient rather than friendly. Even her reading tastes change; instead of romantic escape fiction, she selects literary classics from the local library.[5] During solitary meals at the local diner, she withholds any distinguishing information about the life she has vacated as a wife and mother, instead posing as "a person without a past" (108). Before long, everyone in the small town of Bay Borough, from the cook and waitress at the local diner to young mothers with their toddlers at the park, welcome her into their associations. Delia is so committed to starting again "from scratch" that when her older sister, having traced her to her new location, visits her and tries to discover the reason for her abrupt disappearance, Delia provides no explanation, asserting simply that she does not intend to return home. Further, she admits that the only aspect of her defection about which she feels any remorse is having taken the family vacation money. She regrets that she "didn't start out with nothing. Start out . . . even with the homeless . . ." (118). Her wish to approximate the condition of "homelessness" discloses her need to wrench herself away from the inner stagnation and entrapment represented by home.

Delia's assertions to her sister signal a new stage in her inner journey, in which she begins to confront more honestly the forces that prompted her abrupt departure. Initially, each night before she falls asleep in her spartan room, she weeps "without a thought in her head" (109). The phrase suggests the degree to which she is grieving without acknowledging either the nature of her emotional state or its sources. As Tyler's language hints, Delia enters a state analogous to the inner stripping that precedes spiritual renewal. "She had always known that her body was just a shell she lived in, but it occurred to her now that her mind was yet another shell—in which case, who was 'she'? She was clearing out her mind to see what was left. Maybe there would be nothing" (126–7).[6] For the first time in her life, Delia begins to examine assumptions that have shaped her identity and to mourn losses that she has not previously acknowledged. Recalling incidents from childhood, she recognizes that "she had always been such a *false* child, so eager to conform to the grownups' view of her" (123, Tyler's emphasis). She had maintained that compliant orientation into adulthood, spending most of her married life to the much-older Sam Grinstead "trying to win [his] approval" (137) as if he were her father rather than her husband. Because Sam is indeed a surrogate for her father, Delia has continued to act like a daughter, a role that her husband has unintentionally reinforced through his often-patronizing comments and behavior.

Twenty-five years after the social transformations catalyzed by the feminist revolution of the 1970s, Delia Grinstead seems altogether untouched by them. Yet, despite Tyler's own expressed distance from feminism,[7] *Ladder of Years* follows a pattern established in earlier feminist fiction: the psychological "awakening" of a woman who has unthinkingly defined herself through conventional female roles. However, in contrast to the "mad housewife" narratives, published during the peak years of women's liberation movement, that focus on women fleeing unhappy marriages and relationships,[8] Delia Grinstead (whose surname suggests "grin instead") has by-passed an even earlier stage of leaving home: separation from one's parents. It becomes imperative for her to leave the place where her role as youngest daughter has merged into those of wife and mother in order to discover her self as a person apart from those roles.

In this sense, Delia may be understood as a late twentieth-century, middle-aged version not of her namesake, Shakespeare's Cordelia, but of Ibsen's Nora Helmer. Nora, a woman similarly enmeshed in the roles of daughter, wife, and mother (though of younger children), is patronized by her husband, who calls her as his "little scatterbrain,"[9] much as Delia's family regards her as "sweet and cute" or "silly and inefficient" (23). *Ladder of Years* may be read as a narrative extension to Ibsen's play that imagines what might happen to a woman like Nora—a decade older and a century later but still virtually untouched by ideas of female independence—after she has emphatically closed the door to her doll's house. However, while Nora Helmer's dramatic exit in *A Doll's House* is represented as a deliberate moral choice, Delia Grinstead's departure is catalyzed by unconscious issues, including aspects of loss and denied mourning. When she reflects on her feelings about her father, Delia concludes that the medication her doctor-husband Sam had given her to enable her to sleep on the night of her father's death had in fact blunted her need to mourn his passing. The morning after he died, she felt that "she had missed something. Now she thought what she had missed was her own grief. . . . Why the hurry to leap past grief to the next stage?" (129). Reflecting on that experience from the perspective of her solitude in Bay Borough, she permits herself to weep and to grieve, this time aware of its sources as well as its necessity. "She felt that something was loosening inside her, and she hoped she would go on crying all night" (129).

Delia's anaesthetized state on the night after her father's death was not only medicinal but emotional. Her husband's complicity in numbing her feelings, compounded by what she regards as excessive restraint in his willingness not to "invade her privacy" (125) after she has established her new life, confirm Delia's belief in the correctness of her having left him. What it also enables her to see is that in mid-life she—like Ibsen's Nora—has never outgrown the compliant behavior of an obedient good child. "She had lived out her married life like a little girl playing house, and always there'd been a grown-up standing ready to take over—her sister or her husband or her father" (127). From her new position of self-reliance, she admits to herself that she had nonetheless expected Sam to come and rescue her, much as Nora Helmer had expected her husband to rescue her from the consequences of her violation of the law. "She resembled those runaway children who never, no matter how far they travel, truly mean to leave home" (126). That childish attitude dates back to the early years of Delia's marriage. Her husband, so much older, had seemed to her "fully formed, immune to doubt, this unassailably self-possessed man who had all but arrived on a white horse to save her from eternal daughterhood" (212). In fact, rather than saving her from that condition, he had—with her complicity—sealed her in that role. The death of her father forces to the surface Delia's home/sickness. Her flight from home is a necessary step in stepping out of the fairy tale, wrenching herself away from her father(s), and shedding the role of "eternal daughter."

If Delia grieves as a daughter, she also grieves as a mother who has left her children—or, more accurately, whose children have emotionally left her. The children for whom she longs are not the nearly grown daughter and two adolescent sons of current time. Rather, it is the "younger versions" (134) of them—and of herself as a mother who was once central in their lives—for whom she grieves. Indeed, in longing for the earlier avatars of her children, Delia mourns time's passage and her own stagnation in it. Even though on the surface she feels contented with her new, more austere and solitary life in Bay Borough, just below the veneer lies a layer of sadness and regret. She feels as if "her exterior self was instructing her interior self. . . . It was not that her sadness had left her, but she seemed to operate on a smooth surface several inches above the sadness. . . . Although every so often something would stab her" (138), bringing to awareness details from the lives of her children (though seldom of her husband).

Following the discovery of her whereabouts, members of Delia's family intermittently send cards and messages in the mail; rarely do her children do so, apart from sarcastic cards on her birthday. In a note of response to a communication from her mother-in-law, Delia explains that she left home not because of a particular person but "because I just like the thought of beginning again from scratch" (139). With a hint of sarcasm, her mother-in-law responds, "When you've finished starting over, do you picture working up to the present again and coming home?" (143) Ironically, as Delia delves more deeply into herself, her new life threatens to resemble the one she thought she'd shed. She even acquires a stray cat whose ingratiating habits recall those of the cat she left behind. Noticing some of these repetitive patterns, she decides to leave her secretarial position because her employer's expectations that she will make coffee and feed parking meters resemble too closely the thankless tasks she performed as her father's and husband's secretary/servant/flunky at home.

Her acceptance of a new position as a "live-in woman" for a man whose wife has left him and their preadolescent son may seem almost too contrived a plot twist, an inverted image of Delia's defection from her own marriage and children. But the explicit mirroring enables Tyler to explore Delia's further self-discovery in a situation once-removed from her habitual roles that fittingly reframes the psychological issues with which she struggles. As if operating in a kind of parallel universe, Delia unconsciously chooses positions in her new life that enable her to replay and examine the roles she has played in her former life and home. Thus, having felt that her own husband and children have become strangers to her, Delia turns the circumstances from passive to active: she *chooses* to be a substitute mother (though not substitute wife) to total strangers.

Before she takes the live-in position, Delia mulls over its appeal, revealing her anxieties about her own maternal role and, perhaps behind it, about her own mother who died during Delia's childhood: "a hireling would in some ways be *better* than a mother—less emotionally ensnarled, less likely to cause damage. Certainly less likely to suffer damage herself" (160, emphasis in original). Unlike Delia's own family, her surrogate son and his father—a finicky high school principal whose pet peeve is creeping slang and the resulting deterioration of the English language—cherish her rather than taking her for granted. As Delia manages twelve-year-old Noah's schedule, cooks meals, and attends to miscellaneous household tasks, she discovers to her pleasant surprise that she is a far more capable and indispensable person than she had been for her own family. "She seemed to have changed into someone else—a woman people looked to automatically for sustenance" (183). Yet, as she struggles to find the proper distance she should maintain from Noah, Delia realizes how easy it is to "fall back into being someone's mother" (172).

Just as Noah begins to metamorphose from an engaging child into a more complicated adolescent like her own sons, Delia's actual sons arrive in

Bay Borough. The older one disappoints her by not even attempting to see her; the younger one bluntly confronts her with the effects of her desertion, including his fear that Delia's older sister is making a play for their father. Delia, sidestepping the latter detail but acknowledging how much she has missed her children, also admits to herself a less socially acceptable feeling: that they were "partly what she was running from" (210). While her children had "turned into semistrangers" as she became less important in their lives, it is also true, as she understands from her current vantage point, that "they, in fact, had become just a bit less overwhelmingly all-important to her" (211). She even rationalizes that her younger son "had not appeared ruined by her leaving. He had survived just fine, and so had his brother and sister" (210). In the interest of retaining Delia's perspective narratively, Tyler implicitly asks her readers to discount (as Delia herself does) the effect on her children of her "parental truancy."[10]

While her substitute son, Noah, is away at camp for two weeks, Delia vacations in Ocean City by herself, as if to replay—but this time, on her own terms—the previous summer's family outing to the shore. She even finds herself reading the same paperback romance she had taken with her to the beach the year before. The key word in its title, *captive,* reminds her and signals the reader how far Delia has traveled from home since then. Her serenity as a solitary traveler emphasizes the degree to which she has escaped the captivity of her traditional roles and discovered, for the first time in her life, how to be alone with herself. However, the emotional and spiritual stripping process is still not complete, as is suggested by the imagery of layers and self-exposure. When Delia enters the ocean for a swim, she "spen[ds] forever submerging, like someone removing a strip of adhesive tape by painful degrees"; later, when she peels off her swimsuit in her motel room, "a second suit of fish-white skin lay beneath it" (250). The latter image echoes that of Delia's first shower in her boarding house in Bay Borough a year earlier, when she rinsed off the "grime and sweat and sunblock" from her day at the beach, exposing "a whole new layer of skin" (97).

The woman in the narrative whose situation most closely resembles Delia's, Noah's mother Ellie, becomes an unexpected ally in Delia's process of emotional and spiritual reorientation. Considering Ellie's question whether this is her first vacation alone, Delia wonders to herself "whether traveling alone to Bay Borough qualified as a vacation or not. (And if it did, when had her vacation ended and her real life begun?)" (252). As the two women compare marriage with single life, Ellie describes her experience in words that also characterize Delia's position as an estranged wife:

"In a way, the whole marriage was kind of like the stages of mourning. . . . Denial, anger . . ." (254, Tyler's final ellipsis). Significantly, she only identifies the first two stages of grief, yet the others—bargaining, depression, and acceptance—are also pertinent to Delia's circumstances.[11] If bargaining may be understood as Delia's rationalizations about leaving her husband and children, she ultimately moves from denial/isolation and anger through bargaining, depression and, ultimately, acceptance: of her father's death, her children's increasing independence, and her husband's (and her own) aging.

What emerges in the final stage of Delia's inner journey is her realization that, in running away from home, she has been trying to escape not simply from her traditional roles as wife and mother but also from time and mortality. Early in the narrative, in response to the young man Adrian's admiration of her face, Delia had examined her image in a mirror and had regarded as "unfair" the fact that "she should be wrinkling around the eyes without ever losing the prim-featured, artless, triangular face of her childhood" (26).[12] Although she is only forty, her father's death and the onset of angina in her considerably older husband soon afterward serve as reminders of time's lengthening shadow.

Tyler further develops the theme of aging through the figure of Nat Moffatt, Noah's grandfather. Sixty-seven years old and living in a nursing care facility because of his physical frailties, Nat possesses the heart and spirit of a much younger man and makes no apologies for his challenge to conventional views of aging. As he phrases it in the passage that provides the novel's title metaphor, "I've always pictured life as one of those ladders you find on playground sliding boards—a sort of ladder of years where you climb higher and higher, and then, *oops!,* you fall over the edge and others move up behind you" (193–4). The topography of Senior City duplicates this one-way ladder, with the most infirm residents occupying the building's top floor. During Delia's year in Bay Borough, Nat thoroughly upsets the "ladder of years"[13] that structures the living arrangements as well as the underlying age-based assumptions of Senior City's residents, marrying a divorcée half his age—several months earlier than planned because she is pregnant—and fathering their child. Yet, despite Nat's irreverent and unconventional attitudes toward age, even he later concedes the difficulty of "starting over." Regarding his infant son, he laments, "I must have thought I could do the whole thing over again, properly this time. But I'm just as short-tempered with James as I ever was with my daughters" (321).

In some ways, Tyler's narrative is structured like a fairy tale in modern dress: who wouldn't like to return to certain decisive moments in the past with the opportunity to play out different choices? As in a fairy tale, the proverbial kiss from a handsome young man precipitates a woman's awakening, followed by her departure from home and inner transformation. Adrian's kiss offers Delia a tempting invitation to renewed passion and romantic escape. A year later, another spontaneous kiss, this one from Noah's father, reminds her again of that potentiality and indirectly propels her back into her husband's waiting arms. However, the aspect of Delia's transformation that is least affected by her year in Bay Borough is her sexuality. Eschewing the second opportunity for a sexual liaison as she had refused the first, Delia ultimately returns to her husband as faithful wife, albeit one who has finally outgrown the role of daughter/child.[14]

What immediately triggers Delia's return home is a call from her former life not as a wife but as a mother: the wedding of her daughter Susie. Somewhat improbably, Delia feels so distant from her old life after more than a year's absence from it that she momentarily wonders whether her status will be that of guest or mother of the bride. The visit home obliges her to repeat her earlier defection, this time leaving her surrogate family— much as she had done the year before—without their "live-in woman."

When Delia arrives at her former home in Baltimore for the wedding, neither her actual family nor the house seem particularly "welcoming" (276). She later learns that the configuration of the place has radically changed during her absence; only her husband actually lives in it at this point, the others having left for diverse reasons. Sam, her children, and the extended family and friends who have arrived for the wedding are surprisingly nonchalant about Delia's presence. In a sense, they still take her for granted, unthinkingly expecting that she will simply resume her customary functions, ranging from doing laundry to preparing meals, right where she left off more than a year before. "She glanced toward Sam for some cue (the kitchen wasn't hers anymore; the household wasn't hers to feed), but he didn't help her" (291). Far from understanding the transformation that has occurred within Delia during her extended absence, members of her family and others who knew her before simply place her in "a convenient niche" in their minds, one of those "eccentric wives" who live in one place while their husbands live somewhere else. "Nobody gave it a thought" (285). Only her daughter, who postpones the wedding for reasons of her own, manages to articulate her anger about her mother's defection: "your children . . . orphaned, and me setting up a whole wedding on my own without my mother! . . . Was it him? Was it us? What was so terrible? What made you run out on us?" (293).[15]

Delia's response is as close as she comes to explaining actions that neither her daughter nor anyone else in her family or outside of it will ever fully comprehend. As she explains to Susie, "I never meant to hurt you; I didn't even mean to leave you! I just got . . . unintentionally separated from you, and then it seemed I never found a way to get back again" (293, Tyler's ellipsis). Certainly a key word in Delia's apology is "separated." Her spontaneous separation from her children, her husband, and her enmeshed life as daughter/wife/mother is an essential stage in her redefinition of her relation to home. Yet Delia's extended absence has, at least in her view, catalyzed the process of separation for her children in ways more successful than her own at their ages. Her daughter, barely out of college, has already started a successful business and planned her own wedding. Her sons, in college and high school respectively, have become more self-sufficient in the absence of the mother whom they took for granted as household functionary.

As the narrator describes it, it is the same "process of inaction, of procrastination (much like the one that had stranded her so far from home in the first place)" (294) that leads Delia to remain at her former home until the crisis of Susie's wedding is successfully resolved. The degree to which her second "family" in Bay Borough replicates the demands of her first in Baltimore becomes both comically and painfully apparent. Delia is "called home" several times by a desperate Noah, whom she reassures that she will be "home before long" (308)—though that turns out not to be the case. "Home" ultimately means for Delia the original one she left in Baltimore, not Bay Borough.

Although she endeavors to keep them separate, Delia's parallel lives finally converge when Nat Moffatt arrives from Bay Borough to beg her return. Nat's good-natured presence alters the tone of the family gathering. Delia invites him to stay overnight and, significantly, places him in the room that used to be her father's—a room that, during the months after his death, she had insisted on keeping unoccupied. Before Nat retires, Delia "press[es] her lips to his forehead, the way she used to do with her father all those nights in the past" (323). The scene is particularly allusive of the moment of forgiveness Lear experiences with Cordelia, although in Tyler's reworking of the story it is daughter who gives the tender kiss to her elder rather than the reverse. In effect, the unconventional Nat occupies the position of a more benevolent, accepting father to Cordelia, enabling her to achieve reconciliation and to release herself from the fairy-tale role of eternal good daughter. In doing so, Delia resolves the process of mourning both for her actual father and for the outgrown role of filial compliance.

Nat's idea of his journey as a "time trip" (322) also describes Delia's. Tyler's story of necessary separations concentrates not only on the reorientation of intimate relationships but on their intersections with time. At one point, Delia wonders "how humans could bear to live in a world where the passage of time held so much power" (213). Not long after she kisses Nat goodnight, she joins Sam in bed, waiting for (and receiving) words that signal his wish to have her back home with him. However, their reunion begs some of the questions raised earlier in the narrative. Delia returns, seemingly without reference to her grievances, to the husband from whom she has been not only geographically but emotionally estranged for a year and a half. The novel ends with her privately concluding that she has returned a different person to a different home than the one she had vacated so impulsively, without addressing whether or not her husband has changed accordingly.

> It had *all* been a time trip—all this past year and half. Unlike Nat's, though, hers had been a time trip that worked. What else would you call it when she'd ended up back where she'd started, home with Sam for good? When the people she had left behind had actually traveled further, in some ways?
> Now she saw that June beach scene differently. Her three children, she saw, had been staring at the horizon with the alert, tensed stillness of explorers at the ocean's edge, poised to begin their journeys. And Delia, shading her eyes in the distance, had been trying to understand why they were leaving.
> Where they were going without her.
> How to say goodbye. (326, Tyler's emphasis)

Unlike Homer's classical epic of departure and return, Tyler's narrative is ultimately less about reunion than about relinquishment: the necessity to separate from one's parents and eventually to mourn their deaths, to let go of children who are no longer dependent, to relinquish moribund or false versions of the self. Although at times the balance between comic and serious dimensions of that process is precarious, through Delia's "lost" year (272), Tyler exposes and explores a particularly female anxiety about being trapped both at home and in time, remaining stuck in roles, routines, and relationships in which the self has stagnated. Acting on a deep inner impulse, Delia "travels in time" as well as in space. Leaving home and temporarily assuming another life enables her to examine and dissolve the calcified roles she has maintained and to recover her authentic/lost self. In the process, she confronts more honestly the inevitable grievances and losses that accumulate as people age, parents die, marriages evolve, and children grow up. Passing through and resolving the stages of grief and mourning, Delia Grinstead is enlightened in both the emotional and spiritual senses of the word. Home/sickness, first propelling her away from home, finally leads her to an emotionally transformed landscape. She returns as an adult who has revised her relation to home by learning how to leave it.

◇ 6 ◇

Hom(e)age to the Ancestors:
Praisesong for the Widow,
Paule Marshall

The note was a lamentation that could hardly have come from
the rum keg of a drum. Its source had to be the . . . bruised
still-bleeding innermost chamber of the collective heart.

—Praisesong for the Widow

Like Julia Alvarez, Paule Marshall was born on an island in the West
Indies (Barbados) and grew up in the United States (Brooklyn).
Like Alvarez's Yolanda García, Marshall's Avey Johnson is in transit
between her current residence in the United States and the West Indian
islands and other homes that come to represent her individual and cultural
histories. For both authors, islands signify the geographical equivalent of
memory-places where the past is housed (and contained) and from which
it continues to exert its complex influence. However, more like Anne
Tyler's Delia Grinstead than Alvarez's Yolanda García, the widowed Avey
Johnson is also middle-aged; considerably more of her life is already behind
her when Marshall's narrative begins. Given the protagonist's age and circumstances, *Praisesong for the Widow* (1983) might be regarded as the representation of a midlife crisis somewhat like that experienced by Tyler's Delia
Grinstead, who also discovers herself by precipitously leaving home.
Though superficially it is this, it is also considerably more. The narrative
encompasses not only personal but cultural dimensions of mourning for a
lost self, a lost past, and a lost culture, tracing what Marshall overtly names
"the theme of separation and loss"[1] for Avey in both her individual and
collective history.

Marshall's narrative thus addresses the elements of separation and loss, home and homeland, that shape each individual's history and consciousness, whether she chooses to be aware of them or not. In fact, much of the narrative traces her central character's deep resistance to being made aware of that history. Only an involuntary reorientation obliges Avey Johnson to see the significance of her ancestral cultures—African, Caribbean, and African American—within the lineaments of her personal identity. During and after her travel on a Caribbean cruise with two friends, Avey imaginatively visits sites not on her planned itinerary. Among those sites are her previous and current homes: the house in a white neighborhood in *North White* Plains, where she has lived alone since the death of her husband Jerome four years earlier, and her home on Halsey Street in Brooklyn, where she lived during the early years of married life. Before either of these is the place where, as a small child, she spent summer vacations with her father's great-aunt Cuney on Tatem Island, a sea island off the South Carolina coast that (like Naylor's Willow Springs in *Mama Day*, discussed in a later chapter in this study) possesses strong links with ancestors from Africa and the cultural memory of the Middle Passage. Over the course of the narrative, Marshall's protagonist discovers that she has become estranged from all but her most recent—and most materialistic—home. In effect, Avey Johnson is an unacknowledged exile from both her own younger self and her collective history.

Each of those homes is also associated with a different dimension of Avey Johnson's inwardly fractured self, aspects of which are distinguished by different names. Originally named Avatara after her great-aunt Cuney's grandmother, Avey Williams eventually married Jerome (Jay) Johnson and became so much a product of their marriage that she came to know herself only as his extension—Avey Johnson. In middle age, when she observes a "stylishly dressed matron" reflected in a mirror or store window, initially she does not recognize the image as herself (49). Only at the very end of the narrative, after she has undertaken a painful but ultimately healing journey back in time and recovered her authentic self as part of a larger web of connections does she resume her original name and "recognize" herself.

Avey Johnson's sense of malaise begins during the Caribbean cruise. Something "come[s] over her" quite abruptly (28), prompting one of the few spontaneous actions of her recent life. Like Anne Tyler's Delia Grinstead, who spontaneously decides to leave her family, Avey suddenly decides to abandon the cruise in midjourney and return home. Her impulse is prompted in part by the return of disturbing dreams and daytime visions that disrupt her psychic equilibrium. Melding memories of past experiences with the present moment, the dreams and visions oblige her to review earlier times in her life when she had felt less self-estranged and more connected to others. Early in that process, before she begins to grasp the significance of these intrusive visions, Avey feels "like someone in a bad dream who discovers that the street along which they are fleeing is not straight as they had believed, but circular, and that it has been leading them all the while back to the place they were seeking to escape" (82–3).

Recurrent figures and images mark the several stages of Avey's literal and spiritual journeys. First is the frequent appearance in her dreams of her great-great-aunt Cuney, a phantom who beckons, summons, and even wrestles with Avey to draw her into the domain that she resists visiting: the past. Other figures beckon or touch her to draw her further along her journey or to aid her during times of helplessness or resistance. The disruptive dreams and visions also bring together in the same narrative plane different realms in time and place. Events in the narrative present are intercut nonchronologically with incidents from Avey's childhood and young adulthood. Blurring the line between past and present, Marshall narratively expresses the fact that all individuals are the sum of their experiences, even those they have forgotten or repressed, and that recollections of experiences that may prompt reawakening occur in a deliberately disruptive, asynchronic sequence.

Aunt Cuney's appearance provokes Avey to recall and imaginatively revisit Tatem Island, a place strongly associated not only with her own childhood but with a legendary piece of cultural history to which she has given little notice. She recalls accompanying Aunt Cuney each summer on a long walk, their destination a narrow spit of land where "the waters in and around Tatem met up with the open sea. On the maps of the county it was known as Ibo Landing" (37). Aunt Cuney had brought the young Avey to the place, known by the people of Tatem simply as the Landing, to relate the story of a miraculous event that was witnessed by Cuney's own grandmother, Avatara, as a child. According to the story handed down to Cuney, soon after slave ships docked at the landing, a cargo of Ibo slaves was brought to shore. Although the Africans were chained at the ankles, wrists, and necks with iron fastenings—"'Nuff iron to sink an army. And chains hooking up the iron" (39)—they instantly sized up the situation. Seeing into the future—their destiny as chattel and, beyond that, the Civil War and ".everything after that right on up to the hard times today" (38)—the Ibos refused it outright. Instead, they walked back to the water, past the slave ships, and across the Atlantic to Africa and home. Having witnessed this miraculous event, the first Avatara insisted that "Her body . . . might be in

Tatem but her mind . . . was long gone with the Ibos . . ." (39). Many years
after Avatara's death, Aunt Cuney was visited by her grandmother's spirit,
who instructed her to pass her name on to Avey at her birth.

When the puzzled Avey had asked her great-aunt why the Ibos "didn't
drown" (39), Aunt Cuney had reminded her of the story of Jesus walking
on water, suggesting that the account of the Ibos' return home is a sacred
story, chronicling a miracle that resists ordinary explanations.[2] Avey had
later realized that Aunt Cuney, in telling her the legend of Ibo Landing,
had "entrusted her with a mission she couldn't even name yet had felt duty
bound to fulfill. It had taken her years to rid herself of the notion" (42).
Only belatedly does Avey reverse that process, re-engaging with the mission to keep alive and pass on her African heritage.

However, before Avey achieves that life-affirming reorientation, the
visions that confront her both before and immediately after she leaves the
cruise ship—pointedly named *Bianca Pride*—are associated with death,
decay, and destruction. Sounds produced during a shipboard game of shuf-
fleboard suggest to her "some blunt instrument repeatedly striking human
flesh and bone" (56) and bring to mind a disturbing sight she had witnessed
years before from her apartment window, the brutal beating of a black man
by a policeman with a billy stick. Not long after this recollection disturbs
Avey's serenity, a "shriveled old man" (58) on the ship startles her by grab-
bing her skirt and beckoning her to sit near him. "In a swift, subliminal
flash, all the man's wrinkled sunbaked skin fell away, his thinned-out flesh
disappeared, and the only thing to be seen on the deck chair was a skeleton
in a pair of skimpy red-and-white striped trunks and a blue visored cap"
(59). The images of death approach much closer to Avey herself when she
arrives on the nearby island of Grenada, intending to fly home the following day, and finds herself recalling the Eskimo practice in which elders are
left alone to die on the ice.

The images of death, isolation, and destruction—tropes for the condition of Avey's spirit—ultimately coalesce in her recollections of the home
she has previously regarded as her sanctuary. Questioning her hasty decision
to abandon the cruise, she tries to comfort herself by summoning the
shapes of familiar material possessions in her suburban domicile. However,
instead of their "reassuring forms,"

> she kept seeing with mystifying clarity the objects on display in the museum
> in the town of St. Pierre at the foot of Mt. Pelée . . . the twisted, scarcely
> recognizable remains of the gold and silver candlesticks and snuff boxes,
> jewelry, crucifixes and the like that had been the prized possessions of the

well-to-do of St. Pierre before the volcano had erupted at the turn of the
century, burying the town in a sea of molten lava and ash.

She might enter the dining room tomorrow night to find everything
there reduced to so many grotesque lumps of metal and glass. . . . (83)

For Avey, the corresponding inner volcanic disturbance is the relentless
eruption from her unconscious of long-buried memories and feelings.
Moreover, although part of her inner journey is a questioning and, ultimately, a rejection of a life dominated by the material possessions that came
with (and signified) upward mobility, in another sense she is obliged to
confront the temporality of all material things.

From her dreams, Avey's husband arrives to scold her for abandoning
the cruise—for apparently relinquishing so casually an entitlement of the
affluent life for which he struggled so obsessively that it destroyed him. His
presence triggers Avey's memories of their entire life together, including
the early years of marriage when they had lived in a cramped walk-up
apartment in Brooklyn. In her troubling retrospective dreams, Avey realizes
that the confining Halsey Street apartment, despite its associations with pri-
vation, was actually an expansive emotional space. There, the couple's deepest connection and truest passions—for each other, for music, for dancing,
for life—flourished. The hardwood floor, painstakingly restored by Jay and
"stained earth brown," was "like the rich nurturing ground from which she
had sprung and to which she could always return for sustenance" (12).

Avey's nostalgic memories of the brief ecstatic phase of her married life
also associate plenitude—including sexual orgasm—with the emotional
intensity of childhood. Thus, her yearning for that lost plenitude is in a
sense nostalgia for childhood itself: "[F]or a long pulsing moment she was
pure self, being, the embodiment of pleasure, the child again riding the
breakers at Coney Island in her father's arms, crowing in delight and terror.
The wave she was riding crested, then dropped. . . . It was a long, slow, joyous fall which finally, when it had exhausted itself, left her beached in a
sprawl of limbs on the bed, laughing wildly amid tears" (128). The similar-
ity of the words *Coney* (Island) and (Aunt) *Cuney* suggest that Avey's recovery of vitality pivots on her repossession of the related meanings of these
key experiences and people from her childhood.

Avey also nostalgically recalls the small rituals of early marriage, including the Sunday mornings she and Jay had spent dancing, listening together
to gospel songs, and reciting fragments of old poems over breakfast. Those
rituals represented "an ethos they held in common . . . [that joined] them
to the vast unknown lineage that had made their being possible" (137).

However, those links to a shared ethnic heritage as well as their spontaneous delight in each other were dissolved by Jay's "joyless ethic" (131) of
puritanical self-improvement. As they drew apart both physically and
emotionally, the marriage entered a "downward slide." From its passionate
peak of connectedness, their love evolved to a kind of mutual slavery, a
"burden . . . [l]ike a leg-iron which slowed [Jay] in the course he had set
for himself" (129). When Avey allows herself to recall how material prosperity replaced intimacy, she finally truly mourns her husband—"not his
death so much, but his life" (134). Moreover, if Jerome Johnson had sold his
soul to the devil, Avey concedes that she had been a full collaborator in that
Faustian bargain. In recalling the stranger in the coffin at her husband's
funeral—the "cold face laughing in Mephistophelean glee" (135)—Avey
asks herself four years later, "What kind of bargain had they struck? How
much had they foolishly handed over in exchange for the things they had
gained . . . ?" (139–40)

Belatedly grieving for her husband and their lost passion and intimacy,
Avey also grieves for her own lost self. In the course of her marriage to
Jay/Jerome, what had disappeared was her "proper axis" (254). "'Avey' or
even 'Avatara'" had vanished. "The woman to whom those names
belonged had gone away, had been banished along with her feelings and
passions to some far-off place—not unlike the old Eskimo woman in the
strange recurring vision that had troubled her" (141). Only when Avey
finally permits her anger and grief to surface and acknowledges her sense
of loss and self-betrayal is she able to move beyond mournful nostalgia
toward integration and recovery of her authentic self.

To that end, the next stage of a journey on which she does not yet recognize she is engaged begins on the Caribbean island of Grenada. There,
during her first night she dreams of a perspiring infant who needs changing, only to discover that she herself, having fallen asleep in her clothes, is
the baby bathed in sweat. The image anticipates the reversed journey that
leads Avey first, regressively, into the physical dependencies of childhood
and then, progressively, to spiritual rebirth. Later that day on Grenada, she
takes a solitary walk on the beach and is nearly overcome by heat and panic
as she realizes that she is far from her hotel and in danger of missing the
afternoon departure of the flight that will convey her home. Once again,
mysterious hands beckon her and draw her past her own resistances. Seeking shelter from the intense heat, she stumbles into a rickety rum shop on
the beach where "through the [door's] opening there came a cool dark current of air like a hand extended in welcome. And without her having anything to do with it . . . the hand reached out and drew her in" (157).

The image of the skeletal man who confronted Avey on the cruise ship reappears more positively in the form of the proprietor of the rum shop, an ancient, lame man named Lebert Joseph. To his insistent questions, "[W]hat you is?" and "What's your nation?" (166–67), Avey has no answers. Ignorant of both "who she is" and her own "nation" or cultural origin— her personal and collective identities—she describes herself merely (and accurately) as an outsider, "a visitor, a tourist, just someone here for the day . . ." (167). However, despite her irritation at the ancient man's blunt questions, she finds herself confiding to him the peculiar sequence of events that prompted her impulsive decision to leave the cruise ship and return home. As the old man reads her thoughts even without her speaking words, Avey realizes that he is no ordinary rum shack proprietor. Rather, Lebert is a wise man who "possessed ways of seeing that went beyond mere sight and ways of knowing that outstripped ordinary intelligence . . ." (172).

Their conversation turns to a discussion of the imminent Carriacou Island Excursion, explained by Lebert in his island patois as an annual cele- bration by out-islanders in tribute to the "Old Parents" who came from Africa. During the festivities, islanders venerate and ask forgiveness of their ancestors and renew family connections through ritual dancing and singing. Avey declines Lebert's invitation to join the Excursion and festivi- ties, protesting that she wants to leave the island immediately and "plan[s] on being home tonight, in [her] own house" (181). However, her plans are challenged not only by Lebert but by her own disruptive inner visions. Once again, an invisible hand pulls her in another direction besides the one she consciously chooses, reconfiguring her idea of home before her very eyes. When she tries to summon in her imagination the sanctuary of her suburban home, what comes to mind instead is a site of desolation and devastation. "Home again, she entered the dining room only to find that it had turned into the museum at the foot of Mount Pelée in the wake of the eruption that had taken place during her absence, and which had reduced everything there to so many grotesque lumps of molten silver and glass" (181).

As Lebert, whose name alludes to the Afro-Caribbean trickster god, Legba,[3] cajoles Avey to join the Excursion, Marshall represents as a literal battle her protagonist's resistance to opening herself to her cultural past as well as to deeper dimensions of her own experience. In her struggle to resist Lebert's entreaties, Avey feels "as exhausted as if she and the old man had been fighting—actually, physically fighting, knocking over the tables and chairs . . .—and that for all his appearance of frailty he had proven the stronger of the two" (184). Earlier in the narrative, Avey struggles similarly with the phantom of her great-aunt Cuney, who, appearing in the dream vision, summons her to return to Tatem and the Landing. Avey's resistance to that "call" leads to a "tug-of-war" that becomes a "bruising fist fight" (45). During the struggle, her pricey fur stole is virtually stripped from her body, prefiguring the stripping that accompanies her spiritual conversion.[4]

However, ultimately capitulating to Lebert's power, Avey becomes "as obedient as a child" (186) and prepares to embark on the Carriacou Excursion. Waiting on the wharf triggers her memory of another key moment in childhood, when she and her family joined a number of black families for another annual celebratory occasion, an excursion up the Hudson River. The communal boat trip had elicited in the child Avey an image identical to one she had experienced in Tatem when she had watched the church elders perform a collective dance, the Ring Shout. The parallels are Marshall's way of expressing the fundamental overlapping elements of Avey's repressed personal and collective histories:

> As more people arrived to throng the area beside the river and the cool morning air warmed to the greetings and talk, she would feel what seemed to be hundreds of slender threads streaming out from her navel and from the place where her heart was to enter those around her. And the threads went out not only to people she recognized from the neighborhood but to those she didn't know as well. . . .
>   . . . .
>   Then it would seem to her that . . . the threads didn't come from her, but from them, from everyone on the pier. . . . She visualized the threads as being silken, like those used in the embroidery on a summer dress, and of a hundred different colors. And although they were thin to the point of invisibility, they felt as strong entering her as the lifelines of woven hemp that trailed out into the water at Coney Island. . . .
>   While the impression lasted she would cease being herself, a mere girl in a playsuit . . . ; instead, for those moments, she became part of, indeed the center of, a huge wide confraternity. (190–91)

In this central image of the narrative, Marshall, stressing the powerful intangible connections between bodies and among spirits, captures the sense of Avey's original childhood kinship with others both known and unknown. Avey experiences her self as part of a larger whole—"her heart [entering] those around her"—that she has since forgotten in her materially comfortable but spiritually impoverished adult life. The navel is obviously the physical mark of one's lifeline, the bond of lineage from which

Avey has become radically disconnected. Her vivid recovered memory of the extensive/expansive network of threads occurs just before she departs with the Carriacou Excursion, signaling the beginning of her reconnection to the web of kinship with her African and African American ancestors.

However, Avey's transformation is not without suffering; like a religious initiate, she must first be purged and cleansed.[5] During the schooner voyage to Carriacou, hands again reach out to aid and guide her. Several elderly women on the boat, distinguished by their attitude of "maternal solicitude" (197) and supportive attention, soothe Avey physically, as a mother would a child, during a rough interval. "Their murmurous voices . . . set about divesting her of the troubling thoughts, quietly and deftly stripping her of them as if they were so many layers of winter clothing she had mistakenly put on for the excursion" (197). Avey is further reduced to the state of a child, shrinking almost like the fictional Alice in Wonderland who accidentally tumbles down the rabbit hole:

> [A]s [Avey's] mind came unburdened she began to float down through the gaping hole, floating, looking, searching for whatever memories were to be found there. . . . And the deeper [she] went, the smaller everything became. The large, somewhat matronly handbag on her lap shrank to a little girl's pocketbook of white patent leather containing a penny for the collection plate. . . . (197)

As distant memories merge with present events to elicit the unpleasant visceral sensation of nausea, Avey's seasickness leads to her body's revolt: vomiting followed by voiding of her bowels. Following the cathartic episode, she is gently conducted by the "mothers" to the schooner's deck cabin. There, she imaginatively identifies with her African ancestors in suffering, experiencing the cabin as the hold of a slave ship crammed with a multitude of bodies "packed around her in the filth and stench of themselves, just as she was. Their moans, rising and falling with each rise and plunge of the schooner, enlarged upon the one filling her head. Their suffering—the depth of it, the weight of it in the cramped space—made hers of no consequence" (209). With the passage from Grenada to Carriacou symbolically doubling as Avey's own Middle Passage, Avey is purged of the bloated, satiated feeling that has plagued her for much of her journey. Only after she is "emptied-out . . . with the sense of a yawning hole where her life had once been" (214) can she begin to replace that emptiness with something affirmative. Appropriately, when she is brought to the Carriacou home of Lebert's daughter, Rosalie Parvay, Avey surveys her surroundings "with a look almost of humility" (215). Afterwards, she learns that her mentor and guide, Lebert Joseph, had sat awake in the house the whole night while she was incapacitated, functioning as a kind of guardian or spiritual father working in tandem with her spiritual mother, Aunt Cuney, to assist in the (re)birth of Avey's soul.

Not only humbled but reduced to a child by this point in her journey, Avey is further reduced to the helplessness of infancy—virtually like "a baby that had soiled itself" (217) and who is entirely dependent upon maternal hands for bathing and cleansing. Another of the several maternal figures who assist Avey during her journey, Rosalie (whose surname, Parvay, connotes her function as a purveyor of both physical and spiritual sustenance), performs a ritual bathing and oiling of her body while Avey simultaneously experiences herself as the "child in the washtub" (221) being bathed by her great-aunt Cuney in Tatem. Rosalie's gentle and discrete ministrations, accompanied in island patois by a "praisesong" or chant whose origins are African,[6] effect a spiritually restorative "laying on of hands" (217). Marshall thus situates Avey's rite of passage within a larger African cultural context of social transition and spiritual transformation.

Rosalie's gentle massage culminates for Avey in an orgasmic moment analogous to the one she associates with both passionate lovemaking and the sensation of visceral joy—the "embodiment of pleasure" (128) that she had experienced as a child riding the Coney Island breakers with her father.

> [T]his warmth and the faint stinging reached up the entire length of her thighs. . . . Then, slowly, they radiated out into her loins: When, when was the last time she had felt even the slightest stirring there? . . . The warmth, the stinging sensation that was both pleasure and pain passed up through the emptiness at her center. Until finally they reached her heart. All the tendons, nerves and muscles which strung her together had been struck in a powerful chord, and the reverberation could be heard in the remotest corners of her body. (223–4)

Lebert's daughter assists in the process of "putting [Avey] back together again" (229), referring not only to her recent shipboard indispositions but to her longstanding physical and spiritual self-estrangement.

The several strands of Avey's literal and inner journeys finally converge during the rituals of the Carriacou fête that follow later that evening. Even the absolute darkness Avey witnesses as she climbs the small hill to the site of the celebrations reminds her of Tatem. "Avey Johnson hadn't experienced darkness like this since Tatem, since those August nights when she would accompany her great-aunt along the moonless roads to visit a sick friend or to stand with her across from the church when the Ring Shouts were being held" (231). Again, Avey realizes that Lebert Joseph is more than he appears to be—or, rather, that it is his appearance that keeps changing. One moment he seems a decrepit gnome "of an age beyond reckoning, his body more misshapen and infirm than ever before" (233). The next moment, "the crippled figure up ahead shifted to his good leg, pulled his body as far upright as it would go (throwing off at least a thousand years as he did), and was hurrying forward with his brisk limp to take her arm" (233). As a shape-shifter, the trickster Lebert Joseph "tricks" Avey into recovering her true identity.

Initially, Avey takes a sideline seat for the ritual events of the evening fête of drumming, singing, shouting, and dancing that draws from both Afro-Caribbean and African sources. Each ritual is part of a ceremony of remembrance: of origins, of kin, of culture, of the home/lands in Africa from which all of the participants, through their ancestors, feel exiled. The celebration begins with the "Beg Pardon" led by Lebert Joseph, in which those present petition their ancestors for forgiveness, not only on their own behalf but on behalf of absent relatives and friends scattered throughout the diaspora. Next, the elder members of the group dance the "nation dances" to the gentle beat of the keg drums. As Temne, Banda, Arada, Moko, and other nations are called out by name, Avey experiences the direct presence of the Old People as "kin, visible, metamorphosed and invisible, repeatedly circled the cleared space together . . ." (239). Under the influence of the chanting and the drum rhythms, Avey feels for a moment her own kin—her great-aunt Cuney—standing next to her.

Although the Carriacou fête is somewhat less grand than Avey had anticipated, she finds herself not disappointed but drawn even further into its imaginative dimension. Like Avey herself in the process of regeneration, the ceremonies reflect a process of stripping down to the elemental core. "It was the essence of something rather than the thing itself she was witnessing. . . . All that was left were a few names of what they called nations which they could no longer even pronounce properly, the fragments of a dozen or so songs, the shadowy forms of long-ago dances and rum kegs for drums. The bare bones. The burnt-out ends" (240). Through the image of skeletons that recurs in different forms throughout the narrative and in the statement as a whole, Marshall pointedly laments the lost traditions and wisdom that have almost perished, having been reduced to their "bare bones" as African cultural identities have been dispersed and attenuated over time.

The final movement of the Carriacou fête, the Creole dances, signify the mingling of the cultures in an island "creole" of singing and dancing, both of which modulate into a more rapid rhythm. Lebert Joseph, "his head perform-ing its trickster's dance" (243), is the "hub, the polestar" (243), the master of ceremonies who personally guides Avey and prompts her to participate in the dance. As drums plumb the depths of Avey's awakened spirit, she surrenders to the suggestive power of the reverberations. A particularly resonant note struck on a goatskin drum captures for her "the theme of separation and loss" and the "unacknowledged longing" she has finally recognized within herself as a part of a larger cultural entity. "The note was a lamentation that could hardly have come from the rum keg of a drum. Its source had to be the heart, the bruised still-bleeding innermost chamber of the collective heart" (245).

As the mood of the ceremony shifts from the creole Juba to a carnival-like Trinidadian jump, Avey moves from observer to participant, joining the elderly dancers on the periphery of the circle. Doing so, she acknowledges how far she has retreated from the joyous dancing of her early years of mar-riage and, before that, from the spiritual "confraternity" that she had known as a child. The dances and other elements of the ceremonial fête on Carria-cou enable their participants to mourn, neutralize, and imaginatively heal cultural loss, to override the condition of literal and spiritual exile from their ancestral people and cultures of origin, and to celebrate their deeper cultural connections.[7] Avey Johnson, entering into the "counterclockwise" dance (247), the "flatfooted glide and stamp" (248) of the Carriacou Tramp, is also re-enacting the steps of the Ring Shout that she had observed during her childhood in Tatem. In fact, they are the same dance. One scholar of the rela-tionship between African and African American cultural rituals documents the unequivocal centrality of the Ring Shout in the maintenance of cultural identity for people who were wrenched from their African homelands:

> Wherever in Africa the counterclockwise dance ceremony was performed—
> it is called the ring shout in North America—the dancing and singing were
> directed to the ancestors and gods, the tempo and revolution of the circle
> quickening during the course of movement. The ring in which Africans
> danced and sang is the key to understanding the means by which they
> achieved oneness in America.[8]

In Marshall's novel, Avey recalls how, as a child standing on the road across from the church where the dancers had engaged in the Ring Shout, "she used to long to give her great-aunt the slip and join those across the road. She had finally after all these decades made it across. The elderly

Shouters in the person of the out-islanders had reached out their arms like one great arm and drawn her into their midst" (248–9). The passage repeats the image of the supportive arms and hands that assist Avey at crucial points in her spiritual journey. Additionally, the phrase, "making it across," alludes to the legendary Ibos who made it across the water in their defiant refusal of slavery and return to Africa. Avey finally "makes it across"— enters into active commemoration of her African, Caribbean, and African American ancestors—as she understands the deeper meaning of the dances.

Through her protagonist's transformation, Marshall reweaves the threads of Avey's experience, and of the novel's key movements, by recapitulating the image from Avey's childhood that signifies her spiritual connection to others: "for the first time since she was a girl, she felt the threads, that myriad of shiny, silken, brightly colored threads. . . . [S]he used to feel them streaming out of everyone there to enter her, making her part of what seemed a far-reaching, wide-ranging confraternity" (249). In the midst of her engaged participation in "the Carriacou Tramp, the shuffle designed to stay the course of history" (250), Avey is astonished when first Lebert, then his daughter Rosalie and others, stop and bow reverentially before her. Their gestures implicitly acknowledge that she has earned her ancestral name, becoming "Avey, short for Avatara" (251), an avatar of their shared ancestry.[9]

As Avey departs from Carriacou, she suspects that the island is in fact a kind of magical space, "more a mirage rather than an actual place. Something conjured up perhaps to satisfy a longing and need" (254)—in other words, something generated by Avey's own deepest longings. With the aid of several "conjurers" in the outside world and within herself, Avey Johnson finally finds her way home. Moreover, if in response to that longing finally satisfied, she returns home a different person, so also is home a transformed place. By the time she arrives back in the United States, she has determined to sell her suburban house outside of New York City and fix up the house in Tatem left to her by Aunt Cuney. Most importantly, she plans to have her grandsons visit her there each summer as she had visited her Aunt Cuney as a child. "And at least twice a week in the late afternoon . . . she would lead them, grandchildren and visitors alike, in a troop over to the Landing" (256), where she intends to share with them the legend of the Ibos who miraculously returned home to Africa.

Although Avey's journey commences with a reluctant nostalgia—uninvited, unwelcome, and unproductive—it comes to serve a reparative rather than regressive longing for belonging. Beginning with the appearance of her Aunt Cuney, Avey's dreams and visions compel her to revisit previous phases of her life and the places associated with them as preliminary stops along the route to an unanticipated destination. The dreams, visions, and rituals that she experiences are essential elements in her healing journey from displacement to belonging. In effect, Avey must first acknowledge and actively mourn lost dimensions of her self in order to achieve a fuller assimilation of the lost cultural past. Midlife nostalgia thus serves as a vital catalyst, precipitating the knowledge of loss and grief for a vanished wholeness—understood in both physical and spiritual, individual and cultural senses—as a precondition for the integration of lost (repressed) contents of the psyche and of a collective ethnic history.

Like several other narratives considered in this study, Marshall's *Praisesong for the Widow* both represents and expresses cultural mourning. Though on the surface Avey Johnson's mourning is more immediate and personal, ultimately she brings to consciousness a deeper and broader dimension of grief as she recognizes her profound disconnection from lost ancestors and from her own African and African American heritage.[10] Her experience at the Carriacou fête both acknowledges—"begs pardon" of— the Old People or ancestors and mediates that grief. The meaning of Ibo Landing on Tatem Island has not been lost; indeed, Avey Johnson commits herself to its preservation and retelling. Importantly, the ancestors' miraculous resistance to oppression and the transcendent return to the African homeland encodes a cultural memory not of injury and loss but, rather, of a defiant reversal, a figurative undoing of the collective trauma of the Middle Passage itself. Avey Johnson's "re-membering" enables her to re-establish the threads that connect her to her tradition. Marshall's invocation of cultural mourning and loss is essential to the process, both personal and collective, of resolving grief and "fixing" the past, achieving spiritual affirmation and recovery. As she has phrased it elsewhere, "In order to develop a sense of our collective history, I think it is absolutely necessary for black people to effect this spiritual return [to African roots]. As the history of people of African descent in the United States and the diaspora is fragmented and interrupted, I consider it my task as a writer to initiate readers to the challenges this journey entails."[11]

Praisesong for the Widow is thus an hom(e)age to the ancestral past and its traditions that literally melds a midlife reassessment and the potentiality for renewal with the personal and cultural significations of home. Initially signaled by Avey Johnson's recollections of her actual house, the longing for home evolves into a more pervasive yearning—and mourning—that, like the recurring image of the volcano that springs from dormancy into active eruption, powerfully disrupts and exposes Avey's comfortable but sterile life. Revitalized by her discoveries, Avey is inspired to revive the "threads" that link her, from the navel and the heart, to others across time and space. As the reborn Avatara, she becomes a go-between in the tradition of her own avatars—the first Avatara, Aunt Cuney, Lebert Joseph, Legba. Accepting her liminal role, she re-enters and reclaims history, finding her true home at the spiritual crossroads of geography and genealogy.

◇ 7 ◇

Haunted Longing
and the Presence of Absence:
Jazz, Toni Morrison

Jazz always keeps you on the edge. There is no final chord. There may be a long chord, but no final chord. There is always something else that you want from the music. I want my books to be like that—because I want that feeling of something held in reserve and the sense that there is more—that you can't have it all right now.

—Toni Morrison, Interview with Nellie McKay

As Toni Morrison explained early in her writing of what was to become a trilogy of loosely-related narratives—*Beloved* (1987), *Jazz* (1992), and *Paradise* (1998)—"the thread that's running through the work I'm doing now is this question—*who is the Beloved?*"[1] In fact, her interest in the identity of the "beloved"—and of the complex nature of love itself—dates from the beginning of her writing career. In a 1977 interview she observed, "Actually, I think, all the time that I write, I'm writing about love or its absence. Although I don't start out that way. . . . Each one of us is in some way at some moment a victim and in no position to do a thing about it. Some child is always left unpicked up at some moment. In a world like that, how does one remain whole. . . ?"[2] Subsequently, Morrison elaborated on the relationship between this central literary preoccupation and a central theme of the blues: "my notion of love—romantic love—probably is very closely related to blues. There's always somebody leaving somebody, and there's never any vengeance, any bitterness. There's just an observation of it, and it's almost as though the singer says, 'I am so miserable because you don't love me,' but it's not unthinkable."[3]

Such blues complaints might be understood as the musical rendering of nostalgia, of longing mingled with the emotional pain of lost love. Like the penetrating expression of a blues lament and its recapitulation in the instrumental variations of a jazz improvisation,[4] Morrison's lament on "love or its absence" has both developed and deepened in expression during the course of her fiction, coming to represent the experience of loss felt by individuals who have been separated from lovers, spouses, parents, or children. In some instances that lament springs from the emotional history of an entire group whose members have been scarred, directly or indirectly, by a legacy of cultural dislocation, personal dispossession, and emotional (if not actual) dismemberment.[5]

What Morrison calls the "absence of love" I term the *presence of absence* because most individuals experience it not merely as something missing but as a lack that continues to occupy a palpable emotional space; the presence of absence is the presence of unresolved mourning. As I have previously proposed, mourning may be understood not only in individual but cultural contexts, a response not only to personal losses but to collective traumas and their ramifications over time. For African Americans, that collective trauma occurred generations earlier when their ancestors, forcibly transported to the United States as slaves, were subjected to involuntary separations, physical abuses, and emotional trauma. Ineradicably woven into the fabric of African American experience is the cultural memory of lost cultures, lost lives, lost possibilities, lost parents and children, lost parts of the body, lost selves. As the character Baby Suggs expresses it in *Beloved,* "Not a house in the country ain't packed to its rafters with some dead Negro's grief."[6] Naming and embodying that grief, Toni Morrison expresses the responsibility that she feels for "all of these people; these unburied, or at least unceremoniously buried, people made literate in art."[7]

Jazz, set during the 1920s, an era of emerging cultural optimism for African Americans, initially seems to establish a mood much lighter than those associated, as in Marshall's *Praisesong for the Widow,* with the "absence of love," grief, and loss. A series of linked episodes reflects a cultural moment of vibrant social and aesthetic transformations in the years following the Great Migration and World War I, when, as Morrison has noted elsewhere, "black culture, rather than American culture, began to alter the whole country and eventually the western world. It was an overwhelming development in terms of excitement and glamour, and the sense of individualizing ourselves swept the world."[8] In the novel, Morrison imagines the histories of half a dozen characters whose lives converge in the City. A central story within the several overlapping ones is a romantic love triangle involving a middle-aged married couple, Violet and Joe Trace, and Dorcas Manfred, the eighteen-year-old girl with whom Joe has a brief love affair and whom he eventually kills when he realizes that he is about to lose her to another man. Their liaison is, as the narrator informs us in a deliberately understated announcement of the violent action that frames the narrative, "one of those deepdown, spooky loves that made [Joe] so sad and happy he shot her just to keep the feeling going."[9] Though most of the action in *Jazz* takes place in the City—never named but understood as Harlem—several flashbacks are set in rural Virginia, including the self-contained story of a mulatto named Golden Gray, whose history intersects symbolically with Joe and Violet Trace's.

The narrative owes its structural complexity and originality to the musical forms of blues and jazz.[10] Some years before she wrote *Jazz*, Morrison described her affinity for the structural openness of jazz as well as its haunting quality of "something held in reserve and the sense that . . . you can't have it all right now."[11] The "something held in reserve" also suggests the presence of absence that recurs throughout her fiction. More recently, Morrison made explicit the analogies she endeavored to create between the formal elements of jazz and the narrative structure of *Jazz*. Considering how to tell the story, she explains that she created a narrator who did not know exactly where the story was going:

> It reminded me of a jazz performance in which the musicians are on stage. And they know what they are doing, they rehearse, but the performance is open to change, and the other musicians have to respond quickly to that change. Somebody takes off from a basic pattern, then the others have to accommodate themselves. That's the excitement, the razor's edge of a live performance of jazz. . . . I was trying to align myself with more interesting and intricate aspects of my notion of jazz as a demanding, improvisatory art form. . . .[12]

Structurally, Morrison manages to have it two ways. On the one hand, the narrative unfolds as a series of intersecting stories in the tradition of modernist fiction, drawing readers into the psychological realities of her characters. On the other, a postmodern, "improvisatory" posture deliberately contests the illusion that a reader can know either characters or their stories. A different kind of "unreliable narrator"—one who ultimately confesses not only that she invents the stories as she goes along but that she does not always know the "true" version of events or characters—underscores the irreducible fictionality of the text. These complementary modes of representation are captured in an image early in *Jazz* that expresses the shifting relationship between surface and depth, theme and variation. Naming as "cracks" in Violet Trace's normalcy the disruptive actions that reveal her underlying emotional disarray, the narrating voice further describes these "dark fissures in the globe light of the day": "The globe light holds and bathes each scene, and it can be assumed that at the curve where the light stops is a solid foundation. In truth, there is no foundation at all, but alleyways, crevices one steps across all the time. But the globe light is imperfect too. Closely examined it shows seams, ill-glued cracks and weak places beyond which is anything. Anything at all" (22–3). The globe light may illuminate "consciousness," that primary subject for the modernists.[13] At the same time, it also exposes the "cracks and weak places" that, in the postmodern sense, betray the absence of a "solid foundation" and permit the narrator to create "anything"—either a continuous or a discontinuous world—for the reader to ponder. Morrison slyly alludes to that bifurcated vision through her central character, Joe Trace, who has "double eyes. Each one a different color. A sad one that lets you look inside him, and a clear one that looks inside you" (206).

Similarly, the narrative looks both ways as the narrator's construction of the characters' inner lives and histories vie with the narrator's skepticism and uncertainty about them, suggesting that beneath the words we read lie other variations: unarticulated stories that may contradict the ones the narrator produces. The narrator of *Jazz* is, uniquely, "without sex, gender, or age," a presence Morrison designates as the "voice" in order to highlight its function not as a person (of either gender) but as "the voice of a talking book . . . as though the book were talking, writing itself, in a sense."[14] Through this strategy, Morrison "signifies" intertextually on the trope of the Talking Book, a tradition with sources in the slave narrative.[15]

Initially, the narrating voice of *Jazz* exults as it applauds the emergence of a new order: "Here comes the new. Look out. There goes the sad stuff. The bad stuff. . . . History is over, you all, and everything's ahead at last" (*Jazz* 7). The voice fervently celebrates the era of the "New Negro" along with the emergence of opportunity, cultural pride, and vibrant new musical idioms. However, beneath these exuberant expressions a contrary one insinuates itself—a "complicated anger" (59) interwoven with strands of danger, sorrow, and loss. As eventually becomes clear, the narrating voice is distracted, as much as are the people it observes/fabricates, by the enticements of urban life at the dawn of a new age:"Round and round about the town. That's the way the City spins you. Makes you do what it wants, go where the laid-out roads say to. All the while letting you think you're free. . . . You can't get off the track a City lays for you" (120).

From the perspective of the characters' inner lives, the phantoms of the "absence of love" that appear in this novel, as in Morrison's previous novels, call attention to the haunted longings that disrupt the narrative's jazzy surface. Such longings often have sources in a child's experience of involuntary separation from or actual psychological abandonment by one or both parents. Implicitly, such abandonments in Morrison's fiction recapitulate the actual and emotional displacements of African American historical experience, beginning with the genocide of African people who were ripped from their families and communities and placed on slave ships bound for the West. Untold numbers of them did not survive the Middle Passage; those who did survive were destined to live out the losses upon which slavery was predicated—the horrifying deprivations, degradations, and abuses of body, mind, and being that are so graphically rendered by Morrison in *Beloved*. Like a jazz variation prompted by a blues lament, *Jazz* takes up in a minor key the lingering emotional effects of those traumatic displacements. The relocations of the Great Migration—"the wave of black people running from want and violence" (33)—were similarly infused with cultural loss and mourning for disrupted lives as well as for people and places left behind.

Representing the traces of this experience of loss at both individual and communal levels, orphans figure prominently in *Jazz,* beginning with the major figures in the love triangle/tragedy introduced on the first page.[16] Joe and Violet Trace and Dorcas Manfred are each the offspring of dead, missing, or emotionally unavailable parents. Joe, abandoned at birth and raised by another family, gave himself a surname that marked the presence of absence: the parents who "disappeared without a trace" (124). Dorcas, Joe's eighteen-year-old lover, was orphaned in childhood when her parents became innocent victims of the violent race riots that consumed East St. Louis in 1917, leaving more than two hundred African Americans dead. Dorcas's friend Felice is, if not an actual orphan, arguably an emotional one. Raised by her grandmother while her parents worked on the railroad line in other cities, Felice knew her father and mother primarily through the brief visits that punctuated their much longer absences. As she phrases it, "I would see them once every three weeks for two and a half days, and all day Christmas and all day Easter. . . . Thirty-four days a year" (198).

More literally than Felice and like her younger rival, Dorcas, Violet Trace was orphaned during adolescence. Her "phantom father" (100) deserted his family to seek his fortune, leaving his wife, Rose Dear, to raise their five young daughters. When Rose Dear was brutally dispossessed from her sharecropper's hut, she moved her family to an abandoned shack. Before long, however, she found her hardscrabble life unendurable and, broken in spirit, drowned herself in the well when Violet was twelve, leaving her daughters in the care of their grandmother, True Belle.[17]

Violet was convinced by her mother's suffering and despair that she never wanted children of her own. Many years and several miscarriages later, the inner emptiness produced by that decision haunts her in the form of a "mother-hunger" (108) so intense that she sleeps with dolls and even snatches a baby from a carriage momentarily left unguarded. Violet imagines her husband's lover Dorcas as "a girl young enough to be that [lost] daughter" of her failed pregnancies and, torn between regarding her as "the woman who took the man, or the daughter who fled her womb" (109), she finally acts out her anguish by mutilating the dead girl's face during her funeral. Later, the narrator speculates that Violet's violent action may be understood as "a crooked kind of mourning for a rival young enough to be a daughter" (111).

The term "mother-hunger" may be understood another way: not only Violet's hunger *to be* a mother to appease her belated longing for children but also her hunger *for* her lost mother. Of the lingering effect of her mother's self-annihilation, the narrator observes, "the children of suicides are hard to please and quick to believe no one loves them because they are not really here" (4). Morrison commented in a 1977 interview that "What [black] women say to each other and what they say to their daughters is vital information."[18] Further (in Nancy J. Peterson's paraphrase), "Without this passing down of wisdom, the daughters cannot have 'livable' lives and an entire generation of African Americans will be affected adversely because of the wounds these motherless or sisterless black women carry with them."[19]

Both Violet and Joe Trace are Morrison's representations of another kind of haunted longing: the loss of youth, or what the narrator describes as a hunger for "the one thing everybody loses—young loving" (120). In a historical moment and place where being young and "hep" (114) seem to be everything, "there is no such thing as midlife. Sixty years, forty even, is as much as anybody feels like being bothered with" (11). Although the narrator imagines Joe Trace as in some sense still a boy—"one of those men who stop somewhere around sixteen" (120)—from the perspective of Dorcas's friend, Felice, Joe is "really old. Fifty" (201). As if to counter the fact of their middle age, both Joe and Violet associate themselves with the upbeat jazz culture that emphasizes youth and appearance: he sells Cleopatra beauty products for women and she is a hairdresser who does "fancy women's hair" (84). For both Traces, Dorcas catalyzes their longing for lost youth and passion. When Joe grieves for his dead lover, Violet wonders if "she isn't falling in love with [Dorcas] too" (15).

Before Joe fell in love with the girl who made him feel "fresh, new again" (123), he had recognized the loss of intense feeling that he associates with his youth and had "resigned himself to . . . the fact that old age would be not remembering what things felt like" (29). He defends himself to the woman whose room he rents to pursue his tryst with Dorcas by explaining that his wife has behaved oddly since she underwent "her Change" (46). "Violet takes better care of her parrot than she does me. Rest of the time, she's cooking pork I can't eat, or pressing hair I can't stand the smell of. Maybe that's the way it goes with people been married long as we have" (49).

Violet, lamenting the loss of Joe's affection, speaks with Dorcas's aunt, Alice Manfred, who becomes her confidant. The women share a sorrowful realization that their age (and gender) blocks them from access to the intensities of love and passion that they observe all around them and hear amplified in the sensual music of blues and jazz. "Songs that used to start in the head and fill the heart had dropped on down, down to places below the sash and the buckled belts. Lower and lower, until the music was so low-down you had to shut your windows . . ." (56). Violet laments the absence of love and passion, wondering, "Is this where you got to and couldn't do it no more? The place of shade without trees where you know you are not and never again will be loved by anybody who can choose to do it? Where everything is over but the talking?" (110) From the perspective of her own years of loneliness, Alice fervently advises her, "You got anything left to you to love, anything at all, do it" (112). Later, Violet admits to Dorcas's friend Felice that she has messed up her life by wishing she could be someone else—someone "White. Light. Young again" (208).

Similarly, Joe Trace reaches midlife still attempting to fill the "inside nothing" (37) where the minimal trace of his lost parentage has expanded to form a space of enormous longing. Although he never finds the woman who abandoned him, in the Virginia woods where he grew up he discovers the denlike home of the woman referred to only as "Wild." The description of his arrival in Wild's primitive den is especially evocative of the archetypal fantasy of return to the womb followed by rebirth: "He had come through a few body-lengths of darkness and was looking out the south side of the rock face. A natural burrow. . . . Unable to turn around inside, he pulled himself all the way out to reenter head first. . . . Then he saw the crevice. He went into it on his behind until a floor stopped his slide. It was like falling into the sun" (183).

If Joe Trace is in any way reborn, however, it is in an ironic sense, precipitating an even deeper need. The trail that leads him to his putative mother's burrow becomes emotionally entangled with the trail that leads to his young lover. The "little half moons [that] clustered under [Dorcas's] cheek bones, like faint hoofmarks" (130) signal her wild animal link to Joe's mother with her "deer eyes" (152). For a time, Dorcas occupies the empty space of the "inside nothing" in Joe's heart, becoming the beloved in a way that temporarily assuages the unappeased hunger he feels for the woman who abandoned him at birth. Confiding to Dorcas details of his life that he has never before shared with another person, Joe explains that she is the central figure in his vision of Paradise, "the reason Adam ate the apple and its core. . . . You looked at me then like you knew me, and I thought it really was Eden. . . ." (133)

Nostalgia for a vanished Eden or Paradise is a fantasy that encodes our knowledge of the inevitable original loss at the personal level: separation from infantile bliss. (The suggestive meanings of Paradise obviously continue to interest Morrison, as demonstrated by the novel that immediately follows *Jazz, Paradise,* which is discussed in the final section of this book.[20]) Especially for actual orphans like Joe Trace, there never could have been a true interlude of infantile bliss experienced as unconditional love. Nonetheless, the longing to "recover" something that never existed in the first place endures as an emotionally powerful imperative.[21] As the Jungian analyst Mario Jacoby observes, despite the fact that "the harmonious world which is now regarded as lost . . . never really existed," the image of Paradise "as an inner image or expectation . . . lives on within us, creating a nostalgia the intensity of which is in inverse proportion to the amount of external fulfillment encountered in the earliest phase of life."[22]

In *Jazz,* Joe Trace's nostalgic fantasy of Paradise and of his irrecoverably absent/lost mother fuels a need so insistent that, even into middle age, it demands an outlet for its expression. Soon after he discovers Wild's dwelling among the rocks, he asks plaintively, "But where is *she?*" (184) Following a significant narrative pause (produced by the white space of a chapter break), the response—"There she is" (187)—reveals Morrison's consummate narrative sleight of hand as well as her psychological compass (and perhaps also an allusion to Virginia Woolf[23]). The ambiguous pronoun no longer refers to Joe Trace's mother but to her emotional substitute, his young lover, Dorcas. The slippage between the two female pronoun referents is both formally and psychologically significant. If one regards the white spaces of the novel's chapter breaks as structurally meaningful, then they may be understood to signify the space of absence, the space once occupied by the lost love object who survives in the emotional imagination despite—or, more accurately, because of—its absence through loss or death.[24] To the extent that a child's earliest primary attachment has been disrupted or severed, he or she—or the adult whose psychological reality has been shaped by those critical childhood experiences—yearns for a substitute who might replace the absent beloved, who might fill the emotional space that persists in the form of unresolved mourning.

In his studies of the effects of bereavement, loss, and grief, object-relations psychoanalyst John Bowlby theorized that the loss of a parent during early childhood "gives rise not only to separation anxiety and grief but to processes of mourning in which aggression, the function of which is to achieve reunion, plays a major part."[25] Bowlby also describes a complication of mourning in which the person who has experienced a loss "mislocates" the absent figure in some other figure in his or her life, regarding that person as "in certain respects a substitute for someone lost."[26] Similarly, Morrison's Joe Trace, "a long way from . . . Eden" (180) in every sense, and haunted by the ambivalent feelings of loss and aggression that characterize his futile search for his mother, follows the trail from "*where is she?*" to "*There she is*"—that is, from the phantom of his absent mother in the woods to his absenting-herself young lover in the City who becomes her substitute. As he soliloquizes, "In this world the best thing, the only thing, is to find the trail and stick to it. I tracked my mother in Virginia and it led me right to her, and I tracked Dorcas from borough to borough. . . . [I]f the trail speaks, no matter what's in the way, you can find yourself in a crowded room aiming a bullet at her heart, never mind it's the heart you can't live without" (130).

Locating Dorcas at a jazz party in the City, Joe is angered when he discovers that his beloved prefers a younger man named Acton (whose name implies "action"). In defense of her decision to drop her middle-aged lover for a younger, more exciting man who has "no white strands grow[ing] in [his] mustache" (188), Dorcas privately thinks, "This is not the place for old men; this is the place for romance" (192). As if to punish the original Beloved whose unendurable abandonment is about to be repeated, Joe shoots her emotional surrogate. In doing so, he acts out what may be understood as an ambivalent wish both to reunite with and to punish the woman who, like his mother many years before, has deserted him: "I had the gun but it was not the gun—it was my hand I wanted to touch you with" (130–1). From that aggressive "touch," Dorcas bleeds to death. Later, when Dorcas's friend Felice asks Joe, "' Why'd you shoot at her if you loved her?'" Joe replies, with a candor that makes explicit the deficiency that has stunted his emotional life, "' Scared. Didn't know how to love anybody'" (213).

Like a blues lament that repeats the same primary musical themes in different keys, another orphan's story in *Jazz* recapitulates and amplifies the emotional issues at the heart of Joe and Violet Trace's stories. The most enigmatic character of the narrative, Golden Gray is a young man of an earlier era and place—antebellum South—who also seeks an unknown and radically absent parent. The son of a "phantom father" who never knew of his paternity and a white woman who never acknowledged her motherhood, he is also, figuratively, the child of a black slave woman—Violet's grandmother, True Belle—who was obliged to leave her own children in order to become a surrogate mother for the child with beautiful golden skin and hair. Because he is suggestively both mulatto and androgynous—both black and white, both male and female—he is the boundary-straddling, liminal figure upon whom others, including the narrating voice itself, project and construct multiple, and contradictory, meanings.

When Golden Gray reaches the age of eighteen, he learns the identity of his father from the woman who "lied to him about practically everything including the question of whether she was his owner, his mother or a kindly neighbor" (143). Tracking his father in same Virginia woods in which, many years later, Joe Trace attempts to track his mother, Golden Gray finds the cabin of the woodsman called "Henry Lestory or LesTroy" (148). The uncertain surname signals the narrative's self-conscious fictionality. Morrison, blending modernist narrative cues with postmodernist strategies that employ displaced or unreliable narrative voices, thus emphasizes the irreducible provisionality—the fictionality—of narrative knowledge. Implicitly, she invokes a particular vision of *le story*—the problematic history of a racially-mixed South—through a character whose story contains decidedly Faulknerian echoes.[27]

Golden Gray, awaiting the arrival of the man reputed to be his father, describes his feelings regarding his missing parent as an amputee might describe his experience of a phantom limb, in language that most explicitly

articulates the "inside nothing" produced by a child's experience of abandonment or radical estrangement from a parent:

> Only now . . . that I know I have a father, do I feel his absence: the place
> where he should have been and was not. Before, I thought everybody was
> one-armed, like me. Now I feel the surgery. . . .
> . . . . I don't need the arm. But I do need to know what it could have been
> like to have had it. It's a phantom I have to behold and be held by. . . . I will
> locate it so the severed part can remember the snatch, the slice of its disfig-
> urement. (158–9)

With this passage, Morrison echoes the image of dismemberment that
recurs throughout her fiction as a trope for the legacy of damage inflicted
on African Americans by slavery and its aftermath. Remembering—"remembering" (Morrison's own play on the word[28])—is a crucial compensatory process that might begin to ameliorate the pain of actual and
figurative, individual and communal, severances that cumulatively persist as
cultural mourning.

Significantly, Golden Gray's expression of the ineradicable presence of
absence occurs just before another birth. The pregnant woman known
only as Wild, whom Golden Gray finds injured on the road and takes to his
putative father's cabin, gives birth to a son. Just as Golden Gray's father
rejects his son, so does this mother reject hers. Their complementary refusals
link the several stories of abandoned children and lost parents that com-
pose the narrative of *Jazz*. Wild's story also hints at an explanation for the
lost mother sought years later by Joe Trace. Morrison, pointing out that
"the dates are the same" for the disappearance of Sethe's daughter at the
end of *Beloved* and the birth of Joe Trace in *Jazz*, has explained that "Wild
is a kind of Beloved":

> You see a pregnant black woman naked at the end of *Beloved*. It's at the same
> time. . . . [I]n the Golden Gray section of *Jazz*, there is a crazy woman out
> in the woods. The woman they call Wild (because she's sort of out of it from
> the hit on the head) could be Sethe's daughter, Beloved. When you see
> Beloved towards the end [of *Beloved*], you don't know; she's either a ghost
> who has been exorcised or she's a real person who is pregnant by Paul D,
> who runs away, ending up in Virginia, which is right next to Ohio.[29]

Morrison's provocative suggestion that Wild may be both Joe Trace's
mother and "*a kind of Beloved*" underscores the encompassing psychological

truth embodied in that figure of longing. It represents the lost/dead daughter named by the bereaved slave mother who took her child's life in order to "save" it. More broadly, it represents what I term the *beloved imago*, that phantom of the vanished love object, the missing/lost part of the original parent-child bond that persists psychologically in the form of haunted longing and nostalgic mourning.

Indeed, the *beloved imago*—the idealized, disembodied/embodied presence that Morrison refers to as the "dead girl" in *Beloved*—evolves in *Jazz* into another "dead girl." As Morrison has explained,

> I call her Beloved so that I can filter all these confrontations and questions that she has in that situation [the circumstances of her death and reappearance in *Beloved*] . . . and then . . . extend her life . . . her search, her quest, all the way through as long as I care to go, into the twenties where it switches to this other girl [Dorcas, in *Jazz*]. Therefore, I have a New York uptown-Harlem milieu in which to put this love story, but Beloved will be there also.[30]

Morrison only later realized the full implications of the recurring image of the "dead girl" in her fiction, noticing that "bit by bit I had been rescuing her from the grave of time and inattention. Her fingernails maybe in the first book; face and legs, perhaps, the second time. Little by little bringing her back into living life. . . . She is here now, alive. I have seen, named and claimed her—and oh what company she keeps."[31]

The phantom "dead girl" represents the psychic core of collective loss and mourning that Morrison, over the course of her fiction, has been figuratively working through and resolving. Whether intentionally or not, Morrison's language recalls Freud's own considerably more clinical description of the "work" of mourning. As he phrases it in his classic essay on mourning and melancholia,

> Normally [following the loss of the loved object], respect for reality gains the day. Nevertheless, its orders cannot be obeyed at once. They are carried out bit by bit, at great expense of time and cathectic energy, and in the meantime the existence of the lost object is psychically prolonged. Each single one of the memories and expectations in which the libido is bound to the object is brought up and hyper-cathected, and detachment of the libido is accomplished in respect of it. Why this compromise by which the command of reality is carried out piecemeal should be so extraordinarily painful is not at all easy to explain in terms of economics. . . . The fact is, however, that when the work of mourning is completed the ego becomes free and uninhibited again.[32]

In gathering together those parts of the body, in reclaiming "bit by bit" those parts of the self, Morrison narratively attempts to reverse, by "re-membering," the historical traces of actual and figurative dismemberment that persist as cultural mourning in the African American imagination.

As the phantom of the "dead girl" signifies the *beloved imago,* the phantom of Golden Gray accomplishes a similar psychological and narrative function as a representation of haunted longing. Although Violet Trace never met the golden-haired boy whom her grandmother mothered and adored, she was nonetheless obsessed by him; "I knew him and loved him better than anybody except True Belle who is the one made me crazy about him in the first place" (97). Violet later concludes that when Joe first courted her as a girl, "standing in the cane, he was trying to catch a girl he was yet to see, but his heart knew all about, and me, holding on to him but wishing he was the golden boy I never saw either. Which means from the very beginning I was a *substitute* and so was he" (97, my emphasis).

Only after Dorcas's death do the Traces relinquish their phantoms of longing, resolving their mourning for lost love objects and the lost youth that is associated with them. To the narrator's own surprise, their story resolves not violently, with another murder, but amicably. Dorcas's friend, Felice, brings the Traces—and, implicitly, the story's other traces—together through her revelation that Dorcas is responsible for her own death. She "let herself die" (204) by resisting help for what proved to be a fatal gunshot wound. That revelation partially releases Joe from responsibility for his young lover's death. With Violet's acceptance of her husband's attempts at reconciliation, the couple moves toward a new intimacy of midlife based less on flesh than on spirit. "They reach, grown people, for something beyond, way beyond and way, way down underneath tissue" (228).

Through the narrative's blues lament—the longing for "the heart you can't live without" (130), as Joe Trace puts it—*Jazz* dramatizes both thematically and structurally Ralph Ellison's famous observation that the blues originated in "an impulse to keep the painful details and episodes of a brutal experience alive in one's aching consciousness, to finger its jagged grain, and to transcend it, not by the consolation of philosophy but by squeezing from it a near-tragic, near-comic lyricism."[33] Accordingly, *Jazz,* while not autobiographical, is a lyrical chronicle of the transformations of longing and loss. As the narrator improvises the literary equivalent of a jazz/blues lament for the absent beloved, the subtext in effect expresses variations on that theme in the minor key: the longing to fix the past by resolving mourning for the unrecoverable figures of past/lost loves or, at least, to appease the phantoms of haunted longing.

Part IV

Nostalgia for Paradise

◇

◇ 8 ◇

Memory, Mourning, and Maternal Triangulations: *Mama Day*, Gloria Naylor

. . . everything got four sides: his side, her side, an outside, and an inside. All of it is the truth.

—Miranda Day in *Mama Day*

As has been suggested throughout this study, the original home is less an actual place than a site located in memory and fantasy, a psychic space invested with nostalgia for an idealized notion of wholeness. By the time it can be imagined, home is always already lost; the movement from rapture to rupture is the universal human trajectory. Nostalgia for Paradise may be understood as the collective memory-trace of home's emotional meaning. An imaginary site that ameliorates imperfection, it exists both in the lost past and in a longed-for future. Gloria Naylor's *Mama Day* (1988) and Toni Morrison's *Paradise* (1998) elaborate on the dialectic between the wish for rapture and the reality of rupture by exploring the meanings of Edenic space and time. Both narratives make central the impact of the historical past on individual women and their communities; both pivot on the interventions of nurturing women with spiritual powers who resist what they regard as the destructive values of patriarchal thinking. Encompassing several different time frames of personal and/or historical significance to their characters, both narratives interrogate the longing for belonging and the yearning for Paradise in a world in which relationships are imperfect and change and loss are inevitable.

◇ ◇ ◇

Any discussion of Naylor's *Mama Day* must acknowledge early on the effect of the novel's unique narrative design on its meanings. Commencing in the narrative future, 1999, (the novel was published in 1988) when Cocoa Day's husband, George Andrews, has been dead for fourteen years, the story moves backward in time, intermittently revisiting events that occurred not only during the five years of the relationship between Cocoa and George but during the extended history of the Day family during the five generations before Cocoa's time. The prologue to the narrative is articulated by what might be called the collective voice of Willow Springs, despite the speaker's paradoxical claim that there "ain't nobody really talking to you . . . the only voice is your own."[1] Of the narrative's two major sections, the first, detailing the courtship and marriage of Cocoa and George, is set in New York; the second, the unraveling of those events culminating in the near-death of Cocoa and the actual death of George, is set in Willow Springs. Over the course of the narrative, Cocoa and George reconstruct for each other—and for the reader—the details of their courtship and marriage, along with their struggle to locate the bridge that might connect the incompatible worlds they represent. The narrative thus unfolds in what I term the *holographic present tense,* to amplify Mama Day's conviction that there are four sides to everything: "his side, her side, an outside, and an inside. All of it is the truth" (230). Moreover, although this conclusion is not available to the first-time reader until late in the narrative, *Mama Day* pivots on the nostalgic perspective of Cocoa Day who, fourteen years after her husband George's death, still mourns her loss. One strand of the narrative is thus a memorialization of romantic love interrupted—but not terminated—by death.

Another central relationship in *Mama Day* offers a competing narrative of love and fierce attachment. Although Cocoa's biological mother is dead by the time she begins to tell her story, her powerful surrogate mother still lives in the person of Mama Day, who is actually Cocoa's great-aunt. (The story of a powerful great-aunt who resides on an island and who influences the central character's destiny may remind a reader of Avey Johnson and her great-aunt Cuney in Paule Marshall's *Praisesong for the Widow,* discussed in an earlier chapter.) Though the conjure woman Miranda Day is literally childless, people on the island of Willow Springs regard her as "everybody's mama" (89). During the narrative, Mama Day recovers the meaning of her own lost history—not as a mama but as a daughter. Not long afterward, she secures the life of her surrogate daughter, Cocoa, at the cost of Cocoa's husband.

In juxtaposing these two overlapping—and conflicting—trajectories of attachment and loss, memory and mourning, the narrative traces a complex triangulation between different modes of relationship: romantic/erotic and maternal/filial love. As these oppositions imply, the novel depicts a world sharply divided between conflicting dimensions of being. The matriarchal world of Willow Springs and all it comes to represent—female, spiritual, cyclical, intuitive, emotionally connected, and Afrocentric—are consistently contrasted with the patriarchal world of George Andrews and all he comes to stand for—male, secular, linear, rational, emotionally detached, and Western.[2] Though for a time it appears that Cocoa (Ophelia) Day will be sacrificed in the collision of opposing worldviews, ultimately it is her husband, George Andrews, whose death permits her and the matriarchal world of Willow Springs to prevail.

As the narrative moves along the axis of time, it also moves across an axis of space, encompassing two contrasting geographical locations: the New York City that George Andrews regards as home and the island of Willow Springs that Cocoa Day, even after having lived in New York for seven years, refers to as "home home" (22). Home/land in this narrative may be understood not only as current domicile but as the original, idealized space of childhood and the past. As the narrative voice of Willow Springs evokes the nostalgic view in her meditations on home, "Folks call it different things, think of it in different ways. For Cocoa it's being around living mirrors" (48) of her childhood self, like Abigail and Miranda Day. In another attempt to define the nature of home, the narrator associates it with what is inevitably lost: "You can move away from it, but you never leave it. Not as long as it holds something to be missed" (50).

Ironically, Cocoa meets (I use the holographic present tense) George Andrews in New York just after her job at a home insurance company ends. George's home is about as far away from Cocoa's home island as it can be. Manhattan—if not George's home on still another island, Staten Island—represents an urban, fast-paced, tough, sophisticated world that (from Cocoa's perspective) lacks a sense of intimacy and community. By contrast, the rural, close, and (from George's perspective) closed community of Willow Springs is sharply distinguished in both space and time from the urban New York world. Located in "no state" (4), the barrier island is situated off the coast of Georgia and South Carolina but belongs to neither. It is linked to the mainland by only a single bridge and "even that gotta be rebuilt after every big storm" (5).

Willow Springs is presented as a kind of timeless, Edenic space beyond change; the only thing that seems to alter is the seasons. Real estate developers from the mainland are keen to develop the island as yet another "vacation paradise" (4). Visitors crossing the bridge from the mainland project their own fantasies of Eden onto Willow Springs. Visiting for the first time, George Andrews exclaims that Cocoa "had not prepared [him] for Paradise" (175) and even proposes to her, "Let's play Adam and Eve" (222). However, he fails to understand that Willow Springs is truly an enchanted domain where mediations and transformations—some initiated by magic and conjure, others by more mundane events—occur.[3]

Equally important for what happens during the course of the narrative, the island is a maternal space, dominated by empowered mother/matriarchs, particularly Mama Day and her sister, Abigail, Cocoa Day's grandmother. Indeed, the image that links the several stories and counterstories of *Mama Day* is the matriarch—the lost mother whose absence is central to the personal histories of Miranda and Cocoa Day and also of George Andrews. Cocoa is parentless: her father disappeared long before she was born and her mother, Grace, died during Cocoa's childhood. However, she has a history of family attachments that the orphaned George envies: "To be born in a grandmother's house, to be able to walk and see where a great-grandfather and even great-great-grandfather was born. You had more than a family, you had a history. And I didn't even have a real last name" (129). George is alone in the world; like Toni Morrison's Joe Trace of *Jazz,* he is both parentless and childless. The son of a young prostitute who abandoned him soon after birth, he was raised in another kind of home, a shelter for homeless boys that operated with few if any maternal features. By contrast, Cocoa has been lavishly nurtured, even spoiled, by both her grandmother and her great-aunt, whose complementary strengths have shaped her. As she explains to George, "if Grandma had raised me alone, I would have been ruined for any fit company. It seemed I could do no wrong with her, while with Mama Day I could do no right. . . . [I]n a funny kind of a way, together they were the perfect mother" (58). That composite perfect mother partially compensates Cocoa for the loss of her actual, imperfect mother, Grace, who abandoned her by dying during her childhood.

The principal daughter-figure of *Mama Day* has three names, each of which aligns her with a different value system and degree of intimacy and attachment: Ophelia, Cocoa, and Baby Girl. George calls her Ophelia, a name rarely used in Willow Springs, where, despite (or, more likely, because of) the fact that she shares the name of Mama Day's mother who died by suicide, she is addressed as either Cocoa or Baby Girl. While Cocoa is a pet name that refers to her light skin color, the third and most intimate name signals her identity as "Baby Girl," the object of maternal affection. Over the course of her life, Cocoa has found it difficult to grow up and beyond that affectionate but limiting epithet. In Willow Springs, Cocoa is continuously reminded of her childhood self by "living mirrors with the power to show a woman that she's still carrying scarred knees, a runny nose, and socks that get walked down into the heels of her shoes"(48), as the communal narrator phrases it. When, later in the narrative, Cocoa suffers acutely from the effects of poison placed in her scalp by a jealous rival, she is further infantilized, literally reduced to a baby girl who requires continuous nurturing care.

Although consciously Mama Day wants Cocoa to find happiness in her married life, unconsciously she also resists surrendering to George her possessive power over her "Baby Girl" at precisely the time in her life when Cocoa hopes to become a mother herself. Though the poisoning that Cocoa suffers is administered by a woman who mistakenly considers her a sexual rival, in another sense the poison-induced illness is the physical manifestation of Cocoa's emotional predicament: she is the object of a struggle to the death between competing claims for affection and intimacy from mother (surrogate) and lover. From "outside," the deeper struggle for Baby Girl's soul is between two competing dimensions of love: the maternal and the erotic, signified by the matriarchal and maternal bonds of Willow Springs on the one hand and heterosexual passion on the other. From "inside," Cocoa struggles against divided loyalties: to whom is she most deeply attached and whose "baby girl" will she continue to be when a choice is demanded?

When she first returns to Willow Springs with George, such a choice seems unnecessary. She believes that she is "a very fortunate woman" (177), loved by and belonging to both George and her matriarchal relatives. Nonetheless, she finds it awkward to make love with her husband in the bedroom that is so strongly associated with her filial identity. "I felt as if we were going to have an illicit affair. I had never slept with a man in my grandmother's house. . . . [T]ry as I might, I became a child again in this house" (177). As she voices to George her wish to balance different roles, "Ophelia and Cocoa could both live in that house with you. And we'd leave Willow Springs none the worse for the wear" (177). However, subsequent events prove otherwise.

Significantly, the fever and other symptoms induced by the deadly nightshade embedded in Cocoa's scalp soon after she returns to Willow

Springs precipitate an acute psychological regression, a retreat from hetero-sexual passion in the direction of the succoring maternal embrace. Cocoa experiences herself as

> a little girl again and it was so nice. My head cradled in Grandma's soft bosom, her hands stroking my forehead as she coaxed me to take small sips of that awfully bitter tea. I liked it when she was there to promise me a new dress or a set of real silk ribbons if I'd take just one more swallow, while Mama Day would have promised me a spanking if I didn't open my locked mouth. Are you feeling better, baby? Yes, call me baby again. You'll be the one to make the gray light disappear. (261)

In her infantilized condition, Cocoa perceives George as threatening and seeks maternal protection from "that strange man peering over [Grandma's] shoulder. He reached out to touch me and I shrank away" (261).

When Mama Day spoons marrow tea and chicken broth into the help-less Cocoa's mouth, "like feeding her when she was a baby, propping up her chin, prying open her lips with the tip of the spoon" (265), she admits to herself that she wishes Cocoa were still a child under her (and her sister's) protection, "that she'd never left to go beyond the bridge and still belonged only to them" (265). The possessive element of maternal love is explicitly placed in opposition to the pull of erotic love represented by the male lover and the perilous world that exists "beyond the bridge." As a result of her mother's absence in her own emotional history, Mama Day unconsciously resists relinquishing her surrogate daughter. Concurrently, Cocoa, having returned to Willow Springs with George as a prelude to becoming a mother herself, finds herself in thrall to the powerful and possessive mater-nal embrace of Mama Day.

Nancy Chodorow and other feminist scholars have argued that females are, from infancy, more psychologically fused with their mothers than are males, whose individuation is predicated on separation from their female parent. Whereas boys achieve gender identity and individuation by defin-ing themselves as other than mother/female, girls achieve gender identity and individuation by mirroring their mothers. Becoming mothers them-selves, they reproduce the pattern of attachment to the (typically) female figure who originally mothered them.[4] However, Naylor's *Mama Day* sug-gests a different set of consequences for the mother-daughter attachment. The daughter's unconscious, ambivalent desire to remain within the pro-tective maternal embrace in adulthood is potentially destructive for her maturation because it impedes her achievement of separation and psychological independence, marked by the capacity to form and maintain heterosexual erotic attachments.

If Cocoa is the "baby girl" torn between filial and erotic attachments and loyalties, Willow Springs itself reinforces the sense of matriarchal power. The island is the home of the archetypal "Great Mother" (111) herself, specifically embodied in the founding mother, the legendary African conjure woman, Sapphira Day. George Andrews, considering the legend of Sapphira he has heard from Cocoa, comments, "it was odd . . . the way you said it—she was the great, great, grand, Mother—as if you were listing the attributes of a goddess" (218). Cocoa is specifically identified as an avatar or daughter of the Goddess. As Mama Day, reflecting on her light-skinned great-niece, dotingly observes, "*the* Baby Girl brings back the great, grand Mother. . . . [I]t's only an ancient mother of pure black that one day spits out this kinda gold" (48, Naylor's emphasis).

One tribute to the Goddess or Great Mother of Willow Springs is the island's alternative to Christmas, Candle Walk; the celebratory festival of light takes place on December 22, the winter solstice and the shortest day of the year. In one sense, the struggle represented in *Mama Day* is indeed the perennial mythical struggle between the forces of Day and night, of matriarchy and patriarchy. However, if the Goddess and her avatars are sources of light, George Andrews is a deliberately ambiguous figure rather than an avatar of darkness. Neither evil nor dangerous, he is only unenlightened. As the embodiment of rationalism and patriarchal values, George is nonetheless a sympathetic figure because he genuinely cherishes Cocoa Day, despite the significant differences between them and their worlds.[5] Yet in another sense he is indeed a force of darkness: a man who wants to possess Cocoa absolutely, separating her from her matriarchal home and history.

That history is gradually revealed as one not only of matriarchal power but of a pattern of losses that extends back for many generations, expressed through narrative doublings and repetitions of images of engulfment and drowning. Two of Cocoa's maternal ancestors died by water: Mama Day's sister Peace drowned in a well during childhood; Cocoa's great-grandmother, Ophelia (whose allusively Shakespearean name Cocoa shares), drowned herself in the island's Sound in grief over her daughter's drowning. Other images of drowning and engulfment throughout the narrative heighten the symbolism. George Andrews's mother died by drowning; he is haunted by dreams of his own drowning. Not long after Cocoa and George arrive on the island, they have the same dream: George is swimming across the Sound, trying desperately to reach Cocoa, who is calling out to him. In George's version of the dream, "A wave of despair went over me as I began sinking, knowing I'd never reach you" (184). His sense of desperation may be compounded by the fact (revealed much later in the narrative) that George cannot "swim a stroke" (263). In Cocoa's dream, George is swimming in the wrong direction, away from rather than toward her cries. The dream of watery engulfment recurs when Cocoa almost succumbs to poison-induced fever; she is convinced that it is not she but George who has "gone under" (253). When she awakens from the nightmare, she thinks at first that she is in the embrace of her grandmother, not George. This and later images of watery engulfment suggest Cocoa's drift toward death and, symbolically, the regressive thrall of the maternal embrace: the (impossible) return to the womb.

For Mama Day the imagery of watery engulfment is more ambiguous. Just after the hurricane that slams the island of Willow Springs and makes the waters around the island rise to engulf the single bridge to the mainland, Mama Day goes to visit the "other place" (254), the ancestral, original home. The Day homestead functions in the narrative as the symbolic center where time and space converge. Even from the perspective of an outsider like George, the ancestral place "resonate[s] *loss. A lack of peace*" (225, Naylor's emphasis). At that location, Mama Day retraces the emotional trajectory from rupture to back to rapture, thinking back through her foremothers—"past the mother who ended her life in The Sound, on to the Mother who began the Days" (262).[6] There, she discovers that a true understanding of the past is necessary to make possible the future she hopes for.

In the attic of the other place, Mama Day stumbles on several artifacts of her family's history, most importantly a ledger containing the bill of sale of her great-grandmother. Only the first two letters of the First Mother's name, "Sa," appear in the document, and Miranda grieves that she doesn't even know the full name of the founding mother of her family. "A loss that she can't describe sweeps over her—a missing key to an unknown door somewhere in that house. The door to help Baby Girl" (280). But imagination supplies what time has effaced, so that "in her dreams she finally meets Sapphira" (280). Her journey through a series of figurative doors that open into and reveal the lost past ultimately leads her to "a vast space of glowing light" in which she experiences herself in a way that she has not permitted herself to feel for most of her life: as a daughter. In that moment of enlightenment, she brings to full awareness her knowledge of lost maternal plenitude.

There's only the sense of being. Daughter. Flooding through like fine streams of hot, liquid sugar to fill the spaces where there was never no arms to hold her up, no shoulders for her to lay her head down and cry on, no body to ever turn to for answers. Miranda. Sister. Little Mama. Mama Day. Melting, melting away under the sweet flood waters pouring down to lay bare a place she ain't know existed: Daughter. And she opens the mouth that ain't there to suckle at the full breasts, deep greedy swallows of a thickness like cream, seeping from the corners of her lips, spilling onto her chin. Full. Full and warm to rest between the mounds of softness, to feel the beating of a calm and steady heart. (283)

Mama Day's literal and psychological return home thus culminates in a nostalgic memory: the paradisal fantasy of succor and rapture at the mother's breast.[7] Imaginatively "remembering," she mourns the inevitably vanished experience of infantile bliss, a loss compounded by her mother's suicide. Through her recuperative fantasy, Mama Day is strengthened to confront the space of longing—the enduring presence of absence in her emotional history—by examining the "bottomless pit" (284) where her sister drowned in early childhood. The death of the child named Peace was also the death of peace, precipitating her mother's emotional and literal drowning in grief. Curiously, the first Ophelia's name is absent from the genealogical chart of the Day family that Naylor places at the front of the novel. Mama Day, "looking past the pain" (284) and bringing to consciousness the depth of her own losses, recovers the erased figure of Ophelia and restores her within her own emotional history as a daughter. The experience fortifies her in her determination to save Baby Girl, the surrogate daughter who doubles, in name and emotional importance, for her own lost mother.

Mama Day's efforts to recover memories deeply buried in her emotional history, triggered by her distress over Cocoa's illness and drift toward death, lead her to revise her understanding of her maternal history. According to legend, the African-born Sapphira Day, after having borne seven sons to her Norwegian husband/owner, Bascombe Wade, mysteriously left by wind (152). Several permutations of the legend suggest that Sapphira murdered Wade—variously, by dagger, poison, or suffocation (3)—after having secured from him the deeds to his land. As Mama Day searches through memory and imagination as well as through the actual rooms of the ancestral house, she concludes that the story of her progenitors was distinguished not by homicide but by grief and loss. Sapphira did not murder Bascombe Wade. Rather, refusing to be owned, she left the man who "had claim to her body, but not her mind" (225). Her abandonment "broke his heart 'cause he couldn't let her go" (308). Later, Mama Day amplifies her speculation, concluding that Wade had "freed 'em all but [Sapphira], 'cause . . . she'd never been a slave. And what she gave of her own will, she took away" (308). Mama Day's version makes more sense than do the other explanations for Wade's deed of land on the island to Sapphira and the conjure woman's influential legacy of power that has passed down on the female side of the Day family for five generations.

From her newly illuminated perspective as daughter of both "Sapphira [who] left by wind" and "Ophelia [who] left by water" (152) and also of Bascombe Wade, Mama Day determines that maternal power, while vital, is not always sufficient. Indeed, "looking past the losing was to feel for the man who built this house. . ." (285). She believes that she needs George, whose confident belief in his own rational powers mirrors that of the paternal side of Mama Day's own family and would complement her own intuitive gifts. "[T]ogether they could be the bridge for Baby Girl to walk over. Yes, in his very hands he already held the missing piece she'd come looking for" (285). However, Mama Day also knows that "George [does] not need her" (285); he is capable of saving Cocoa on his own. George is thus the object of Mama Day's ambivalence, since she perceives him as both necessary to her aspirations for the Day "line"—Cocoa's eventual offspring—and a rival to her unacknowledged possessive maternal love. Motivated by conflicting purposes, she chooses to regard George not as a man but as a child—"'it's gonna take a man to bring her peace'—and all they had was that boy" (263)—thereby reducing his male power to something within her maternal control.

Thus propelled by conflicting goals, Mama Day sets George a challenge that, impeded by his stereotypical Western male rationality, he almost surely cannot meet. Giving him two tokens from her own family that she has found in the process of searching her ancestral home, she asks him to go to the henhouse and seek "the old red hen that's setting her last batch of eggs. . . . [S]earch good in the back of her nest, and come straight back here with whatever you find" (295). What she hopes he will find is not a material object but a new kind of understanding. George, failing either to grasp the nature of the test or to master the symbolic task demanded by Mama Day, succeeds only in destroying both hen and eggs and himself.

Throughout *Mama Day,* hens and eggs function as symbols for Mama Day's life-generating powers. George's aggressive encounter with "the old red hen that's setting her last batch of eggs" signifies his combative struggle with the elderly Miranda over Cocoa's future as well as his inability to comprehend the meaning of eggs and "henhouse"—the female principle associated with intuitive knowledge. Angry at Mama Day for compelling him to undertake a task that he regards as a "wasted effort" (301), he privately voices his possessive feelings toward Cocoa: "these were *my* hands, and there was no way I was going to let you go" (301, Naylor's emphasis). His attitude allies him with Mama Day's own forefather. Like Bascombe Wade five generations earlier, George Andrews becomes, in Mama Day's judgment, "another [man] who broke his heart 'cause he couldn't let [his woman] go" (308). To support this view, Mama Day must overlook her own defensive reluctance to let go of Cocoa.

Soon after George returns, bloodied and angry, from his aggressive confrontation with the old red hen, his heart fatally attacks him. Determined that he is "not going to let [Cocoa] go" (301), he manages to return to Cocoa's grandmother's house in time to rescue her from hallucination-driven engulfment in a bathtub full of water in which she is about to drown. The scene repeats the imagery of watery engulfment that marks George's and Cocoa's recurring nightmares, echoed a final time in the moment that follows George's heart attack: "the road felt like water under my buckling knees" (301). As the couple's repeated nightmares of drowning foreshadow, George is engulfed by events before he can either claim Cocoa or "cross over" (301) to the mainland—the patriarchal world in which he is far more at home.

Naylor's narrative interweaves complementary nostalgic stories, each with its own counterstory of "fixing"—recovering, repairing—the lost past that encompasses both succor and grief. In the narrative of heterosexual romantic love, Cocoa and George are the central figures. Cocoa nearly loses her life as the victim of misdirected sexual jealousy but, aided by her maternal heritage, instead loses her husband. In the nostalgic counternarrative—the story retold by Cocoa and the spirit of George years after his actual death—loss is offset in the very fact of George's spiritual survival beyond the grave. The enduring nature of the love between Cocoa and George is narratively represented by the alternating monologues that form the holographic present tense of the novel: the complex and evolving history of their relationship. George's status as a phantom presence from the "other side" with whom Cocoa intimately communicates suggests the unresolved mourning that underlies her narrative. As she phrases it, "You're never free from such a loss. It sits permanently in your middle, but it gets less weighty as time goes on and becomes endurable" (308). Her narrative memorializes her relationship with George, ostensibly still unfolding retrospectively fourteen years after his death: "each time I go back over what happened, there's some new development, some forgotten corner that puts you in a slightly different light. . . . When I see you again, our versions will be different still" (310–11). The romantic narrative of love and loss, of suffering and sacrifice, exists in a state of continuous revision.

The underlying and competing love story, the maternal one, also traces a nostalgic narrative of loss and mourning and a counternarrative in which both death and erotic desire are neutralized. In that story, the central figure is Miranda Day. Virtually all commentators on the novel admire Mama Day as an unambiguously positive character, "that true and perfect maternal figure we all yearn to have known."[8] I regard her as a more ambiguous mediator in the narrative's triangulations of attachment, separation, and loss. As the daughter of Ophelia, the erased maternal figure whom she lost during childhood, and the great-aunt of another Ophelia (Cocoa) who also lost her mother during childhood, Mama Day struggles to save her spiritual daughter at all costs. Her possessive attachment to Baby Girl—in her words, "the closest thing I have to calling a child my own" (294)—is her defense against loss. Cocoa compensates her for maternal abandonment and for the absence of a daughter of her own.

Yet that possessive attachment is ultimately incompatible with Cocoa's relationship with her husband. In the maternal counternarrative, Mama Day, rather than allowing George to save his wife Ophelia on his own terms, sets a symbolic task that frustrates his rationalism and dooms him to failure and, ultimately, death. Though Mama Day had reasoned that together she and George "could be the bridge for Baby Girl to walk over" (285), as events unfold, one part of the "bridge" is destroyed: George is sacrificed to achieve Cocoa's survival. Further, his death releases Mama Day from the competition for possession of "Baby Girl," securing Cocoa for her own reconciliation with the past and vision of the future.

It would appear that the Great Mother Sapphira, whose contemporary avatar is Mama Day, triumphs and matriarchy prevails through the sacrifice of the (not-quite-perfect) romantic male lover on the altar of maternal love. But not entirely. While Mama Day mends the pain of the loss of her own mother and mediates the survival of her surrogate daughter, Cocoa survives to assume the legacy of longing and unresolved mourning—the "vacant center" (309) that marks the Day family history. As readers learn near the end of the narrative, some years after George's death Ophelia/Cocoa marries a "good second-best man" (309) of whom even

Mama Day approves. With him, she lives neither in a metropolis ("I couldn't stay up in New York" [305]) nor on an island ("I couldn't hide in Willow Springs forever" [308]) but on the mainland ("it was easier in Charleston; we'd never been there together" [308]). Yet, while married to a "decent guy" (309) whose significance to her story is so slight that he remains nameless, Cocoa remains spiritually married to George Andrews. From Cocoa's perspective, his essential presence in her life, and in her narrative, is testimony to the enduring power—even beyond death—of romantic love and erotic union. From Mama Day's perspective, George has become part of the history of the failure of such possessive attachments—another man who "broke his heart 'cause he couldn't let [his woman] go" (308). Indeed, Cocoa's story virtually mirrors George's: she cannot "let him go," even in death.

Although Cocoa eventually succeeds in her desire to become a mother herself, she gives birth to sons rather than daughters. Thus, the legacy of the Great Mother is not absolute. In fact, the matriarchal line that Miranda Day hoped would extend through Cocoa in fact ends with her. By the novel's conclusion, the multiple "sides" to the story suggested by Mama Day—the overlapping narratives and counternarratives of *Mama Day*—remain incompletely resolved.[9] In Naylor's complex triangulations, Cocoa Day remains divided as daughter, lover/wife, and mother, figuratively straddling the emotional spaces of mother and home, mourning and loss. There can be no complete resolution of longing because the intersecting narratives of love and possession are incompatible. The narrative ends inconclusively, not only because Cocoa's own story is still in progress but because "there are just too many sides to the whole story" (311).

Willow Springs may be Paradise, but that is not where Cocoa Day lives.

Amazing Grace and the Paradox of Paradise: *Paradise,* Toni Morrison

The force behind the movement of time is a mourning that will not be comforted. That is why the first event is known to have been an expulsion, and the last is hoped to be a reconciliation and return. So memory pulls us forward, so prophecy is only brilliant memory—there will be a garden where all of us as one child will sleep in our mother Eve, hooped in her ribs and staved by her spine.

—Marilynne Robinson, *Housekeeping*

As Gloria Naylor's *Mama Day* suggests, the ancestral homestead, the "other place" on Willow Springs, is not simply a literal place but an imaginative location, a space created by longing and nostalgia for idealized notions of succor, contentment, and wholeness. Toni Morrison, pondering the convergence of similar ideas in her fiction, has acknowledged that "matters of race and matters of home are priorities in [her] work."[1] Recognizing the danger of dwelling in "nostalgia for the race-free home I have never had and would never know" (4), she nonetheless identifies the ultimate protected space—"social space that is psychically and physically safe"—by the term "home" ("Home" 10). This place of succor and inclusion, existing outside of the "established boundaries of the racial imaginary" (9) that perpetuates racial stereotyping and racism is not only home but Paradise, an imaginary site shaped by memory and desire.

Paradise (1998), the novel in which Morrison explores these ideas, is the final novel in a series of three loosely related narratives.[2] What I have termed the *beloved imago* evolves in this final volume of the series into the image of a woman whose nurturing and all-forgiving qualities signify her Christlike role as the bridge between human and divine. The character Consolata functions as the figure who links—and comes to embody—secular and sacred conceptions of *mother, home,* and *Paradise.*

An abiding sense of damage and injury, ranging from physical or sexual abuse and trauma to betrayal and loss, suffuses the pages of the ironically titled *Paradise.* Virtually all of the women whose names form the nine chapter headings, as well as many of the narrative's other characters of both sexes, have suffered some form of emotional or spiritual injury. In one instance, a young woman continues to injure her body in an ambivalent attempt to repeat and to neutralize traumas experienced early in her life from which she has never fully healed. Many of the men are also emotionally and spiritually injured, though their destructive urges are directed outward rather than toward themselves; nearly all are veterans of war, whose fields of military action range "from Bataan to Guam, from Iwo Jima to Stuttgart" (6).

Interestingly, the original title for the novel was *War;* for commercial reasons, Morrison's publisher persuaded her to change it.[3] Yet the imagery of war and aggression remain prominent in the narrative. The current time of the narrative, the 1970s, is the era of the Vietnam War and the Civil Rights movement. The men of Ruby, Oklahoma, while in most cases fortunate enough to have survived the wars in which they fought (though Steward Morgan's two sons die in Vietnam), returned home apparently uninjured but in fact inwardly scarred and tipped in the direction of aggressive behavior by their exposure to bloodshed, violence, and death. When they feel angry, threatened, or helpless, they "want to shoot somebody,"[4] an impulse that reveals the barely contained aggression simmering just beneath the superficial tranquillity of Ruby's "paradise." The narrative itself is framed by gunshots. The mansion in which the rampage occurs is curiously shaped like a "live cartridge" (71), which figuratively explodes twice in the novel, once at the beginning and a second time at the climactic moment that recapitulates it near the narrative's end. As the narrator queries, "in that holy hollow between sighting and following through, could grace slip through at all?" (73) Indeed, if *Jazz* is framed by one shooting that anticipates another one that does not occur,[5] *Paradise* is similarly framed, with the crucial difference that the shooting described at the beginning is repeated late in the narrative, this time with the reader's knowledge of the unfolding history of the Convent and the community of Ruby inserted between "sighting and follow through."

Two physical structures in the narrative serve as organizing images for Morrison's narrative exploration of aggression, injury, and victimization on the one hand, and nurturance, healing, communion, and spiritual transcendence on the other. One is the Oven, a structure originally built as a communal cooking utility by the African American residents of a small Oklahoma town. The town, named Haven (besides its obvious connotations of sanctuary and refuge, the name also resembles and suggests "heaven") was established in 1890 by a group of freedmen and their families who walked from Mississippi and Louisiana after the Civil War to find a safe haven, along with economic and social independence, outside of the South. Over the nearly century-long time frame of the narrative, both that community and the Oven that comes to stand for its original covenant evolve with each generation. Originally functioning as a "community kitchen" (99) associated with nurturance and intimate affiliation, the Oven "both nourished them and monumentalized what they had done" (7). Over time, it has evolved from a "utility" to a "shrine" (103) as, concurrently, it has absorbed and reflected dissonant attitudes within the community itself, including sexual indulgence, political dissent, and, finally, self-righteous vengeance. Presaging the horrific scenes that bracket the narrative—the invasion of the Convent and slaughter of its five female occupants by nine men of Ruby—it is at the Oven that the perpetrators are overheard "cooking" up (269) their vicious and vengeful assault.

Linking home with nurturance, food is a recurring image and central symbol in the narrative. In addition to the obvious symbolism of the Oven itself, a significant number of events occur within the context of nourishment being prepared, served, shared, or received, as Morrison emphasizes the centrality of hunger and the gratification or denial of appetites both physical and spiritual. Virtually all of the women in the narrative, both those who live in the Convent and those who reside in the community of Ruby, are associated with literal food or symbolic nurturance or both.

Like the Oven, the Convent contains a history that embraces opposing meanings and functions, including several that pre-exist the town that comes to repudiate it. The Convent functions as a complementary and opposing structure that, over time, acquires some of the functions and meanings of the original Oven, including its associations with community and affiliation as well as food and nurturance. For example, the place is typically suffused with the aroma of rising dough. Even the townspeople of Ruby who disdain the Convent nonetheless seek out the bread, hot peppers, barbecue, and other foods produced on its land or prepared in its oversized kitchen. In an ironic sense the house might be said to have evolved, like the community Oven, from "utility" to "shrine." In an earlier era, the mansion erected by a rich landowner of dubious reputation was dubbed an "embezzler's folly" (3); to judge from fixtures that hint at its use as a place of sexual exploitation of women, it presumably operated as a brothel. The suspected house of ill repute later evolved into a more benign kind of retreat: a school for Native Girls, administered by a small coterie of Catholic Sisters. Years later, its decorations and symbols conflate those antithetical functions through the iconographies of sacred and profane traditions. Nude Venuses, carved nymphs, and faucets that mimic the shapes of male and female genitalia share space with images of martyrdom, including a "space where there used to be a Jesus" (12) and a woman with an "I-give-up face"—identified as Saint Catherine of Siena—"serving up her breasts like two baked Alaskas on a platter" (74, 73).[6] Further, "nursing cherubim" and "nipple-tipped doorknobs" (72) suggest an ambiguous erotic/maternal iconography of breasts. The maternal ambience of the Convent is suggested not only through the images of food and nurturance but through associations with birth and the presence of infants. At least two babies are born in the Convent; the sounds of children's laughter and singing are frequently heard by the women who live there. The narrative itself is divided into nine chapters, concluding with both death and deliverance. (However, antithetically, the men who storm the Convent and deliver death are also nine in number.)

Although the religious Sisters are long gone from the Convent by the 1970s—the narrative's current time frame—a spiritual sisterhood nonetheless unites the women who find shelter within its walls. In its contemporary incarnation, the Convent functions as an empowering place, a home away from home, a kind of *safe house* for spiritually—and often also literally—starving (female) souls. Within the Convent's sphere, women who have been betrayed, abandoned, abused, or otherwise delegitimized in the world discover a place where they may mend their injuries and vanquish the monsters that haunt them. The only behavior not permitted within the Convent is lying. The liberating and authenticating potentiality of the place is so powerful that the women who accidentally stumble into its welcoming embrace ultimately discover that they have no desire to leave "the one place they [are] free to leave" (262).

Unlike the Oven, whose functions change over time but whose meanings the community of Ruby struggles to preserve unaltered, the meanings of the Convent are fluid and unstable. Not only do they shift during the course of the narrative but they also differ depending on the perspective, values, and gender of the observer. For Mavis, Grace, Seneca, and Pallas, along with Soane and Dovey Morgan and Lone DuPres—three women of

Ruby who are estranged from that community's puritanical values—the Convent is a vitally sustaining, "unjudgmental" (48) home and safe place, "a protected domain, free of hunters but exciting too" (177), where a person might "meet herself . . . an unbridled authentic self . . ." (177). Yet precisely because the women value the Convent's atmosphere of freedom and its "blessed malelessness" (177), the tradition-bound men of Ruby regard the Convent's occupants as more "coven" than "convent." In their view, the dissolute "outlaw women" exercise illegitimate liberties that challenge Ruby's hierarchical, patriarchal idea of paradise; outrageously, in their view, the Convent women "don't need men and . . . don't need God" (276). From the threatened male perspective, the Convent comes to be regarded as the certain source of "catastrophes" (11) occurring in their town and lives and, ultimately, as the site of "defilement and violence and perversions beyond imagination" (287).

A significant tension between these vastly different kinds of communities—the group of "unbridled" women who reside at the Convent and the repressed, static, insular town of Ruby—comes from the colliding visions of "home" as opposed to the "Out There" that threatens it. "Out There" functions in Morrison's narrative as a symbolic space and the necessary psychological opposite of "home." However, the oppositeness is gender-inflected. While the women of the Convent and of the town regard "Out There" as the expansive domain of dreams and mysteries, corresponding with what Morrison has elsewhere called the "concrete thrill of borderlessness—a kind of out of doors safety" ("Home" 9), the men see it as a threatening, unmonitored space where "random and organized evil erupted when and where it chose" and where "your very person could be annulled" (*Paradise* 16). The very exclusiveness and rigidity of Ruby press its patriarchs toward the denial of the Other, which they construe as the true enemy "Out There"—the dangerous, anarchic, fluid void that undermines their certainties.

Throughout her fiction, Morrison has remained interested in inclusion and exclusion, insiders and outsiders. Her narratives frequently explore the relationship between members of a community and the "others" who are defined in opposition to it—pariahs, outlaw figures, and scapegoats; orphans also figure prominently in her fiction.[7] In *Paradise*, Morrison focuses not only on individual orphans and pariahs but on the condition of being "orphaned" in the collective sense: an entire community repudiated by other African Americans on the basis of gradations of skin color. The legendary original group of fifteen families who left the South in 1890 to found the town of Haven consisted of nine "intact" families along with "fragments" (188) of a number of others. The group's identity was shaped by their individual and collective status as orphans, "the absences that hovered over their childhoods and the shadows that dimmed their maturity. Anecdotes marked the spaces that had sat with them at the campfire. . . . They talked about the orphans, males and females aged twelve to sixteen, who spotted the travelers and asked to join, and the two toddlers they simply snatched up . . ." (189). The sojourners took pride in their steadfast commitment to racial purity and their fiercely protected "unadulterated" bloodlines. Having served as field hands rather than as house slaves before the Civil War, they were proud to have escaped the legacy of miscegenation; the women, never forced to submit to sexual demands from white slaveholders, never gave birth to racially mixed offspring.

However, the group's racial "purity" ultimately evolved into its greatest liability. When they attempted to resettle in the ironically named black town of Fairly, Oklahoma, the wayfarers were cast out by residents who disdained them on the basis of their darker skin hue. "The sign of racial purity they had taken for granted had become a stain" (194). Shamed and humiliated by what they termed the "Disallowing" (189), the wayfarers set out to establish a "pure" community of their own, protected by an unspoken "blood rule." The bargain they made with God dictated that no one among the "8–rocks"—a term derived from coal mining to signify and dignify the group's "pure" blue-black skin color—could marry "out" or engage in sexual union either extramaritally or with a lighter-skinned partner. As Patricia Best, Ruby's self-appointed historian and genealogist, phrases it, "Unadulterated and unadultered 8–rock blood held its magic as long as it resided in Ruby. . . . That was their deal. For Immortality" (217).

In this regard, Ruby, Oklahoma, embodies a key characteristic of traditional myths of Paradise: immortality.[8] The "deal" made by its inhabitants seems to have been successful. Although a few of Ruby's residents have died elsewhere, no one has died in Ruby in the twenty years since the demise of the woman after whom the town was named. However, by the current time of the narrative, several generations of intermarriage, "unadulterated" inbreeding, and insularity have resulted in sterile men, infantilized women, and defective babies.

Since the community of Ruby is based on "the fathers' law" (279)— principles regarding racial and sexual purity established by the Old Fathers and strictly maintained by their descendants, the New Fathers—the greatest threat to it is what might be termed "the mothers' law." As Pat Best speculates, "everything that worries [the men of Ruby] must come from women" (217). In contrast to the communities of Haven and Ruby, the

Convent might be said to operate on the values of "the mothers' law": affiliation, nurturance, and disregard for such social distinctions as age, class, race, and skin color. Accordingly, the opening line of the narrative—"They shoot the white girl first" (3)—announces that one of the women who lives at the Convent is white, but Morrison deliberately develops the narrative in such a way that the reader can never know with certainty which one it is.[9] As she has indicated elsewhere, she wanted to create in imaginative terms a space where "race both matters and is rendered impotent" ("Home" 9).

As different as are the communities of Ruby and the Convent, they have something essential in common: the residents of both have been "disallowed"—that is, spiritually stunted by shame, rejection, and exclusion. Moreover, the history of the one is as inextricably related to the history of the other as the Oven is to the Convent (the first word is literally contained in the second). Though the diverse women who arrive at the Convent do not intentionally seek it out, they are united in that space as they flee from traumatic circumstances in their lives. Each woman has been "disallowed" by someone in her own family, shamed or damaged in her sense of her self through a betrayal or desecration of her deepest attachments. Either she has been an abused wife who turned her destructive actions toward her own children (Mavis) or a daughter betrayed or implicitly or explicitly abandoned by her mother (Consolata, Gigi, Seneca, Pallas).

Mavis, the first wanderer to seek solace at the Convent, leaves her Maryland home following the deaths of her newborn twins, who suffocated in the heat of a closed car as a result of her own negligence. Subsequently, she uses that car (her husband's cherished Cadillac) as her escape vehicle, leaving behind her abusive husband and three other children. Following a brief stay with her own mother, she drives across the country and ultimately finds herself—having run out of gas in more than the literal sense—in the Convent's nonjudgmental embrace. Grace, nicknamed Gigi, is a runaway from San Francisco, the daughter of an "unlocatable" (257) mother and a father doing time on death row. For Gigi, the journey that ends at the Convent begins with a riot in Oakland during which a black child bleeds from a mortal gunshot wound. Though the circumstances of her early history are vague, Gigi's central preoccupation is eros. Her travels are prompted by a futile search for the location of a mythical couple locked in erotic union—a "man and woman fucking forever" (63) in a desert location suggestively called Wish, Arizona. Even those who disdain the mythical couple's unrestrained sexuality secretly need them, "needed to know they were out there" (63). The image captures an entirely different sense of "out there" from the one that preoccupies the repressed town fathers of Ruby. Though Gigi never locates the legendary couple, once she reaches the safety of the Convent she legitimizes her own wish for erotic freedom, shedding her clothes, sunbathing naked, and engaging in a sexual liaison with the nephew of one of Ruby's most powerful patriarchs.

Seneca is another of the narrative's actual and emotional orphans. Abandoned in a public housing project in Indiana at the age of five by an adolescent mother whom Seneca believed was her sister, she was eventually found and placed in foster care, only to suffer sexual abuse from her foster brother. Before Seneca finds succor in Consolata's home for lost souls, she is exploited in a manner only hinted at by a woman she meets on the road who pays her a large sum of money to keep her as a sexual "pet" for several weeks. The last of the four women to arrive at the Convent, Pallas, is also an emotional orphan and runaway. A "sad little rich girl" (259), she runs from the Los Angeles home of her affluent father, traveling to San Francisco with her boyfriend (a Latino maintenance man at her high school) to find the mother whom she has not seen for thirteen years. When they find her, the boyfriend decides he prefers the mother—named Divine Truelove—to the daughter. (Despite the obvious irony, the mother's name underscores several of the narrative's central preoccupations.) Betrayed by both lover and mother, Pallas runs again and is forced into a lake in the dark by cruel boys. She arrives at the Convent traumatized into speechlessness.

The antidote to each of the runaway women's experiences of "disallowance" is what might be termed "allowance": the unconditional forgiveness and tolerance that permeates the Convent, signified by the sustenance dispensed by Consolata that feeds both body and soul. Though Pallas's appetite had been "killed" (178) by her lover's and her mother's mutual betrayal, soon after her arrival at the Convent she, like the other women, recovers her appetite. Under the influence of Consolata's nurturing acceptance—signaled by a table overflowing with delectable food—the women slowly evolve from soul-ravaged to ravenous.

If one of Morrison's ongoing concerns in *Paradise,* as in the two novels that precede it, is the meaning of the *beloved imago*—the idealized, lost love object who is imaginatively constructed through nostalgic longing—in this narrative the notion is developed within the contexts of maternal nurturance and unconditional love, both human and divine. In the chapter entitled "Divine," significantly positioned at the midpoint of *Paradise,* a wedding ceremony is delayed while two ministers of different spiritual persuasions struggle to define the terms of human beings' relation to God. As the bride-to-be waits impatiently for the traditional opening words of the wedding ceremony—"Dearly Beloved, we are gathered here" (149)—the Methodist guest preacher, Reverend Pulliam, chastens the couple and the waiting congregation with the reminder that love is "divine only and difficult always. . . . It is a learned application without reason or motive except that it is God" (141). The Baptist Reverend Misner privately feels that his senior peer's homily is less a disinterested exhortation than an oblique sortie in an ongoing ideological battle between two men of God regarding the best way to guide their respective congregations toward the divine. In contrast to Reverend Pulliam's Old Testament view of a judgmental God whose love is arbitrary and almost unattainable, Reverend Misner regards God's relation to human beings in more forgiving New Testament terms. In his view, love is the capacity for "unmotivated respect" (146) for others, a capacity for caring earned for human beings through Christ's sacrifice.

The arguments forwarded by the two ministers illustrate different nuances of the ideal of spiritual love termed *agape*.[10] Through the ministers' polarized debate about the nature of spiritual love or *agape*, the human relation to the divine, and the relation of both to tradition and change, Morrison revises conventional Christian constructions of divinity by reinserting the idea of the maternal divine. If the figure of the father—epitomized by the Old Fathers of Haven and the New Fathers of Ruby who strictly emulate their model—is the central representative of the patriarchal dispensation, the figure of the mother is central not only to the matriarchal dispensation but to the embracing vision of Paradise itself.

Unlike the stern patriarchal god of Reverend Pulliam's homily, the Reverend Mother who resides at the Convent until her demise embodies a more spiritually nurturing, matriarchal—and maternal—model of divine love. Even as she lapses into Latin gibberish in the days before her death, Reverend Mother is concerned that those who arrive at the Convent are well-succored. She queries Consolata, "You're feeding them properly? They're always so hungry. There's plenty, isn't there?" (48) Epitomizing her almost-divine spiritual presence, Reverend Mother is described as "see[ing] everything in the universe" (47). Consolata instructs the newly arrived Mavis, "She is my mother. Your mother too" (48). Together, these statements suggest not only a Godlike female being but, in psychological terms, an idealized maternal figure—one who, besides gratifying her child's appetites, is perceived by the child as both omniscient and omnipotent.

Many years before, Reverend Mother—then Sister Mary Magna—had discovered the abandoned child, Consolata, in a heap of street garbage in Brazil and had "kidnapped" the nine-year-old orphan back to the United States. At the Convent, Consolata began what turned out to be a spiritual apprenticeship. Over the course of her thirty years of service to the woman who was her mother-surrogate and eventually the Mother Superior of the Convent, Consolata has "offered her body and her soul to God's Son and His Mother as completely as if she had taken the veil herself" (225).

However, sometime before the four runaway women arrive at the Convent, Consolata, at the age of thirty-nine, met a man and, consumed by erotic desire for the first time in her life, almost consumed him instead.[11] "Being love-struck after thirty celibate years took on an edible quality" (228), so much so that she inadvertently brought their union to an end by biting her lover's lip during lovemaking. Still later in the narrative, her lover is revealed to be the secretly adulterous Deacon Morgan, one of the most powerful and self-righteous men among the upstanding and ostensibly morally pure citizens of Ruby. Only after losing him as a result of her consuming sexual appetite does Consolata acknowledge to herself that she had confused divine love with human passion. Too "bent on eating [her lover] like a meal" (239), she had lapsed "from Christ, to whom one gave total surrender and then swallowed the idea of His flesh, to a living man" (240).

The equation between consumption and Communion suggestively links parallel meanings in the narrative. Eros and agape are equated through acts of incorporation and submission, understood in the seemingly antithetical contexts of surrender of the self: physical passion and spiritual renunciation. Consolata eventually concludes that her devouring "gobble-gobble love" had not meant that she "want[ed] to eat him. [She] just wanted to go home" (240)—that is, she wanted to recapture through eros the all-encompassing embrace that she had experienced through *agape* and spiritual surrender. Consolata's implicitly self-imposed punishment for her excess of worldly desire is the onset of light-blindness, the inward-turning "bat vision" (241) that also signifies her deepening spiritual vision and enlightenment. The visionary gift possessed by the nun Mary Magna and acquired by her spiritual apprentice is suggested through similar defects in their literal vision. While Reverend Mother is severely myopic, Consolata wears sunglasses to protect her light-weakened eyes from the aura of intense illumination that emanates from the Reverend Mother in the months before her death—"the whiteness at the center" that observers find "blinding" (46). Her own eyes turning inward so that only the whites appear, Consolata eventually comes to see "nothing clearly except what [takes] place in the minds of others" (248).

Consolata's inward-turning vision is the source of her capacity to "trick" death—an unorthodox power she learns not from Mary Magna but from a woman of the town, the motherless midwife Lone, who also possesses special healing gifts and spiritual powers. Lone teaches Consolata how to "step in" or "see in" (247) to the spirit of a dying person by concentrating intensely on the fading light that signifies his or her fragile link to life and then drawing it back into the realm of the living. Through that intervention, Consolata saves the dying son of Deacon Morgan, the man who had awakened her physical passion years before. Thus, whatever claims to "immortality" the town of Ruby celebrates, at least one bargain with death is achieved through Consolata's unique "in sight" (247) and her function as a midwife mediating the boundary between death and life.

As the spiritual daughter and figurative child of Mary and as a woman possessed of the ability to "[raise] the dead" (242)—characteristics that associate her with Christ—Consolata uses her special powers to extend the life of Reverend Mother long beyond her normal time. Moreover, her spiritual midwifery functions in the opposite direction as well. On the day that even such profound devotion is insufficient to prevent Mary Magna from finally leaving her earthly body, Consolata figuratively becomes the mother of her mother, delivering Reverend Mother into the afterlife much as a mother delivers her infant. She enfolds Reverend Mother's dying body "in her arms and between her legs" so that she enters "death like a birthing . . ." (223). "And so intense were the steppings in, Mary Magna glowed like a lamp till her very last breath in Consolata's arms" (247). When Reverend Mother dies, Consolata feels herself "orphaned" (247) a second time.

Transfigured through her bond with Mary Magna, Consolata occupies her spiritual mother's place at the "center" of the Convent, becoming the source of maternal nurturance and unconditional love. As the "new and revised Reverend Mother" (265), she functions in the narrative's overlapping iconographies as spiritual midwife, mother surrogate, mother goddess, and—given her identification as the figurative daughter of Mary (Magna) and her ability to override death—Christ figure. However, before Consolata fully achieves that position, she enters a dissolute and desolate phase, a "slug-like existence" (221) in which she is engulfed in mourning for the two beloveds of her life, Mary Magna and Deacon Morgan. Punishing herself for having succumbed to "excessive human love" (247) for both, she drowns her self-pity and shame by liberally imbibing the wine that stocks the cellar of the former mansion. There, "craving only oblivion" (221), Consolata retreats from the society of the other women living in the Convent and wishes for her (and their) death.

What decisively alters Consolata's drift toward self-annihilation is a visitation by a phantom presence. Like the phantom "Friend" whom Dovey Morgan sees several times in her garden, a benign male figure approaches the Convent and speaks with Consolata. The figure wears a cowboy hat like that of Steward Morgan, Deacon's identical twin whom, years earlier, Consolata had once mistaken for her lover. Beneath the hat, the presence reveals long "tea-colored hair" (252) and green eyes—physical characteristics of Consolata herself. The phantom presence is thus suggestive of her own hidden androgyny. The singular visitation of a figure who is both Other and self awakens Consolata from her spiritual malaise. Wresting herself away from inebriation and despair, she turns her attention to the "disorder, deception . . . and drift" (221–2) that have eroded the serenity of the Convent as the runaway women have brought their own quarrels and tensions into it. Drawing on her spiritual legacy from the Reverend Mother, Consolata begins to guide her figurative daughters away from their infantile behavior and "babygirl wishes" (222) along a path of emotional recuperation and spiritual discipline. In the characteristic nurturing setting of a table spread with food, she advises them, "I will teach you what you are hungry for" (262) and feeds them an alternative eucharist of "bloodless food and water alone to quench their thirst . . ." (265).

Under Consolata's guidance, the women enact a healing ritual. Making outlines of their naked bodies on the Convent's cellar floor, they use paints and chalk to express within these "templates" or "moulds" their deepest feelings about what has happened to/in their bodies. In effect, they *re-mould* themselves, beginning to purge their self-hatred, self-destructive compulsions, and emotional histories of victimization. For example, Seneca has for years lacerated herself, carving in her own flesh a pattern of abuse initiated by others during her childhood. During the moulding ritual, when she felt "the hunger to slice her inner thigh, she chose instead to mark the open body [template] lying on the cellar floor" (265).

While the exclusive and static paradise of Ruby slowly unravels in response to its own very worldly internal divisions, abetted by its history of insularity and rigidity, the inclusive maternal space of the Convent nudges its occupants in the opposite direction. To the damaged women—one who has been a "bad mother" herself and the others who have been damaged by abusive or neglectful "bad mothers"—Consolata functions as the idealized "good mother" before psychological separation during infancy. She becomes for them—as had the Reverend Mother for her—that indulgent nurturing figure who "seemed to love each one of them best; who never criticized, who shared everything but needed little or no care; required no emotional investment; who listened; who locked no doors and accepted each as she was . . . this ideal parent, friend, companion in whose company they were safe from harm . . ." (262).

In the spiritual sense, Consolata functions for the emotionally needy women as the embodiment of a compassionate, all-forgiving, maternal Christ, intuitively revising the traditional Christian conceptions of love debated in the narrative by the Reverends Pulliam and Misner. Interestingly, a contested phrase on the communal Oven whose history is bound up with the evolution of the town of Ruby is jestingly revised by Anna Flood (one of the few liberal women of the town) from "Beware the Furrow of His Brow" (86) to "Be the Furrow of *Her* Brow" (159, Morrison's emphasis). The characterization of Christ in female/maternal terms dates to the Middle Ages when devout and visionary writers articulated visions of the deity with female and maternal attributes.[12] These medieval religious writers' representations of God or Christ as "a woman nursing the soul at her breasts, drying its tears, punishing its petty mischief-making, giving birth to it in agony and travail, are part of a growing tendency to speak of the divine in *homey* images and to emphasize its approachability. . . . Seeing Christ or God or the Holy Spirit as female is thus part of a later medieval devotional tradition that is characterized by increasing preference for analogies taken from human relationships. . . ."[13]

Morrison uses the idealized maternal/divine figure to explore both secular and spiritual senses of sanctuary, devotion, home, and Paradise: *being safe* becomes analogous to *being saved*. As the women in the Convent gain power over their private demons and come to accept themselves and their bodies, Consolata instructs them in the inseparability of body and spirit. She shares with them her most profound discovery, acquired through her complementary unions with Reverend Mother and her male lover, that eros and *agape* are indivisible. In her Portuguese-accented English, she intones,

> My child body, hurt and soil, leaps into the arms of a woman who teach me my body is nothing my spirit everything. I agreed her until I met another. My flesh is so hungry for itself it ate him. When he fell away the woman rescue me from my body again. Twice she saves it. When her body sickens I care for it in every way flesh works. I hold it in my arms and

between my legs. . . . After she is dead I can not get past that. My bones on
hers the only good thing. Not spirit. Bones. No different from the man. My
bones on his the only true thing. . . . Never break them in two. Never put
one over the other. Eve is Mary's mother. Mary is the daughter of Eve. (263)

As Consolata becomes more clearly associated with the maternal divine,
the correspondences in the narrative between *home* and *Paradise* also
become more evident. The more liberal of the two conventional ministers,
Reverend Misner, sermonizes to Pat Best on the subject of overlapping
worldly and spiritual conceptions of the original home, stressing a view
that developed during the Civil Rights movement: that the true home of
African Americans is Africa. To Pat's defense of the community of Ruby as
proudly American—"This is their home; mine too. Home is not a little
thing" (213)—Misner replies,

> "But can't you even imagine what it must feel like to have a true home? I
> don't mean heaven. I mean a real earthly home. Not some fortress you
> bought and built up and have to keep everybody locked in or out . . . but
> your own home, where if you go back past your great-great-grandparents,
> past theirs, and theirs, past the whole of Western history, past the beginning
> of organized knowledge, past pyramids and poison bows, on back to when
> rain was new, before plants forgot they could sing and birds thought they
> were fish, back when God said Good! Good!—there, right there where you
> know your own people were born and lived and died. . . . That place. Who
> was God talking to if not to my people living in my home?" (213)

Imbedded in Reverend Misner's question is a larger yearning. "That place"
embodies the nostalgic longing for the (idealized) original home: Paradise.
Morrison's narrative explores the collision between competing visions of
"that place" of imagined perfect safety, succor, and wholeness: secular/
sacred, Old Testament/New Testament, patriarchal/matriarchal, even liberal
and conservative conceptions of an idyllic place beyond change.[14]

Consolata's insistence on the possibility of wholeness—the indissolubil-
ity of flesh and spirit—is similarly associated with home and Paradise. She
shares with the women of the Convent her vision of an enchanted location, an unearthly realm near the sea distinguished by "scented cathedrals
made of gold where gods and goddesses sat in the pews with the congregation . . ." (263–4). Its presiding presence is Piedade, a figure who sings but
never speaks and whose (Portuguese) name means compassion or pity.
Later, drawing on nostalgic fantasies from childhood, Consolata embellishes
her vision of Paradise and of Piedade, the beneficent nurturing figure who,

as she phrases it, "bathed me in emerald water. Her voice made proud women weep in the streets. . . . Piedade had songs that could still a wave, make it pause in its curl listening to language it had not heard since the sea opened. . . . Travelers refused to board homebound ships while she sang. At night she took the stars out of her hair and wrapped me in its wool" (284–5). The celebration of that idealized succoring figure and the place of ultimate embrace and union with her—home as mother/Paradise—is strategically, and ironically, positioned in the narrative just before the nine men of Ruby stage a demonic massacre that expresses and enacts the antithesis of Paradise: an unleashing of sanctioned violence typically associated with aggression and war.

When Soane and Lone DuPres—spiritually awake women of Ruby who have secretly communicated and sympathized with Consolata over the years—hasten to the Convent after the massacre, they find Consolata bleeding from an apparently mortal bullet wound to the head. They "close the two pale eyes but can do nothing about the third one, wet and lidless, in between" (291). The image of the "third eye"—literally, the site of the bullet wound in Consolata's forehead—also suggests the third eye of esoteric spiritual traditions[15] and Consolata's own gift of "in sight." Significantly, Consolata's final word is "Divine" (291).

Virtually the only thing that people can agree on concerning the rampage at the Convent and the mysterious disappearance of its apparently slaughtered female occupants is that there is no single version of events about which everyone concurs. Apart from Deacon Morgan, who remains silent, "every one of the assaulting men had a different tale" (297). Lone DuPres, the Cassandra figure whose warnings are never heeded by the men of Ruby, is convinced that God performed a miracle comparable to Christ's ascension—that He "swept up and received His servants in broad daylight . . . for Christ's sake!" (298) The Reverends Pulliam and Misner, who try to account for the version of events that has begun to take on the status of "gospel" (297)—the presumably murdered women "took other shapes and disappeared into thin air" (296)—inevitably disagree on "the meaning of the ending" (297). One meaning is the (re)introduction of mortality into Paradise. The brutal assault on the Convent women by the nine men of Ruby who represent and enact the community's deepest fears of lawlessness and threat of Otherness is closely followed by the death of the (symbolically named) defective child, Save-Marie, the first person to die in that "town full of immortals" (296) for an entire generation.

Only three people of Ruby are permitted to glimpse another "meaning of the ending." The first is Deacon Morgan who, having failed to prevent his twin from firing the shot that fatally wounds Consolata, repudiates the men's rationalization that they acted against the Convent women in "self-defense" (290). Uncharacteristically, he advises the other agents of the rampage, "This is our doing. Ours alone. And we bear the responsibility" (291). Later, the repentant Deacon begins a "long remorse at having become what the Old Fathers cursed: the kind of man who set himself up to judge, rout and even destroy the needy, the defenseless, the different" (302). The others who are granted insight into the "meaning of the ending" are Reverend Misner and Anna Flood, who later return to the Convent to try to make sense of what happened there. Drawn to its garden, filled with evidence of the perennial cycle of "blossom and death" (304), each senses the beckoning of an entrance into another realm, a door or window to "the other side" (305).

Through that opening in the Garden, the patient reader is granted a glimpse of the state of grace that each of the novel's lost women achieves: consolation and reconciliation. The final segment of *Paradise* provides a series of what (to invoke the Homeric epic tradition) might be termed "recognition scenes." Each of the four wayfarers who discovered her self in the Convent appears once more as if herself a phantom presence from Out There—this time, understood as the "other side" of the beckoning door/window. In each instance, the woman appears either to affirm a relationship with a beloved person from her past or to claim a kind of reparation from one who absolutely betrayed or "disallowed" her. Appropriately, given the narrative's emphasis on the wished-for gratification of appetites both worldly and otherworldly and on parent-child relationships, all of the meetings involve an encounter between a daughter and her mother (or, in one instance, her father); further, the two positive recognitions occur within the context of sharing bread. Gigi, appearing to her startled father during his lunch break at a prison farm, gently assures him that he will indeed "hear from [her]" again (310). Also over lunch, Mavis meets her surprised daughter Sal in what leads to a vivid and emotionally moving reconciliation. In response to the daughter's question, "You okay?" Mavis responds, "I'm perfect." Sal adds, "I always loved, always, even when," to which Mavis responds, "I know that, Sal. Know it now anyway" (315), as she kisses her daughter's cheek and disappears into a crowd.

By contrast, Pallas and Seneca appear to the mothers who betrayed or abandoned them and withhold forgiveness or reconciliation. By disdaining connection in any form, each in effect mirrors the original rejection by the "bad mother" who "disallowed" her. Though "the smile on Pallas' face" is "beatific" (311), it is not intended for the astonished mother to whom she appears. Rather, just as the daughter lost the power of speech in response to her mother's betrayal and her later traumatizing experience in a lake, Divine Truelove is struck voiceless, unable to call out to capture her daughter's attention. Similarly, when Seneca's mother sights her in a crowd, Seneca—"blood running from her hands" like stigmata (316)—denies the identification. In a comment that, like each of the other Convent women's statements, is open to double meaning, she adds, "That's okay. Everybody makes mistakes" (317). In Morrison's parable of spiritual growth, it is not the proud, self-declared "immortal" inhabitants of Ruby but the wayward, flawed women of the Convent who are given the opportunity to "fix" their damaged pasts and who are granted (narratively, at least) transcendence over death.

Paradise concludes with an image that recapitulates one final time the nostalgic "wish for permanent happiness" (306) associated with the title word. Pertinently, the image is framed in a setting that embodies the earliest experience of mother/home/Paradise. The sea gently lapping the beach suggests the paradigmatic site of home as womb: prenatal, amniotic bliss. Piedade sings a lullaby of solace as two unidentified women—one older and "black as firewood" (318), the other younger, with skin "all the colors of seashells," "tea brown hair," and "emerald eyes" (318) like Consolata—ponder memories "neither one has ever had: of reaching age in the company of the other; of speech shared and divided bread smoking from the fire; *the unambivalent bliss of going home to be at home—the ease of coming back to love begun*" (318, my emphasis). When, reminiscent of the maternal associated with giving birth, "the ocean heaves[,] sending rhythms of water ashore," Piedade looks "to see what has come. Another ship, perhaps, but different, heading to port, crew and passengers, *lost and saved*, atremble, for they have been *disconsolate* for some time. Now they will rest before shouldering the endless work they were created to do down here in Paradise" (318, my emphasis).

The inverted echo of Consolata's name and her visionary fantasy of Piedade's realm thus anticipate the novel's concluding word: "Paradise." Although Morrison does not invoke the Portuguese word that is closely related to *piedade*—*saudade*—its signification of nostalgic longing saturates the closing images of the novel: consolation (Consolata), pity (Piedade), and solace. Yet the novel's idyllic coda is a decidedly qualified and even ironic one since, as the story of Ruby demonstrates, perfection is a static (and humanly unattainable) condition. The dynamics of internal division and change—processes occurring not only within communities but within individuals—make the tranquil changelessness of Paradise impossible. In the novel, Reverend Misner observes, "How exquisitely human was the wish for permanent happiness, and how thin human imagination became trying to achieve it" (306). As Morrison has mused elsewhere on the destructive potentiality that exists within even the most virtuous causes, "The overwhelming question for me . . . was how does it happen that people who have a very rich, survivalist, flourishing revolutionary impetus, end up either like their oppressor, or self-destructive in a way that represents the very thing they were running from."[16] Speaking at a symposium entitled "Imagining Paradise," Morrison reiterated her conviction that an "exclusionary paradise" is an inevitable "part of the history of western thought: 'Be good so you go to heaven and won't be with bad people.'"[17] Inherent in a vision of perfection based on a principle of exclusion and "disallowance"—the suppression (and repression) of the Other—is the destructive potentiality that intrudes from both inside and outside the community and the self.

Despite Morrison's expressed intention to imagine a paradise that is neither exclusive nor static,[18] the paradoxical image with which the novel closes belies these intentions. The final sentence suggests an Edenic space where the women (no men are mentioned) pause before resuming their tasks in the ordinary world—"the endless work they were created to do down here in Paradise" (318). In the imaginary space where maternal nurturance and filial affection are celebrated/elevated, where racial differences cease to matter, and where earthly and spiritual desires converge, even the most injured and wayward daughters may achieve a state of grace. In that paradoxical Paradise, they find themselves both safe and saved: at home at last in the idyllic but—in more than one sense—exclusive embrace of the Go(o)d Mother.

Fixing the Past,
Re-Placing Nostalgia

Birth is your first experience of exile, the Greeks maintained. That's why a child bellows when it is born: it discovers into what life it has been thrust. The second exile is
never really to belong. . . . And the third exile is to forget
the enormity of your loss.

—William Gass, *Literature in Exile*

This is the use of memory:
For liberation—not less of love but expanding
Of love and beyond desire, and so liberation
From the future as well as the past.

. . . .

We shall not cease from exploration
And the end of all our exploring
Will be to arrive where we started
And know the place for the first time.

—T. S. Eliot, "Little Gidding," *Four Quartets*

Although it may be true that one "can't go home again," the eight
writers considered in this study express a variety of ways to return
imaginatively, through memory and art, to the original home—
the place that represents emotional succor, intimacy, and plenitude. If the
past may be understood as the home/homeland from which we are all

exiles, literary nostalgia expresses a reparative vision, memorializing the imagination's subversive desire to "fix" the past. Mother is our first home, the original *safe house*—or the idealized fantasy of such a person and place—by which all later spaces of belonging are measured. Retracing the path from rupture back (or forward) to rapture represents, for the characters whose homesickness or nostalgia shapes a number of these narratives, the impulse to secure but also to recover, repair, restore, or discover a more enduring meaning in events that shape the unfoldings of time, emotional history, and memory.

The answer to the double question posed in the title of the first section, "Is mother home?" is equivocal. It depends on whether the past is construed as "fixed" (set, unalterable) or as amenable to "fixing" (imaginative revision). *To the Lighthouse* lyrically illuminates Woolf's successful resolution of deferred mourning for—and denied anger toward—her lost mother of childhood, memorializing nostalgic longing through a double artistic vision that fixes the past. In this sense, nostalgia also functions as a fixative: something that makes permanent, prevents fading. Lily Briscoe, emulating her surrogate mother's gift in her own artistic medium, strives to "make of the moment something permanent" (*To the Lighthouse* 161). By contrast, Doris Lessing, mourning the mother lost to her not through death but emotional abandonment and the home lost to her through geographical exile, concedes that the past is ultimately a kind of fiction created through the involuntary omissions and embellishments of memory as well as the voluntary shapings of art. However, moving beyond the skepticism expressed in *The Golden Notebook* regarding "lying nostalgia"—memory's distortion of the unretrievable "true" version of past experiences—she permits the middle-aged protagonist of *Love, Again* something she denied her younger characters from Martha Quest to Anna Wulf. Sarah Durham, engaging with the phantoms of past loves that haunt her emotional life, discovers a "corrective" vision; through it, she views her emotional history as if without the distortions that time and the vagaries of memory exact on past experiences. Her memories of infancy and childhood are analogous to Woolf's memories of the foundational scenes of early childhood at St. Ives, albeit with the emotional tone of desolation rather than rapture.

Complementary solutions to the equation between mother and home and the tension between longing and belonging are central to the transformations that structure the experiences of a number of characters in novels by the six contemporary American writers considered in this study, beginning with Barbara Kingsolver's three narratives. *Animal Dreams* traces a woman's efforts to recover imaginatively the mother who, like Woolf's, died during her childhood and for whom she has deferred mourning, at a high emotional cost. Additionally, Codi Noline struggles to find the truth of a family history from which she has been disconnected as a result of her father's falsifications. Ultimately, she reaches the healing knowledge that "all griefs are bearable" (*Animal Dreams,* 327). Reconnecting with her own maternal sources in both directions, as it were, she resolves mourning, fixing (securing) the memory of her lost mother and fixing (repairing) the lost pregnancy of her youth by *choosing* motherhood with the same man as the child's father a second time. Kingsolver also complicates the notions of home and loss represented in the work of Woolf and Lessing. Codi's Native American lover functions as her spiritual guide to a deeper "ground orientation"—the Native American spiritual vision of home/mother as the land itself. The outcome of Codi's multilayered personal salvaging operation is a reparative vision of herself within a larger web of belonging: a community, a reclaimed family history, and spiritual grace.

The narratives discussed with reference to cultural dislocation engage with larger contexts for nostalgia and mourning that extend some of the issues raised in the work of Woolf and Lessing. The matter of home becomes inseparable from issues of homeland, exile, and loss that bear on an entire cultural group or community. Thus, Kingsolver's Taylor Greer, arbitrarily thrust into motherhood across cultures, discovers the profound cultural disruptions and dislocations upon which her attachment to a Cherokee child is predicated. Julia Alvarez's Yolanda García of *How the García Girls Lost Their Accents* engages nostalgia as a way to fix/repair the path home across cultural and linguistic boundaries. Her narrative both defines and embodies a reparative vision that neutralizes and transmutes loss. By figuratively unraveling and reknitting into a different and more satisfying design the strands of her family's history and her own experience of exile, Yolanda fixes the past: geopolitical dislocation is repatterned to articulate a restorative hybrid vision of cultural and linguistic identity. Unlike Kingsolver's Codi Noline and Taylor Greer—both, like Yolanda García, young women on the verge of adult life and generativity—Alvarez's Yo affirms herself in a manner more like Woolf's Lily Briscoe: as an independent artist rather than as either daughter or mother.

The narratives considered in "Midlife Nostalgia and Cultural Mourning," written by authors a generation older than Kingsolver and Alvarez, focus on characters approaching the coming of *age.* Tyler's Delia Grinstead, Marshall's Avey Johnson, and Morrison's Violet and Joe Trace trace different trajectories of the journey home and produce different resolutions of nostalgia as a psychic defense against loss. Of the female characters considered here, the one who most explicitly fixes her past by literally revising her life is Anne Tyler's Delia Grinstead. As Delia impulsively runs away from home and installs herself in a parallel life, Tyler traces an improbable comic trajectory that discloses a darker subtext. Although Delia's mother died during her childhood, Tyler makes little of that fact, though it may account for some of Delia's anxieties about her own maternal role. It is her father who shapes Delia's orientation toward attachment and loss. Ultimately, through belatedly mourning his death, Delia (also belatedly) acknowledges and resolves mourning for earlier phases of herself. Fathoming the underlying meaning of her home/sickness, she surrenders the outdated versions of herself as daughter, mother, and child-wife—roles that have persisted, ironically, as a result of her never having left the original safe house of her filial home and domestic space.

Paule Marshall's widowed Avey Johnson, compelled to confront not only her personal history but the cultural history from which she is equally disaffected, ultimately returns home transformed by her island sojourn. Gaining, like Kingsolver's Codi Noline, a new "ground orientation," signified by her participation in ceremonial African dances of reparation and renewal, she confronts her spiritual disaffection and discovers her home within a larger cultural history and geography. Avey, like Codi, is aided in her homeward journey by a male spiritual guide who steers her past obstacles in her progress toward a more authentic vision of herself and her history. Finally, like Codi, Avey moves from "no-line" to recover her "line" within a vital communal web of spiritual kinship.

In Toni Morrison's *Jazz*, what I have termed the *beloved imago* functions as the embodiment of individual longing/mourning for the absent/lost love object who stands for an entire collective history of loss. Both Joe and Violet Trace are haunted by "mother-hunger." Dorcas functions imaginatively as both lost mother (for Joe) and lost daughter (for Violet). Additionally, she is the sacrificial figure through whom both Joe and Violet accommodate themselves to the loss of youth and passion during a period when—as Morrison imaginatively renders what was happening to African Americans living on the edges of the Jazz Age—America itself seemed obsessed with both. Combining stories and figures from different emotional and cultural histories and times, Morrison melds several facets of cultural dislocation and longing for belonging in African American experience during Reconstruction and the Great Migration, rendering the cultural mourning that signifies a collective loss with sources in an even earlier era of involuntary exile and dislocation.

The self-reflexive narrating voice of *Jazz* fixes the past in still another sense. Revising several stories in the very process of telling them, the voice exemplifies the postmodern understanding that the past is not a set of fixed facts but a fluid matrix out of which stories assume diverse forms. History becomes fiction or—to invoke Morrison's postmodern word play—it becomes *"le story."* In this sense, the past, because it remains open to multiple interpretations, is neither irreparable nor fixed but indeterminate. Thus, fiction *can* imaginatively fix (secure, reset) events that happened in the past. The reconciliation of Joe and Violet Trace, ironically made possible by Dorcas's death, revises longings and acknowledges losses that might have resulted—as the "unreliable" narrator had anticipated—in a destructive outcome.

Cocoa Day of Naylor's *Mama Day,* motherless and childless like Kingsolver's Codi Noline, struggles within a more polarized legacy, in this instance mediated by the maternal great-aunt who stands in for her lost mother. Whereas in Kingsolver's *Animal Dreams,* Loyd Peregrina functions as both nurturing lover and spiritual guide, Naylor's George Andrews is an earnest but more ambiguous lover/spouse who lacks the spiritual knowledge sustained by Mama Day and the Great Mother of Willow Springs. In her multivoiced narrative, Naylor interweaves the romantic love story of Cocoa and George with the counter love story: Mama Day's need to protect—and to possess—her surrogate daughter as a defense against abandonments and losses in her own emotional history. However, the "four-sided story" of *Mama Day* resists "fixing" despite Mama Day's ambivalent collaboration/contest with George Andrews over Cocoa's deliverance and despite Cocoa's own efforts to mediate between competing desires and loyalties.

Morrison's *Paradise* fittingly concludes this study, defining the outer limits of the meanings of longing and belonging, mother and home, emotional loss and spiritual reparation. Through Consolata, the soul-damaged women who reside at the pointedly named Convent find a safe house and a nurturing spiritual mother and guide. But ironies abound in *Paradise* (if not in Paradise): competing visions of perfection are placed in direct confrontation with each other. Like Naylor's *Mama Day, Paradise* traces a struggle between matriarchal and patriarchal power and complementary visions of home and Paradise. Further, Morrison narratively articulates a reparative fantasy, a defense against the soul-destroying experiences of social and psychological "disallowance" in African American historical experience. Yet that healing vision ironically betrays the limits of a nostalgic vision of Paradise. As rendered by Consolata, the fairy tale realm presided over by Piedade—characterized by "the unambivalent bliss of going home to be at home" (*Paradise* 318)—is a timeless, static place of female exclusivity.

Moreover, if Paradise is defined as a site of changelessness in a timeless present, neither the past nor the future can be fixed (revised).

Each narrative considered here describes a trajectory of discovery, but also one of longing or mourning balanced to a greater or lesser degree by a corrective vision that enables—narratively, at least—healing and renewal. In most instances, the central character arrives at a deeper understanding, altering her comprehension of her attachment to—or loss of—mother/home, culture or community, and/or personal and collective history. Several of the authors considered here employ homesickness as a narrative vehicle for releasing their characters from longing. In those narratives, the female character moves through and past nostalgia to solace. Relinquishing her longing for the fantasied, idealized mother who gave birth to her, she figuratively gives birth to her own revitalized self. Other characters transmute the losses that inevitably accompany passage through life—whether conceptualized as phantoms of the mother, earlier (and younger) versions of the self, or memory traces of home/land/ancestral culture—into new visions of themselves within their personal and cultural histories.

Resolving mourning—whether for lost parents, lost ancestors, lost selves, lost youth and possibilities, lost lives, lost places, lost cultures—is a means of imaginatively fixing the past by revising its meanings in—and for—the present and future. Through nostalgia, authors provide their characters with a vehicle for discovery or transformation of consciousness. For the authors themselves, narrative nostalgia provides opportunities to work through mourning, to revisit and revise the emotional sites of loss. Such healing transformations are, of course, narrative and fictive ones. My insistence on the potential for "fixing" the past must ultimately be understood as metaphor. However, the transformation of grief into art may be the vehicle for and the resolution of nostalgic mourning in real terms as well. As Virginia Woolf discovered in writing *To the Lighthouse,* "I suppose that I did for myself what psycho-analysts do for their patients. I expressed some very long felt and deeply felt emotion. And in expressing it I explained it and then laid it to rest" ("Sketch," *Moments* 81). Or, as Doris Lessing phrases it, "Myth does not mean something untrue, but a concentration of truth" (*Laughter* 35).

Across diverse geographies, histories, ethnicities, cultures, and phases of the life course, the literary imagination collaborates with memory and desire to re-*place* nostalgia: to override or neutralize loss through reparative transformations of emotional pain associated with past experience. Home matters not simply as a place but as the imagination's *place marker* for a vision of personal (and cultural) re/union, encompassing both that which actually may have been experienced in the vanished past and that which never could have been. Even as the remembered/imagined vision of home is a construction, it also constructs—and stokes, and sometimes even heals—the longing for belonging. Home functions in the (literary) imagination not as a tangible place but as a liminal site, what cultural anthropologist Victor Turner defines as "a place that is not a place, and a time that is not a time."[1] In that domain, in that transitional space or time where meanings remain temporarily open or suspended, the characters considered here—and their authors and readers—may discover that home is ultimately a state of mind. It may even be, for a few, a state of grace.

Notes

Home Matters: Longing and Belonging

1. See Simone de Beauvoir, *The Second Sex,* trans. and ed. H. M. Parshley (1953; rpt., New York: Knopf, 1971); and Betty Friedan, *The Feminine Mystique* (1963; rpt., New York: Dell, 1964).

2. A number of novels by women published during the late 1960s and the 1970s mirrored those views, representing the perspective of the trapped woman or "mad housewife" who felt compelled to leave home to escape from the tyranny of domesticity and to find herself. Representative novels include Sue Kaufman, *The Diary of a Mad Housewife* (New York: Random House, 1967); Anne Richardson Roiphe, *Up the Sandbox* (New York: Simon and Schuster, 1970); Erica Jong, *Fear of Flying* (New York: Holt, Rinehart and Winston, 1973); and Marilyn French, *The Women's Room* (New York: Summit, 1977).

3. Susan Stanford Friedman uses the phrase "locational feminism" to suggest an expanded feminist discourse based upon "the assumption of changing historical and geographical specificities that produce different feminist theories, agendas, and political practices. . . . Locational feminism requires a geopolitical literacy that acknowledges the interlocking dimension of global cultures, the way in which the local is always informed by the global and the global by the local." *Mappings: Feminism and the Cultural Geographies of Encounter* (Princeton: Princeton University Press, 1998), 5.

4. The exiled Somalian writer Nuruddin Farah joins the political and metaphysical meanings of exile in his answer to his own question, "What is the topic of literature? It began with the expulsion of Adam from Paradise. What, in fact, writers do is to play around either with the myth of creation or with the myth of return. And in between, in parentheses, there is that promise, the promise of return. While awaiting the return, we tell stories,

create literature, recite poetry, remember the past and experience the present. Basically, we writers are telling the story of that return—either in the form of a New Testament or an Old Testament variation on the creation myth. It's a return to innocence, to childhood, to our sources." Qtd. in William Gass, "The Philosophical Significance of Exile" (interview with Nuruddin Farah, Han Vladislav, and Jorge Edwards) in *Literature in Exile*, ed. John Glad (Durham: Duke University Press, 1990), 4. Like many comments by male writers regarding the effects of exile on their writing, Farah's observation omits mention of the female dimension: Eve's expulsion, with Adam, from Paradise. For feminist postcolonial approaches to the notion of home, see Rosemary Marangoly George, *The Politics of Home: Postcolonial Relations and Twentieth-Century Fiction* (Cambridge and New York: Cambridge University Press, 1996); and Caren Kaplan, "Territorializations: The Rewriting of Home and Exile in Western Feminist Discourse," *Cultural Critique* 6 (1987): 187–98.

5. Virginia Woolf's *A Room of One's Own* (1929) was the foundational text for bookshelves of studies elaborating on and qualifying this conjunction of ideas. Among the most influential studies in feminist critical scholarship is Sandra Gilbert and Susan Gubar's elucidation of the figurative meanings of domestic spaces, *The Madwoman in the Attic.* Focusing on nineteenth-century British women writers, Gilbert and Gubar's groundbreaking study inaugurated a central premise in feminist literary criticism: that literary narratives might be more fully understood through the intersecting contexts not only of culture and history but of gender and patriarchal ideology. Figurations—and configurations—of space derive their power as metaphors from social arrangements and imbedded ideological assumptions about differences in gender. See *The Madwoman in the Attic: The Woman Writer and the Nineteenth-Century Literary Imagination* (New Haven: Yale University Press, 1979). Annette Kolodny's work also pivots on spatial conceptualizations of women's writing. See *The Lay of the Land: Metaphor as Experience and History in American Life and Letters* (Chapel Hill: University of North Carolina Press, 1975).

6. Roberta Rubenstein, *Boundaries of the Self: Gender, Culture, Fiction* (Urbana: University of Illinois Press, 1987).

7. See Nancy Chodorow, *The Reproduction of Motherhood: Psychoanalysis and the Sociology of Gender* (Berkeley: University of California Press, 1978); and Carol Gilligan, *In a Different Voice: Psychological Theory and Women's Development* (Cambridge: Harvard University Press, 1982).

8. In *Narrating Mothers: Theorizing Maternal Subjectivities,* Brenda O. Daly and Maureen T. Reddy coin the term "daughter-centricity" to highlight the one-sided emphasis in second wave feminist theory and criticism on the daughter's subjectivity at the expense of the mother's (Knoxville: University of Tennessee Press, 1991), 2. Marianne Hirsch provides a needed balance by analyzing the mother as *subject* rather than object in fiction by women. See

The Mother-Daughter Plot: Narrative, Psychoanalysis, Feminism (Bloomington: Indiana University Press, 1989).

9. As psychoanalyst Pietro Castelnuovo-Tedesco phrases it in his exploration of the meaning of nostalgia, homesickness may be "resolved or alleviated by a return home or even simply by the promise of such a return, but no such ready solution is effective for the nostalgic's plight, inasmuch as what he yearns for belongs to another time." "Reminiscence and Nostalgia: The Pleasure and Pain of Remembering," in *The Course of Life: Psychoanalytic Contributions Toward Understanding Personality Development*. Vol. III: *Adulthood and the Aging Process*, ed. Stanley I. Greenspan and George H. Pollock (Washington, DC: DHHS Pub. No. (ADM) 81–1000), 120.

10. The word nostalgia was coined by Johannes Hofer in 1688, combining the Greek *nostos,* return or the return home, with *algos,* pain or sorrow. See Mario Jacoby, *Longing for Paradise: Psychological Perspectives on an Archetype,* trans. Myron B. Gubitz (Boston: Sigo Press, 1985), 5. In pre-twentieth century Europe, when doctors were still ignorant of infectious agents as the source of disease, they regarded nostalgia as the source of organic diseases as diverse as gastroenteritis and pleurisy. See Jean Starobinski, "The Idea of Nostalgia," *Diogenes* 54 (1966): 81–103. In other words, according to David Lowenthal, "To leave home for long was to risk death." *The Past is a Foreign Country* (Cambridge: Cambridge University Press, 1985), 10. The idea that a person's separation from home could produce an organic disease named "nostalgia" gave way in the twentieth century to its construction as an emotional disturbance related not to the workings of the body but to "the workings of memory" (Starobinski, 89–90) and characterized less by the risk of literal death than by a yearning for something of emotional significance that an individual regards as absent or lost.

11. Starobinski (paraphrasing Kant), 191.

12. Beverley Raphael describes mourning as the process through which an individual "gradually undoes the psychological bonds that bound him to the deceased." *The Anatomy of Bereavement* (New York: Basic Books, 1983), 33. Psychoanalyst George H. Pollock conceptualizes the idea of mourning more broadly, proposing that what he terms the "mourning-liberation process" is a universal, lifelong series of adaptations to significant losses and changes, from which no individual is immune. The process may produce different outcomes, ranging from normal resolution (liberation) to arrested mourning or depressive disorders. The acute experiences of grief and bereavement precipitated by the death of a significant love object are a subset of this lifelong developmental process of mourning and reconciliation. *The Mourning-Liberation Process,* 2 vols. (Madison, CT: International Universities Press, 1989), vol. 1, 105.

13. Marsha H. Levy-Warren observes that "a move from one's culture of origin can be seen as similar to the loss of a loved person, which initiates a process

of mourning." "Moving to a New Culture: Cultural Identity, Loss, and Mourning," in *The Psychology of Separation and Loss: Perspectives on Development, Life Transitions, and Clinical Practice,* ed. Jonathan Bloom-Feshbach, Sally Bloom-Feshbach, et al. (San Francisco: Jossey-Bass, 1987), 305.

14. A number of feminist scholars have explored the idea of nostalgia from literary and psychoanalytic perspectives. For example, Donna Bassin regards nostalgia in psychoanalytic terms as a fantasy "devoid of a sense of internal agency" and thus one in which an individual "remains trapped in a process of endless seeking." See Donna Bassin, Margaret Honey, and Maryle Mahrer Kaplan, eds., *Representations of Motherhood* (New Haven: Yale University Press, 1994), 168. According to Mary Jacobus, nostalgia for the "lost mother" of childhood occurs despite the fact that "there never was a prior time, or an unmediated relation for the subject (whether masculine or feminine), except as the oedipal defined it retroactively. The mother is already structured as division by the oedipal; no violent separation can be envisaged without an aura of pathos, because separation is inscribed from the start. . . ." *First Things: The Maternal Imaginary in Literature, Art, and Psychoanalysis* (New York: Routledge, 1995), 18. Gayle Greene, in her analysis of feminist uses of memory in women's fiction, distinguishes between nostalgia and what she judges "more productive forms of memory": "nostalgia and remembering are in some sense antithetical, since nostalgia is a forgetting, merely regressive, whereas memory may look back in order to move forward and transform disabling fictions to enabling fictions, altering our relation to the present and future." "Feminist Fiction and the Uses of Memory," *Signs: Journal of Women in Culture and Society* 16, no. 2 (Winter 1991): 298. Janice Doane and Devon Hodges, evaluating the implicit message of novels and nonfictional works written mostly by male writers during the 1970s and 1980s, argue that nostalgia represents a reactionary male wish for women to return to the separate sphere (home) that they occupied prior to the social changes catalyzed by feminism and the women's movement. It signifies a "retreat to the past in the face of what a number of writers—most of them male—perceived to be the degeneracy of American culture brought about by the rise of feminist authority." *Nostalgia and Sexual Difference: The Resistance to Contemporary Feminism* (New York: Methuen, 1987), xiii.

Emphasizing the framework of culture rather than gender in his study of the "homing" tendency frequently expressed in narratives by Native American writers, William Bevis argues that "The connotations of 'regression' are cultural: not all people equate their 'civilization' with 'discontents,' and therefore a return to a previous status quo is not necessarily a romantic 'escape' from an unbearable present of cultural or individual maturity and anxiety." "Native American Novels: Homing In," in *Recovering the Word: Essays on Native American Literature,* ed. Brian Swann and Arnold Krupat (Berkeley: University of California Press, 1987), 590. Representing a middle ground between the view of nostalgia as regressive or reactionary and Bevis's counterargument for its culturally relative meaning, sociologist Fred Davis captures the contradictory orientations of nostalgia in his observation that "Nostalgia manages at one and the same time to celebrate the past, to diminish it, and to transmute it into a means for engaging the present." *Yearning for Yesterday: A Sociology of Nostalgia* (New York: The Free Press/ Macmillan, 1979), 45. Or, as Edward S. Casey phrases it, "Nostalgia leads us to invoke the following principle: in remembering we can be thrust back, transported, into the place we recall. . . . Rather than thinking of remembering as a form of re-experiencing of the past *per se,* we might conceive of it as an activity of *re-implacing:* re-experiencing past places." *Remembering: A Phenomenological Study* (Bloomington: Indiana University Press, 1987), 201 (emphasis in original).

Chapter 1
Yearning and Nostalgia: Fiction and Autobiographical Writings of Virginia Woolf and Doris Lessing

1. Doris Lessing, *The Golden Notebook* (1962; rpt., New York: Harcourt Brace Jovanovich, 1989), 137. Future references in the text are to this edition, abbreviated as *Notebook.*
2. Doris Lessing, *Under My Skin* (New York: HarperCollins, 1994), 12, Lessing's emphasis.
3. Virginia Woolf, "A Sketch of the Past," in *Moments of Being: Unpublished Autobiographical Writings,* ed. Jeanne Schulkind (New York: Harcourt Brace Jovanovich, 1976), 75. Subsequent references in the text are to this edition, abbreviated as *Moments* and (for the essay) as "Sketch."
4. Such vivid, almost photographically exact images are termed *eidetic* images. Barbara G. Myerhoff offers an especially rich description of such memories: "Memory is a continuum ranging from vague, dim shadows to the brightest, most vivid totality. It may offer opportunity not merely to recall the past but to relive it, in all its original freshness, unaltered by intervening changes and reflections. Such magical Proustian moments are pinpoints of the greatest intensity, when a sense of the past never being truly lost is experienced. The diffuseness of life is then transcended, the sense of duration overcome, and all of one's self and one's memories are felt to be universally valid. Simultaneity replaces sequence and a sense of oneness with one's past is achieved. Often such moments involve childhood memories, and then one experiences the self as it was originally, and knows beyond doubt that one is the same person as that child who still dwells within a time-altered body." "Re-membered Lives," *Parabola* V, no. 1 (February 1980): 76.
5. *A Room of One's Own* (1929; rpt., New York: Harcourt Brace Jovanovich, 1989), 76.

6. Doris Lessing, *African Laughter: Four Visits to Zimbabwe* (New York: Harper-Collins 1992), 11. Subsequent references in the text are abbreviated as *Laughter.*

7. Doris Lessing, "My Mother's Life," *Granta* 17 (Fall 1985): 236.

8. Doris Lessing, *Martha Quest,* vol. 1 of *Children of Violence* (1952, rpt., New York: Simon and Schuster, 1964), 32. Subsequent references in the text are to this edition.

9. Judith Kegan Gardiner, focusing on the effect of exile on Lessing's writing, draws different conclusions from mine, observing that "Lessing expresses a nostalgia for the space of the colony as opposed to the civilization of the center, nostalgia not for home but for homelessness, for boundlessness." "The Exhilaration of Exile: Rhys, Stead, and Lessing," in *Women's Writing in Exile,* ed. Mary Lynn Broe and Angela Ingram (Chapel Hill: University of North Carolina Press, 1989), 145.

10. Doris Lessing, *A Proper Marriage,* in vol. 1 of *Children of Violence* (1954; rpt., New York: Simon and Schuster, 1964), 341. In her analysis of the uses of memory in women's fiction, Gayle Greene discusses nostalgia in Lessing's *Children of Violence* and *The Golden Notebook* (see especially 302–3 and 308–10). She argues that, although nostalgia is not gender specific, it has "different meanings for men and women. Though from one perspective, women might seem to have more incentives than men to be nostalgic—deprived of outlets in the present, they live more in the past . . .—from another perspective, women have little to be nostalgic about, for the good old days when the grass was greener and young people knew their places was also the time when women knew their place, and it is not place to which most women want to return." "Feminist Fiction and the Uses of Memory," *Signs: Journal of Women in Culture and Society* 16, no. 2 (Winter 1991): 296.

11. Betsy Draine, focusing on the relation between formal elements and meaning within Lessing's fiction, argues that Anna's nostalgia conveys a longing less for place than for a more abstract sense of order through achieved form—"a yearning for the recovery of the sense of form, the stage illusion of moral certainty, innocence, unity, and peace. In effect, this yearning is a desire for unreality and nonexistence. Since the yearning can never be fulfilled, it always leads to painful frustration and often to nihilism and despair" (71). Moreover, the notebooks each express a "pattern of opposition between nostalgia and awareness . . ." (72), including Anna-Ella's "long battle with nostalgia for the lost condition of naive commitment to an order of meaning . . ." (81). *Substance Under Pressure: Artistic Coherence and Evolving Form in the Novels of Doris Lessing* (Madison: University of Wisconsin Press, 1983).

12. Elsewhere, I have explored these issues in greater detail, concluding that "there is no single authoritative view of events" in *The Golden Notebook* and that "all versions of Anna's experiences are fictions, though each is true in its own way. . . . The 'truth' is not in any one version of Anna's experiences

but in what she—and we—understand by imaginatively fusing the various fragments and perspectives together" (102, 105–6). See Roberta Rubenstein, *The Novelistic Vision of Doris Lessing: Breaking the Forms of Consciousness* (Urbana: University of Illinois Press, 1979). See also Greene, 308–10.

13. Thanks to Ellen Cronan Rose for sharpening this observation.

14. Jennie Taylor, exploring *Going Home* as a text of colonial writing that blends autobiographical and political discourses, emphasizes the "interaction of difference, assimilation, and exile" (60). Speaking of the irony of the title, she observes, "*Going* Home addresses and constructs an alien reader, looking at Africa from outside, whom the writer is leaving in order to inform. Going *Home* implies arriving somewhere familiar, seeing it through a pentimento of memories, overlapping biographical and historical time, but as an alien who cannot be assimilated, either by the dominant white or subordinate black culture" (57, Taylor's emphasis). Although Taylor does not use the term *nostalgia*, her argument that Lessing "reinvents" crucial scenes from her past life in Africa "through the replacement of memory by desire" (63) coincides with what I term nostalgia. "Memory and Desire on Going Home: The Deconstruction of a Colonial Radical," in *Doris Lessing*, ed. Eve Bertelsen (Johannesburg: McGraw-Hill, 1985).

15. Doris Lessing, *Going Home* (1957; rpt., New York: Ballantine, 1968), 55. Subsequent references in the text are to this edition.

16. In "Impertinent Daughters," Lessing describes the extraordinary richness and variety of wildlife that inhabited the bushland of her childhood: "Every kind of animal lived there: sable, eland, kudu, bushbuck, duiker, anteaters, wild cats, wild pigs, snakes. There were flocks of guineafowl, partridges, hawks, eagles, pigeons, doves—birds, birds, birds. Dawns were explosions of song; the nights noisy with owls and nightjars and birds whose names we never knew; all day birds shrilled and cooed and hammered and chattered. But paradise had already been given notice to quit. The leopards and baboons had gone to the hills, the lions had wandered off, the elephants had retreated to the Zambesi Valley, the land was emptying." *Granta* 14 (Winter 1984): 65. In another installment of her memoirs, she reiterates the "miracle of good luck" of her African childhood: "We were surrounded by every kind of wild animal and bird, free to wander as we wanted over thousands of acres, solitude the most precious of our gifts . . . but our mother lay awake at night, ill with grief because her children were deprived, because they were not good middle class children in some London suburb." "My Mother's Life," *Granta* 17 (Fall 1985): 235, Lessing's ellipsis.

17. Mario Jacoby, *Longing for Paradise: Psychological Perspectives on an Archetype*, trans. Myron B. Gubitz (Boston: Sigo Press, 1985), 66.

18. Doris Lessing, *Briefing for a Descent into Hell* (1971; rpt., New York: Bantam, 1972). Subsequent references in the text are to this edition, abbreviated as *Briefing*.

19. The image of an Edenic city occurs throughout Lessing's work. It is a leit-motif of *Children of Violence,* from the adolescent Martha Quest's visionary fantasy of an ideal city in *Martha Quest* to the concluding volume of the *Children of Violence* series, pointedly titled *The Four-Gated City.* As I have noted elsewhere, "The image of the city also reproduces the configuration of the sacred city, laid out with four cardinal orientations whose center symbolizes the sacred center of the universe." *Novelistic Vision,* 127; see also 37–8, 56, and 164. Ellen Cronan Rose traces the sources of the image of the *città felice* in Lessing's work to its sources in medieval texts. See "Doris Lessing's *Città Felice,*" in *Critical Essays on Doris Lessing,* ed. Claire Sprague and Virginia Tiger (Boston: G. K. Hall, 1986), 141–53. Claire Sprague, in a chapter pertinently titled "From Mud Houses to Sacred Cities," also considers the persistence of the image and its conflation of past and future fantasies; she cites Frank E. Manuel and Fritzie P. Manuel's observation, in their study of utopian thought, that "' the nostalgic mode has been an auxiliary of utopia'" (155). Sprague traces the image of the "archetypally lost city" from *Children of Violence* through Lessing's series of intergalactic novels, *Canopus at Argos.* See *Rereading Doris Lessing: Narrative Patterns of Doubling and Repetition* (Chapel Hill: University of North Carolina Press, 1987), 168–80.

20. Doris Lessing, *Canopus in Argos: Archives. Re: Colonised Planet 5: Shikasta* (New York: Knopf, 1979), 6–7. Subsequent references in the text are to this edition, abbreviated as *Shikasta.*

21. Virginia Woolf, *Mrs. Dalloway* (1925; rpt., New York: Harcourt Brace Jovanovich, 1990), 34. Subsequent references in this text are to this edition.

22. Elizabeth Abel also observes a kind of nostalgia in the narrative, though one quite different in emphasis than the one I explore here. As she phrases it, "Critics frequently note the elegiac tone which allies *Mrs. Dalloway* with the modernist lament for a lost plenitude, but nostalgia in this text is for a specifically female presence absent from contemporary life" (42). She reads the recollected scene between Clarissa and Sally Seton, interrupted by Peter Walsh's appearance, as a "psychological allegory": "the moment of exclusive female connection is shattered by masculine intervention . . . [suggesting] a revised Oedipal configuration: the jealous male attempting to rupture the exclusive female bond, insisting on the transference of attachment to the man, demanding heterosexuality" (32–33). *Virginia Woolf and the Fictions of Psychoanalysis* (Chicago: University of Chicago Press, 1989).

23. Woolf describes the "seductions by half-brothers" in two different autobiographical accounts: "A Sketch of the Past" and "22 Hyde Park Gate," in *Moments of Being: Unpublished Autobiographical Writings,* ed. Jeanne Schulkind (New York: Harcourt Brace Jovanovich, 1976), 69, 155, 182. Louise DeSalvo, exploring the implications of Virginia Woolf's sexual abuse during childhood, concludes that "the pattern of abuse lasted for many, many years, from roughly 1888, when [Woolf] was six or seven, through 1904; that she

was abused by more than one family member; that it was a central formative experience for her; and that a pattern of abuse existed within the Stephen family." *Virginia Woolf: The Impact of Childhood Sexual Abuse on Her Life and Work* (Boston: Beacon Press, 1989), 101. Some Woolf scholars have disputed several of DeSalvo's assertions.

24. "Old Bloomsbury," in *Moments of Being*, 161.

25. Pietro Castelnuovo-Tedesco argues that, "Although different objects from various periods of one's life can evoke nostalgic yearnings, ultimately they are derivative substitutes for the pre-oedipal mother." "Reminiscence and Nostalgia: The Pleasure and Pain of Remembering," in *The Course of Life: Psychoanalytic Contributions Toward Understanding Personality Development*, vol. III: *Adulthood and the Aging Process*, ed. Stanley I. Greenspan and George H. Pollock (Washington, DC: DHHS Pub. No. (ADM) 81–1000), 121.

26. In an early autobiographical commentary written during her twenties, Woolf describes the relationship between her mother and her older half-sister, Stella, in terms that both idealize the bond and suggest her own unfulfilled desires for merger with the mother they shared: "It was beautiful, it was almost excessive; for it had something of the morbid nature of an affection between two people too closely allied for the proper amount of reflection to take place between them; what her mother felt passed almost instantly through Stella's mind; there was no need for the brain to ponder and criticize what the soul knew." "Reminiscences," in *Moments of Being*, 43.

27. *To the Lighthouse* (1927; rpt., New York: Harcourt Brace Jovanovich, 1989), 51. Subsequent references in the text are to this edition, abbreviated as *Lighthouse*.

28. Thomas C. Caramagno, tracing the ramifications of Woolf's mood disorder through her fiction and autobiographical writings, proposes that such intense nostalgia might have been generated by her bipolar emotional illness. While "normal" individuals react to the death of a parent or loved one with "sadness, mourning, and loneliness," the "biochemically depressed" respond to such events to an emotionally intensified degree that typically includes "an intense sense of abandonment and certain doom." Further, "convinced that they alone are inadequate and impotent, and feeling as helpless and as vulnerable as infants, these patients often look back nostalgically to what now seems to them an idyllic childhood union with an idealized parent, as they bemoan their loss or blame themselves for this fateful turn of events." *The Flight of the Mind: Virginia Woolf's Art and Manic-Depressive Illness* (Berkeley: University of California Press, 1992), 115.

29. A number of Woolf scholars have focused on the problematic relationship between Lily and Mrs. Ramsay in *To the Lighthouse*, including the possible parallels that may be drawn between the fictional characters and Virginia Woolf's relationship with her own mother, Julia Stephen. Using psychoanalytic approaches, Ellen Bayuk Rosenman and Elizabeth Abel both identify

the intense, regressive, and ambivalent elements of the interrupted mother-daughter relationship as Woolf represented it through Lily's attachment to Mrs. Ramsay before and after her death. Rosenman, grounding her reading in object-relations psychology, observes that "Woolf's memory of Julia, written forty-seven years after her death, is specifically infantile, reconstructing the time when the mother is the child's whole environment. In Woolf's mind, Julia remains this idealized figure as if no other understanding of her had intervened since childhood." *The Invisible Presence: Virginia Woolf and the Mother-Daughter Relationship* (Baton Rouge: Louisiana State University Press, 1986), 7–8. Rosenman also suggests that "The original loss, for Woolf, is the loss of the mother, the 'centre' of St. Ives and childhood who is no longer present and who can only be approached through the compensatory gestures of art" (16).

Abel, revising elements of classic Freudian psychoanalysis from a feminist perspective, emphasizes the ambivalence of the attachment, noting that Lily is "buffeted by opposing impulses toward merger and autonomy in a pattern unbroken (and perhaps even intensified) by Mrs. Ramsay's death. . . . Lily functions simultaneously as the middle-aged artist whose completed painting 'of' Mrs. Ramsay concludes the novel that assuages Woolf's adult obsession with her mother and as an infant longing both to fuse and to separate." Abel, 68–9. From a somewhat different position, Mark Spilka explores the consequences of what he terms Woolf's "impacted grief" (120). He argues that in *To the Lighthouse*—Woolf's "elegy for her dead mother" (15)—the author "returns to the childhood sources of her own blocked grief and successfully conveys the release of impacted feelings in a young spinster woman like herself; but, to avoid sentimentality and confusion, she circumvents the death which created that impaction, oversimplifies the life histories of her major characters, and so leaves untouched the most secret causes for her initial inability to grieve" (9). *Virginia Woolf's Quarrel with Grieving* (Lincoln: University of Nebraska Press, 1980). Suzanne Raitt suggests that the idealized portrait of Mrs. Ramsay extends beyond Woolf's personal biography into an ambivalent attitude toward traditional and unconventional female roles: through her emphasis on Mrs. Ramsay's "feminine beauty," Woolf "appears to feel nostalgic for, as well as critical of, the ideal of Victorian womanhood." *Virginia Woolf's* To the Lighthouse (New York: St. Martin's Press, 1990), 57. Thomas C. Caramagno argues that "Woolf's preoccupation with her mother . . . stood for more than a neurotic longing to escape into the past. Julia became an emblem for Woolf's search for self" (153). Moreover, *To the Lighthouse* dramatizes Woolf's achievement of psychological as well as aesthetic equilibrium; Lily's resolution of her feelings about Mrs. Ramsay through her painting demonstrates that "the longing for mothering, for an idyllic past and manic omnipotence to overcome depressed helplessness, is replaced by adult self-sufficiency" (245). By the end of the narrative, "the body of the mother has been demystified; it is no longer seen as the only source of nurture and stability. . . . Woolf no longer desired to sacrifice her autonomy for the sake of becoming a child again" (269).

30. In describing the "mourning-liberation process," psychoanalyst George H. Pollock argues that "the successful completion of the mourning process results in creative outcome. This end result can be a great work of art, music, sculpture, literature, poetry, philosophy, or science, where the creator has the spark of genius or talent that is not related to mourning per se. Indeed the creative product may reflect the mourning process in theme, style, form, and content, and it may itself stand as a memorial." *The Mourning-Liberation Process*, 2 vols. (Madison, CT: International Universities Press, 1989), vol. 1, 114.

31. Virginia Tiger notes the correspondences between the autobiographical Maude Tayler and the figures of May Quest of Lessing's *Children of Violence* and Maudie of *The Diaries of Jane Somers*. "Doris Lessing, 'Impertinent Daughters' and 'Autobiography (Part Two): My Mother's Life'" (review), *Doris Lessing Newsletter* 10, no .2 (Fall 1986): 14. Claire Sprague elaborates on Lessing's multiple fictional representations and revisions of her knotted relationship with her mother. Sprague 108–28.

32. *Memoirs of a Survivor* (1975; rpt., New York: Bantam, 1979), front dust jacket. Subsequent references in the text are to this edition, abbreviated as *Memoirs*.

33. Lessing's mother later chose to go by her middle name, Maude. "Impertinent Daughters," 53.

34. Lessing remarked, in response to an interviewer's question about her mother's self-proclaimed unsatisfying life in Southern Rhodesia, "Well, of course she wanted to go Home. . . ." Eve Bertelsen, "Interview with Doris Lessing," in *Doris Lessing*, ed. Eve Bertelsen (Johannesburg: McGraw-Hill, 1985), 104.

35. Jacoby, 7.

36. Doris Lessing, *Love, Again* (New York: HarperCollins, 1995), 216. Subsequent references in the text are to this edition.

37. Greene, 298.

Chapter 2
Home is (Mother) Earth: *Animal Dreams*, Barbara Kingsolver

1. Barbara Kingsolver, *Animal Dreams* (New York: HarperCollins, 1991), 13. Subsequent references in the text are to this edition.

2. Interview with Donna Perry, *Backtalk: Women Writers Speak Out* (New Brunswick, N J: Rutgers University Press, 1993), 147.

3. Eliot acknowledged his significant indebtedness to Jessie Weston's now-classic study of the Grail Legend, *From Ritual to Romance*, and to James Frazer's *The Golden Bough*. Weston posited the central elements of the Waste Land story: "a close connection between the vitality of a certain King, and the prosperity of his kingdom; the forces of the ruler being weakened or

destroyed, by wound, sickness, old age, or death, the land becomes Waste, and the task of the hero is that of restoration" (23). Later she clarifies the sources of these legends in ancient rituals of fertility: "in the earliest, and least contaminated, version of the Grail story the central figure would be dead, and the task of the Quester that of restoring him to life . . ." (120). Weston, *From Ritual to Romance* (1920; rpt., Garden City, New York: Doubleday, 1957). My reading of *Animal Dreams* with reference to the wasteland theme is not based on any statements by Kingsolver concerning Eliot's poem or its antecedents. Rather, given the wealth of allusions to the motif that appear in the narrative, I assume the author's familiarity with the archetypal story.

4. In *Ceremony,* a young man of mixed Laguna (Pueblo) and white blood returns to his New Mexican pueblo after the Second World War and struggles with his profound feelings of loss and alienation, believing that he is somehow personally responsible for the multiyear drought in his area. Through various healing ceremonies of fertility and renewal, he is ultimately reconnected to the land and to himself. See Roberta Rubenstein, "Boundaries of the Cosmos," in *Boundaries of the Self: Gender, Culture, Fiction* (Urbana: University of Illinois Press, 1979), 190–202. In an interview, Kingsolver affirmed her "kinship" (159) with Leslie Silko, whom she regards as one of her favorite writers, and acknowledged that her own worldview is closer to the Native American than to the Judeo-Christian position. See Donna Perry, *Backtalk,* 148. At least one other Native American author, Jim Welch, incorporates the wasteland motif in his novel, *Winter in the Blood* (1974). See Kenneth Lincoln's analysis of the wasteland parallels in Welch's narrative in *Native American Renaissance* (Berkeley: University of California Press, 1983): 153, 155, 162. Several other narratives by Native American authors represent an ailing protagonist whose cure comes as he recovers his tribal identity. See William Bevis, "Native American Novels: Homing In," in *Recovering the Word: Essays on Native American Literature,* ed. Brian Swann and Arnold Krupat (Berkeley: University of California Press, 1987): 580–620.

5. Carlo's vocation may be an ironic allusion to ancient fertility myths: the dismemberment and recovery of the "severed parts" of Adonis/Osiris were associated with rituals of renewal and fertility. See Sir James George Frazer, *The Golden Bough,* abridged ed. (New York: Macmillan, 1940): 365–6, 378–9.

6. ". . . the Doctor, or Medicine Man, did, from the very earliest ages, play an important part in Dramatic Fertility Ritual . . . that of restoring to life and health the dead, or wounded, representative of the Spirit of Vegetation." Weston, 109. In Silko's *Ceremony* there are several healers, including the Medicine Man Betonie and the spirit woman, Ts'eh, through whose intervention Tayo reconnects with his Laguna tradition, participates in ceremonies of purification and renewal, and recovers from his inner deadness.

7. The language echoes another Homeric event: Odysseus outwits the Cyclops by identifying himself as "Nobody." Kingston has acknowledged the presence in *Animal Dreams* of "references to Homer's *Odyssey. . . .*" *Backtalk,* 153.

8. Paula Gunn Allen, *The Sacred Hoop: Recovering the Feminine in American Indian Traditions* (Boston: Beacon Press, 1986), 210–11.

9. Bevis, 582.

10. Ibid., 585.

11. Ibid., 587–8.

12. Allen, 119.

13. J. E. Cirlot, *A Dictionary of Symbols,* 2nd ed., trans. Jack Sage (New York: Philosophical Library, 1971), 251.

14. *The Tempest,* I, ii: 396, in *The Complete Works of William Shakespeare* (rpt. New York: Oxford University Press, 1964), p. 6.

15. See Weston. The Gracelas sisters, whose progeny populates the town of Grace, may also allude to the three Graces of Greek mythology: the sisters Aglaia (brightness), Euphrosyne (joy), and Thalia (bloom) were fertility goddesses.

16. According to Diana Kappel-Smith, "Nolinas are relatives of yucca. Their flower spike when fully unfolded in bloom is a fragrant, insect-infested affair the size of a family Christmas tree. These are not minor events, and they are not common. One ranger [in Joshua Tree National Monument, California] has a nolina in his yard that hasn't bloomed for 17 years." As a result of unusually plentiful rains during two previous winters, it produced three flower stalks in the same season. "Fickle desert blooms: opulent one year, no-shows the next," *Smithsonian* 25, no. 12 (March 1995): 86.

17. T. S. Eliot, *Collected Poems, 1909–1962* (London: Faber and Faber, 1963), 31.

18. Ibid., 46.

Chapter 3
Home/lands and Contested Motherhood:
The Bean Trees and *Pigs in Heaven,* Barbara Kingsolver

1. Barbara Kingsolver, *The Bean Trees* (1988; rpt., New York: HarperCollins, 1992), 10. Subsequent references in the text are to this edition.

2. Interview with Donna Perry, in *Backtalk: Women Writers Speak Out* (New Brunswick, N J: Rutgers University Press, 1993), 165.

3. Barbara Kingsolver, *Pigs in Heaven* (New York: HarperCollins, 1993), 61. Subsequent references in the text are to this edition.

4. Kingsolver did not learn of her Cherokee blood until she was "much older." "My Cherokee great-grandmother was quite deliberately left out of the family history for reasons of racism and embarrassment about mixed blood. But her photograph captured my imagination when I was a little girl,

and I always felt a longing to have known her. I felt that there was some sort of wisdom there that I needed." *Backtalk,* 148.

5. Barbara Kingsolver, *Homeland and Other Stories* (New York: Harper and Row, 1989), 18.

6. According to Thomas E. Mails, a scholar of Cherokee culture, "The celestial cluster that the Cherokees called the Seven Stars was regarded with particular reverence." *The Cherokee People: The Story of the Cherokees from Earliest Origins to Contemporary Times* (Tulsa, OK: Council Oak Books, 1992), 160. Mails cites the principal nineteenth-century ethnographer of Cherokee culture, John Howard Payne, who recorded a different version from the one Kingsolver uses. According to Payne's informants, the legend was based on "a family of eight brothers who once sneaked into the town council house and beat the sacred drum kept there for ceremonial purposes. Some of the elders of the town caught and reproved the brothers, who became angry, seized the drum, and flew upwards into the sky with it, defiantly beating upon it as they went. Finally, seven of the brothers became seven stars. The other brother, however, fell back to the ground so hard that his head stuck deep into it, and he became a cedar tree. This tree would stand forever, and it had the peculiar ability to bleed like a human being whenever it was bruised or cut." *The Cherokee People,* 160.

Chapter 4
Inverted Narrative as the Path/Past Home:
How the García Girls Lost their Accents, Julia Alvarez

1. Amy Kaminsky, *Reading the Body Politic: Feminist Criticism and Latin American Women Writers* (Minneapolis: University of Minneapolis Press, 1993), 30; emphasis in original. Kaminsky's study focuses on Latina writers in exile who write in their native language.

2. Ibid., 33.

3. Julia Alvarez, *Something to Declare* (Chapel Hill, N C: Algonquin Books, 1998), 139. Subsequent references in the text are to this edition, abbreviated as *Declare.*

4. Julia Alvarez, *How the García Girls Lost Their Accents* (1991; rpt., New York: Penguin Plume, 1992), 8. Subsequent references in the text are to this edition, abbreviated as *García Girls.*

5. Jonathan Mandell, "Uprooted but Still Blooming," *New York Newsday,* 17 November 1994, sec. B, p. 4.

6. Alvarez credits her reading of Kingston's *The Woman Warrior: Memoirs of a Girlhood among Ghosts* (1976) as a turning point in her conception of writing because it showed her the possibility of articulating her own bicultural experience. Kingston "used Chinese words and had Chinese characters, and she talked about being in the middle of two worlds, those mixed loyalties,

those pulls in different directions, and I read that and I said 'Oh my God, you *can* write about this.'" Mandell, sec. B, p. 12, emphasis in original. Acknowledging her major literary influences, Alvarez notes, "When I read a page of my own writing, it's as if it were a palimpsest, and behind the more prominent, literary faces whose influence shows through the print (Scheherazade, George Eliot, Toni Morrison, Emily Dickinson, Maxine Hong Kingston), I see other faces: real-life ladies who traipsed into my imagination with broom and dusting rag. . . ." *Declare* 149.
7. Jean Starobinski, "The Idea of Nostalgia," *Diogenes* 54 (1966): 130.

Chapter 5
Home/sickness and the Five Stages of Grief:
Ladder of Years, Anne Tyler

1. Several commentators on Tyler's fiction have noted the centrality of the theme of homesickness in her novels. Commenting on Tyler's *Dinner at the Homesick Restaurant*, Joseph Voelker observes that "homesickness" comes to encompass several different meanings, including "not only sickness for home (longing, nostalgia), but also sickness of it (the need to escape from the invasiveness of family) and sickness from it (the psychic wounds that human beings inevitably carry as a result of having had to grow up as children in families). " *Art and the Accidental in Anne Tyler* (Columbia: University of Missouri Press, 1989), 76. John Updike proposes that Tyler's fiction pivots on the tensions between "stasis and movement, between home and escape. Home is what we're mired in; Miss Tyler in her darker mode celebrates domestic claustrophobia and private stagnation." "Loosened Roots," in *Critical Essays on Anne Tyler,* ed. Alice Hall Petry (New York: G. K. Hall, 1992), 89.
2. Anne Tyler, *Ladder of Years* (New York: Knopf, 1995), 15. Subsequent references in the text are to this edition, abbreviated as *Ladder.*
3. Anne Tyler, *Celestial Navigations* (New York: Knopf, 1974), 125–6.
4. Doris Lessing, "To Room Nineteen," in *A Man and Two Women* (New York: Simon and Schuster, 1963), 278–316.
5. Virginia Schaefer Carroll proposes that the changes in Delia's reading habits track the stages of her inner transformation, evolving from "virtuous repression of preference in the name of self-improvement" (102) to critical reading for the purpose of "construct[ing] meaning and synthesis" (103). "Wrestling with Change: Discourse Strategies in Anne Tyler," *Frontiers* 19, no.1 (1998).
6. The word "nothing" links Delia's inner stripping with that of King Lear, who initially is angered by what he regards as betrayal by his youngest and favorite daughter, Cordelia. Only belatedly does he come to understand another meaning in the phrase, "nothing will come of nothing."
7. Correcting an earlier comment in which she expressed her distaste for "novels by liberated women," Tyler noted, "Certainly I don't hate liberated

women as such. . . . I assume I'm one myself, if you can call someone liberated who was never imprisoned." Qtd. in Alice Hall Petry, "Tyler and Feminism," in *Anne Tyler as Novelist,* ed. Dale Salwak (Iowa City: University of Iowa Press, 1994), 33.

8. For the titles of several "mad housewife" narratives of the late 1960s and the 1970's, see n. 2 in notes for *Home Matters: Longing and Belonging,* above.

9. Henrik Ibsen, *A Doll's House,* trans. Peter Watts (1879; rpt., Harmondsworth: Penguin, 1965), 148.

10. Benjamin DeMott, "Funny, Wise, and True," in *Critical Essays on Anne Tyler,* ed. Petry, 112 .

11. There are several different descriptive models for stages of grief and mourning. Tyler apparently draws on Dr. Elisabeth Kübler-Ross's five-stage model, developed through her observations of and discussion with patients dying of terminal diseases: denial and isolation, anger, bargaining, depression, and acceptance. *On Death and Dying* (New York: Macmillan, 1969).

12. Issues concerning bodily changes and other manifestations of aging are developed in a number of midlife (and post midlife) narratives, including Doris Lessing's *The Summer Before the Dark* (1973) and Tyler's own *Breathing Lessons* (1988). For a discussion of the latter novel along with *Ladder of Years* as narratives about the transitions of menopause, see Virginia Schaefer Carroll, "Wrestling with Change"; for a broader discussion of representations of midlife transformations in women's fiction, see Margaret Morganroth Gullette, *Declining to Decline: Cultural Combat and the Politics of the Midlife* (Charlottesville: University Press of Virginia, 1997).

13. Pertinently, Virginia Schaefer Carroll notes that "ladder of years" is a "direct reference to the climacteric, a word derived from the Greek *klimakter,* which literally means 'rung of a ladder'" ("Wrestling with Change," 88). Carroll analyzes Tyler's novel as an exploration of a woman's life-reorientation precipitated by (peri)menopause.

14. Several commentators have noted Tyler's avoidance, throughout her fiction, of the subject of sexual passion. Writing about *Earthly Possessions,* Nicholas Delbanco observes that "violence and lust are rare, or offstage; the characteristic emotions are abstracted ones—anger comes to us as vexation, bliss as a kind of contented release." *Critical Essays on Anne Tyler,* ed. Petry, 87. Even more emphatically, Edward Hoagland contends that throughout her fiction Tyler "touches upon sex so lightly, compared with her graphic realism on other matters, that her total portrait of motivation is tilted out of balance." *Critical Essays on Anne Tyler,* 144.

15. Susie's words echo the grievance—and guilt—experienced by several of Tyler's characters who are victims of parental abandonment. Cody Tull of *Dinner at the Homesick Restaurant* dreams that he asks his father, who vanished years before, "Was it something I said? Was it something I did? Was it something I didn't do, that made you go away?" (New York: Knopf, 1982), 47.

Chapter 6
Hom(e)age to the Ancestors: *Praisesong for the Widow*, Paule Marshall

1. Paule Marshall, *Praisesong for the Widow* (New York: G. P. Putnam's, 1983), 44. Subsequent references in the text are to this edition, abbreviated as *Praisesong*.
2. Barbara Christian observes that the legend of "Africans who were forced to come across the sea—but through their own power, a power that seems irrational, were able to return to Africa—is a touchstone of New World black folklore. Through this story, peoples of African descent emphasized their own power to determine their freedom, though their bodies might be enslaved. They recalled Africa as the source of their being." *Black Feminist Criticism: Perspectives on Black Women Writers* (New York: Pergamon, 1985), 151–2.
3. According to several scholars, Lebert Joseph represents the Yoruba trickster god Esu-Elegbara, one of whose avatars is Legba, the Haitian and Afro-Caribbean god of households and thresholds. As Eugenia Collier notes, "Like Lebert Joseph, Legba is a lame old man in ragged clothes. Intensely personal and beloved, Legba is the liaison between man and the gods. . . . An African Hermes, psychopomp, guide of souls, god of the crossroads, Lebert Joseph leads Avey along the path to self-discovery. . . ." "The Closing of the Circle: Movement from Division to Wholeness in Paule Marshall's Fiction," in *Black Women Writers (1950–1980): A Critical Evaluation,* ed. Mari Evans (Garden City, New York: Anchor/Doubleday, 1984), 312. Karla F. C. Holloway regards Lebert Joseph as "the incarnation of [Avey's] Ibo ancestors." *Moorings and Metaphors: Figures of Culture and Gender in Black Women's Literature* (New Brunswick, N J: Rutgers University Press, 1992), 118. See also Abena P. A. Busia, "What is your Nation? Reconnecting Africa and Her Diaspora through Paule Marshall's *Praisesong for the Widow,*" in *Changing Our Own Words: Essays on Criticism, Theory, and Writing by Black Women,* ed. Cheryl A. Wall (New Brunswick and London: Rutgers University Press, 1989), 204.
4. Kimberly Rae Connor regards Avey Johnson as an "involuntary convert"—one who undergoes a spiritual conversion despite her strong resistance to the process. *Conversions and Visions in the Writings of African-American Women* (Knoxville: University of Tennessee Press, 1994).
5. According to Barbara Christian, the title of this section of the narrative, "Lavé Tête," refers to a Haitian voodoo ceremony in which the initiate is "washed clean." *Black Feminist Criticism,* 154.
6. Abena P. A. Busia describes praisesongs as traditional African "ceremonial social poems" that are "recited or sung in public at anniversaries and other celebrations, including funerals of the great. Praisesongs may embrace the history, myths, and legends of a whole people or their representative and

can be used to celebrate communal triumph or the greatness of rulers, and the nobility of the valiant and brave, whether in life or death. . . . They can also be sung to mark social transition. Sung as a part of rites of passage, they mark the upward movement of a person from one group to the next." "What is your Nation?" 198.

7. Sterling Stuckey, analyzing the continuity between African rituals and African American cultural practices that survived despite the horrifying abuses of slavery and its aftermath, observes that "The final gift of African 'tribalism' in the nineteenth century was its life as a lingering memory in the minds of American slaves. That memory enabled them to go back to the sense of community in the traditional African setting and include all Africans in their common experience of oppression in North America." *Slave Culture: Nationalist Theory and the Foundations of Black America* (New York: Oxford University Press, 1987), 3.

8. *Slave Culture,* 12. Stuckey traces the transformation of the circular rituals of West African tribal groups into the Ring Shout as it was practiced in North America. During the nineteenth century, the spiritual ritual was so pervasive that it was regarded as a threat to Christian conversion (93). The Ring Shout significantly shaped not only the evolution of African-American religious experience but, through its rhythms, the development of unique musical forms. According to Marshall Stearns, the "continued existence of the ring-shout is of critical importance to jazz, because it means that an assortment of West African musical characteristics are preserved, more or less intact, in the United States—from rhythms and blue tonality, through the falsetto break and the call-and-response pattern, to the songs of allusion and even the motions of African dance." Qtd. in Stuckey, 95.

9. As Helen Lock phrases it, Avey's given name suggests that she is "an avatar of all the past and present consciousnesses that have contributed to the making of Avey Johnson." "'Building Up from Fragments': The Oral Memory Process in Some Recent African-American Written Narratives," in *Race-ing Representation: Voice, History, and Sexuality,* ed. Kostas Myrsiades and Linda Myrsiades (Lanham, MD: Rowman and Littlefield, 1998), 205.

10. Barbara Christian argues that "Marshall's entire opus focuses on the consciousness of black people as they remember, retain, develop their sense of spiritual/sensual integrity and individual selves against the materialism that characterizes American societies" (149). A vital part of Avey Johnson's "journey back to herself" in *Praisesong for the Widow* is "the African wisdom still alive in the rituals of black societies in the West." *Black Feminist Criticism,* 183. According to Abena Busia, Marshall "articulates the scattering of the African peoples as a trauma—a trauma that is constantly repeated anew in the lives of her lost children. The life of the modern world and the conditions under which Afro-Americans have to live, the sacrifices they must

make to succeed on the terms of American society, invariably mean a severing from their cultural roots, and, as Avey learns to her cost, this is tantamount to a repetition, in her private life, of that original historical separation." "What is your Nation?" 197. Thomas Couser observes that Avey's experience in Carriacou signifies the "return of the repressed tribal consciousness." Additionally, readers of the narrative, "regardless of their own ethnicity, [are enlisted] in the reconstruction of the lost history of the minority group." Couser, "Oppression and Repression: Personal and Collective Memory in Paule Marshall's *Praisesong for the Widow* and Leslie Silko's *Ceremony*," in *Memory and Cultural Politics: New Approaches to American Ethnic Literatures,* ed. Amritjit Singh, Joseph T. Skerrett, Jr., and Robert E. Hogan (Boston: Northeastern University Press, 1996), 117.

11. "Return of a Native Daughter: An Interview with Paule Marshall and Maryse Condé, trans. John Williams, *SAGE: A Scholarly Journal on Black Women* 3, no. 2 (1986): 52. More recently, Marshall has stressed the importance of the multiple geographical and ethnic dimensions of her personal history, commenting, "my way of seeing the world has been . . . profoundly shaped by my dual experiences, those two communities, West Indian and African-American. Those two great traditions . . . nurtured me, they inspired me, they formed me. I am fascinated by the interaction of the two cultures, which [are] really, as I see it, one tradition, one culture." "An Interview with Paule Marshall," Daryl Cumber Dance, *Southern Review* 28, no. 2 (Winter 1992): 16.

Chapter 7
Haunted Longing and the Presence of Absence: *Jazz*, Toni Morrison

1. Marsha Darling, "In the Realm of Responsibility: A Conversation with Toni Morrison" (1988), in *Conversations with Toni Morrison,* ed. Danille Taylor-Guthrie (Jackson: University Press of Mississippi, 1994), 254 (Morrison's emphasis).

2. Jane Bakerman, "'The Seams Can't Show': An Interview with Toni Morrison," in *Conversations,* ed. Taylor-Guthrie, 40.

3. Anne Koenen, "The One Out of Sequence: An Interview with Toni Morrison," in *Conversations,* ed. Taylor-Guthrie, 71.

4. Virtually all music scholars concur that jazz developed from and elaborates on the characteristic elements of the blues, including the basic twelve-bar structure with flatted third, fifth, and seventh notes, and the call-and-response pattern. As Mary Ellison describes the essential relationship between the two forms, "Jazz and blues have always been different genres of the same music[,] with jazz emphasizing the instrumental and blues the vocal content. Jazz has consistently been dependent on the blues, from its

inception to its most recent developments." *Extensions of the Blues* (New York: Riverrun, 1989), 19. Moreover, as Albert Murray has pointed out, within blues music there is often a contradiction between the vocal expression—which may and often does verbalize melancholy—and the instrumental expression: "more often than not even as the words of the lyrics recount a tale of woe, the instrumentation may mock, shout defiance, or voice resolution and determination." *Stomping the Blues* (1976; rpt., New York: Vintage, 1982), 69.

5. A number of scholars have discussed Morrison's preoccupation throughout her fiction with absence and loss. Of *Beloved,* Rafael Pérez-Torres notes the "interplay between presence and absence" that shapes the several narrative levels and thematic concerns of the narrative. "Knitting and Knotting the Narrative Thread—*Beloved* as Postmodern Novel," in *Toni Morrison: Critical and Theoretical Approaches,* ed. Nancy J. Peterson (Baltimore: Johns Hopkins University Press, 1997), 93. According to Patricia McKee, "In African-American life Morrison identifies both material losses—missing persons, and parts of persons—and nonmaterial losses—lost relations, lost possibilities—whose absence is historically significant." "Spacing and Placing Experience in Toni Morrison's *Sula,*" in Peterson, ed., 59. Phillip Novak's focus on elements of mourning in *Sula* parallels my argument for the recurrent presence of what I have termed *cultural mourning* in Morrison's work as a whole. As he phrases it, "To grieve for Sula—to 'miss' her, in Morrison's term—is . . . to grieve for an African American cultural past the novel, from its inception, imagines as irrevocably lost. Such grieving can never be completely worked through." However, "Morrison's efforts to transform mourning into melancholia are paradoxically therapeutic. . . . [S]uch a transformation is aimed not only at paying tribute to the past but also at securing the present." "'Circles and Circles of Sorrow': In the Wake of Morrison's *Sula,*" *PMLA* 114, no. 2 (1999): 191. See also Robert Grant, "Absence into Presence: The Thematics of Memory and 'Missing' Subjects in Toni Morrison's *Sula,*" in *Critical Essays on Toni Morrison,* ed. Nellie Y. McKay (Boston: G. K. Hall, 1988), 90–103; Emily Miller Budick, "Absence, Loss, and the Space of History in Toni Morrison's *Beloved,*" *Arizona Quarterly* 48, no. 3 (Autumn 1992): 117–38; and Mae G. Henderson, "Toni Morrison's *Beloved*" in *Comparative American Identities: Race, Sex, and Nationality in the Modern Text,* ed. Hortense J. Spillers (New York: Routledge, 1990), 62–86.

6. Toni Morrison, *Beloved* (New York: Knopf, 1987), 5.

7. "A Conversation: Gloria Naylor and Toni Morrison," in *Conversations,* ed. Taylor-Guthrie, 209.

8. Angels Carabi, "Interview with Toni Morrison," *Belles Lettres* 10, no. 2 (1995): 41.

9. Toni Morrison, *Jazz* (1992; rpt., New York: Plume/Penguin, 1993), 3. Subsequent references in the text are to this edition.

10. Considering the correspondences between musical and narrative techniques in *Jazz,* Eusebio L. Rodrigues contends that Morrison employs punctuation, repetition, rhythm, and other linguistic elements in distinctive ways to mimic jazz and to transform the text into "a musical score" (246), whereby "the reader has to actively participate in the process of musicalizing the text before it will yield up all its meanings." "Experiencing *Jazz,*" in Peterson, ed., 249. Paula Gallant Eckard further proposes that in effect, jazz is "the mysterious narrator of the novel" (11) and that "jazz as narrator constructs the text" (18). "The Interplay of Music, Language, and Narrative in Toni Morrison's *Jazz,*" *CLA Journal* 38, no.1 (1994). The analogies between the improvisatory nature of jazz and the fluid structure of literary narrative operate in the other direction as well, according to ethnomusicologist Paul Berliner, who proposes that jazz improvisations might be likened to storytelling:

> In part, the metaphor of storytelling suggests the dramatic molding of creations to include movement through successive events "transcending" particular repetitive, formal aspects of the composition and featuring distinct types of musical material. . . . Paul Wertico advises his students that in initiating a solo they should think in terms of developing specific "characters and a plot. . . . You introduce these little different [musical] things that can be brought back out later on; and the way you put them together makes a little story. That can be [on the scale of] a sentence or a paragraph. . . . The real great cats can write novels." *Thinking in Jazz: The Infinite Art of Improvisation* (Chicago: University of Chicago Press, 1994), 202 (ellipses and brackets in original).

11. Nellie McKay, "An Interview with Toni Morrison," in *Toni Morrison: Critical Perspectives Past and Present,* ed. Henry Gates Louis, Jr. and K. A. Appiah (New York: Amistad, 1993), 411.

12. Carabi, 41–42.

13. Morrison wrote her M.A. thesis at Cornell on the theme of alienation and suicide in the novels of Woolf and Faulkner. Virginia Woolf's important manifesto of modernism, "Modern Fiction," provides an interesting intertextual echo of the passage from *Jazz* quoted above: "Life is not a series of gig lamps symmetrically arranged; life is a luminous halo, a semi-transparent envelope surrounding us from the beginning of consciousness to the end. Is it not the task of the novelist to convey this varying, this unknown and uncircumscribed spirit, whatever aberration or complexity it may display, with as little mixture of the alien and external as possible?" "Modern Fic-

tion," *The Common Reader,* First Series, ed. Andrew McNeillie (1925; rpt.,
New York: Harcourt, 1984), 150. In a meditation on the similarities and differences between Woolf and Morrison (addressed as if to Morrison), Barbara T. Christian notes, "although your and Virginia's views of the novel
might seem to be worlds apart, both of your writings are riveted on the
relationship between the inner life of your characters and the world within
which they find themselves, the object in fact of their consciousness." "Layered Rhythms: Virginia Woolf and Toni Morrison," in Peterson, ed., 28.

14. Carabi, 42.

15. Henry Louis Gates, Jr., tracing the history of the "voice in the text" in
African American literature, proposes that the "trope of the Talking Book"
embodies the "paradox of representing, of containing somehow, the oral
within the written. . . ." *The Signifying Monkey: A Theory of Afro-American
Literary Criticism* (New York: Oxford University Press, 1988), 131–2.

16. Morrison's novels before *Jazz* also feature a number of orphaned children—whether understood literally, like Cholly Breedlove (*The Bluest Eye*),
who was abandoned at birth by his mother in a dump heap and whose
father never knew of his existence; and Sethe (*Beloved*), who was separated
by slavery from her mother and never knew her father; or emotional
orphans, like Pecola Breedlove (*The Bluest Eye*) and Sula Peace *(Sula),* who
experience themselves as radically estranged from their parents; or cultural
orphans, like Jadine Childs (*Tar Baby),* who, besides being literally parentless,
wobbles ambivalently between black and white worlds. Using a telling
metaphor, Ann Douglas has observed that African Americans, "whose
ancestors were kidnapped from their native land and sold into slavery in an
alien country, were, in fact, America's only truly orphan group." *Terrible
Honesty: Mongrel Manhattan in the 1920s* (New York: Farrar, Straus and
Giroux, 1995), 83.

17. Gurleen Grewal argues that the "theme of dispossession" is a central theme
of the novel. *Circles of Sorrow, Lines of Struggle: The Novels of Toni Morrison*
(Baton Rouge: Louisiana State University Press, 1998), 129.

18. Morrison interview with Ntozake Shange, quoted by Nancy J. Peterson in
"'Say make me, remake me': Toni Morrison and the Reconstruction of
African-American History," in Peterson, ed., 209.

19. Ibid.

20. Marianne DeKoven, using the term *utopia* rather than *paradise,* stresses the
"intensity of Morrison's . . . utopian desire" in the "push of [her] literary
writing toward transcendence" in *Beloved.* However, during the historical
moment in which *Beloved* is set, "both the New World Eden and white
Abolitionism are vitiated by slavery and racism." "Postmodernism and Post-
Utopian Desire in Toni Morrison and E. L. Doctorow," in Peterson, ed., 116.

21. Understood psychoanalytically, the figure of the mother "remembered"
from infancy is a not a true memory but a fantasy of her, a phantom or

imago—"a kind of stereotyped mental picture that forms in the unconscious, reflecting not only real experiences" but also other early experiences that occur before a child's emotional differentiation from its mother and that are thus attributed to her. See Janine Chasseguet-Smirgel, "Being a Mother and Being a Psychoanalyst: Two Impossible Professions," in *Representations of Motherhood,* ed. Donna Bassin, Margaret Honey, and Maryle Mahrer Kaplan (New Haven: Yale University Press, 1994), 115.

22. Mario Jacoby, *Longing for Paradise: Psychological Perspectives on an Archetype,* trans. Myron B. Gubitz (Boston: Sigo Press, 1985), 5, 8.

23. The phrase recalls the final line of *Mrs. Dalloway,* when Clarissa returns to her party; from Peter Walsh's perspective, "For there she was." *Mrs. Dalloway* (1925; rpt., New York: Harcourt Brace Jovanovich, 1990), 194.

24. Again, Woolf comes to mind, particularly in the evocation of the blank space of absence signified by the loss of the mother in the elegiac "Time Passes" section of *To the Lighthouse* (1927; rpt., New York: Harcourt Brace Jovanovich, 1989).

25. John Bowlby, *Loss: Sadness and Depression,* vol. 3 of *Attachment and Loss,* 3 vols. (New York: Basic, 1980), 37.

26. Ibid., 161.

27. Morrison has acknowledged her debt to Faulkner, commenting, "William Faulkner had an enormous effect on me, an enormous effect. . . . My reasons, I think, for being interested and deeply moved by all his subjects had something to do with my desire to find out something about this country and that articulation of its past that was not available in history." "Faulkner and Women," in *Faulkner and Women: Faulker and Yoknapatawpha, 1985,* ed. Doreen Fowler and Ann J. Abadie (Jackson: University Press of Mississippi, 1986), 296. Both Charles Bon of Faulkner's *Absalom, Absalom!* and Golden Gray of *Jazz* are effeminate, light-skinned mulattos. Each, illegitimate and defined by the radical absence of the father who rejected or deserted him, is haunted by the wish to be emotionally legitimized and acknowledged by that father. Thomas Sutpen's legitimate son and Golden Gray's putative father are both named Henry. See Roberta Rubenstein, "History and Story, Sign and Design: Faulknerian and Postmodern Voices in Toni Morrison's *Jazz,*" in *Unflinching Gaze: Morrison and Faulkner Re-Envisioned,* ed. Carol A. Kolmerten, Stephen M. Ross, and Judith Bryant Wittenburg (Jackson: University Press of Mississippi, 1997), 152–64.

28. In her acceptance of the Robert F. Kennedy Award for Fiction, Morrison used the term "re-member"—emphasizing the hyphenation—in her comments about writing *Beloved.* American University, Washington, DC, May 13, 1988, videocassette. Barbara G. Meyerhoff credits the anthropologist Victor Turner with the origination of the hyphenated word, which emphasizes "the reaggregation of one's members, the figures who properly belong to one's life story, one's own prior selves, the significant others without

which the story cannot be completed." "Re-membered Lives," *Parabola* V, no. 1 (February 1980): 77.

29. Carabi, 43.
30. "A Conversation: Gloria Naylor and Toni Morrison," in *Conversations,* ed. Taylor-Guthrie, 208.
31. Ibid., 217.
32. Sigmund Freud, "Mourning and Melancholia," 1915, 1917, *The Standard Edition of the Complete Psychological Works of Sigmund Freud,* vol. 14, trans. and ed. James Strachey (London: Hogarth Press, 1957), 244–5.
33. Ralph Ellison, *Shadow and Act* (New York: Random House, 1964), 78–9.

Chapter 8
Memory, Mourning, and Maternal Triangulations:
Mama Day, Gloria Naylor

1. Gloria Naylor, *Mama Day* (New York: Ticknor & Fields, 1988), 10. Subsequent references in the text are to this edition.
2. In Susan Meisenhelder's view, George has been so co-opted by white patriarchal values that he is a black cultural orphan, trained to be a parody of the stereotypical white male. "'The Whole Picture' in Gloria Naylor's *Mama Day,*" *African American Review* 27, no. 3 (1993): 407. A number of commentators on the novel, including—besides Meisenhelder—Lindsey Tucker, Helen Fiddyment Levy, and Bonnie Winsbro, discuss its polarized perspectives. See Tucker, "Recovering the Conjure Woman: Texts and Contexts in Gloria Naylor's *Mama Day,*" *African American Review* 28, no. 2 (1994): 173–88; Levy, *Fiction of the Home Place: Jewett, Cather, Glasgow, Porter, Welty, and Naylor* (Jackson: University Press of Mississippi, 1992); and Winsbro, *Supernatural Forces: Belief, Difference, and Power in Contemporary Works by Ethnic Women* (Amherst: University of Massachusetts Press, 1993).
3. Lindsey Tucker observes that Willow Springs alludes to the island of Shakespeare's *The Tempest.* "Miranda's name (which means 'worker of wonders') suggests Shakespeare's *Tempest* with a radical rewriting of the father-daughter relationship. Ophelia's name also has Shakespearean associations, especially in view of the fact that the grandmother, also named Ophelia, has gone mad and committed suicide by drowning." Tucker, 184. Peter Erickson, exploring Shakespearean allusions in Naylor's work, argues that in *Mama Day,* Naylor "create[s] a black female equivalent to Prospero" while "largely ignoring Caliban" and subversively reconfiguring elements of race, class, and gender in *The Tempest.* "'Shakespeare's Black?': The Role of Shakespeare in Naylor's Novels," in *Gloria Naylor: Critical Perspectives Past and Present,* ed. Henry Louis Gates, Jr. and K. A. Appiah (New York: Amistad Press, 1993), 243.

4. Chorodow's feminist revision of Freudian theory arises from her close attention to the diverse trajectories of the preoedipal phase of psychological development for females and males. She argues that, "Because of their mothering by women, girls come to experience themselves as less separate than boys, as having more permeable ego boundaries. Girls come to define themselves more in relation to others" (93). Moreover, "being a grown woman and mother also means having been the daughter of a mother, which affects the nature of her motherliness and quality of her mothering" (98). Additionally, "girls do not 'resolve' their oedipus complex to the same extent as do boys. They neither repress nor give up so absolutely their preoedipal and oedipal attachment to their mother, nor their oedipal attachment to their father. This means that girls grow up with more ongoing preoccupations with both internalized object-relationships and with external relationships as well. These ongoing preoccupations in a girl grow especially out of her early relationship to her mother. They consist in an ambivalent struggle for a sense of separateness and independence from her mother and emotional, if not, erotic, bisexual oscillation between mother and father—between preoccupation with 'mother-child' issues and 'male-female' issues" (168). *The Reproduction of Motherhood: Psychoanalysis and the Sociology of Gender* (Berkeley: University of California Press, 1978).

5. Suzanne Juhasz regards George as the "maternal hero—that fantasy women create so that true love is possible for us as grown women living in a patriarchal culture. . . ." *Reading from the Heart: Women, Literature, and the Search for True Love* (New York: Viking, 1994), 193.

6. As Virginia Woolf phrased it so memorably in another context, "we think back through our mothers if we are women." *A Room of One's Own* (1929. Reprint, New York: Harcourt Brace Jovanovich, 1989), 76.

7. Helen Fiddyment Levy proposes that the nurturing mother figure that Mama Day experiences is the "goddess" Sapphira. "Arising out of a historical memory, a racial memory as well as a female memory, Sapphira's name comes only when Miranda passes through rationality, through male myth, coming at last through dreams to the first seer" (219). Sapphira, Mama Day, and Cocoa "form a sort of woman's trinity with mother, daughter, and spirit" (220). *Fiction of the Home Place,* 220.

8. Virginia C. Fowler, *Gloria Naylor: In Search of Sanctuary* (New York: Twayne, 1996), 118.

9. Bonnie Winsbro argues that Cocoa ultimately reconciles the opposing worlds of George and Mama Day. "Cocoa discovers, after her loss of the world she shared with George, the power to construct a new world—one that is fixed in neither Willow Springs nor New York but that is founded on beliefs drawn from both worlds, supplementing a belief in self with a belief in external powers." *Supernatural Forces,* 125. Suzanne Juhasz proposes that

"As a ghost, George has shed the encumbrances of his masculinity. . . . Cocoa and George do get to be together always, in a space that is safe from the evils of the patriarchy (to which George no longer belongs)." *Reading from the Heart,* 203–4.

Chapter 9
Amazing Grace: The Paradox of Paradise: *Paradise,*
Toni Morrison

1. Toni Morrison, "Home," in *The House That Race Built,* ed. Wahneema Lubiano (New York: Pantheon, 1997), 4. Subsequent references in the text to this essay are abbreviated as "Home."

2. It is tempting to consider parallels between Morrison's trilogy and Dante's *Divine Comedy. Beloved* recounts the Hell of slavery and its immediate aftermath, while *Paradise* not only shares the title of the final book of Dante's trilogy but traces a journey towards divine grace. However, the middle novel of Morrison's trilogy, *Jazz,* does not readily correspond to Purgatory. Anna Mulrine characterizes the trilogy as an "arc of inquiry into the dangers of excessive love—for children, mates, or God." "This Side of 'Paradise,'" *U. S. News and World Report,* 19 January 1998: 71.

3. Ibid.

4. Toni Morrison, *Paradise* (New York: Knopf, 1998), 96. Subsequent references in the text are to this edition.

5. As Nancy J. Peterson phrases it, "we read the entire novel waiting for a second shooting that never happens." "'Say make me, remake me': Toni Morrison and the Reconstruction of African-American History," in *Toni Morrison: Critical and Theoretical Approaches,* ed. Peterson (Baltimore: Johns Hopkins University Press, 1997), 213.

6. Either intentionally or inadvertently, Morrison has conflated details from the lives of more than one martyred saint. Agatha of Sicily and several other female martyrs were tortured by having their breasts cut off and at least one offered the severed breasts to her persecutors. However, this was not true for Catherine of Siena, who martyred herself through continuous fasting and "holy anorexia." See Caroline Walker Bynum, *Holy Feast and Holy Fast: The Religious Significance of Food to Medieval Women* (Berkeley: University of California Press, 1987), 83, 86–88.

7. See n. 16 in chapter 7 of this study.

8. In his typology of such myths, Mircea Eliade notes that "the supreme *paradisiac* element" is "immortality." *Myths, Dreams, and Mysteries,* trans. Philip Mairet (New York: Harper and Row, 1960), 59, emphasis in original.

9. As Morrison has explained her reason for withholding this information, "The tradition in writing is that if you don't mention a character's race, he's white. Any deviation from that, you have to say. What I wanted to do was

not erase race, but force readers either to care about it or see if it disturbs them that they don't know. Does it interfere with the story? Does it make you uncomfortable? Or do I succeed in making the characters so clear, their interior lives so distinctive, that you realize (a) it doesn't matter, and (b) more important, that when you know their race, it's the least amount of information to know about a person." Qtd. in David Streitfeld, "The Novelist's Prism," *The Washington Post*, 6 January 1998, sec. B, p. 2.

10. According to the scholar of religion, Anders Nygren, "*agape* is spontaneous and 'unmotivated'. . . . When it is said that God loves man, this is not a judgment on what man is like, but on what God is like" (85). Furthermore, "there is from man's side no way at all that leads to God. . . . God must Himself come to meet man and offer him His fellowship. There is thus no way for man to come to God, but only a way for God to come to man: the way of Divine forgiveness, Divine love" (89). "Agape and Eros," in *Eros, Agape, and Philia: Readings in the Philosophy of Love*, ed. Alan Soble (New York: Paragon, 1989).

11. The episode recalls a central episode in Faulkner's *Light in August:* Joanna Burden also experiences erotic desire late in life and nearly consumes her lover, Joe Christmas, before he murders her; she is instead consumed by the fire that destroys her house. See William Faulkner, *Light in August* (1932; rpt., New York: Vintage Random, 1990).

12. Caroline Walker Bynum notes that, for twelfth-century Cistercian monks, for example, "the most frequent meaning of mother-Jesus . . . [was] compassion, nurturing, and union" (151). In the fourteenth century, the anchoress Julian of Norwich, "whose vision of God as mother is one of the greatest reformulations in the history of theology" (136), delineated in her book of *Showings* the maternal qualities of Jesus. See *Jesus as Mother: Studies in the Spirituality of the High Middle Ages* (Berkeley: University of California Press, 1982). In representative passages, Julian of Norwich writes,

> And thus Jesus is our true Mother in kind, by our first making; and he is our true Mother in grace by his taking our kind that is made. All the fair working and all the sweet kindly office of dearworthy motherhood are appropriated to the Second Person. . . .
>
> But now it is necessary to say a little more about this "forth-spreading": as I understand it in our Lord, it means how we are brought again by the motherhood of mercy and grace into our natural home where first we were made by the motherhood of kind love, and this kind love, it will never leave us.
>
> Our kind Mother, our gracious Mother, for he would be wholly our mother in every way. . . ." *Revelations of Love*, trans. and ed. John Skinner (New York: Doubleday, 1997), from sections 59 and 60, 132–3.

13. Bynum, *Jesus as Mother*, 129 (my emphasis).

14. Mircea Eliade notes that the universal "nostalgia for Paradise" has as its source "those profound emotions that arise in man *[sic]* when, longing to participate in the sacred with the whole of his being, he discovers that this wholeness is only apparent, and that in reality the very constitution of his being is a consequence of its dividedness." *Myths, Dreams, and Mysteries,* 98.

15. The third eye is located "between and slightly above the eyebrows, at the center of the forehead. It is . . . regarded by occultists as the seat of psychic and paranormal powers." Neville Drury, *Dictionary of Mysticism and the Occult* (San Francisco: Harper and Row, 1985), 255.

16. Diane McKinney-Whetstone, "Interview with Toni Morrison," *BET Weekly, The Washington Post,* February 1998, 15.

17. "Toni Morrison Honored at Princeton Conference," *Toni Morrison Society Newsletter* 6, no. 1 (Spring 1999): 4.

18. Ibid.

Fixing the Past, Re-Placing Nostalgia

1. Victor Turner, *Dramas, Fields, and Metaphors: Symbolic Action in Human Society* (Ithaca: Cornell University Press, 1974), 239.

Works Cited

Abel, Elizabeth. *Virginia Woolf and the Fictions of Psychoanalysis.* Chicago: University of Chicago Press, 1989.

Allen, Paula Gunn. *The Sacred Hoop: Recovering the Feminine in American Indian Traditions.* Boston: Beacon Press, 1986.

Alvarez, Julia. *How the García Girls Lost Their Accents.* 1991. New York: Penguin Plume, 1992.

———. *Something to Declare.* Chapel Hill, NC: Algonquin Books, 1998.

Bakerman, Jane. "'The Seams Can't Show': An Interview with Toni Morrison." In *Conversations with Toni Morrison,* ed. Danille Taylor Guthrie, 30–42. Jackson: University Press of Mississippi, 1994.

Bassin, Donna. "Maternal Subjectivity in the Culture of Nostalgia: Mourning and Memory." In *Representations of Motherhood,* ed. Donna Bassin, Margaret Honey, and Maryle Mahrer Kaplan, 162–73. New Haven: Yale University Press, 1994.

Bassin, Donna, Margaret Honey, and Maryle Mahrer Kaplan, eds. *Representations of Motherhood.* New Haven: Yale University Press, 1994.

Berliner, Paul. *Thinking in Jazz: The Infinite Art of Improvisation.* Chicago: University of Chicago Press, 1994.

Bertelsen, Eve. "Interview with Doris Lessing." In *Doris Lessing,* ed. Eve Bertelsen, 93–118. Johannesburg: McGraw-Hill, 1985.

Bevis, William. "Native American Novels: Homing In." In *Recovering the Word: Essays on Native American Literature,* ed. Brian Swann and Arnold Krupat, 580–620. Berkeley: University of California Press, 1987.

Book of the Month Club promotional flyer on Toni Morrison's *Paradise,* 1997.

Bowlby, John. *Loss: Sadness and Depression.* Vol. 3 of *Attachment and Loss.* 3 vols. New York: Basic, 1980.

Busia, Abena P. A. "What is your Nation? Reconnecting Africa and Her Diaspora through Paule Marshall's *Praisesong for the Widow.*" In *Changing Our Own Words:*

Essays on Criticism, Theory, and Writing by Black Women, ed. Cheryl A. Wall, 196–211. New Brunswick: Rutgers University Press, 1989.

Bynum, Caroline Walker. *Holy Feast and Holy Fast: The Religious Significance of Food to Medieval Women.* Berkeley: University of California Press, 1987.

————. *Jesus as Mother: Studies in the Spirituality of the High Middle Ages.* Berkeley: University of California Press, 1982.

Carabi, Angels. "Interview with Toni Morrison." *Belles Lettres* 10, no. 2 (1995): 40–43.

Caramagno, Thomas C. *The Flight of the Mind: Virginia Woolf's Art and Manic-Depressive Illness.* Berkeley: University of California Press, 1992.

Carroll, Virginia Schaefer. "Wrestling with Change: Discourse Strategies in Anne Tyler." *Frontiers* 19, no.1 (1998): 86–109.

Casey, Edward S. *Remembering: A Phenomenological Study.* Bloomington: Indiana University Press, 1987.

Castelnuovo-Tedesco, Pietro. "Reminiscence and Nostalgia: The Pleasure and Pain of Remembering." In *The Course of Life: Psychoanalytic Contributions Toward Understanding Personality Development.* Vol. III: *Adulthood and the Aging Process,* ed. Stanley I. Greenspan and George H. Pollock, 115–27. Washington, DC: DHHS Pub. No. (ADM) 81–1000.

Chasseguet-Smirgel, Janine. "Being a Mother and Being a Psychoanalyst: Two Impossible Professions." In *Representations of Motherhood,* ed. Donna Bassin, Margaret Honey, and Maryle Mahrer Kaplan, 113–28. New Haven: Yale University Press, 1994.

Chodorow, Nancy. *The Reproduction of Motherhood: Psychoanalysis and the Sociology of Gender.* Berkeley: University of California Press, 1978.

Christian, Barbara. *Black Feminist Criticism: Perspectives on Black Women Writers.* New York: Pergamon, 1985.

————. "Layered Rhythms: Virginia Woolf and Toni Morrison." In *Toni Morrison: Critical and Theoretical Perspectives,* ed. Nancy J. Peterson, 19–36. Baltimore: Johns Hopkins University Press, 1997.

Cirlot, J. E. *A Dictionary of Symbols.* 2nd ed. Translated by Jack Sage. New York: Philosophical Library, 1971.

Collier, Eugenia. "The Closing of the Circle: Movement from Division to Wholeness in Paule Marshall's Fiction." In *Black Women Writers (1950–1980): A Critical Evaluation,* ed. Mari Evans, 295–315. Garden City, New York: Anchor/Doubleday, 1984.

Connor, Kimberly Rae. *Conversions and Visions in the Writings of African-American Women.* Knoxville: University of Tennessee Press, 1994.

Couser, G. Thomas. "Oppression and Repression: Personal and Collective Memory in Paule Marshall's *Praisesong for the Widow* and Leslie Silko's *Ceremony.*" In *Memory and Cultural Politics: New Approaches to American Ethnic Literatures,* ed. Amritjit Singh, Joseph T. Skerrett, Jr., and Robert E. Hogan, 106–20. Boston: Northeastern University Press, 1996.

Daly, Brenda O., and Maureen T. Reddy, eds. *Narrating Mothers: Theorizing Maternal Subjectivities.* Knoxville: University of Tennessee Press, 1991.

Dance, Daryl Cumber. "An Interview with Paule Marshall." *Southern Review* 28, no. 1 (Winter 1992): 1–20.

Darling, Marsha. "In the Realm of Responsibility: A Conversation with Toni Morrison." (1988). In *Conversations with Toni Morrison,* ed. Danille Taylor-Guthrie, 246–54. Jackson: University Press of Mississippi, 1994.

Davies, Carol Boyce. *Black Women, Writing and Identity: Migrations of the Subject.* New York: Routledge, 1994.

Davis, Fred. *Yearning for Yesterday: A Sociology of Nostalgia.* New York: The Free Press/Macmillan, 1979.

DeKoven, Marianne. "Postmodernism and Post-Utopian Desire in Toni Morrison and E. L. Doctorow." In *Toni Morrison: Critical and Theoretical Perspectives,* ed. Nancy J. Peterson, 111–30. Baltimore: Johns Hopkins University Press, 1997.

Delbanco, Nicholas. Review of *Earthly Possessions.* In *Critical Essays on Anne Tyler,* ed. Alice Hall Petry, 85–87. New York: G. K. Hall, 1992.

DeMott, Benjamin. "Funny, Wise, and True." In *Critical Essays on Anne Tyler,* ed. Alice Hall Petry, 111–14. New York: G. K. Hall, 1992.

DeSalvo, Louise. *Virginia Woolf: The Impact of Childhood Sexual Abuse on Her Life and Work.* Boston: Beacon Press, 1989.

Doane, Janice, and Devon Hodges. *Nostalgia and Sexual Difference: The Resistance to Contemporary Feminism.* New York: Methuen, 1987.

Douglas, Ann. *Terrible Honesty: Mongrel Manhattan in the 1920s.* New York: Farrar, Straus and Giroux, 1995.

Draine, Betsy. *Substance Under Pressure: Artistic Coherence and Evolving Form in the Novels of Doris Lessing.* Madison: University of Wisconsin Press, 1983.

Drury, Neville. *Dictionary of Mysticism and the Occult.* San Francisco: Harper and Row, 1985.

Eckard, Paula Gallant. "The Interplay of Music, Language, and Narrative in Toni Morrison's *Jazz.*" *CLA Journal* 38, no.1 (1994): 11–19.

Eliade, Mircea. *Myths, Dreams, and Mysteries.* Translated by Philip Mairet. New York: Harper and Row, 1960.

Eliot, T. S. *Collected Poems, 1909–1962.* London: Faber and Faber, 1963.

Ellison, Mary. *Extensions of the Blues.* New York: Riverrun, 1989.

Ellison, Ralph. *Shadow and Act.* New York: Random House, 1964.

Erickson, Peter. "'Shakespeare's Black?': The Role of Shakespeare in Naylor's Novels." In *Gloria Naylor: Critical Perspectives Past and Present,* ed. Henry Louis Gates, Jr. and K. A. Appiah, 231–48. New York: Amistad Press, 1993.

Fowler, Virginia C. *Gloria Naylor: In Search of Sanctuary.* New York: Twayne, 1996.

Frazer, Sir James George. *The Golden Bough.* Abridged ed. New York: Macmillan, 1940.

Freud, Sigmund. "Mourning and Melancholia." 1915, 1917. *The Standard Edition of the Complete Psychological Works of Sigmund Freud.* Vol. 14. Translated and edited by James Strachey. London: Hogarth Press, 1957, 243–58.

Friedman, Susan Stanford. *Mappings: Feminism and the Cultural Geographies of Encounter.* Princeton: Princeton University Press, 1998.

Gardiner, Judith Kegan. "The Exhilaration of Exile: Rhys, Stead, and Lessing." In *Women's Writing in Exile,* ed. Mary Lynn Broe and Angela Ingram, 134–50. Chapel Hill: University of North Carolina Press, 1989.

Gass, William. Interview with Nuruddin Farah, Han Vladislav, and Jorge Edwards. "The Philosophical Significance of Exile." In *Literature in Exile,* ed. John Glad. Durham: Duke University Press, 1990, 1–7.

Gates, Henry Louis, Jr. *The Signifying Monkey: A Theory of Afro-American Literary Criticism.* New York: Oxford University Press, 1988.

Gates, Henry Louis, Jr., and K. A. Appiah, eds. *Gloria Naylor: Critical Perspectives Past and Present.* New York: Amistad Press, 1993.

George, Rosemary Marangoly. *The Politics of Home: Postcolonial Relations and Twentieth-Century Fiction.* Cambridge: Cambridge University Press, 1996.

Gilbert, Sandra M., and Susan Gubar. *The Madwoman in the Attic: The Woman Writer and the Nineteenth-Century Literary Imagination.* New Haven: Yale University Press, 1979.

Gilligan, Carol. *In a Different Voice: Psychological Theory and Women's Development.* Cambridge: Harvard University Press, 1982.

Greene, Gayle. "Feminist Fiction and the Uses of Memory." *Signs: Journal of Women in Culture and Society* 16, no. 2 (Winter 1991): 290–321.

Grewal, Gurleen. *Circles of Sorrow, Lines of Struggle: The Novels of Toni Morrison.* Baton Rouge: Louisiana State University Press, 1998.

Gullette, Margaret Morganroth. *Declining to Decline: Cultural Combat and the Politics of the Midlife.* Charlottesville: University Press of Virginia, 1997.

Hirsch, Marianne. *The Mother-Daughter Plot: Narrative, Psychoanalysis, Feminism.* Bloomington: Indiana University Press, 1989.

Hoagland, Edward. "About Maggie, Who Tried Too Hard." In *Critical Essays on Anne Tyler,* ed. Alice Hall Petry, 110–44. New York: G. K. Hall, 1992.

Holloway, Karla F. C. *Moorings and Metaphors: Figures of Culture and Gender in Black Women's Literature.* New Brunswick, NJ: Rutgers University Press, 1992.

Ibsen, Henrik. *A Doll's House.* Translated by Peter Watts. 1879. Reprint, Harmondsworth: Penguin, 1965.

Jacobus, Mary. *First Things: The Maternal Imaginary in Literature, Art, and Psychoanalysis.* New York: Routledge, 1995.

Jacoby, Mario. *Longing for Paradise: Psychological Perspectives on an Archetype.* Translated by Myron B. Gubitz. Boston: Sigo Press, 1985.

Jones, Anne G. "Home at Last, and Homesick Again: The Ten Novels of Anne Tyler." *The Hollins Critic* 23, no. 2 (April 1986): 1–14.

Juhasz, Suzanne. *Reading from the Heart: Women, Literature, and the Search for True Love.* New York: Viking, 1994.

Julian of Norwich. *Revelations of Love.* Translated and edited by John Skinner. New York: Doubleday, 1997.

Kaminsky, Amy. *Reading the Body Politic: Feminist Criticism and Latin American Women Writers.* Minneapolis: University of Minneapolis Press, 1993.

Kaplan, Caren. "Territorializations: The Rewriting of Home and Exile in Western Feminist Discourse." *Cultural Critique* 6 (1987): 187–98.

Kappel-Smith, Diana. "Fickle desert blooms: opulent one year, no-shows the next." *Smithsonian* 25, no.12 (March 1995): 79–91.

Kingsolver, Barbara. *Animal Dreams.* New York: HarperCollins, 1991.

———. *The Bean Trees.* 1988. New York: HarperCollins, 1992.

———. *Homeland and Other Stories.* New York: Harper and Row, 1989.

———. *Pigs in Heaven.* New York: HarperCollins, 1993.

Koenen, Anne. "The One Out of Sequence: An Interview with Toni Morrison." *Conversations with Toni Morrison,* ed. Danille Taylor-Guthrie, 67–83. Jackson: University Press of Mississippi, 1994.

Kolodny, Annette. *The Lay of the Land: Metaphor as Experience and History in American Life and Letters.* Chapel Hill: University of North Carolina Press, 1975.

Kübler-Ross, Elisabeth. *On Death and Dying.* New York: Macmillan, 1969.

Lessing, Doris. *African Laughter. Four Visits to Zimbabwe.* New York: HarperCollins 1992.

———. *Briefing for a Descent into Hell.* 1971. Reprint, New York: Bantam, 1972

———. *Canopus in Argos: Archives. Re: Colonised Planet 5: Shikasta.* New York: Knopf, 1979.

———. *Going Home.* 1957. Reprint, New York: Ballantine, 1968.

———. *The Golden Notebook.* 1962. Reprint, New York: Bantam, 1973.

———. "Impertinent Daughters." *Granta* 14 (Winter 1984): 51–68.

———. *Love, Again.* New York: HarperCollins, 1995.

———. *Martha Quest.* Vol. 1 of *Children of Violence.* 1952. Reprint, New York: Simon and Schuster, 1964.

———. *Memoirs of a Survivor.* 1975. Reprint, New York: Bantam, 1979.

———. "My Mother's Life." *Granta* 17 (Fall 1985): 227–38.

———. *A Proper Marriage.* In Vol. 1 of *Children of Violence.* 1954. Reprint, New York: Simon and Schuster, 1964.

———. "To Room Nineteen." *A Man and Two Women.* New York: Simon and Schuster, 1963, 278–316.

———. *Under My Skin: Volume One of my Autobiography to 1949.* New York: HarperCollins, 1994.

Levy, Helen Fiddyment. *Fiction of the Home Place: Jewett, Cather, Glasgow, Porter, Welty, and Naylor.* Jackson: University Press of Mississippi, 1992.

Levy-Warren, Marsha H. "Moving to a New Culture: Cultural Identity, Loss, and Mourning." In *The Psychology of Separation and Loss: Perspectives on Development, Life Transitions, and Clinical Practice,* ed. Jonathan Bloom-Feshbach, Sally Bloom-Feshbach et al., 300–15. San Francisco: Jossey-Bass, 1987.

Lincoln, Kenneth. *Native American Renaissance.* Berkeley: University of California Press, 1983.

Lock, Helen. "'Building Up from Fragments': The Oral Memory Process in Some Recent African-American Written Narratives." In *Race-ing Representation: Voice, History, and Sexuality,* ed. Kostas Myrsiades and Linda Myrsiades, 200–12. Lanham, MD: Rowman and Littlefield, 1998.

Lowenthal, David. *The Past is a Foreign Country.* Cambridge: Cambridge University Press, 1985.

Mails, Thomas E. *The Cherokee People: The Story of the Cherokees from Earliest Origins to Contemporary Times.* Tulsa, OK: Council Oak Books, 1992.

Mandell, Jonathan. "Uprooted but Still Blooming." *New York Newsday,* 17 November 1994: B4–5, 12.

Marris, Peter. *Loss and Change.* 2nd ed. London: Routledge, 1996.

Marshall, Paule. *Praisesong for the Widow.* New York: G. P. Putnam's, 1983.

———. "Return of a Native Daughter: An Interview with Paule Marshall and Maryse Condé," translated by John Williams. *SAGE: Scholarly Journal on Black Women* 3, no. 2 (1986): 52–53.

Martin, Biddy and Chandra Talpade Mohanty. "Feminist Politics: What's Home Got to Do with It?" In *Feminist Studies/Critical Studies,* ed. Teresa de Lauretis, 191–212. Bloomington: Indiana University Press, 1986.

McKay, Nellie. "An Interview with Toni Morrison." In *Toni Morrison: Critical Perspectives Past and Present,* ed. Henry Gates Louis, Jr. and K. A. Appiah, 394–411. New York: Amistad, 1993.

McKee, Patricia. "Spacing and Placing Experience in Toni Morrison's *Sula.*" In *Toni Morrison: Critical and Theoretical Perspectives,* ed. Nancy J. Peterson, 37–62. Baltimore and London: Johns Hopkins University Press, 1997.

McKinney-Whetstone, Diane. "Interview with Toni Morrison." *BET Weekly, The Washington Post.* February 1998, 15–16.

Meisenhelder, Susan. "'The Whole Picture' in Gloria Naylor's *Mama Day.*" *African American Review* 27, no. 3 (1993): 405–19.

Meyerhoff, Barbara G. "Re-membered Lives." *Parabola* V, no. 1 (February 1980), 74–77.

Morrison, Toni. *Beloved.* New York: Knopf, 1987.

———. "Faulkner and Women." In *Faulkner and Women: Faulker and Yoknapatawpha, 1985,* ed. Doreen Fowler and Ann J. Abadie, 295–302. Jackson: University Press of Mississippi, 1986.

———. "Home." In *The House That Race Built,* ed. Wahneema Lubiano. New York: Pantheon, 1997, 3–12.

———. *Jazz.* 1992. Reprint, New York: Plume/Penguin, 1993.

———. *Paradise.* New York: Knopf, 1998.

———. Robert F. Kennedy Book Award Acceptance Speech. American University, Washington, DC, May 13, 1988. Videocassette.

Mulrine, Anna. "This Side of 'Paradise.'" *U. S. News and World Report,* 19 January 1998: 71.

Murray, Albert. *Stomping the Blues.* 1976. Reprint, New York: Vintage, 1982.

Naylor, Gloria. "A Conversation: Gloria Naylor and Toni Morrison." In *Conversations with Toni Morrison,* ed. Danille Taylor-Guthrie, 188–217. Jackson: University Press of Mississippi, 1994.

————. *Mama Day.* New York: Ticknor & Fields, 1988.

Novak, Phillip. "'Circles and Circles of Sorrow': In the Wake of Morrison's *Sula.*" *PMLA* 114, no. 2 (1999): 184–93.

Nygren, Anders. "Agape and Eros." *In Eros, Agape, and Philia: Readings in the Philosophy of Love,* ed. Alan Soble, 85–95. New York: Paragon, 1989.

Pérez-Torres, Rafael. "Knitting and Knotting the Narrative Thread—*Beloved* as Postmodern Novel." In *Toni Morrison: Critical and Theoretical Perspectives,* ed. Nancy J. Peterson, 91–109. Baltimore: Johns Hopkins University Press, 1997.

Perry, Donna. Interviews with Barbara Kingsolver and Gloria Naylor. *Backtalk: Women Writers Speak Out.* New Brunswick, N. J.: Rutgers University Press, 1993, 143–69 and 217–44.

Peterson, Nancy J. "'Say make me, remake me': Toni Morrison and the Reconstruction of African-American History." In *Toni Morrison: Critical and Theoretical Approaches,* ed. Nancy J. Peterson, 210–21. Baltimore: Johns Hopkins University Press, 1997, .

————, ed. *Toni Morrison: Critical and Theoretical Approaches.* Baltimore and London: Johns Hopkins University Press, 1997.

Petry, Alice Hall. "Tyler and Feminism." In *Anne Tyler as Novelist,* ed. Dale Salwak, 33–42. Iowa City: University of Iowa Press, 1994.

————, ed. *Critical Essays on Anne Tyler.* New York: G. K. Hall, 1992.

Pollock, George. *The Mourning-Liberation Process.* 2 vols. Madison, CT.: International Universities Press, 1989.

Raitt, Suzanne. *Virginia Woolf's To the Lighthouse.* New York: St. Martin's Press, 1990.

Raphael, Beverley. *The Anatomy of Bereavement.* New York: Basic Books, 1983.

Rodrigues, Eusebio L. "Experiencing Jazz." In *Toni Morrison: Critical and Theoretical Perspectives,* ed. Nancy J. Peterson, 245–66. Baltimore and London: Johns Hopkins University Press, 1997.

Rose, Ellen Cronan. "Doris Lessing's *Città Felice.*" In *Critical Essays on Doris Lessing,* ed. Claire Sprague and Virginia Tiger, 141–53. Boston: G. K. Hall, 1986.

Rosenman, Ellen Bayuk. *The Invisible Presence: Virginia Woolf and the Mother-Daughter Relationship.* Baton Rouge: Louisiana State University Press, 1986.

Rubenstein, Roberta. *Boundaries of the Self: Gender, Culture, Fiction.* Urbana: University of Illinois Press, 1987.

————. "Fixing the Past: Yearning and Nostalgia in Woolf and Lessing." In *Woolf and Lessing: Breaking the Mold,* ed. Ruth Saxton and Jean Tobin, 15–38. New York: St. Martin's, 1994.

————. "History and Story, Sign and Design: Faulknerian and Postmodern Voices in Toni Morrison's *Jazz.*" In *Unflinching Gaze: Morrison and Faulkner Re-*

Envisioned, ed. Carol A. Kolmerten, Stephen M. Ross, and Judith Bryant Wittenburg, 152–64. Jackson: University Press of Mississippi, 1997.

———. *The Novelistic Vision of Doris Lessing: Breaking the Forms of Consciousness.* Urbana: University of Illinois Press, 1979.

———. "Singing the Blues/Reclaiming Jazz: Toni Morrison and Cultural Mourning." *Mosaic:* The Interarts Project, Part II: Cultural Agendas, Vol. 31, no. 2 (1998): 147–63.

Silko, Leslie Marmon. *Ceremony.* 1977. Reprint, New York: New American Library, 1978.

Spilka, Mark. *Virginia Woolf's Quarrel with Grieving.* Lincoln: University of Nebraska Press, 1980.

Sprague, Claire. *Rereading Doris Lessing: Narrative Patterns of Doubling and Repetition.* Chapel Hill: University of North Carolina Press, 1987.

Starobinski, Jean. "The Idea of Nostalgia." *Diogenes* 54 (1966): 81–103.

Streitfeld, David. "The Novelist's Prism." *The Washington Post,* 6 January 1998, sec. B, pp. 1–2.

Stuckey, Sterling. *Slave Culture: Nationalist Theory and the Foundations of Black America.* New York: Oxford University Press, 1987.

Taylor, Jenny. "Memory and Desire on Going Home: The Deconstruction of a Colonial Radical." In *Doris Lessing,* ed. Eve Bertelsen, 55–63. Johannesburg: McGraw-Hill, 1985.

Taylor-Guthrie, Danille, ed. *Conversations with Toni Morrison.* Jackson: University Press of Mississippi, 1994.

Tiger, Virginia. Review: Doris Lessing, "Impertinent Daughters" and "Autobiography (Part Two): My Mother's Life." *Doris Lessing Newsletter* 10, no. 2 (Fall 1986): 7, 14.

"Toni Morrison Honored at Princeton Conference." *Toni Morrison Society Newsletter* 6, no. 1 (Spring 1999): 1–4.

Tucker, Lindsey. "Recovering the Conjure Woman: Texts and Contexts in Gloria Naylor's *Mama Day.*" *African American Review* 28, no. 2 (1994): 173–88.

Turner, Victor. *Dramas, Fields, and Metaphors: Symbolic Action in Human Society.* Ithaca: Cornell University Press, 1974.

Tyler, Anne. *Celestial Navigation.* New York: Knopf, 1974.

———. *Dinner at the Homesick Restaurant.* New York: Knopf, 1982.

———. *Ladder of Years.* New York: Knopf, 1995.

Updike, John. "Loosened Roots." In *Critical Essays on Anne Tyler,* ed. Alice Hall Petry, 88–91. New York: G. K. Hall, 1992.

Voelker, Joseph C. *Art and the Accidental in Anne Tyler.* Columbia: University of Missouri Press, 1989.

Weston, Jessie. *From Ritual to Romance.* 1920. Reprint, Garden City, NY: Doubleday, 1957.

Winsbro, Bonnie. *Supernatural Forces: Belief, Difference, and Power in Contemporary Works by Ethnic Women.* Amherst: University of Massachusetts Press, 1993.

Woolf, Virginia. "Modern Fiction." *The Common Reader,* First Series, ed. Andrew McNeillie. 1925. Reprint, New York: Harcourt, 1984.

———. *Moments of Being: Unpublished Autobiographical Writings,* ed. Jeanne Schulkind. New York: Harcourt Brace Jovanovich, 1976.

———. *Mrs. Dalloway.* 1925. Reprint, New York: Harcourt Brace Jovanovich, 1990.

———. *A Room of One's Own.* 1929. Reprint, New York: Harcourt Brace Jovanovich, 1989.

———. *To the Lighthouse.* 1927. Reprint, New York: Harcourt Brace Jovanovich, 1989.

Index

30, 33; in *Mama Day*, 129, 130,
136, 139, 141; in *Paradise*, 142, 145,
153, 154, 157, 158, 163, 164–5; in
Pigs in Heaven, 59–61, 62, 63; in
Praisesong for the Widow, 95, 96,
98–9, 100, 101, 107, 108; in
Virginia Woolf, 23, 24; running
away from, 83–4, 87, 89
homeland, home/land, 37, 38, 57, 159,
164; "Homeland" (story), Barbara
Kingsolver, 60; in *Animal Dreams*,
7–8, 37, 38, 63, 77; in *The Bean
Trees*, 57, 63, 77; in *How the García
Girls Lost Their Accents*, 66, 67, 68,
71, 74, 75; in *Pigs in Heaven*, 60,
62, 63, 64; in *Praisesong for the
Widow*, 105, 106, 108
homelessness, in *Animal Dreams*, 44; in
The Bean Trees, 55,63; in *Ladder of
Years*, 85; in *Paradise*, 146; in *Pigs
in Heaven*, 63
Homer (*The Odyssey*), 2, 4, 38, 93, 156,
179n.7
homesickness, 2, 4, 5, 38, 81, 181n.1; in
The Bean Trees, 55; in *How the
García Girls Lost Their Accents*, 70,
72, 73, 75; in *Jazz*, 81; in Doris
Lessing, *The Golden Notebook*,
16–17; in "Impertinent
Daughters," 30; in *Martha Quest*,
15–16; in *The Memoirs of a
Survivor*, 30–31; in *Praisesong for
the Widow*, 81; in Anne Tyler,
181n.1; home/sickness, in *Ladder
of Years*, 81, 82, 87, 94, 162

Ibsen, Henrik (*A Doll's House*), 86, 87
imago, 189n.21
See also: *beloved imago*

Jacobus, Mary, 170n.14
Jacoby, Mario, 21, 118, 169n.10,
177n.35

jazz (music), 185–6n.4; in Morrison's
fiction, 113, 117, 123,
187n.10
Juhasz, Suzanne, 191n.5, 191n.9
Julian of Norwich, 193n.12

Kaminsky, Amy, 64, 180n.1
Kaplan, Caren, 168n.4
Kappel-Smith, Diana, 179n.16
Kingsolver, Barbara, 7, 66, 77,
161; *Animal Dreams*, 7–8, 37–51,
53, 54, 77, 160, 161, 163; *The
Bean Trees*, 37, 53–9, 61, 64, 66,
77, 161; "Homeland" (story), 60;
Pigs in Heaven, 37, 59–64, 77,
161
Kingston, Maxine Hong, 75, 181n.6
Kolodny, Annette, 168n.5
Kübler-Ross, Elisabeth, 182n.11

Lessing, Doris, 6–7, 8, 12–22, 24,
28–33, 37, 51, 160, 161, 164;
African Laughter, 2, 13, 15, 17,
18–20, 32, 164; *Briefing for a
Descent into Hell*, 20–22; *Going
Home*, 15, 18; *The Golden
Notebook*, 14, 16, 17, 20, 24, 32–3,
160; "Impertinent Daughters," 8,
30, 173n.16, 177n.33; *Love, Again*,
31–2, 160; *Martha Quest*, 15–16;
The Memoirs of a Survivor, 29–31;
"My Mother's Life," 15; *A Proper
Marriage*, 16; *Shikasta*, 22; *The
Summer Before the Dark*, 182n.12;
"To Room Nineteen," 84; *Under
My Skin*, 29
Levy, Helen Fiddyment, 191n.7
Levy-Warren, Marsha, 169n.13
liminal, 8, 165; in *Praisesong for the
Widow*, 109; in *Jazz*, 120
Lincoln, Kenneth, 178n.4
Lock, Helen, 184n.9
Lowenthal, David, 169n.10